ELIZABETH PETERS
& JOAN HESS

THE PAINTED QUEEN

Constable • London

CONSTABLE

First published in the USA in 2017 by HarperCollins Publishers

First published in Great Britain in 2017 by Constable

1 3 5 7 9 10 8 6 4 2

A CIP catalogue record for this book
is available from the British Library.

ISBN: 978-1-47212-682-5

Typeset in Dante MT by SX Composing DTP, Rayleigh, Essex
Printed and bound in Great Britain by CPI Group (UK) Ltd, Croydon CR0 4YY

Papers used by Constable are from well-managed forests
and other responsible sources.

Constable
An imprint of
Little, Brown Book Group
Carmelite House
50 Victoria Embankment
London EC4Y 0DZ

An Hachette UK Company
www.hachette.co.uk

www.littlebrown.co.uk

TO

BARBARA MERTZ,

with love and respect

FOREWORD

EGYPTOLOGISTS TOGETHER: AMELIA PEABODY,
ELIZABETH PETERS, AND BARBARA MERTZ

SALIMA IKRAM,

Distinguished Professor in Egyptology,
American University in Cairo

O NE OF THE great delights of the Amelia Peabody books is
that in each one, Amelia combines murder, mayhem and
mystery with solid doses of Egyptology and history. As a
scholar, Barbara Mertz (Elizabeth Peters) meticulously researched
every historical point in her Peabody novels, and these root the series
and give it a life beyond its pages, illuminating the world of the ancient
Egyptians, historic events of the nineteenth and twentieth centuries
and the lives and discoveries of Egyptologists. Through her books,
Barbara managed to seduce readers into caring not only about Amelia,
Emerson and their circle, but also about Egyptology. She managed
to educate without bludgeoning people with too many facts; she
humanised archaeologists and explained what we do in the field, dull
though it often is, with its endless sifting of sand in the quest for telling
'odds and ends'.

Barbara's inspirations for each Amelia book varied. They were often
triggered by a particular moment in the history of Egyptology that
intrigued her, a site that she loved or a single artifact that was iconic,
both to her and to the world – particularly ones that had good stories
attached to them, with a hint of intrigue, and which still today remain
the subjects of Egyptological speculation (though some might rudely
call it gossip). The inspiration for *The Painted Queen* falls into the latter

categories: the famous Nefertiti bust (discovered in December 1912 by German archaeologist Ludwig Borchardt) is an iconic object with a muddy past and a contentious present, her discovery and departure from Egypt the subject of endless speculation by archaeologists and aficionados of ancient Egypt.

I remember when Barbara first told me about starting *The Painted Queen*. 'You'll never guess what I am going to tackle next! It will be such fun, and hopefully set the cat among the pigeons – and everyone will be happy as we are going back to Amarna!' From that moment on, she embarked on a frenzy of research, reading all she could on the topic, whether it was Borchardt's excavation reports, diaries and letters from the time, newspaper reports about the appearance and disappearance of Nefertiti, the opinions of scholars past and present about the bust or websites dealing with the exit and return of Nefertiti. All the while she kept track of what Egypt and Europe were like in the early part of the twentieth century. She also polled her Egyptological friends, asking their opinions about Borchardt's character, whether German governmental officials might have conspired to remove Nefertiti illegally from Egypt and keep her in Germany, and their thoughts on the accuracy of modern studies on the Nefertiti bust. Barbara's Egyptological friends entered into the spirit of the book, and sent her any relevant material that they thought might be of interest, whether it was a new book in German about the history of the German Institute that figures prominently in this book (the Deutsche Orient-Gesellschaft, at that time), or visiting the actual house that belonged to the German Institute in Cairo, and where Nefertiti might have temporarily rested (and where people were imprisoned) or obscure notes and opinions about the queen and her excavators.

The controversy about the bust of Nefertiti is one of the great debates of Egyptology. Was the bust found on 6 December 1912, as reported by excavator Borchardt (Barbara took some liberties with this portion of the tale – libel is unattractive), and later illegally removed by Borchardt? And how did Borchardt accomplish this removal? Did he

hide the bust, disguise it with a liberal application of plaster or put pres-
sure on Gustave Lefebvre, the young inspector who had come to select
the finds that were to remain in Cairo? If Lefebvre did *not* examine all
the contents of the boxes, and used only the list of items that Borchardt
had prepared (after all, he was a senior and very well respected scholar
who had been working in Egypt for a long time), he would have merely
noted that this was a bust of gypsum, as Borchardt had been economical with the truth. The bust was of limestone with its gypsum covering
and paint still surviving – a rarity. By misleading Lefebvre, it was speculated that Borchardt defrauded Egypt of its rightful share of the finds
at Amarna. In Berlin, the bust was displayed publicly for just one day,
after which it was whisked off to the home of James Simon (appear-
ing here as James Ridgemont), who had funded the excavation, and
remained with him (but visitable by a select few) until 1920. The fact
that Borchardt failed to publish news of the bust's discovery until 1923,
although details of other items from the same excavation made it into
print earlier, fuelled the controversy as to whether Nefertiti had been
'kidnapped'. Private letters and papers in Germany, and official complaints made by the Egyptian Antiquities Service, fed into speculation
about the exit of Nefertiti from Egypt. Additionally, later allegations
that Hitler fell under the spell of the bust and took the original, leaving
a fake in its place, only strengthened the Nefertiti mystique, making
her discovery a prime candidate for a mystery that Barbara (and Joan)
– and Amelia – had to tackle.

Barbara's books were always well researched on Egyptological and
historical levels, as she remained an Egyptologist and scholar at heart.
Although she never excavated in Egypt, she had visited more sites than
many archaeologists. I particularly remember a bumpy ride to the
rarely visited Abu Rawash, a site that Barbara had wanted to see for
some time, as she was thinking of featuring it in a new book. When we
got there, we carried out an almost total suspension of Barbara over
the burial pit of the pyramid so that she could see what it looked like,
and concluded with an Amelia-style picnic at the edge of the pyramid,

in the mortuary temple. While travelling through Egypt, Barbara was happy to try anything (I had the privilege, all in the name of research, of introducing her to *sheesha* smoking), talk to anyone and had a very real 'feel' for the country and its archaeological sites. She knew the ins and outs of an excavation, having visited many and interrogated their directors, à la Amelia, about the techniques that they used. It is this intimate knowledge of Egypt and its sites that makes Amelia's experiences so immediate for the reader. When she writes of crawling through bat guano, handling ancient bones, inspecting mummies, trudging through sand or enjoying the cool north breeze on the Nile, it is because Barbara had experienced all of this firsthand. Luckily for us, Joan accompanied Barbara on one of her trips, thus she too has had a 'taste of Egypt'.

Perhaps this intimacy with Egypt is why so many Egyptologists are devotees of the Amelia Peabody series. No other fiction author has spoken so directly and truly to us, skilfully blending historic fact with fiction, giving a very real sense of place, including in-jokes, all while telling a ripping tale. It is with great sadness that I bid farewell to the idea of enjoying any new adventures of the indomitable Amelia and Emerson, the 'most brilliant archaeologist of the nineteenth and twentieth centuries'. However, I find comfort in knowing that I have the old stories to return to, and, no doubt, even if they are not being chronicled as before, Amelia continues to contend with another ruined shirt as she and Emerson embark on fresh adventures.

PREFACE

JOAN HESS

I MET BARBARA THIRTY years ago at a mystery convention, when I timidly approached her as a wide-eyed fan. We clicked because of a shared sense of humour (sardonic) and perspective (jaded), and became close friends over the years. She offered wisdom as I floundered through the publishing world. We laughed often, engaged in a lengthy exchange of weird presents involving sheep and had weekend parties with our clever friends. She invited me to accompany her on one of her annual trips to Egypt, where she was revered by local shopkeepers and international Egyptologists. On the occasion of her eightieth birthday party, I rented a camel.

I was still stunned by her death three years ago when I arrived at Mertz Manor for the funeral. Beth (her daughter), Dominick Abel (her agent and dear friend), and I were sitting at the kitchen table when the topic turned to Barbara's unfinished manuscript. I will admit my gut froze as I sensed the inevitable question: would I complete *The Painted Queen*? My first response was an adamant refusal. The idea of attempting to capture her voice, her erudite style, her wit and her vast knowledge of archaeology in the early twentieth century, seemed ludicrous. I lost that one, obviously.

Barbara and I had discussed the plot in the preceding months, and I'd made suggestions. I was assured that she had made extensive notes and plotted the entire thing. I knew better. Yes, the notes were extensive – to a certain point. Interesting things were happening, and I suspect that she intended to let the plot develop as she wrote. Her illness overcame her.

I kept almost all of Barbara's prose, although some changes were necessary. Salima Ikram and I brainstormed via Skype to come up with the how, the who, the why. Beth offered comments and referenced earlier novels. Ray Johnson and Dennis Forbes gently corrected my missteps. It took me nearly three years to complete *The Painted Queen* due to personal health issues, but I am pleased with the result.

All factual and translation errors are Salima's fault. Or somebody else's, anyway. Maybe Google's.

I still miss Barbara.

INTRODUCTION

THE TRUSTEES OF THE
BARBARA MERTZ TRUST

I T IS OUR sad duty to introduce this last of the Amelia Peabody Emerson volumes. The devoted Editor of Mrs Emerson's memoirs, Elizabeth Peters, died in August of 2013 while in the midst of working on the manuscript of *The Painted Queen*. She had contemplated this project with excitement, knowing that publishing Mrs Emerson's recollections from this time would shed new light on a famous moment in the history of Egyptology. With her usual thoroughness, she had begun research on many aspects of the event in question, hoping to clarify some of the more difficult-to-decipher entries in Mrs Emerson's journals from this time. It bears noting that she had made the effort of writing out the final page of *The Painted Queen* before she died, a page that is reproduced herein verbatim. Happily, as she worked on this last manuscript, Ms Peters was in constant conversation with her dear friend and fellow mystery writer, Joan Hess, who valiantly took on the very difficult task of completing the work. Ms Hess sought the help of another close friend of Ms Peters, the distinguished archaeologist Dr Salima Ikram, in working through the nitty-gritty of the Egyptological details. Dennis Forbes, editor of *Kmt*, and Dr Raymond Johnson read the penultimate draft and offered suggestions as well.

We all owe Joan Hess an enormous debt of gratitude for the years of work she devoted to this undertaking, persevering through unimagined difficulties and prioritising this work over all else during this time. Greater friendship one could not imagine.

For many years, Elizabeth Peters (and her alter ego, Barbara Mertz) relied on the calm, constant and utterly reliable guidance of her agent, Dominick Abel, who also became a cherished friend and ally. As they always have shared a dislike of maudlin sentiment, we won't elaborate further. Even a skilled editor like Ms Peters needed help with her manuscripts – although she would have told you that she didn't suffer foolish edits gladly; thus it is a real testament to the skill of her longtime editor, Jennifer Brehl, that Ms Peters approved of (and even privately admitted to enjoying!) the work they did together.

Ms Peters accumulated a group of other friends over many years in the book business, including fellow authors, who carried one another through highs and lows. Their exploits at various conventions (including their own 'GroucherCon') and elsewhere probably are best left undescribed. Let us just say that they certainly could hold their own with Amelia when it came to beverages of genial and other types – and that their commentaries shared with Emerson a literate, if at times intemperate, character. And that leads us also to Ms Peters's comrades-in-arms within Egyptology and allied fields, similarly sturdy companions through all kinds of adventures. The prefaces of previous Amelia volumes are filled with specific acknowledgements of individual scholars and sources – but they name only a small swathe of the colleagues she counted as friends.

We hope she would forgive us for saying that her friendly and warm embrace extended broadly across family and friends, from nearby neighbours to far-flung pen pals – despite her attempts to pass as a curmudgeon. We miss her wicked sense of humour, her warmth, her intense curiosity, and the enthusiasm she used to create a sense of adventure in even the most mundane of settings.

And finally, we are certain that Ms Peters would want to thank her and Amelia's 'dear Readers' for decades of shared enjoyment in this adventure. As many readers know, for some years now the books in this series have been going back in time to fill in missing seasons in the saga. *The Painted Queen* does just this, also. The final chapter of the tale chronologically was published some years ago, in *Tomb of the Golden Bird*, allowing Amelia and Emerson to exit triumphantly, on their own terms. And now we come to the moment when we must allow Amelia's very dedicated editor to depart in the same fashion.

Indeed, there have long been striking similarities between Elizabeth Peters and Amelia Peabody – not the least of which being that they both liked to have the last word. To honour this preference, we close with some admonitions that Ms Peters included in her 1986 preface to *Lion in the Valley* – which we find to be just as appropriate now as they were then:

In this . . . volume of the memoirs of Amelia Peabody Emerson (Mrs Radcliffe Emerson), the editor once again deems it expedient to explain certain anomalies and obscurities in the text. Mrs Emerson was not as careful as she might have been about noting the dates of her entries. She seems to have picked up the current volume of her journal and scribbled away until something happened to distract her . . .

As the editor has had occasion to mention, the names of most of the persons involved have been changed, in order to spare the feelings of descendants of said individuals. The informed reader will recognise some names as those of well-known archaeologists, who appear only peripherally. Mrs Emerson seems to have been fairly accurate in describing their activities; however, it would be a serious error to assume that she was equally accurate in reporting their conversations with her for, like her distinguished husband, she had a decided tendency to attribute to other people opinions of her own.

Another obscurity in the ur-text (if the editor may so describe the journals themselves) arises from the fact that at some point Mrs Emerson apparently decided to edit them for eventual publication . . . Since she was as inconsistent about her revision as she was about dating her pages, the result is sometimes a peculiar blend of journalistic and novelistic styles.

In other words, none of the eccentricities of the present volume are the responsibility of the editor.[1] She has done the best she could and would suggest that complaints, criticisms and other pejorative comments be addressed to the heirs of Professor and Mrs Emerson, not to her.

[1] Or, we hasten to add, of those who laboured to finish *The Painted Queen.*

THE
PAINTED QUEEN

ONE

FROM THE HARBOUR, the port of Alexandria is an attractive sight, its whitewalled houses and red tiled roofs framed by azure sky and sea. Since I had been there many times, I knew that the walls were disfigured by dried mud and rude graffiti and that the streets were inches deep in evil-smelling debris. I never arrived in Alexandria without wishing to leave it as soon as possible.

However, our welcome was warm enough to cheer the saddest heart. Our arrival had been heralded by the mysterious network of communication that operates in countries such as Egypt, and cries of greeting arose as our ship approached the dock. '*As-salaam-u-alaykum*, o Father of Curses. *Marhaba, ya* Sitt Hakim!'

Egyptians enjoy inventing soubriquets, and that of Emerson, I believe, requires no elucidation. As I have often said, and never tire of saying, my husband is the greatest Egyptologist of the nineteenth century (of the Christian era), and although the present century is still in its infancy, I do not doubt he will dominate it as well. His physical endowments are no less remarkable than his intellectual skills. As he stood beside me at the rail, his thick black hair was dishevelled by the breeze, and his sapphirine orbs shone with anticipation, for we were returning to a particularly intriguing excavation that certain events of a particular nature had prevented us from finishing the previous season.

My own name, Sitt Hakim, means Lady Doctor, and although I had never acquired formal training in medicine, I could not help but feel that I had done some good. My excellent spouse's comment 'No one would dare die if you told them to live' was no doubt meant as sarcasm, but it held a seed of truth. A positive attitude is vital to recovery, and so is confidence in one's medical attendant.

But I digress.

Emerson shouted greetings in response to the respectful saluta-tions of his numerous disreputable 'old friends' (of whom he had far too many, in my opinion). I waved my parasol in a jovial manner, and was amused to observe certain members of the receiving committee back off a few steps. My parasol was regarded by the more superstitious of the fellahin as a device of potent magical power. It certainly was a useful weapon, not only because the victim was not expecting attack by parasol, but because my parasols were made to my specifications, having a rather sharp tip and a stout steel shaft.

With the assistance of some of Emerson's admirers (whose devo-tion was not so great as to refuse the baksheesh he dispersed), we got ourselves and our belongings onto the train to Cairo. A similar scene ensued when the train arrived at the Cairo station. How the word of our arrival had got out so quickly I do not know, but more of Emerson's old friends awaited us on the platform. I had resigned myself to the inevitable delay when an individual in formal morning dress pushed through the crowd and addressed my husband. 'Professor Emerson?' he inquired unnecessarily. (There is no mistaking Emerson; his stal-wart form is known the length and breadth of Egypt.) 'I come from M. Maspero,' he went on. 'He asks that you do him the honour of calling upon him as soon as is possible.'

'Oh dear, what have you done now?' I cried. Emerson's uneasy rela-tions with the director of the Service des Antiquités certainly justified the question, but seeing his eyes flash and his chin protrude, I went on with (I am proud to say) scarcely a pause, 'What task that would have daunted a lesser man have you accomplished, to win the commenda-tion of M. Maspero? For I do not doubt that he wishes to congratulate you, or, what is more likely, enlist your aid in solving—'

Emerson interrupted me with a loud 'Hmph!' I decided I might have been overdoing it just a bit.

'Inform M. Maspero that I will respond to his request after we have arranged for accommodations and rested from the journey,' said Emerson to the individual in question. Emerson's tone left no room for debate. The young man bowed and backed away.

'Really, Peabody,' said Emerson to me. 'Must you lower your dignity by running on at such length? A curt nod and a frosty stare would have been good enough for a cursed Frenchman.'

Let me hasten to explain that Emerson had no particular prejudice against the French, who had been allowed to continue their control of the Antiquities Department when the British took over the other departments of government. No indeed! Emerson takes an unbiased and candidly critical view of most people: archaeologists who do not live up to his professional standards (most of them); all bureaucrats, tourists and journalists; and the majority of the officials of the Service des Antiquités.

'Emerson,' I said, taking his arm. 'Speaking of accommodations, those on the steamer—'

'Were not up to your standards? Well, my dear, what with one thing and another I think you deserve a few days at Shepheard's.'

That was precisely what I intended to do, but I had expected it would take a while to convince Emerson, who hates elegant hotels. Our dahabeeyah was still in Luxor, but it would have been just like Emerson to suggest we stay with one of his old friends or go to one of the plainer (i.e., less sanitary) hotels. This unexpected and courteous acquiescence touched me deeply. I told Emerson so and gave his arm a loving squeeze.

We were greeted as the honoured guests we were, and after a brief interlude (which involved the relocation of the occupants thereof) were shown to our usual quarters.

'Well, well,' said Emerson, trying not to look at the pile of luggage that awaited unpacking. 'I believe I will just – er – run round to see Maspero. Rude to keep him waiting.'

Emerson's is not a nature that lends itself to successful subterfuge. Never in his life had he given a curse (as he would have said) about offending M. Maspero.

'Emerson,' I said, 'you intend to call on Maspero? *Without me?*'

Emerson might, with some reason, have pointed out that I had not been included in the invitation. Instead he replied with a remark to the effect that if I meant to make an issue of it, he would delay his visit. His tone was so emphatic and the number of swear words he used so numerous that I could not doubt his asseveration. 'I will just take a little stroll and renew old acquaintances,' he said. 'Will you be all right alone?'

I looked at him in surprise. 'Of course, my dear. What could possibly happen to me here?'

Loofah, towels and soap in hand, I made my way to the bath chamber and filled the tub. The wisps of steam rising from the water and the scented bubbles called to me with a siren song. I sank into the water with a sigh of contentment.

In past years, when accommodations at Shepheard's were in great demand, some of the commodious bath chambers had been converted into temporary bedrooms, with doors opening onto the hallway. I had not given the matter much thought until a hitherto unobserved door gave way and a large man burst in.

He did not see me at first, since the tub was in an alcove out of the line of sight of someone standing in the doorway, so I had ample time to observe him as he turned ponderously from side to side. Heavily built, with large calloused hands and coarse features, he was neatly dressed in a tweed coat and trousers, except for one singular feature – a gold-rimmed monocle in his left eye.

I was unarmed, having assumed it was unnecessary to carry weapons into the bath chamber. I have always been of the opinion that the best defence is a prompt and vigorous attack, but my current position rendered certain options untenable. My only weapons were a bar of soap, a loofah and a towel. Thanks to the scented soap bubbles I was more or less covered, which would not be the case should I rise to my feet. I was still considering strategies when the man advanced farther into the room and caught sight of me. His arms rose, his fingers curled in a most menacing fashion as he gave me a cruel (and somewhat demented) smile. 'You!'

'Sir,' I said in my iciest tones, 'you were perhaps unaware that this room was already occupied. Kindly remove yourself at once.'

His response was as remarkable as his sudden appearance. Touching one hand to his throat, he gasped, 'Murder!' and collapsed onto the floor.

The *suffragi* appeared in the doorway, eyes staring and mouth agape. It is the duty of these fellows to patrol the hallways, directing visitors to the proper room and preventing guests from annoyance. Obviously Ali's performance in this latter matter was not up to his usual standards.

'Ali,' I said irritably as he scuttled into the room like a lame spider. 'What the devil is going on? Where were you when this person intruded upon me?'

The answer was what I expected: he had been attending to the needs of another patron and had not observed the intruder.

'Summon the manager at once,' I ordered. 'And close the door behind you.'

'But, Sitt, there is a body—'

'Close it!'

I waited until the door was shut before I emerged from the tub and assumed my dressing gown and slippers. I was reasonably certain that the fellow on the floor was dead (the hilt of a knife protruding from his back assisted me in this diagnosis) but duty demanded I ascertain whether he was beyond assistance.

He was. Having felt for a pulse and found none, I was about to begin investigating his pockets when the door was again flung open and I beheld Emerson, looming head and shoulders over the group of people behind him. Even in such a short space of time the sensation seekers had gathered, no doubt due to Ali's bleats of distress as he went downstairs to the lobby. There was some pushing and shoving, and a few irritated comments. One strident voice rose above the hubbub. 'Out of the way, you chaps! Don't you know who I am?'

No one did, or no one cared; the crowd continued to enlarge. Emerson appeared somewhat agitated; he was breathing quickly and his face was flushed, but he controlled himself admirably. 'Curse it,' he remarked. 'What the devil are you up to now, Peabody? Who is the person lying on the floor? Anyone we know?'

'I believe not, Emerson. I had just begun searching him in the hope of finding a means of identification.'

'Allow me, Peabody.' He turned the body onto its side. The fellow's features were no more prepossessing in death; they were set in a snarl and the staring eyes were like dull brown pebbles.

'Hmph,' said Emerson, going through the fellow's pockets and removing a few papers. 'Receipts and bills . . . and this.'

It was a piece of pasteboard, the same size as an ordinary calling card, blank except for a single hand-printed word.

'Judas,' Emerson and I said in unison.

'What the devil does that mean?' Emerson asked, solo.

'Could it be an accusation?' was my response. 'Judas was, of course, the betrayer of Jesus. The ultimate betrayer. But to the best of my knowledge I haven't betrayed anyone.'

'Here's another odd item,' Emerson went on. 'It appears to be a monocle.'

'He was wearing it when he came in,' I explained. 'It must have fallen from his eye when he crumpled.'

He sat back on his heels and stared at me. 'I believe this is the first time I have heard of a thug wearing a monocle. It wouldn't have suited him. One would expect a more aristocratic, not to say refined, looking person.'

'I expect it is the insignia of a secret society, Emerson.'

'A secret society??' Emerson exclaimed. (I assure the Reader that two interrogation points scarcely convey the vehemence of his question.)

'Close the door, Emerson,' I said, regarding with distaste the gaping faces that fringed it on either side. When he had obliged, I said, 'I have never seen him before, so someone must have hired him to, ah, dishabilitate me on a permanent basis. As for the monocle, you know as well as I that they are rare these days, even at Court. It must serve as a way for members of a discreet and unsavoury alliance to recognise one another.'

'I say,' said the same voice that had spoken earlier from the hallway. 'Isn't someone going to call the police?'

The manager, Mr Baehler, was the next to appear. At the sight of the body he let out a heartfelt groan. 'Good Gad, Mrs Emerson – not again!' he exclaimed.

Resenting the implication I replied, 'I assure you, Mr Baehler, I take no pleasure in having people murdered in my vicinity. Have you called the police?'

'Someone has already done so,' was the reply, followed by a deep sigh. Managers of fine hotels prefer not to call the police but in this case he had no choice. Based on volume, the spectators outside the door now extended a good distance down the corridor in either direction.

'Quickly, Peabody, into our rooms,' said Emerson, rising to his feet. 'I believe I heard the heavy footsteps of the law approaching. I will fend them off as long as possible. Do me the favour of assuming proper attire with as much celerity as you can command.'

He bolted the door behind us and went on into the sitting room while I debated what my proper mode of attire should be. I had a new tea gown I had anticipated wearing for Emerson; it was his favourite colour, scarlet, covered with black polka dots and trimmed extensively with black lace. However, I was forced to conclude that if the day went on in this manner, it might be advisable for me to be armed and ready.

My working costume, refined season by season, consisted of stout boots a divided skirt of ample proportions and modest length, a shirtwaist, and a coat covered with pockets. My belt of useful tools completed this costume, but I decided against putting it on since Emerson complained about the jangling noise it made and the sharp edges on certain objects. I did take my parasol with me when I proceeded into the sitting room, where I found Emerson leafing through the papers he had removed from the dead man's pockets.

'Sit down, Peabody,' he said, making room for me on the sofa next to him. 'I have a question for you. What have you been up to lately?'

'I beg your pardon, Emerson?'

'It is early days for you to be targeted by an assassin, my dear. I am accustomed to this sort of thing occurring later in the season, but you have not had time enough to instigate such an attack. That is . . . Have you?'

'I fail to see the point you are attempting to make, Emerson.'

'It is simple enough. If you have done nothing in the past two hours to inspire murderous fury in someone, it must have been inspired by an action at some earlier time. Does anything occur to you?'

'I cannot say that it does.' I pondered the suggestion. 'If you like I will make one of my little lists.'

'Lists of old enemies? That would take too long.'

I decided not to reply to this remark, which was intended to be provocative. 'Have you found anything useful among those papers?'

'A slip of paper with your name and the number of our suite.'

'Interesting,' I said. 'It is evident that I was to be his victim. Anything else?'

He handed me another slip of paper and I read it aloud. 'Octavius Buddle. No address. I have no idea who Mr Buddle might be, but he is obviously the next intended victim. He must be warned.'

'Against what?' Emerson demanded. 'A dead assassin?'

'Assassins sometimes travel in gangs, Emerson.'

Emerson's eyes opened very wide. 'Peabody, where do you get these notions? Assassins do not travel in gangs. Furthermore, how do you plan to warn Mr Buddle when you don't know who he is or where he is?'

'That does present a difficulty,' I acknowledged. 'I forgot to ask – did the putative assassin have a weapon on his person?'

'He didn't need one,' Emerson said grimly. 'Those hard hands of his could have held you underwater long enough. Your habits of cleanliness are no doubt admirable, my dear, but I sometimes think you spend too much time in bathtubs.'

Except for the tramping of heavy boots in the bath chamber, audible even through the sturdy door, nothing transpired for a time. The post had been brought up and a neat pile of messages and letters begged for my attention, so while I waited for the expected visit from the police I sorted through these missives. Some were welcoming notes from our archaeological acquaintances. I put them aside, for among them was the letter I had hoped to find.

Though our last season had been successful from a professional point of view, it had ended in a series of distressing events, particularly to our foster daughter, Nefret.

I thought of her as a daughter, and so did Emerson, though we had never made the relationship official. Nefret had been thirteen when we first encountered her in a remote oasis in the Western Desert. Her father, fleeing the bloody Mahdist revolt in the Sudan, had found refuge there, and there his daughter had grown up, revered as High Priestess of Isis. It was certainly an unusual background for an English girl of impeccable lineage and, as we later learned, considerable wealth. We had of course brought her back to England with us and had watched with proud affection as she grew up to be a trained physician and surgeon. She had founded a clinic in Luxor, which served any woman, respectable wife or prostitute, in need of medical care, and had engaged excellent female physicians to staff it.

Her failings – everyone has a few, even I – were a quick temper and an impetuous nature. It was this last that had led her into a disastrous marriage with a man who had turned out to be a consummate villain. His violent death had led her to suffer a miscarriage, which given her husband's character, might have been regarded as a blessing in disguise. However, she did not so regard it. Upon the advice of our dear family physician, Dr Willoughby, I had taken her to a renowned psychiatric institution in Paris. With the strength of character I knew she possessed, she had made an excellent recovery and had, most sensibly in my opinion, gone on with her medical studies. There is nothing like hard work and a goal in life to assist mental healing.

'Emerson,' I exclaimed. 'This is from Nefret. Good news, my dear!' For he had turned towards me, anxiety writ large upon his handsome countenance. I went on, 'She is joining us here within a few days.'

'Do you think she is up to it?'

'Here, read the letter for yourself.'

His frown smoothed out as he read. 'She sounds quite her old self. Are you sure she—'

'Youth is resilient, my dear. Nefret is too well balanced an individual to spend her life reliving old sorrows and mistakes. Learn from the past and then put it behind you. Get on with—'

'Well put, my dear,' said Emerson rather loudly. 'That is good news indeed. What the devil are they doing next door?'

'Removing the body, I trust.'

'Quite. It is a decided inconvenience to have a corpse in one's bath chamber.'

'Why, Emerson,' I exclaimed. 'I believe you are being ironic.'

'What?' His heavy brows drew together. From his pocket he removed a folded paper, unfolded it, stared at it, refolded it and replaced it in his pocket.

'You say the fellow uttered a few words before he died?'

'Two words, to be precise,' I replied. '"You" and "murder".'

'Stating the obvious, wasn't he?' Emerson took out the paper, unfolded it and stared at it, frowning. 'Are you certain that is what he said?'

'I assure you, Emerson, my hearing is unimpaired.'

'No doubt; but the ability of a dying man to articulate clearly *is* impaired.'

'You have, I presume, an alternative suggestion?' My tone was, I admit, a trifle sarcastic.

'As a matter of fact,' said Emerson, 'I have not.'

'Then why did you question my hearing?'

'Because you are always hearing words like "murder". Never mind what he may or may not have said; the most important thing is that bit of pasteboard with the word "Judas". I feel certain it is a vital clue.'

'It is a possibility worthy of . . . Emerson, will you please stop doing that and pay attention?' For once again he had removed the paper from his pocket. 'What is so absorbing about that paper? Where did it come from?'

'It had been pushed under the door,' he muttered.

'It is a message, then,' I said, feeling as if I were fighting through a jungle of non-communication. 'For heaven's sake, Emerson, stop mumbling. Is that message addressed to you, or to me?'

'To neither. No direction was necessary,' said Emerson between his teeth. 'It reads "Where were you?" The meaning is obvious. "Where were you when your wife was being murderously attacked?" And, to continue the equally obvious corollary, "It's a good thing I was watching over her".'

'That is surely reading too much—'

'Someone was watching over you. Someone stabbed the murderous bastard in the back before he could get to you.' His voice rose to a pitch that rattled the windows. 'And it wasn't I!'

Emerson could contain himself no longer. He leapt to his feet and headed for the door, intent, I assumed, on racing up and down the corridors knocking people down and shouting at them. I was about to call him back when I decided the exercise would do him good and help him work off his annoyance. It would have no other useful effect. Sethos was not likely to be still in the hotel and Emerson would not recognise him if he were. Our old enemy was a master of disguise.

The author of the note had to be Sethos. He must have been in the crowd that morning. No one else could arouse Emerson's wrath so effectively as the Master Criminal, or, as I sometimes called him, the Genius of Crime. Emerson objected to both titles, on the grounds that they were first, ridiculously theatrical, and second, subtly flattering.

We had never known his true name or his antecedents. The soubriquet Sethos referred, as my Readers must know, to the Egyptian god Set, who was the enemy of the benevolent Osiris and Osiris's son Horus, and who was therefore regarded as evil. But Egyptian religion is seldom so simple. Set could be evil or benevolent according to his circumstances. He had many functions, which I will not go into here because they would necessitate a long and (to some Readers) boring digression. I refer said Readers to any decent volume on Egyptian religion.

Like his chosen tutelary deity, our old foe had a few good qualities, at least from my point of view. He had a strange devotion to my humble self and on one memorable occasion I had been his prisoner for several extremely interesting hours. I must say he behaved like a perfect gentleman, even after I had struck him over the head in an abortive attempt to escape. One would suppose that a keen observer like myself would be able to identify him after spending so much time in his presence, and such would have no doubt been the case had he not been – as I have mentioned – a master of disguise. Over the years he had appeared as an elderly, irascible American lady, an effete English aristocrat and a number of other personae. I knew he was tall and well built, but on the occasion I have mentioned his actual features had been obscured by a formidable beard and moustache. I could not even be certain that he was dark haired. Hair colour is one of the easiest means of identification to alter.

Having reached this point in my cogitations – which took far less time than it has taken to write them down – I went to the main door, asked Ali to have tea sent up, and settled back to await the next development.

This would be, I assumed, a visit from the police. Seldom in a case of murder do the authorities have an eyewitness to the crime, and if I may be allowed a slight touch of vanity, such an experienced witness. However, I had had dealings with the Cairo police before and found them strangely reluctant to call on me for assistance. After waiting for what I considered a reasonable length of time I was about to go to them when there was a knock at the door.

Ali entered with the tea trolley, followed close behind by another man. Recognising him, I got to my feet with an exclamation of pleasure. We were old friends, Thomas Russell and I, and I took it as a personal compliment that he had come in person instead of sending an underling. Formerly commissioner at Alexandria, he recently had been appointed chief of police in Cairo. One could not have called him classically handsome, but he was a fine-looking man, with light blond hair and steady brown eyes.

After congratulating him on his well-deserved promotion, I said with a smile, 'Is this a professional call, Mr Russell, or may I invite you to take tea with me?'

'I would be honoured to join you for tea, Mrs Emerson, but I must ask a few questions in my professional capacity. When I realised you were involved in this case I decided to come round in person.'

'That was kind of you. Sugar? Milk?'

While I attended to his requests (no milk, three lumps of sugar) he said, 'Not so much kindness, ma'am, as selfishness. I seldom get the chance of questioning an eyewitness to murder.'

'And attempted murder,' I said, adding a third lump of sugar to the cup. 'Emerson is of the opinion that the fellow came there to assassinate me.'

Russell started to laugh, but quickly sobered. 'I beg your pardon. It was your – er – insouciance, your matter-of-fact tone of voice . . .'

'You need not apologise. My attitude may strike some persons as unusual, but one becomes used to that sort of thing after a time.'

'No doubt. However, I am of the same opinion as the Professor,'

Russell said seriously. 'A gentleman does not burst into a lady's bath chamber, or, if he inadvertently intrudes, he immediately apologises and retreats. This fellow was no gentleman. His appearance as well as his behaviour mark him as a lower-class individual. I have seldom seen such a rough countenance.'

'Have you been able to identify him?'

'It is early days yet, Mrs Emerson. He is not a local villain; I have a good memory for such persons, and this man is unknown to me. Did he say or do anything that would give you a clue to his identity or nationality?'

I gave him a brief, well-organised description of what had transpired. 'He had on his person a card on which was written the word "Judas",' I explained.

Russell's well-disciplined features reacted to this admittedly bizarre statement with only a few twitches. 'May I see the card?' he asked.

'Certainly. Oh – I believe Emerson was so agitated that he took it with him. I assure you there can be no doubt about the name. I assume you found the other cardboard rectangles, one with our room number. The thug was headed to this room when he was stabbed in the back. The shock caused him to open the adjoining door. The second card had the curious inscription "Octavius Buddle".'

'And you have no idea what it means?'

I had a number of ideas as to what it might mean, but I saw no advantage in troubling Russell's rigidly logical mind with them. 'Not really,' I said. 'I am sorry I cannot be of more help.'

'But you have been of help.' Russell rose. 'Based on your analysis of his accent, he was British. We will telegraph the fellow's description to Scotland Yard. Please give the Professor my regards and tell him I am sorry to have missed him.'

EMERSON'S COMINGS AND goings are generally impetuous, and he seldom looks to see where he is going. He assumes that any persons in his path will get out of his way and that he can brush aside any impediment. When he flung the door of the sitting room open, he stumbled over an object lying on the threshold. Fortunately he did look down this time, and I was treated to the sight of agitated dance steps as Emerson tried to avoid treading on the object. He had, with his usual acuity, realised at once that it was of some value.

'Where the devil did this come from?' he demanded, carrying the object in question to me.

It was a small wooden head, approximately three inches in height, carefully carved and painted. A fresh break just below the shoulders indicated that it had been part of a larger statuette of an ushebti, one of the servant figurines placed in the tomb to assist the deceased in the afterlife. The head was that of a pharaoh with slanting eyes, pronounced cheekbones, full lips and an elongated chin; it wore the Blue Battle Crown with a uraeus on the brow. I had no difficulty identifying its subject. At only one period of Egyptian history had this particular artistic style prevailed. This was Akhenaton, the so-called Heretic Pharaoh, who had abandoned the multitudinous gods of Egypt in favour of one deity, the Aton, and had left Thebes for a new capital at a place now called Tell el-Amarna.

'Amarna,' I said.

'Obviously,' Emerson rubbed his chin, a habit of his when perplexed or deep in thought. 'What I ought to have asked was who brought it here and why. This remarkable object must have been removed from the site without the knowledge or permission of the excavators. All artifacts discovered are to be kept until the end of the season, at which time the Service des Antiquités inspects them and decides which—'

'I am well aware of that,' I said impatiently. Emerson had recently got into the habit of lecturing instead of answering a simple question, much in the manner of our son, Ramses. I intended to break both of them of it as soon as was possible.

'So to return to your original question,' I went on, 'why was this object brought to us?'

I paused to draw breath, and Emerson said, looking uncharacteristically shy, 'I have a theory.'

'Splendid, my dear,' I said encouragingly.

'The broken figurine is itself a coded message: Amarna – damage, looting, destruction!'

'Well!' I exclaimed. 'I must say, Emerson, that is very ingenious. We may take it, then, as an appeal for help, and an urgent appeal at that. I will send a telegram to Selim immediately, telling him that we are on our way and to get our dahabeeyah there as quickly as possible. If you will assist me in packing your—'

'Curse it!' Emerson shouted. 'We are getting off onto one of those digressions that so often occur when I attempt to have a sensible conversation!'

'Really, Emerson!' I said indignantly.

Emerson went on before I could continue. 'Let us take advantage of this temporary lull to recapitulate. Start from the beginning. How did the dead man end up on the floor of your bath chamber? Be succinct, I beg.'

'There is not much to tell, Emerson. I was enjoying a pleasant soak when the soon-to-be-dead man staggered in and collapsed. He must have been stabbed immediately before he entered, since he could not have gone far in that condition.'

Emerson lit his pipe. 'Weren't you the one who once pointed out to me that an individual wounded by a sharp, narrow-bladed knife often goes some distance before he realises he is injured? His murderer may not have been anywhere near him when he collapsed.'

'True,' I admitted. 'And the deed may have been done so quickly it could have passed unnoticed even by a close witness. A hearty slap on the back, a jovial—'

'Point taken, Peabody.'

'We could ask the *suffragis* if any of them observed such an encounter.'

'Greatly as I enjoy your flights of fancy, my dear, the scenario you have described with such panache is only one of several possibilities.'

'Give me another, then.'

'A shove and a stumble, a helpful hand on the shoulder,' said Emerson promptly. 'A phalanx of purported tourists marching down the hallway and pushing everyone out of their way, engulfing the victim.'

'That is a bit far-fetched, don't you think?'

'Oh, I don't know. You've seen them do it. Frequently led,' Emerson went on, 'by several iron-jawed females who behave as if they owned the hotel.'

Feeling obliged to defend my sex, I said, 'I have seen iron-jawed men behave the same way. Many of them are members of the military.'

'Quite so,' Emerson admitted. 'Let us abandon conjecture and deal with the fact itself.'

'A dead man on my bath chamber floor,' I said helpfully.

'Precisely. It will take them some time to identify the fellow. Need we sit here twiddling our thumbs?'

'I suppose we needn't. Mr Russell has already questioned me.'

'Russell was here?'

'Yes. I took it as a courteous gesture that he would come in person. He said he was sorry to have missed you.'

'Bah,' said Emerson. 'Never mind the pleasantries. I refuse to allow these distractions to interfere with our professional activities any longer.'

'Then perhaps we should visit M. Maspero, as he requested. We will need his permission to excavate.'

'Oh.' Emerson's brow furrowed. 'Curse it, I suppose we must.'

'I will be ready as soon as I find my parasol.'

Another discussion followed, but it was brief, since Emerson had known from the first that I intended to accompany him, and his protests were purely formal. I managed to persuade him to assume a coat and cravat, and I put on a new frock I had purchased in London – yellow silk trimmed with ecru lace and amber beads. It is always advisable,

I feel, to present oneself at one's best when dealing with people like Maspero, who appreciates haute couture.

During the cab ride Emerson managed to work himself up into quite a state of temper. He burst into the director's office without ceremony, brushing aside assorted clerks and assistants.

'See here, Maspero, I refuse to be ordered about. What the devil do you want?'

Maspero's beard was greying and his head balding, but his smile was as warm as ever. Over the years he had become used to Emerson. Rising from behind his desk, he extended a welcoming hand.

'My dear old friend, I would never have the temerity to order you or Mrs Emerson to do anything. I requested your assistance in a delicate matter because I have such confidence in you. Whether you accept or not is entirely up to you, *s'il vous plaît*.'

'Hmph,' said Emerson. After escorting me to a chair, he took another and stared fixedly at Maspero. 'Well? Let us get to the point at once. What is it you want us to do? Kindly reply in the fewest possible words.'

'Spend your winter season at Amarna.'

'At the Workmen's Village? Thank you,' said Emerson with heavy sarcasm. 'But no – it has already been examined. And I doubt Borchardt would relinquish any interesting part of the site to me.'

Maspero hesitated for a moment, and then said, 'I am sure I can depend on you, my friends, to keep the information I am about to disclose confidential. Herr Borchardt had to return to Germany to deal with a family crisis. Herr Morgenstern was sent to replace him. All was well, but now I have been increasingly concerned about him. His behaviour of late has been unusual.'

'In what way?' I asked.

'He has been absent from his excavations for a long period of time, leaving them in the charge of an individual who appears to have little or no experience in archaeology. That is not like Herr Morgenstern, who is well respected in his field. Rumour has it that he is in Cairo.'

Maspero's shrug was melodramatic. 'What is he doing there? It is highly improbable that a woman is involved. A dalliance might distract him for a short while, but he is a dedicated archaeologist who has been given the opportunity to excavate a significant site. Besides that, there has been no gossip. When such things occur, there is always gossip.'

'Are you asking us to find out?' I inquired. 'For it would be impertinent of us to pry into his private affairs without a direct order from you. Herr Morgenstern is not an easy man to get on with; Emerson has never got on with him.'

'Not an order,' Maspero said with a sigh. 'A request. A direct request. An urgent request. Tell el-Amarna must be protected at all costs.'

'We will consider that sufficient authorisation,' I said. 'And we will let you know as soon as is possible what we propose to do.'

'Does your request have anything to do with the dead man who intruded upon Mrs Emerson's bath this morning?' Emerson asked.

'Pardon?' Maspero exclaimed. 'A dead man walked into Mrs Emerson's bath chamber?'

'He wasn't dead until after he came in,' said Emerson, thus adding to Maspero's confusion.

'Allow me, Emerson,' I said, and proceeded to explain the situation in my customary efficient fashion.

'*Mon Dieu!*' the director exclaimed. 'I regret, madame, that you should have been subjected to such a distressing sight.'

'Bah,' said Emerson. 'She thrives on such sights.'

I had brought the broken ushebti with me. 'We found this outside the door of our sitting room this morning,' I said, handing it to the director. 'I believe it is meant to communicate a message.'

'Message?'

'An appeal for help,' I explained.

'Help?' Maspero echoed, staring at the ushebti.

'Please pay attention, monsieur,' I said. 'That object conveys two ideas: first, Amarna, and second, destruction, damage.'

Maspero continued to stare at the ushebti. 'It is Akhenaton,' he muttered. 'He is unmistakable. Where did it come from?'

'That is the question,' I said. 'If it does not come from any collection with which you are familiar, then it must have come from the site of Amarna itself.'

'But not from Morgenstern's excavations,' Emerson said. 'He is excavating the city site. Ushebtis are funerary objects. They would not be found in a private house.'

'Then from a hitherto undiscovered tomb!' Maspero proclaimed. 'The task of discovery would seem to be yours, my friends.'

Emerson is not good at concealing his emotions. 'Smug' might be too strong a word for his expression at that time, but not by much. He had refused to work at several of the most enticing sites in Egypt as a matter of principle (or possibly pure bull-headedness), claiming that sooner or later his expertise would be needed and that he would graciously yield to Maspero's pleas that we return to Amarna. We both had a special affection for that site, where we had first met and (after an interval) become attached to each other in ways that should not require elucidation for my mature Readers. There were few places in Egypt that would have attracted him more. But his steely sense of duty (or pure bull-headedness) forbade the primrose path.

'Impossible,' my husband declared firmly, 'in that we have an unfinished excavation at Zawyet el'Aryan to complete.'

'But my dear fellow, what can Zawyet el'Aryan offer in comparison with Amarna?'

In fact it had a great deal to offer: a Third Dynasty royal burial, to be precise. We had been unable to complete it the previous year because of the distressing events to which I have alluded.

'You excavated at one time at the Workmen's Village at Amarna,' Maspero went on. 'Why not return and finish the job? And, while you are there, search for a new tomb.'

'Aside from the commitment Emerson has mentioned,' I said, before he could offer an opinion that might not coincide with mine, 'our staff is not complete. Our son and his friend David Todros are still in Palestine.'

Momentarily diverted, Maspero asked, 'What is Emerson *fils* doing in Palestine?'

A truthful answer would have been 'I wish I knew'. My annoying son had not refused to answer my questions, but his replies had been so vague and equivocal that I had been unable to pin him down. My fear was that he had got himself involved with the cursed British Secret Service. The Service was always trying to recruit archaeologists. They made ideal agents because they had a legitimate reason for being where they were – Egypt, Palestine, Turkey, Syria – and in most cases they spoke the local language. Ramses was a natural linguist; his German, Turkish and Arabic were of native fluency. From early childhood he had lived part of the year in Egypt and was as much at home there as he was in England. In short, he was a perfect spy and I knew that British intelligence would give a great deal to enlist him.

And I would make certain that they did not succeed.

'He will be joining us soon,' I said with fervour. 'At Amarna.'

TWO

'WE CANNOT ABANDON Zawyet!'

When seen in print, this statement lacks a certain portentousness. When uttered in Emerson's deep, resonant basso, it has the effect of a decree from on high. Very high.

We had retired to our room after dinner. Emerson was disrobing in his typical slapdash manner, tossing his garments onto the floor and leaving his boots in places where one of us was sure to stumble over them. I sat at the dressing table giving my hair its usual one hundred strokes.

I gain no particular satisfaction from regarding my own countenance. Shimmering auburn curls and azure eyes would be more to my taste than my stormy grey eyes, heavy black hair and slightly sallow complexion. However, Emerson finds no fault with these features or with a figure that is fuller in certain regions than I would like. His opinions are the ones that count with me.

Being accustomed to Emerson's emphatic tone, which he often employed, I replied, 'No one is suggesting that we should, my dear. Selim has assured us that there has been no evidence of local interest in the area, but that situation may not continue, and the burial is too important to be left to the vagaries of chance. How many Third Dynasty burials have been found, more or less intact?'

'Precisely what I was about—'

'It shouldn't take too long to complete the job,' I continued affably, avoiding a tedious lecture. 'There is no chance of reconstructing the original arrangement, since it was jumbled about by Geoffrey Godwin. We can only sort and record what is there now.'

Emerson admitted the truth of this with a grudging grumble. 'To-morrow, then,' he said. 'I will send Selim a telegram to notify the men and meet us in Zawyet.'

'Not tomorrow, Emerson. What we must have before we continue is a skilled photographer.'

'Selim,' Emerson began, 'is quite—'

'Selim has acquired considerable skill, but he may need assistance. Arranging the reflectors and changing them as the sunlight shifts, de-ciding how long an exposure requires – these are details best left to someone with more experience. One such person comes to mind, Em-erson. Have you forgotten that Nefret will be arriving soon?'

'Of course not, but we can return to greet her when she arrives, or she can come to us directly. Zawyet is too far for to-ing and fro-ing on a daily basis unless we live in Giza or Saqqara, and even then it takes time. She is capable of joining us at the site without your assistance unpacking her suitcases.'

'I prefer to be here to greet her on her first day back in Egypt since that dreadful experience,' I said. 'Furthermore, if we are to work at Am-arna, the dahabeeyah must arrive from Luxor. I am confident Fatima has thoroughly cleaned the *Amelia* several times from bow to stern, but she will need time to stock the larder. Not even to oblige you, my dear, will I camp out in an abandoned tomb for a lengthy season.' Emerson had, some years back, made a lavishly romantic gesture and acquired a Nile houseboat or dahabeeyah for me, and after refurbishing it fully, named it the *Amelia*. It has been our floating home in Egypt ever since then, being an efficient and practical way of moving from site to site and avoiding camping (although I am fully capable of running a com-fortable and clean camp), as well as travelling through Egypt on the Nile, as was done by the ancient Egyptians for millennia.

'You did once before,' Emerson replied, advancing upon me with a familiar gleam in his sapphirine eyes.

'I was younger then,' I said as his strong arms enclosed me, rekindling the most passionate of memories, 'but I would do it again if it were necessary. I cannot see that a few days . . .' I said no more at that time, for reasons that should be obvious to the sensitive Reader.

Emerson fussed a bit about the delay, but I managed to keep him distracted by one means or another. He is not a companionable shopper; his patience expires long before I have tried on more than three or four hats. I insisted that we purchase some shirts for him, since he is notoriously hard on his wardrobe. With ill-disguised reluctance, he consented to visit Selim's family, where we enjoyed a simple yet sumptuous feast with aunts, uncles and cousins of all ages. Other distractions took place in the boudoir and need not be described.

We were sitting on the hotel terrace taking tea when a cab pulled up at the steps and a familiar face appeared at its window, a delicately sculpted face framed by a halo of golden hair and adorned with a beaming smile. Emerson leapt to his feet, knocking over his chair, and ran down the stairs with the brash ardour of a besotted schoolboy. He plucked Nefret from the cab and held her close, giving me barely a chance to greet her at all.

'My dearest girl,' I said as she turned to embrace me. 'It is wonderful to see you, and even earlier than we had hoped.'

'I left Paris as soon as I heard you were on your way to Egypt,' Nefret replied. 'And here I am, just in time for tea.'

We returned to our table, where Nefret removed her hat and tossed it onto a chair. It was a warm day; heat and perspiration made her gold tendrils of hair cling to her temples and coil over her ears. The waiter who brought her cup and saucer could scarcely keep his eyes in their respective sockets. Several young officers at other tables appeared to have the same difficulty.

'Has the Professor condescended to inform you of where we will be working this season?' Nefret asked with amusement.

It was one of Emerson's more exasperating habits – which I did not find at all amusing – to delay this announcement until the last possible moment. On some occasions he had done so because he had procrastinated about applying for a firman and had in consequence been given a site nobody, including me, wanted.

'Oh yes,' I replied, anticipating Emerson. 'M. Maspero has asked us, as a personal favour, to return to Amarna.'

'Excellent!' she exclaimed.

'Herr Morgenstern has the firman,' I went on. 'Or, to be precise, the Deutsche Orient-Gesellschaft has it. According to M. Maspero, Herr Morgenstern was sent to replace Borchardt, who returned to Germany for personal reasons. Morgenstern has been neglecting his work to linger in Cairo, and we have M. Maspero's official permission to replace him if we believe him to be incapable of carrying out his duties.'

Nefret's lips curved in a smile. 'That leaves you quite a wide latitude.'

'We would never take advantage of that.'

'Of course not, Aunt Amelia.'

'But first we must complete the excavation we began at the end of last season, at Zawyet el'Aryan.' I took her hand in mine. 'If you fear it will cause you grief, you need not accompany us. You could, perhaps, take the train to Luxor and spend a few days at the clinic.'

She shook her head resolutely. 'I will come with you to Zawyet. I have conquered those horrid nightmares and I will not allow melancholic memories to dictate my life.'

I overcame the lump in my throat and assumed a cheerful voice. 'You see, Emerson, it was advantageous for us to wait. We now have a skilled photographer.'

'Yes, Peabody,' he said, his face lowered to hide what I suspected was an errant tear.

WE HAD AGREED not to mention my encounter with the assassin to Nefret; as I had pointed out to Emerson, there was no sense in worrying the girl about matters she could not assist us with. The following day I took the precaution of sending a note to Mr Russell, asking him to call on us at a time when I knew Nefret would be out visiting friends, and he was good enough to comply. When he joined us, I apologised for seeming to press him. 'I know,' I began politely, 'that you would inform us immediately of any new discoveries you have made.'

'I was about to do so when I received your message,' Russell replied. 'The dead man has not been identified. He appears to have no criminal record. He is unknown to Scotland Yard or the Sureté. What is significant about the name "Judas" in this connection? Who is so desirous of revenge upon Mrs Emerson, and is foolish enough to follow her to Egypt? Passage from England is not inexpensive, as you know so well. There surely cannot be many such zealous individuals.'

'Hah!' said Emerson.

'I beg your pardon?' said Mr Russell.

'Never mind,' Emerson muttered. 'I admit you have made a valid point, Russell. Such energetic activity on the part of her antagonist suggests that her perceived offence was of relatively recent date. Whom have you offended lately, Peabody?'

'Offhand I cannot think of anyone, Emerson. The scoundrel who was beating his donkey until I took the stick away and applied it to his shoulders could not have entered the hotel without—'

'Irrelevant and immaterial.'

'No doubt,' I conceded. 'The answer to your question, then, is that I am unaware of having offended anyone to such an extent that he would go to these extremes. Have you located Octavius Buddle? I fear he is the next intended victim.'

Mr Russell sighed. 'Nothing thus far indicates he is in Egypt, but you are familiar with the chaos at the port. Documents and paperwork are filed haphazardly, if at all. Immigration officers are not above bribery. Continue to search your mind, Mrs Emerson. We really cannot have this sort of thing going on.'

Emerson's sigh was longer and gustier. 'Never underestimate my wife, Russell.'

'Why, thank you, my dear,' I said with a modest smile.

ZAWYET EL'ARYAN HAS been described, possibly by me, as one of the more boring sites in Egypt. This is perhaps to do it an injustice, since it does possess the remains of two pyramids, if one can apply that term to crumbled, collapsed structures that resemble piles of meaningless rubble. Of these two so-called pyramids at Zawyet, the Unfinished Pyramid in the north is the only one whose substructure is of interest – particularly as there is virtually nothing of the superstructure preserved. A rock-cut ramp precisely sixty-eight point nine feet long (Emerson demands accuracy) was cut into the bedrock, leading down to a deep shaft in which the burial chamber was constructed. It is quite a nice burial chamber, with foundations and paving of red granite and a limestone skirting, and an elegant pink granite sarcophagus, which was to be set in the pavement. This act was never completed, and we were able to view the sarcophagus, which, unusual for that period, was oval. It had been sealed with plaster, and the excavator had the devil of a time opening it – to find, alas, that it was empty, save for a black stain on the bottom.

However, there was also a burial under one of the paving stones of the ramp. Honesty compels me to admit that we might not have found it had not the stone been left ajar. It had been levered aside and slightly downward, so that there was room for grasping hands to remove whatever contents were within reach. The hands in this case had belonged to Geoffrey Godwin, Nefret's late and unlamented husband. He had been working with a colleague of ours at Giza when we first met him, and although he seemed amiable and competent, Nefret's hasty marriage to him had taken me by surprise. I had not observed evidence of a strong attachment on her part, and I am somewhat of an expert in such matters. It was not until the end of the season that the full extent of Geoffrey's villainy became evident. When he was exposed, he had threatened to shoot me, and I had the distinct impression that he would have enjoyed doing so. Before he could act, Ramses had knocked him into the shaft on the edge of which he stood. Emerson had closely supervised the removal of the body, cursing steadily at the hapless police officers.

We had not had time the previous season (owing to the proceedings I have just mentioned) to complete the excavation of the burial under the paving stone. Emerson had provisionally assigned the burial to the Third or Fourth Dynasty on the basis of the dates of some of the nearby tombs, and a royal burial of this date, or a burial of a person closely enough related to the king to be buried in the pyramid, was an extremely important discovery.

During this period, most mummies (or to be more accurate, corpses, since the elaborate procedures of mummification did not appear until the Fourth Dynasty), were buried in a slightly flexed position, lying on their sides. This individual had been placed on a funerary bed equipped with beautiful ivory legs. What else we had soon learned was that Geoffrey had extracted the front legs of the bed but had been unable to reach any other part of the burial paraphernalia.

Or so we had assumed, until our workmen lifted the stone. The brown skull grinned up at us, as skulls do. Among the brittle bones of the ribs only a few gold beads remained of what must have been an elaborate neckpiece. It might have been ancient tomb robbers who took it, but it seemed more than likely that we should attribute this theft to Geoffrey. Once the burial chamber was accessible, we found that the other two legs of the bed were there, plus a number of jars that had contained food for the hereafter, including a tasty selection of dried meat – haunches of beef, goat and fowl. The poor person could at least count on nourishment in the hereafter. It was not a lavish burial, but a significant find.

Nefret seemed unruffled as she and Selim photographed the interior of the tomb and the contents therein. I discreetly observed her whenever I could, and was relieved by her placid composure. She was quieter than usual, and upon occasion I noted a slight tightness about her jaw, but she did not appear to be beset by ghosts from the past.

Emerson could never be accused of conducting a hasty excavation, but he did hurry the work as much as was possible without violating his professional standards (which are demanding). His temper was not improved by several messages from Maspero asking how much longer it would take us to finish at Zawyet. Finally, to the relief of all concerned, Emerson declared the excavation complete and we made ready to leave for Amarna. The following morning we boarded the train.

THE PLAIN OF Amarna is a rough half circle, with the river as the diameter. The cliffs come down almost to the river at either end of the diameter, so that access to the plain is difficult. The site is rich in archaeological remains: two groups of elegant nobles' tombs, a series of boundary stelae, a workmen's village, and the mournful remains of the once-dazzling city itself. Here Akhenaton, the Heretic Pharaoh, abandoning the city of Thebes and the worship of the extensive pantheon of gods and goddesses, built a new capital on ground that had never belonged to another god, as he declared in his plentiful boundary stelae that delineated the site. It was a short-lived city, active for some seventeen years and deserted not long after Akhenaton's death circa 1336 BC. His successor, young Tutankhamen, returned to Thebes and within less than a decade orthodoxy was re-established.

Akhenaton has been called the first monotheist and although certain other solar deities are mentioned in his inscriptions, it is mere quibbling, in my opinion, to deny that he is entitled to that distinction, any more than it is reasonable to deny that Christianity is monotheism because it worships the Father, the Son and the Holy Ghost.

But to resume.

Minya is the nearest official train station to Amarna, but it was not convenient for us, so the engineer obligingly stopped just across the river from the site. (He was obliging because Emerson had convinced him this act was in his own best interests, which it assuredly was.) This occasioned the usual complaints from the European passengers, which we of course ignored. Our loyal friends were waiting for us, and it did not take long to unload our luggage. It took longer to exchange the embraces and expressions of welcome from Daoud and the rest of the men, who had taken an earlier train. Even now, after so many years, I found myself looking for the stately form and magnificent turban of our former *reis* Abdullah, who had always been among the first to welcome us. Our men had worked for us for many years, and one of them, Abdullah's grandson David, was now a member of our family, having espoused our niece Lia. (The scandal this had caused in the *haut monde* of Kent had fed local gossip for weeks.)

It was like coming home again to see our dear dahabeeyah, which Emerson had named after me, moored at the dock across the river. We got ourselves into the small boats our friends had readied and as we approached the dock, we saw our treasured cook and housekeeper, Fatima, on deck, vigorously waving a towel. We were soon returning her hearty embraces, save for Emerson, who, with difficulty, extracted his hand from hers, which she was wringing with great enthusiasm as she could not embrace him in public, even though she was virtually a member of our family. Mahmoud, our steward, maintained a civil distance, but he was beaming.

I tried to persuade Emerson to allow us to rest a bit and tidy ourselves after the tedious train ride, but he was champing at the bit to get to the site, and Nefret announced that she was, too. Needless to say, I opted to join them.

Some of the rudimentary accommodations we had built previously were still standing, and the men set to work at once cleaning and repairing them. Four erect timbers awaited a canvas tarpaulin; shade was essential under the blistering sun. A small shed set away from the site offered a modicum of privacy in certain situations. The fact that the basic components of the structures remained intact was a tribute to Emerson. Not even the bravest of scavengers would dare risk offending the Father of Curses.

I knew there was no hope that I could keep Emerson away from Morgenstern's excavation. 'Why, Peabody,' he would say reprovingly, 'it is basic courtesy to call on a fellow scholar when one is in the neighbourhood.'

Which was precisely what he did say.

The path was one we knew well, following the river as far as was possible before striking out across the sandy, sun-baked plain towards the ruins of Akhenaton's once-beautiful city. We were still in the blessed shade of the cultivation, the belt of fertile soil on either side of the Nile, when we saw a man striding briskly towards us. He was a comical-looking fellow, with protuberant eyes and hair that poked straw-colored wisps out from under his hat. His white suit was tainted with dust, but his bright red bow tie appeared to be impeccable. He began calling out to us in a shrill voice when we were still some distance away. 'No one is allowed near the excavation! Leave at once!'

'Who the devil are you?' Emerson demanded.

The little man drew himself up to his full height (five and a half feet, at best). 'Octavius Buddle, representing Herr Morgenstern.'

'Good Gad!' Emerson said, startled. He gave me a sharp look. 'Fancy that. Peabody, here is Mr Octavius Buddle, alive and well.'

'I do believe your assessment is accurate,' I replied, 'although we have yet to examine his back. Would you be so accommodating as to turn around, Mr Buddle?'

'I shall do no such thing!'

'Then you leave me with only one option,' I said as I hooked his arm with my parasol and yanked him to one side. 'He is intact and unharmed,' I informed Emerson, who seemed immoderately entertained by the man's yelp of indignation. 'How shall we proceed?' Knowing my husband as well as I do, I knew we were both wondering if we ought to inform him about the card found in the would-be assassin's pocket.

Emerson shrugged. 'Do you know who we are, Mr Buddle?'

He looked us up and down with a cool self-confidence that I feared was bound to irritate my easily irritated spouse. 'Professor and Mrs Emerson, I presume. Herr Morgenstern was particularly insistent that you should not be admitted to the site. Kindly leave at once.'

'Bah,' said Emerson. 'You have given me no reason to suppose you have such authority, Mr Buddle. That Morgenstern should appoint you as his second-in-command is nonsense. I wish to speak with Morgenstern himself.'

'He is not here.'

'Where is he?'

'I see no reason why I should answer that question, Professor, but in fact Herr Morgenstern is in Cairo.'

'Ridiculous,' I said, forestalling a rude response from Emerson. 'He should have been back here some time ago. Be so kind as to tell us when you expect him.'

'I don't see why I should tell you anything, Mrs Emerson,' Buddle said with a priggish frown.

Emerson coolly picked him up and set him aside. 'I do not know you, sir, but I am certain of two facts: first, that you are no archaeologist, dressed as you are; and second, that you have taken it upon yourself, without authorisation, to speak for Morgenstern. Whom the devil do you represent?'

Somewhat taken aback by this blunt accusation, Mr Buddle hesitated for a moment before replying. 'You may not be aware, Professor, that the major contributor to the work of the Deutsche Orient-Gesellschaft is a distinguished gentleman named James Ridgemont. I am a trusted aide of Mr Ridgemont. He has sent me here to make certain his interests are looked after.'

'In other words, to claim the most interesting discoveries,' said Emerson to Nefret and me. 'That is why I have refused to accept sponsorship, even from so good a friend as Cyrus. Why the Service des Antiquités allows these looters to make off with so many unique objects I do not understand. Fortunately, we need not pay any attention to this fellow.'

Followed by Mr Buddle, who was making noises like an incensed chicken, we continued on our way. Suddenly an astonishing figure trotted out from behind one of the small houses. He was a great bear of a man, bulky and extremely hairy; not only did he exhibit a head of hair that resembled a great tangle of black yarn and a long black beard and moustache, even the backs of his hands were covered with black fuzz and more showed at the open collar of his shirt. I believe he had every intention of speaking to us, but before he could do so Emerson leapt upon him and bore him to the ground.

The two rolled back and forth while I stood over them with parasol raised and Nefret danced nimbly around the moving bodies, ready to intervene should it be necessary. She and I were accustomed to Emerson's precipitous actions, though I could not understand what had prompted this one. However, my duty was to assist my spouse, so when the bearish man was uppermost, I struck with my parasol.

Unfortunately the pair had rolled over at the last second, and my blow landed on my dear husband's head. Momentarily stunned, he loosened his grip and the man promptly extricated himself and dashed away as if ravenous hyenas were nipping at his heels.

I was torn between pursuing him and seeing to Emerson, but a moment's consideration informed me that the quarry was retreating at a velocity I could not match. Nor, to be candid, did I know what I would do if I were able to catch up with him.

Emerson sat up, rubbing his cranium.

'I am so sorry, my dear!' I exclaimed.

'Are you all right, Professor?' Nefret asked anxiously.

'Oh quite,' said Emerson, blinking. 'I am accustomed to being whacked on the head by my wife. It occurs more often than you might think.'

'Good heavens,' Mr Buddle blustered. I must give him credit; instead of fleeing, he had remained nearby, hopping up and down and uttering little squawks of alarm. 'Is this sort of behaviour typical, Professor? I find it reprehensible.'

'Should I have permitted him to accost my wife?' Emerson rose to his feet, his expression formidable. 'Are you familiar with the word "assassin"? It comes from the word *"hashshashin"* and was used to describe a sect of Nizari Ismalis formed in the late eleventh century and based in Syria and Persia.'

Emerson's lecture would have gone on at length had I not clutched his arm and gestured at a man hurrying towards us. He would have been a fine-looking young fellow, had it not been for the unseemly scar that disfigured his cheek. I deduced he must be German, since students of that nation take a peculiar pride in such stigmata.

'Mr and Mrs Emerson, I presume,' he began, but he got no further because Emerson leapt upon him and bore him to the ground.

'Emerson, please stop doing that,' I said in vexation. 'You must excuse my husband, Mr – er – '

Emerson, looking somewhat sheepish, removed himself and I assisted the newcomer to his feet and retrieved his hat. 'Allow me the honour of introducing myself,' he said hoarsely. 'Eric von Raubritter, at your service.'

I could not help but admire his self-possession. Few people remember their manners after being knocked down and nearly dismantled.

'How do you do,' I said. 'Allow me to present you to Dr Nefret Forth.'

Von Raubritter had already removed his pith helmet; he bowed in formal German style as Nefret smiled and nodded. Before either could continue with the courtesies, Emerson said, 'Who the devil—'

I raised my voice to a well-bred pitch that can silence even Emerson. 'Herr von Raubritter is obviously one of Morgenstern's staff, my dear. You had no business knocking him down.'

'Then who was that other fellow?'

'What other fellow?' von Raubritter asked.

'The hairy fellow,' Emerson growled. 'Black hair all over him.'

'I did see someone run off,' von Raubritter said, obviously bemused by this description. 'But I saw only his back. We certainly have no such . . .'

'Hirsute man,' I said helpfully. 'Imagine a bear.'

He shrugged. 'None of the men fit that description.'

'Aha.' Emerson gave me a meaningful look. 'You see, Peabody?'

'No, I don't, Emerson.'

'It should be obvious, Peabody.'

'It is not, Emerson.'

Von Raubritter laughed. Little dents at the corners of his lips gave him a good-natured look, as if he were always on the verge of smiling. 'What a pleasure it is to hear such affectionate domestic exchanges. As you deduced, I am Herr Morgenstern's second-in-command. If you will excuse me . . .'

I gestured at Mr Buddle. 'This gentleman claims to speak for Herr Morgenstern.'

Buddle shook his head. 'I merely repeated what he told me. I represent the interests of my employer.'

'He has no authority over the site,' said von Raubritter.

'Well, then,' Emerson said, 'we will just have a quick look round, in case we notice something Morgenstern may have overlooked.'

The sheer effrontery of this statement took the young man aback. 'But – but, sir,' he stammered.

'You needn't come with us,' Emerson said in a kindly manner. 'You have your work to do.'

He did come with us, though he had to run to catch up with us, for Emerson had not lingered. So did Mr Buddle, who had fallen silent, perhaps because he was too out of breath to speak. Once Emerson, Nefret and von Raubritter were far enough ahead to be out of earshot, I caught Mr Buddle's arm and pulled him aside.

'There is something I must tell you,' I said. 'You may be in grave danger.'

'That crossed my mind when your husband began throwing innocent persons to the ground,' he said drily. 'The man you described as bearish is a missionary who has been observing the excavation from time to time. He and Herr Morgenstern are on a friendly basis. Your husband should have given him the opportunity to introduce himself.'

I saw no need to defend Emerson's actions, which were justifiable in the present situation. 'In Cairo we, ah, encountered a criminal who had a card with your name written upon it. He is, ah, no longer a threat, but he may have associates who wish you harm.'

Mr Buddle gaped at me. 'Who is this man?'

'He may have been using the alias "Judas". The police have been unable to identify him properly.'

'A man named Judas who is no longer a threat? Mrs Emerson, I suspect the heat has muddled your senses,' he murmured in a voice laden with condescension. 'Why don't you find a place in the shade to rest, you poor lady?'

Rather than bother to concoct a scathing reply, I increased my pace until I had reached Emerson's side. He gave me a quizzical look, but I was not in the mood to recount the exchange and seriously endanger Mr Buddle's well-being.

Followed by the usual train of curious children and fellahin, we made our way along the edge of the cultivation. We were passing through a cluster of humble houses located in a small grove of palm trees when Emerson stopped short and turned with the panther-like quickness he can display when he chooses. One of the women following us was somewhat taller than the average Egyptian female, and was swathed from head to foot in black, except for a pair of kohl-rimmed dark eyes. Emerson and I are of one mind and one heart; I always know what he is thinking, sometimes before he knows it himself, so when Emerson rushed at the woman I was able to prevent him from knocking her to the ground.

'She is concealing something under her burka!' he exclaimed, trying to fend me off.

There was certainly a bulge, but if Emerson had not been so fixated on potential assassins, he would probably have arrived at the more obvious conclusion. Even after the woman fell to her knees, crying out, he continued to maintain his grip on her shoulder.

'Emerson, what in heaven's name are you doing?' I cried, futilely tugging his arm. 'She is with child.'

'What better disguise for our old enemy Sethos than that of a pregnant female?' Emerson crowed. 'Look at her eyes, Peabody! They are not black but greenish brown.'

'He is not the only one to have eyes of that shade,' I replied. 'He may be able to impersonate a pregnant woman, but this lady is soon to give birth. Not even Sethos could simulate that activity.'

'Oh good Gad!' Emerson let go of the woman as if she had become red hot. 'Are you certain?'

'Yes,' Nefret declared firmly. 'Help us get her into her house.'

Emerson, who had dealt with bloody wounds, including his own, with perfect aplomb, backed off, his eyes wide. 'Never mind,' I said. 'Just go away. Nefret and I can manage.'

Which we did, of course.

Twenty minutes later, we left the house and found Emerson hovering nearby. 'Is she all right?' he asked anxiously. 'The baby?'

'Both are well,' Nefret assured him. 'Her mother was ecstatic to have Sitt Hakim and Nur Misur in her home and was adamant that we have mint tea and figs. After I briefly examined the young woman, I assured her that her baby will be born in the next few days. Although she is only fifteen or sixteen, this is not her first child.' A shadow flickered across her face, but she maintained her gaze.

Once again my sometimes derided (by Emerson) belt of tools proved useful in cleansing hands, for I carry both water and alcohol with me. (The alcohol is in the form of whisky, thus serving in two capacities, those of restorative and disinfectant.) After Nefret dribbled a few drops on a handkerchief and began to rub her hands, I took a discreet sip. If my beloved husband was to continue leaping upon people, I would need fortitude.

Emerson went into the house. I heard a low murmur of conversation, then the metallic chink of coinage, followed by shrieks of delight. If the mother and daughter had borne Emerson ill will, his generosity had consoled them.

We proceeded on our way, following the line of the cultivation as far as was possible before striking out into the desert. Buddle was nowhere in sight, but when we neared the site where Morgenstern's crew was working, I saw von Raubritter watching our approach with a certain air of apprehension. To give the absent Morgenstern his due, he had been working with almost the same degree of expertise Emerson and I would have demonstrated. Having identified what must have been one of the main streets of the city, he was methodically excavating the structures that had lined and thus defined it. They were an interesting mixture, stately villas interspersed with lowly houses and miscellaneous buildings. The men had not yet reached ground level in a debris-riddled courtyard. They stopped at once at a sharp word from von Raubritter.

But the order came too late; only a few inches of sand remained and even I could see a shape too regular to be a natural formation. With a loud exclamation, Emerson dropped to his knees next to the excavated area and took a brush to clear the object of the remaining vestiges of sand. My cry of 'Emerson!' mingled with von Raubritter's 'No, Professor!' was to no avail. Only physical restraint can stop Emerson when he is on the trail of an important find.

'It is the head of a queen or princess,' Emerson pronounced as he stood up. 'Part of a composite statue. The crown would have been a separate piece, attached by means of this protuberance. As you see, Peabody, it was not finished. The surface is unpolished, and the faint vertical line from brow to chin indicates that the sculptor intended to continue working on it.'

Von Raubritter could not constrain himself from displaying superior knowledge. 'This is part of the workroom of a sculptor named Thutmose. I was told that Herr Borchardt was euphoric when he came across an ivory horse blinker amidst the rubbish. It was inscribed with Thutmose's name and job title as official court sculptor of Akhenaton. Since Herr Morgenstern has taken over, we have uncovered more than a dozen plaster casts of faces and full heads, along with tools and jars of pigments.'

Emerson raised his eyebrows. 'It is a woman. Do you suppose it could be Queen Nefertiti?'

I repressed a strong urge to poke Emerson with something sharp, but since I was loath to wield my parasol for a second time in less than an hour, I had to content myself with a whispered reprimand. 'That was not a wise move, Emerson. Look at them.'

'They' were the usual suspects – potential tomb robbers and other miscreants, scattered among the band of folk curious to see what we would do next and who had followed us. They had stopped when we stopped, at a safe distance from Emerson, and there was a good deal of jostling as everyone tried to get the best view. I recognised Mahmud Farouk's blind white eye and frosty brows, the piebald beard of Asmar, the pockmarked countenance of Mustafa Ahmed from our first sojourn at Amarna. If Sethos was among them, he was well disguised.

'They will be back tonight,' I went on, 'for they know that where there is one, there may be more.'

'I shall not allow that,' said Emerson. He raised his voice to his famous bellow. 'I will be here tonight, all night! Let he who would brave the wrath of the Father of Curses—'

'You have made your point, my dear, and very eloquently. Now give the brush to Herr von Raubritter. It has been a busy day and I would like to enjoy a late luncheon and rest.'

Emerson passed von Raubritter the brush and then handed over the head, but with a visible disinclination to trust someone else with his discovery. Squaring his shoulders, von Raubritter said, 'I appreciate your offer to help guard the cache, Professor, but that is my responsibility. With all due respect, I think that Herr Morgenstern would not – er – '

'Appreciate our interfering with another excavator's work,' I supplied. 'You are quite right, Herr von Raubritter. It will not happen again. I doubt you will have any difficulty tonight. I bid you good day. Come along, Emerson.'

Emerson sensed he was in for a scolding, as he would have called it. My mild reminders of proper behaviour were sometimes taken as such by my sensitive spouse. He offered me his arm as we retreated to the dahabeeyah. Once we were in the salon, Nefret tactfully removed herself.

'I suppose,' began Emerson, 'that you are about to lecture me for intruding on the duties of von Raubritter. Curse it, Amelia, I cannot allow—'

I knew I was in disfavour since he had used my given name instead of 'Peabody', which he had originally used as a term of derision, but which had become one of respect and affection. I refused to be put off.

'I have refrained from questioning you about your strange behaviour because I hoped the bond between us would lead you to confide in me voluntarily. That bond seems to have weakened, so I must ask: Why do you keep leaping on people who have done nothing to provoke you? What do you know that I do not? If this has become an involuntary habit—'

'Don't talk nonsense, Peabody!' Emerson snapped, rubbing his chin so vigorously that it reddened. 'I am not subject to involuntary habits. My behaviour is, as always, perfectly rational.'

'In that case you will not object to explaining it to me.'

'Oh the devil,' Emerson muttered, 'I suppose I must. You will get it out of me anyhow. I am somewhat surprised that the same explanation has not occurred to you. Who other than myself would intervene to protect you?'

'Ah,' I said. 'Another assassin here in Amarna, and in disguise. Well, I confess I am relieved. That assumption renders your recent habit of leaping on people explicable, if rash.'

'To be honest, Peabody, that idea had not entered my mind. No assassin would attack when you are surrounded by other people – especially me. We both know Sethos is here. What if he has been awaiting an opportunity to kidnap you again?'

'It seems plausible,' I acknowledged, 'especially since Herr Morgenstern seems to have made a significant discovery. It is a magnet for local thieves as well as those from the Continent. But you must apply reason before you knock people down. For instance, Sethos cannot possibly be Mr Buddle. He is a good six inches shorter than Sethos.'

'I did not knock Buddle down,' Emerson said self-righteously. 'Von Raubritter could be Sethos. He is of the right height, and a scar can be an element of disguise. It distracts one from other features.'

Pleased to hear him argue lucidly, I nodded. 'Well done, my dear. However, a more likely candidate is the gentleman covered with black hair. We cannot keep calling him "the hirsute man"; he must have a name and a plausible reason for being here. Mr Buddle identified him as a missionary who hovered about the site, but we must inquire further. Selim is the obvious person to ask. Where is he?'

'At the bl—blasted Workmen's Village, supervising the men.'

'Where we should have been, rather than encroaching on Herr Morgenstern's concession.'

'It isn't my fault, Peabody. With half my staff missing, there was little to be done today. Where the devil is Ramses? I sent him a letter last month that I need him and David. How can I concentrate on work when there are all these distractions? Protecting you, my dearest, takes precedence over all other things.'

He advanced upon me, arms outstretched, and I allowed him to seize me in a fond embrace. I enjoy Emerson's embraces at all times, and I hoped this one would keep him in a milder frame of mind. Unfortunately his attentions had just reached an interesting stage when a disembodied voice announced, 'Luncheon is served.'

The voice was that of Mahmoud, our excellent steward. He and the other servants liked to know that we were 'being friendly', as one of them had put it, but Emerson did not like to be seen when he was being friendly, and neither did I.

Nefret had decided to dine in her cabin. We ate on the upper deck, as was our custom when the weather was fine, as was the case today. The sky was blue, and the air was so clear we could see the sweep of the enclosing cliffs, bleached to pale yellow by the sunshine.

Upon our arrival, I had sent one of our fellows to fetch Selim. When he appeared, Emerson greeted him with pleasure.

'Good of you to come, Selim. Sit down and join us.'

Selim nodded his thanks and said, 'Father of Curses, I have already questioned the local villagers about the hairy person. His name is Theodor Dullard and he has been preaching to the fellahin about Issa.'

'Jesus!' Emerson exclaimed.

'Emerson!' I exclaimed.

'Merely translating, my dear. As you seem to have forgotten, "Issa" is the Arabic word for Jesus, who is regarded as a great prophet by Moslems. Dullard ought to be warned, Selim. Moslems do not tolerate proselytisers.'

'He is preaching to the Christians,' Selim said.

The Coptic Church has existed in Egypt since the first century. Initially tolerated by the Moslem conquerors, occasionally persecuted, it has flourished in certain areas of Egypt. There was a predominantly Coptic village in the region. We had had very little to do with the residents thereof, since our workmen were all related in some degree to Abdullah, and all were devout Moslems. 'Preaching to the Christians,' as Selim put it, was acceptable since nobody – except perhaps the Copts – cared what they thought.

'So Mr Dullard really is a missionary,' I said.

'They keep popping up, don't they?' Emerson pushed his plate away and reached for his pipe. 'One would suppose they would have realised they have made little headway and give up.'

'When one takes one's orders from God, one does not give up,' I said. 'Emerson, I believe we owe Mr Dullard an apology. I shall invite him to join us for tea. If you concur, that is.'

'Apology be damned!' snapped Emerson. 'I refuse to apologise to that fellow. But by all means ask him to tea. Selim, do you know where he is staying?'

'With the Copts at Deir el-Mowass,' Selim said promptly. 'I will send Daoud with a letter if you like.'

I went to my desk and penned a brief but friendly note. 'Tell Daoud to wait for a reply,' I said.

I take some of the responsibility for what was to happen. Due to fatigue, I failed to have observed a familiar gleam in Emerson's eyes.

THREE

As soon as I received a return note from Mr Dullard accepting our invitation, I requested an expansive tea, with a selection of cakes and tinned strawberry jam to accompany the scones. I have observed that missionaries have excellent appetites when there is an ample supply of food available. No doubt they are kept on short rations by their congregations as examples of Christian fortitude.

On my way to our cabin, I stopped and tapped softly on Nefret's door. There was no reply, so I peeked inside and saw the dear girl was sound asleep. The thought of a nap held immense appeal, but I needed to wash away the soot from the train ride and the dust from the rocky expanse of Amarna, tidy my hair, and don a suitable tea gown for our guest.

Mr Dullard arrived promptly at four o'clock. I tried not to stare at him, but he was certainly an extraordinary figure. Had his feet been bare, I was sure they would have sported the same thick layer of black hair as his hands did. When he greeted me in a precise, high-pitched voice, I had difficulty controlling my reaction because the contrast between his appearance and his speech was so extreme. As I escorted him into the salon, I offered a brief apology for Emerson's assault, since Emerson had made it clear that he himself would do no such thing, under any circumstances whatsoever, and my mere suggestion that he do so was preposterous. At least I think that was what he said, since his bellow echoed in the salon and he had inserted a remarkable number of curse words into his diatribe. While we waited for tea to be served, I lapsed into general remarks about the weather. Our guest replied in kind, while Emerson snorted periodically.

The missionary tucked into the food with good appetite. He was finishing his third cup of tea when Emerson suddenly reached across the table and seized him by the beard.

Dullard dropped his cup and began emitting shrieks of pain and surprise. After several sharp tugs, Emerson released it.

'Really, Emerson!' I cried out. 'Apologise to Mr Dullard at once.'

'I shan't,' Emerson replied with maddening complacency. 'It was necessary for me to ascertain that his hirsute appearance is genuine and not assumed for the purpose of disguise.'

Tears filled Dullard's eyes. 'I take it most unkindly, sir, that you should mock my unfortunate appearance. It is a hereditary family trait, and a source of grief to us, my sisters in particular.'

'For God's sake, man, don't cry!' snapped Emerson. 'And don't grovel! Stand your ground and don't apologise for something you cannot help.'

'Emerson,' I said. 'Look at Mr Dullard's eyes.'

'Why the blazes should I?'

'Look at his eyes. What is the one characteristic of Sethos that he has trouble disguising?'

'Hmph,' said Emerson. He knew the answer but was reluctant to admit he had acted rashly.

'Sethos's eyes are an indeterminate shade between green and brown. Mr Dullard's are dark brown.'

Emerson parried with 'I know that you are aware of the artificial scleral lenses created by Frick, and improved by Girard in the eighteen eighties. A person versed in disguises might have found a way to alter his eye colour.'

'Not at all, Emerson. I had already ascertained that he is not wearing such peculiar things,' I said after a brief stare at our guest's eyeballs.

'Then why did he run away this morning?'

'Because you threw me to the ground and began pummelling me!' Dullard squeaked.

'Then you ran away.'

'It did not seem wise to linger and endure further pummelling.'

'So you took the coward's way out and fled!' Emerson's tone was triumphant.

'My religious beliefs prevent me from injuring any of God's children.' Dullard's left eye, almost hidden under a bristly black eyebrow, twitched. 'Therefore, I had no choice but to leave rather than defend myself.'

Emerson's jaw jutted forward. 'You presume you are capable of injuring *me*?'

'I was a professional wrestler before I was called upon to spread the word of God. For nearly fifteen years, I travelled in a caravan in the Yorkshires. I was known as "Blackbeard". In Germany, they called me "*Schwarbar*", or "Black Bear". I was ne'er defeated by man nor beast.'

'Nor squirrel nor squire,' my husband said with a sneer.

I put an end to this unproductive dialogue by inquiring, 'May I ask, Mr Dullard, what sect or organisation is sponsoring you?'

'The Enlightened Brethren of the Church of the Father, Son and Holy Ghost. We are a small group dedicated to spreading the gospel across the world. Doing so is a hardship, since we have taken vows of poverty and must rely on the charity of strangers.'

Emerson made a strangled noise.

'Another scone, Mr Dullard?' I said brightly.

ACCUSTOMED AS I am to my son's unpredictable habits, his appearance at breakfast next morning produced a resonating exclamation of surprise from me.

'I apologise for startling you, Mother,' Ramses said as he bent down to kiss my cheek. He nodded at Emerson, who had not yet consumed enough coffee to be civil. 'I arrived late last night and decided not to wake you and Father. As I have come to expect of her, Fatima had my room ready for me.'

'It is always ready for you,' said Fatima. She clutched her hands together and gave him a broad smile.

The corners of Ramses's mouth turned up in an answering smile. It gave warmth to a countenance that was normally impassive and difficult to read. His colouring was that of the Egyptians among whom he had spent much of his life – light brown skin and dark eyes, and exuberant black hair with a tendency to curl that Ramses had fought more or less unsuccessfully since childhood. His features were not unpleasing, though his nose was too prominent and his jawline too angular to be deemed handsome. Oddly enough, a surprising number of young ladies found him prepossessing. There were usually a few hanging about him, flapping their eyelashes and cooing nonsense. I will say for Ramses that he did not encourage them. At least I don't think he did. Surely not . . .

I abandoned this train of thought. 'Is David with you?' I asked. He and Ramses are closer than most brothers; Lia and Nefret consider themselves to be sisters and best friends. Such familial affection is a blessing for which I have offered gratitude in many prayers.

'He is outside Cairo, visiting his relatives, but I expect him tonight or tomorrow.'

Fatima set an overflowing plate of eggs and toast in front of him. 'Where is Nefret?' Ramses asked.

'Here,' she announced from the doorway. 'Good morning, Aunt Amelia and Professor. Ramses, it's good to see you again.'

'And you, too.' He rose and gave her what I perceived to be a perfunctory hug. He held her chair for her, and she took her place at the table.

'Eat,' Fatima urged. 'You are too thin, Ramses.'

When Ramses began to eat, Nefret said, 'What's wrong with your arm?'

'It's nothing.'

'Let me see.'

Emerson, finishing his second cup of coffee, was now capable of taking notice of the world around him. He cleared his throat. 'You may as well comply. She'll keep after you until you do.'

With an audible sigh Ramses put down his fork and rolled up his sleeve. Someone, probably David, had wound cloth of questionable cleanliness around a long slash on Ramses's right forearm.

'It needs to be disinfected and rebandaged,' Nefret said sternly.

'Can it not wait until after breakfast? I'm hungry.'

'Oh, I suppose so. You've already contaminated the wound. When did this happen?'

'A few days ago,' Ramses said. 'The freighter David and I took from Palestine encountered nasty weather the entire journey, and both of us felt under the weather when we docked at Alexandria. We stayed in a hotel for two nights and then took the train to Cairo. As I mentioned, David went to his cousins' village. I had some business to attend to, which included' – he glanced at Emerson – 'finding out where you were.'

'Which you did,' Emerson responded blandly as he allowed Fatima to refill his coffee cup. 'You would be hard pressed to find anyone in Cairo who doesn't know where I am at any time.'

'We would appreciate a few more details about this attack, if you don't mind,' I said. I shivered as one of my famous premonitions, which seldom prove false, occurred to me.

'It was rather odd, actually,' Ramses said. 'I went to the Khan el-Khalili to have a little chat with Aslimi about some fake antiquities he has been selling to gullible tourists. I was on my way back when someone jumped me from a dark doorway. I got my arm up in time to protect my throat and managed to disarm the man, but he took to his heels and I lost him in that maze of narrow streets and alleys.' He resumed eating.

That terse description of a deadly encounter was typical of Ramses.

In this case I wanted to ask for more details, but Nefret was tapping her foot and scowling like a thundercloud, so I said, 'Ramses, please go with Nefret and let her tend to that cut.'

'Yes, Mother,' he replied without enthusiasm.

Emerson and I had finished eating when Ramses came back with bandages covering his entire forearm.

'Mother, do I really need all this? It's as if she is planning to mummify me, one appendage at a time.'

'Leave it,' I said, 'or deal with Nefret in her wrath.'

Ramses smiled as Fatima put another platter of food in front of him. 'Nefret felt the need of a sponge bath and a change of attire after dealing with my seeping wound. An eavesdropper might have deemed her the "Daughter of Curses". Her vocabulary was most impressive.'

'Ramses, you must eat so your arm will heal,' Fatima pleaded.

He obediently picked up his fork, and I said, 'Before you begin, Ramses, answer a single question. What did the person who attacked you look like?'

'It was getting dark. I didn't get a look at his features, only his general outline. He was tall for an Egyptian, and not heavily built. He moved with the agility of a young man. The oddest thing was that he was wearing eyeglasses. One lens caught the light, dim as it was—'

'Those were not eyeglasses!' I exclaimed. 'They – it – that was a monocle!'

'A what?' Ramses said.

Emerson opened his mouth.

'I will explain,' I said. 'The situation is somewhat complex and requires a certain amount of background information.'

Emerson closed his mouth, and I went on. 'As you know, the Deutsche Orient-Gesellschaft has the firman for Amarna. M. Maspero gave us permission to excavate at the Workmen's Village.'

'Extraordinary,' said Ramses. 'As a general rule, the concession includes the entire site.'

'Unusual, at least,' I acknowledged. 'My – our – theory is that Herr Morgenstern has run into something of sufficient importance that it has taken precedence over his excavation. We haven't set eyes on him since we arrived. The work is proceeding under his subordinate, a man named von Raubritter, but it is not like Herr Morgenstern to delegate when interesting finds are turning up. Yesterday your father discovered a very beautiful, though unfinished, head, which may be that of Nefertiti. There is compelling evidence of a workroom that belonged to a sculptor named Thutmose.'

Ramses's black eyebrows went up. 'Father discovered the head?'

'He had no business doing any such thing,' I said before Emerson could bully his way into the discourse. 'We had gone to the site on a perfectly open and proper mission – to greet an old friend' – I ignored a sputtered curse – 'and confer with him as to how we should work together. His crew had partially cleared a courtyard and your father . . .' I caught Emerson's eye and amended what I had started to say. 'Your father's trained eye saw – a shape, was it not, Emerson? A shape that told him something of interest lay just out of sight. He could not resist brushing away the sand to expose it. It was wrong of him, but understandable.'

'Wrong be damned,' he growled. 'The greatest sin in archaeology is for the excavator to allow unsupervised digging to go on. We can trust our people to turn over the discoveries to us, but such is not the case with all the men. If a small, easily hidden object turned up, the temptation to tuck it away would—'

'The ushebti,' I said. 'That must have been what happened. One of the men found it, realised its value, and secreted it in—'

'Excuse me, Mother,' Ramses said, a trifle exasperated, 'but at this moment I am less interested in Herr Morgenstern's activities than in your assertion that my assailant wore a monocle. Even you must acknowledge that it was a very peculiar remark.'

'My remark is not the least bit peculiar in that a person wearing a monocle burst into my bath chamber at Shepheard's,' I explained. 'No,

Ramses, kindly do not interrupt my orderly narrative. Eat your breakfast. You may ask questions when I have finished.'

Ramses managed to control himself, although his eyebrows kept going up and down and at one point he let out a choked gurgle. When I finished, he took a very long breath, let it out, and remarked, 'Accustomed as I should be to the – er – busyness of your life, Mother, I hardly know what to say first. The monocles do seem to connect the attacks on us, but what the devil do they mean?'

'I expect they are the insignia of a secret society,' I said. 'If need be, the assassins are able to recognise one another in public.'

'A secret society!' Emerson exclaimed. 'Balderdash! Must you elevate the so-called gang of thugs to a higher rank? Will they soon be agents of a global conspiracy?'

I gave him a cool look. 'Then the fact that both men sported monocles was merely a coincidence?'

Since he could not think of an answer, Emerson was forced to say, 'The monocles are a bizarre element. To judge by the example I examined, they served no practical purpose. The broken lens was of clear glass, without magnification. I suppose it could have been used to start a fire by focusing the sun's rays, but why bother with that when matches are available?'

'Possibly,' Ramses countered, 'because sharp shards of glass can inflict deadly and disfiguring wounds. It is a simple weapon.'

'Oh dear,' I said.

'I would have employed a stronger word,' said Emerson. He shrugged into his coat and started for the door. 'Selim has gathered a full crew, and I am needed.'

'Put on your pith helmet,' I said.

'Why? I always lose the cursed things, and then you complain.'

'Emerson, there are going to be persons present who dislike you. They fear you, yes, but a missile flung by one member of a crowd can be more or less anonymous.'

He slapped the pith helmet on his head with such force that

the impact reverberated for several seconds. He winced slightly. 'Ramses, you have my authorisation to lock up your mother . . . No, just don't let her out of your sight. I want you or Nefret with her every moment.'

'Really, Emerson,' I said. 'Is there any reason why I should not accompany you? Surely I would be safer with you than with anyone else.'

'Well, er, hmph.'

'Mother is correct,' Ramses admitted. 'I'll wait for Nefret, and we should be no more than fifteen minutes behind you. In broad daylight, with the three of us, as well as Selim, Daoud and the crew surrounding her, it would take a very efficient assassin to get anywhere near her.'

It was a reasonable assumption.

EMERSON STOPPED TO speak with Selim, who was waiting on our small dock. I walked on ahead. I had no warning, only a sudden outburst of a thunderous rhythm behind me, before an arm like whipcord wrapped round my waist, lifted me and deposited me with noticeable force upon a hard surface – in this case, a saddle.

He was attired in the voluminous black robe of a Touareg, the traditional blue veil concealing all but his eyes. I knew those eyes, though, and also the voice that remarked, 'Stop squirming, Amelia. If you fall, you will incur some nasty bruises.'

'I have already incurred several nasty bruises,' I retorted angrily. 'What is the meaning of this theatrical performance, Sethos?'

'I thought you enjoyed theatrical performances. What could be more romantic than being snatched up by a veiled rider on a white horse and carried off into the desert? Seriously,' he went on, before I had framed an adequately derisive reply, 'I wanted to have a private conversation with you. It is difficult to find you alone.'

'I will, of course, repeat everything you say to Emerson.'

'That is your privilege.' He slowed the horse to a walk. 'But I can't carry on a reasonable discussion with Emerson stamping and swearing and trying to knock me into the next room.'

'I suggest you be brief, then. Emerson is in hot pursuit.'

Sethos glanced over his shoulder. 'He's quite a bit behind. What I need to ascertain from you is if you have any ideas as to the identity of your assailant. I haven't been able discover anything about him.'

'You were the one who stabbed him, I presume. Didn't you—'

'There wasn't time for me to search him. I was in somewhat of a hurry,' he replied blandly. 'Did you and Emerson discover anything in his pockets that might identify him?'

As a rule I have no difficulty making decisions. Sethos was far more familiar with the network of thieves and rogues that plagued Egyptian society. I quashed the temptation to mention the monocle and cards, and said, 'Nothing.'

He looked back. 'I see Emerson is gaining on us. He can run quite fast for a man of his size, can't he? If it occurs to him to commandeer a horse, he may become a nuisance.' He pulled his steed to a stop and lowered me to the ground. 'If I were a phrenologist I would say you had a hollow where your bump of self preservation should be. Please do your long-suffering husband and me a favour, and try to stay out of trouble. À bientôt, Amelia.'

Sethos was a distant figure when Emerson swept me into his arms. His embrace was such that I could scarcely breathe, but his panting was adequate for the two of us. 'Good Gad, Peabody, are you unharmed?' he demanded as he stepped back and searched my face.

'I'm fine, Emerson,' I said, although I was feeling a bit dizzy. I am unaccustomed to 'theatrical performances' of such intensity and drama.

Emerson glowered at the disappearing rider. 'I needn't bother to ask, I presume,' he said. I shook my head. 'Then we shall discuss this later, Peabody, and in private. Selim and the crew are no doubt standing idle, their mouths agape. We have work to do.'

I FULLY EXPECTED that at breakfast the next day Emerson would have something more to say about the events of the previous morning. However, he appeared to feel that the subject had been sufficiently discussed when we had retired to our cabin after dinner. He had certainly discussed it at length and went on doing so even after he fell asleep; several times I was awakened by a large hand fumbling at me and a voice muttering curses. I had persuaded him not to stand guard at the site the night before. The mere possibility that he might appear from behind a boulder or a wall would be enough to deter potential thieves, some of whom regarded him as having supernatural powers like his son. (Ramses's Egyptian soubriquet, I regret to say, is Brother of Demons.)

There were three of us at table. Nefret had not yet come down. Emerson had just enough energy to ask in dying tones, 'Is there . . . is there coffee?' I at once supplied him with that beverage, for I was familiar with his habits. Knowing it would take several cups to restore his father to coherence, Ramses continued our discussion.

'Mother, I am familiar with your views on proper conversation at table, but this may be the best opportunity to talk about certain matters before Nefret joins us. I must ask you if you have had any new ideas as to the identity of your attacker?'

'Hmm,' I said. 'That is an interesting question. If the fellow was a hired assassin, he was carrying out orders from someone else, his employer. This unknown employer engaged the services of yet another assassin who left that ugly slash on your arm. What happens if the first attempt fails, as it did in both circumstances? Is the original assassin – in your case, obviously – bound to keep on trying? Or, if he has been put out of commission, must he supply a substitute or perhaps return the payment? For we must assume that they demand payment in advance, since—'

'Mother,' Ramses said impatiently, 'please concentrate. Who are these monocled people and why are they bent on our untimely demises?'

At this point the door burst open with such force that it slammed

back against the wall. Framed in the doorway, with the sunlight behind her, Nefret resembled one of the goddesses of vengeance, her
golden hair forming an aureole around her face.

'You were listening at the door,' I said reprovingly.

'Apparently I must since no one in this family trusts me enough to
confide in me!' she retorted, glaring in turn at each of us.

Emerson let out a rumble of protest, and I said, 'My dear girl, we
were only trying to spare you needless concern. There is nothing you
can do—'

'Yes, there is! I can answer Ramses's question.'

FOUR

EFRET CROSSED HER arms. 'Geoffrey.'

Emerson and I exchanged alarmed glances. 'Let me get this straight,' he said. 'Geoffery Godwin? Nefret, my dearest, Geoffrey is—'

'Dead!' she snapped. 'But his influence, his power, did not die with him. He told me a great deal about his family, things I never repeated to you because he professed abhorrence of their activities and assured me he had separated himself from them for ever. They were, and are, the scourge of Cornwall, lawless and unprincipled. They feud among themselves, but if an outsider threatens one of them, they close ranks and go after this enemy with unbridled ferocity. It must be Geoffrey's family members behind these attacks. They meet your criteria, and Geoffrey did mention that they fancied themselves gentlemen because they wore monocles. They are wealthy because they take what they want from the people they terrorise, and they never forget or forgive a perceived injury.'

'That would explain why Ramses and I have been the only ones attacked,' I mused. 'I was the one who exposed Geoffrey as the villain he was, and Ramses – good heavens, they must consider Ramses to be directly responsible for Geoffrey's death! Ramses's blow sent Geoffrey tumbling into the pit and incidentally saved my life. But Ramses tried to pull Geoffrey back. He chose to let go of Ramses's hands.'

'True,' Ramses said without expression, although I knew he was still troubled by his involvement, even if it was warranted. Despite the cruelty and violence that at times seemed indigenous to the Middle East, he has maintained a tender heart. Many of his sworn enemies have survived solely due to his aversion to the taking of a life.

'Those of us nearby were the only ones who saw that,' Emerson said. 'To someone at a distance it might have appeared that Ramses was trying to pry Geoffrey's fingers loose.'

'That is how Geoffrey's family would interpret it,' said Nefret, her upper lip curled in contempt. 'Altruism and mercy are alien concepts to them.'

'Hmph,' Emerson said. 'I believe you have hit the nail on the head, Nefret. If we were in England, we could mount an expedition and rid the shire of the Godwin tribe. Under the present circumstances, our best course is to deal with the assassins themselves. How many of the bl— er – villains are there, do you suppose?'

'Five,' Nefret replied as she sat down at the table.

Emerson stared at her. 'How do you know that?'

Some of the colour had left her cheeks and her voice trembled. 'Geoffrey had five brothers, or half-brothers, to be precise. Their names . . .' She frowned, her mouth pursed. 'Oh yes, how could I forget? Judas, Cromwell, Absalom, Guy and Flitworthy.'

'What extraordinary names!' I exclaimed. 'Judas, the betrayer; Cromwell, responsible for the execution of King Charles I; Absalom, King David's renegade son. The only notorious Guy I can recall offhand was Guy Fawkes, who tried to blow up King James I and Parliament. As for Flitworthy, nothing comes to mind, although it is a rather silly name. Their mother must have been deranged to bestow such names on her sons.'

'Geoffrey escaped with a conventional name solely because he was the product of his mother's first marriage to an ordinary chap.' Nefret said. 'Being married to Geoffrey's vile stepfather would have been a strain on any woman. She endured the births of five more sons. Her choice of names suggests a strong sense of bitterness.'

'So we must assume that the assassin who burst into the bath chamber was Geoffrey's brother Judas,' I said. 'The card he carried was not an accusation, but his own name.'

'Half-brother,' Nefret corrected me. 'Yes, Aunt Amelia, I believe we must. I never met him or the others, but I feel certain that was the equivalent of a calling card. Had he succeeded in his murderous mission, he wanted to be sure he got the credit.'

'It behooves us to find out for certain,' Ramses said. 'I suggest we telegraph Sir Reginald Arbuthnot at Scotland Yard. He is an admirer of Mother's and can inquire of the local constabulary as to the current whereabouts of the Godwin brothers. If they are no longer in their usual habitat, we must face the probability that they are in Egypt.'

'Only four of them now,' Emerson said with grim satisfaction. 'See what you can find out from Scotland Yard, will you, Ramses? I must be off.'

'I will be with you as soon as I have fetched my parasol,' I said, rising. 'And my belt of tools.'

Emerson looked me up and down. 'Very well, Peabody. Despite the events of yesterday morning, you are probably safer with me.'

'Emerson,' I said, putting my hand on his arm, 'I know your feelings about Sethos—'

'No, you don't.'

'But I ask you to consider, fairly and without rancour, whether or not he has been of assistance to us. You share, I believe, the same goal: my protection. Why not make use of him in that capacity? "The enemy of my enemy is my friend," as the Arabic proverb has it. You need not be friends,' I added hastily as Emerson's face darkened to an ominous hue. 'You merely need to be – how to put it – well, non-enemies.'

'Hmph.'

I considered this a good sign. On some occasions Emerson had employed a number of swear words at the mere hint of such an alliance.

After I had found my parasol and donned my belt of tools, we set out.

As always I was ready to defend my husband should the need arise, but on this occasion I felt I could relax my vigilance. Our loyal men would be with him, and Daoud was a pillar of strength by himself. Daoud was a gentle man, not easily stirred to anger, but his giant frame and simple mind made him a formidable opponent. 'Simple' does not mean 'stupid'. Daoud was not stupid, but he had a very direct way of looking at difficulties. If there was a problem, one dealt with it promptly and effectively. Then there was no longer a problem.

Emerson interrupted my train of thought by remarking, 'You are jangling more than usual today, Peabody. Have you added more – er – objects to that belt of yours?'

'I believe you are familiar with all of them, Emerson. My little pistol, my knife, a sewing kit for stitching up wounds, you know—'

'I do know,' said Emerson emphatically.

'A coil of thin but stout cord—'

'For tying up prisoners.'

'A length of cord is useful in a number of ways, Emerson. To continue: a little flask of whisky, a compass, an electric torch, a water bottle, a folding cup for I do not consider it ladylike to swig liquid from a bottle or canteen except when under duress—'

'Splendid,' said Emerson. 'Yes, yes, well done as usual, Peabody.'

Realising I had lost his attention (for, after all, he had heard the list a number of times), I fell silent so I could ponder the question of what Morgenstern had stumbled upon. The sculptor Thutmose's workshop, which contained the plaster casts of practice portrait heads and the ivory horse blinker that von Raubritter had indiscreetly mentioned, was a remarkable find. It is rare that an archaeologist can identify the creator of a sculpture with such sureness, and Morgenstern could publish papers and present lectures long after the excavation was completed. That he would leave the site under the supervision of a subordinate was even more inconceivable. Emerson often had to be discouraged from sleeping at a promising site, but he is, as I am fond of reminding my Readers, the greatest Egyptologist of the nineteenth century, and now the twentieth century. Morgenstern had abandoned a site of great importance, a faux pas worthy of inclusion in the list of deadly sins.

No doubt Emerson had reached this conclusion as well. He had not yet voiced his intentions, but I could read his mind as easily as I read what he derisively calls my 'sensational fiction'. I prefer the term 'contemporary literature'.

As we plodded on through the sand, perspiration trickling down my cheeks, it occurred to me that we ought to construct quarters nearer the remains of the city. Such construction was easily carried out; sundried brick, which the locals were accustomed to making, served quite well unless there was a heavy downpour of rain. Under those circumstances the bricks dissolved into a mass of clay. However, this seldom happened, and the collapsed structure was easily repaired. When the Deutsche Orient-Gesellschaft had been awarded the firman for Amarna, Borschardt did what most archaeologists would have done: constructed a suitable structure designed for long-term residential and professional needs. He had occasionally entertained us in his house, which he had made quite comfortable with brightly woven rugs, sturdy tables and chairs of local manufacture. Bookshelves from the same source held his reference materials, notebooks and correspondence. One room lacked windows and had a stout door with a lock, where objects from the excavations could be stored to be further examined and catalogued. One could not begrudge him such comforts, since there were no hotels nearby in which a person with even minimal standards of hygiene and sanitation could reside. Morgenstern surely had moved in on arrival.

'I have been thinking,' I said to Emerson, 'that since we are going to commandeer the city site—'

'Are we, Peabody? What a novel idea.'

'Which occurred to you the moment you realised that Morgenstern has left the site vulnerable – unless, of course, the idea was conceived in M. Maspero's office.' When he merely gazed at me, I continued. 'We ought to build ourselves a nice dig house.'

'Why bother?' Emerson demanded. 'Here is Morgenstern's. Maspero authorised us to take over his work, which would certainly include his house.'

'Good gracious, Emerson, that is rather disingenuous. I am not at all sure—'

'If Morgenstern were here and in his right mind, he would invite us in,' Emerson said. 'Since he is not here and probably not in his right mind, he can have no objection to our making use of his pleasant little house. If this von Raubritter fellow is in residence, I will instruct him to find other accommodations. We need to be nearer the site, Peabody. The resident vultures have already gathered.'

But when we reached the site we found it deserted. The concavity that had held the sculptures had been filled. We continued to the dig house, which was padlocked. All around, as the poet Shelley has it, the lone and level sands stretched far away.

Or words to that effect. To be strictly accurate, the sands were not level. Humps and hollows broke the surface. Nor were they lone. Camels, donkeys, dogs and people were going about their business, making a colourful variegated pattern: the black garments of the women, the blue-and-white-striped robes of the men, and the sombre indigo robes and turbans of a few Copts.

Hands on his hips, Emerson surveyed the scene with scornful eyes. 'I knew von Raubritter was no archaeologist. He and his crew should be here. And so should Morgenstern.'

He took hold of the padlock and gave it a hard tug. The entire fastening – bolt, padlock and doorframe – came off. Hinges squealed. 'Hell and damnation!'

'Oh dear,' I said. 'Can you mend it, Emerson?'

'Not without tools.' He shoved the door open.

I followed him into the front room. It was as I remembered it, but exceedingly untidy. Fine sandy dust permeates the smallest of cracks, and even if we had not known Morgenstern was absent, the accumulation of sand on every flat surface would have told us as much. I had always considered Morgenstern more fastidious ('finicky', according to Emerson) than most men, but the place was a complete shambles – the bed unmade, unwashed dishes on the table and the stench of rotting refuse filling the air.

'He left in a hurry,' I said, pinching my nose, 'and I can think of only two reasons.'

'I have come up with only one. Please elucidate, Peabody.'

I took a large handkerchief from one of my pockets and wiped a chair seat. Once it met my standards, I sat down. 'Morgenstern could have developed some dreadful medical problem that required him to consult a doctor in Cairo. He might be hospitalised.'

'And no one in Cairo knows this? Gossip about foreigners spreads like a dust storm, as you well know. I've had inquiries about where I've been before I've gone there.'

'Which is why I discarded that theory,' I replied. 'Shall I continue?'

'You needn't bother,' Emerson said. 'Morgenstern has obviously discovered something of great significance, something he was unwilling to show von Raubritter or Buddle. Based on the location of the most recent excavation, we can assume it is a piece of sculpture by Thutmose.'

'Well, yes, that was my primary theory. Morgenstern took it to Cairo to sell to one of the unscrupulous dealers.' I paused, prudently scooting in my chair as Emerson began to pace around the table like a caged tiger. 'Or he could have—'

'Taken it to a forger! He plans to keep the original for himself, or as you suggested, sell it to a dealer. In either case he will return with the forgery and receive acclaim for a discovery of what must be vast importance.' Emerson came to an abrupt halt. I sighed in relief; swivelling my head to watch him was a strain on my neck muscles. 'We must put a stop to this damned scheme, Peabody! We will leave for Cairo as soon as possible. I trust you are not going to suggest we spend the night here.'

'Good heavens, no. But since we intend to occupy the house upon our return, we should at least get rid of the rubbish,' I said.

'Oh, I suppose so. You aren't going to insist on going through it, I hope.'

'I am going to insist on a whisky and soda and a comfortable bed,' I said, smiling. 'But the door is now useless as a barrier, so I shall ask Selim, as a special favour, to send a few of his people to guard the place.'

OUR FRIENDS REPORTED no disturbance during the night, and Mohammed, our carpenter, repaired the door. Fatima sent one of her girls to the house, and under my direction we soon had the place in fairly good order – the bed linens laundered, dust and sand removed, dishes washed and put away. I did a thorough examination and discovered no indication that Herr Morgenstern had shared his accommodations with von Raubritter or Buddle, which I found peculiar since it was customary to do so. By late in the afternoon we completed the task and returned to the dahabeeyah. I was delighted to find David sitting with Nefret and Ramses on the upper deck.

'How are you?' I said as I gave him an enthusiastic hug. 'Is everything well with your family?'

'They send their kindest regards, Aunt Amelia,' he replied, his thin brown face split by a warm smile. 'As does Lia, who is so very fond of you and the Professor. I miss her so much that I can scarcely sleep at night.'

'But when you do,' Nefret said, giggling, 'I'm sure you dream of her. Her letters have become quite boring, since her only topic is how much she misses you.'

'May I read them?' he asked eagerly.

'Of course not. They would make you blush.'

Ramses gave her an odd look as he handed me a whisky and soda. I gave him an equally odd look, but he failed to notice it.

BY THE FOLLOWING morning we were ready to take the early train. Ramses announced his intention of accompanying us, and David did the same; Nefret decided to go to Luxor to visit the clinic and purchase supplies as needed. Daoud beamed all over his large amiable face when I asked if he would like to go. After expressing his pleasure in being able to visit the city, he added vehemently, 'And, Sitt, I will watch every passerby and seize them if they approach too closely.'

We discussed various ramifications of this proposal, and Daoud agreed not to seize people unless they appeared menacing, though I was not certain he understood what I meant by that word, or would accept my definition if he did.

'With you on one side of me and Emerson on the other, and Ramses and David following behind, no one can get near enough to harm me,' I pointed out.

'Camels,' muttered Daoud. 'A rider on a camel—'

'You will, of course, watch out for them, too,' I said, wondering how many innocuous camel riders would be demanding exorbitant baksheesh after being dragged from their saddles.

As it turned out, very few incidents of that sort occurred. (I had never seen a camel move sideways until Daoud made certain it did.)

Once we were established at Shepheard's, we set off for the old market. It had been some time since I had visited the Khan el-Khalili. It was delightful to be there again, traversing the winding pathways under passages through whose latticed roofs rays of sunlight stretched like dusty fingers. The shopkeepers squatted on whitewashed mastaba benches outside their shops; one old acquaintance recognised me and called out, 'Sitt Hakim! I have new, beautiful cloth from Damascus, woven with gold. For you, a special price!'

Which would involve my paying the usual price, after an hour of coffee drinking and pleasurable haggling. 'Not today, Fahim,' I called back. 'Another time, perhaps.'

Harun has been acknowledged as the finest forger in Cairo. We had long suspected that many of his fakes were displayed in museums throughout Europe and the United States, while the originals were held by wealthy collectors of ancient Egyptian art.

His establishment was just around the corner from the Street of the Metalworkers. One of the loungers on the mastaba bench outside the shop rose and offered me his seat (and a cupped hand ready to receive baksheesh). I shook my head, and Emerson and I went into the shop, leaving the rest of our entourage outside in order not to terrify Harun into a heart attack.

There was no one in the small front room, which contained only a chair, a desk and a few shelves displaying oddments of pottery. From behind a door at the back came low voices and clinking sounds. When I tried the door I found it locked – an occurrence so unusual that I stood staring at it for several seconds before announcing my presence.

The door opened just wide enough for one of Harun's eyes to appear. 'Oh, it is you, Sitt!' he said in a poor pretence of surprise. 'And Father of Curses. *Ahlan-wa-salan!* Welcome to my humble shop.'

I put my hand on the hilt of my parasol. 'Are you coming out, or shall we go in?'

It is amazing how expressive a single optic can be to one who has learned to read such signals. His obvious reluctance to admit us only made me more determined to proceed. The sight of Emerson looming behind me may have contributed to his rapid retreat from the door. Or the sight of Ramses and David, who had followed us and were looming as well. I pushed open the door.

Two of Harun's apprentices were seated at a table on whose surface rested blocks of limestone, about twenty inches tall and roughly shaped into what would eventually be a human head wearing a tall crown. As we entered, they leapt to their feet and fled through the back door.

Harun stood with his back to me – an act of rudeness I found hard to understand until I realised he was hunched over, his arms wrapped round what was either a disastrously enlarged stomach or an object of some size.

'Caught in the act,' said Emerson, grinning. 'Put it on the table, Harun. You cannot elude the Sitt Hakim or the Father of Curses.'

'Or the Brother of Demons,' Ramses added ominously.

Harun let out a heartrending groan. 'I know that. But I have done nothing wrong. He will tell you; he comes every day to see her. She is his. He found her, and he has fallen in love with her.'

'Good gracious,' I said. 'Is it Herr Morgenstern of whom you speak?'

Harun nodded vigorously. 'I did not say his name. I gave him my word I would not say it.'

'You have kept your word,' Emerson said impatiently. 'Now let us see it.'

Everyone knows it now. It has become a symbol of Egypt, an icon. But that first sight literally took my breath away. I had never seen anything to equal it. The exquisite face, tinted in the colours of life, the long slender throat and proudly lifted chin, and the tall blue crown that was hers alone.

'Nefertiti,' I said in a long breath. 'How lovely she is, how serene, how regal.'

Ramses took it from Harun's arms and set it on the table. 'Indeed. Her name translates as "a beautiful woman has come". That is an understatement. Thutmose must have been a highly talented sculptor to produce a work of this precision.'

'So this is what Morgenstern found before he deserted his excavation and went dashing off to Cairo,' Emerson muttered. 'What is it doing here, Harun?'

'It is his. He brought it—'

'It is not his,' Emerson said. 'Not unless the Service des Antiquités awards it to him at the final division. Answer my question, Harun. Why did Morgenstern bring it to you?'

Harun was very proud of his long white beard. It extended almost to his waist. I presume he combed and washed it periodically, but hair of that length does tend to collect debris, and Harun's was an untidy profession. He brushed at it as he glanced upward for help from Allah.

'Never mind,' Emerson went on. 'The answer is obvious. You are the one my wife likes to call the Master Forger, the most skilled maker of fakes in Cairo. Morgenstern asked you to make him a copy. Who else asked you to do so?'

'No one, Father of Curses. No one.'

'Your apprentices,' said Emerson, biting off each syllable, 'are working on objects that are clearly copies of the original head. Two objects. One, you say, is for Herr Morgenstern. For whom is the other intended?' He clutched Harun's beard. 'Is it for you, you miserable pile of goat dung? You are renowned for prowess, and you have had ample time to make copies. Are you hoping to sell them on the black market?'

Harun's eyes rolled up so far only the whites were visible. 'No, Father of Curses,' he whined. 'Never would I do such a thing.'

'Damnation!' roared Emerson. 'I haven't the patience to fight my way through the labyrinth of lies this old reprobate will tell us. I think we can deduce the answer, can we not, Peabody?' Had he uttered Sethos's name, flames would have leapt from his blazing eyes. He settled for a particularly vulgar oath.

'Oh yes, Emerson,' I said hastily. 'Shall we seek more salubrious surroundings in which to ponder our options?'

'Harun, I will return tomorrow morning with the proper authorisation from Maspero to seize the head of Nefertiti. If it is not here, I will curse you for this life and the next.'

'Yes, yes, Father of Curses,' Harun mumbled as he scuttled backward in fear.

We started back towards the Muski. Emerson set a rapid pace, and I knew he was anxious to get out of the maze of narrow streets that characterise the old city. The Muski was at that time an odd blend of the old and the new; modern stores, with plate glass windows and actual doors, stood side by side with open-fronted shops whose woven goods were hung from hooks outside and fluttered in the breeze. Glazed pots and elaborately decorated hookahs lined the shelves.

We were passing one of the latter establishments, where oriental carpets framed the entrance, when it happened.

Events occurred so rapidly that I cannot claim I remember them accurately; but as I recall, Daoud let out a bellow of alarm and tried to urge our group forward. 'Twas of no avail; the street ahead was blocked by hordes of people running every which way from a man who stood in the opening to a narrow alley. He was tall, at least six feet in height, and cadaverously thin. Locks of rusty orange hair hung from under his broad-brimmed felt hat. In one hand he held a brown stick approximately a foot long. One end was sparking.

I believe my intelligent Readers need not be told what this object was. The people fleeing from this individual had received some warning of his intent, for seconds earlier he had struck a match to light the fuse. We had not observed this. When the missile came hurtling towards us, we all stood frozen.

All except one. Almost instantly, or so it seemed, there came a deafening explosion, not from where we stood but in the alleyway whence the dynamite had been thrown. As the noise died away I heard Emerson say, 'Well done, my boy. I don't know how you did it, but well done.'

I turned to see Ramses, his arm still raised and his expression more unguarded than usual. 'It was sheer reflex, Father. I didn't have time to think, the fuse was so short. Is he . . .'

A single prostrate form lay unmoving on the street. Luckily most of the bystanders had scurried out of range. Some of them had sustained minor injuries, but many of the storefronts, most of them of flimsy construction, had been reduced to smouldering rubble. Tatters of brightly coloured rugs littered the street, together with broken pots and shards of glass.

I picked my way through the debris to the fallen man. Emerson tried to prevent me from seeing the blackened face and the small fires that licked at his garments, but it was my Christian duty to make certain the fellow was beyond my help.

He was. This was fortunate in one sense; his injuries were too severe to be mended; unfortunate in another, since I had hoped we would be able to capture one of these men alive and persuade him to talk.

'I didn't mean to kill him,' Ramses said in a hollow voice. His countenance was impassive, as always, but I could hear the horror he was attempting to conceal.

'Would you rather he blew us to smithereens?' Emerson cleared his throat noisily. 'I apologise, my boy. I respect your feelings about the taking of human life, but if this is another cursed Godwin, he deserved what happened to him.'

'It must be one of the Godwins, Emerson,' I said. 'They are the only assassins after us just now. I wonder if this one could be Guy?'

'As in Guy Fawkes, the gunpowder enthusiast? Quite possibly. These people don't have much imagination. They formulate what they believe to be a clever plan and stick doggedly to it even when it goes awry. Let us see if this fellow, like Judas, has a calling card.'

I allowed Emerson to search the body. I have dealt with withered mummies and bodies in various stages of disrepair, but the procedure is not one I relish.

The square of pasteboard had been severely damaged, but there was enough left to enable us to make out a name.

'It's Guy, right enough,' said Emerson. He picked up the mangled remains of a monocle and tucked it in his pocket. 'Let us make ourselves scarce, Peabody. I hear the patter of police feet and I think we ought to discuss how much to tell them. Trying to explain this situation is going to tax even your fertile tongue.'

It is not my habit to avoid confrontations with duly appointed representatives of the government, but in this case I had to admit Emerson was right. With a few exceptions police officers have very little imagination and a wholly unjustified prejudice against females. So we retreated to Shepheard's, with Ramses, David and Daoud close behind. Daoud insisted that he would stand guard outside the hotel. I felt a pang of pity for those who would assume they could sweep past him, their noses in the air.

Once we reached our chambers, Emerson went to the sideboard. 'It is early, but after that ghastly episode I think we are entitled to a whisky and soda. Boys, will you join us?'

Ramses stood at the window, his back turned to us. 'No thank you, sir.'

'I most certainly will,' David murmured. 'Explosions always make me thirsty.'

'I propose,' said Emerson, 'that we leave Cairo as soon as we have delivered the bust to Maspero. As we have just had demonstrated, it is too easy to carry out a murderous attack in these crowded streets.'

'I agree, Father. The sooner Mother is away from the city, the safer she will be.'

'We cannot leave yet,' I protested. 'Not until we have ascertained how many copies of the Nefertiti head Harun has already made. We can't have new ones popping up unexpectedly, and we must relieve him of the one he is using as a model. It is the original. I wish we had taken it, even though that would have constituted thievery since it falls under Morgenstern's propriety.'

'Tomorrow morning we will inform Maspero of the situation and call on Harun before taking the midday train,' Emerson said. 'Ramses is right; we must get you away from this cursed city before another Godwin tries to blow you to bits.'

I did not reply.

THE FOLLOWING MORNING, Emerson, being Emerson, had decided over coffee on the hotel terrace not to bother informing M. Maspero of the situation until he had had a chance to examine the sculpture himself. The next day the four of us arrived at Harun's establishment to find that the bird had flown – or, as Emerson put it, 'gone underground like the rodent he is'. Emerson's repeated pounding on the locked and bolted door finally produced a terrified youth who must have been told – perhaps by Harun himself, before he fled out the back door – that if Emerson were not admitted he would kick the door in. The youth claimed he had not the least idea where Harun had gone – and that, in fact, he did not know who Harun was or who he himself was.

The head of Nefertiti was not there. The two unfinished sculpted heads were also missing.

'Hell and damnation!' Emerson shouted. 'I knew we shouldn't have left it here. Let us search the place and make certain we haven't overlooked anything else of importance.'

The boy made good his escape while we searched the premises, finding nothing of interest. Emerson took out his watch. 'We will have to hurry or we will miss the midday train. I believe we have finished here.'

'We have not,' I said. 'There are two dilemmas before us, and we can ignore neither of them. I think we can assume that when Morgenstern discovered the Nefertiti sculpture, he immediately took it here to have a copy made. It appears von Raubritter has made no more than a lackadaisical attempt to continue excavating the site, since he has left it idle and unprotected. How can we anticipate what may still await to be uncovered?'

Emerson's sapphirine orbs glittered as he considered the bountiful possibilities. 'True, Peabody. There may be more of Thutmose's masterpieces beneath the rubble and sand.'

'Yet the site is not secured, and the thieves are gathering like maggots on a carcass. Our men are loyal and trustworthy, but they can be distracted from their vigilance.'

Ramses nodded. 'Rumours about the Nefertiti sculpture may have already spread. Unscrupulous dealers from across Europe and America will be booking passage to Egypt and purchasing Nile cruise tickets.'

'Bloody hell!' Emerson thundered with such vehemence that pedestrians in the street stopped to gape. He added several other explicit sentiments that sent them hurrying on their way.

'Therefore,' I continued mildly, 'you must return to Amarna post-haste to ensure the integrity of the site. Our second dilemma is here in Cairo. Morgenstern is lurking somewhere in the vicinity, waiting for his precious queen to be returned to his arms. Harun must have been promised an exorbitant amount of money for the copy – or copies – to defy your threatened curses. He is likely to have knowledge of Morgenstern's whereabouts. This despicable scheme cannot be allowed to succeed.'

'True, Peabody, but I cannot leave you to be beset by the remaining Godwins. Yesterday that blasted fellow must have followed us to Harun's shop and lain in wait. His remaining brothers are capable of doing the same. You are not even safe at Shepheard's Hotel.'

I was touched by the depth of concern in his voice. 'I shall take precautions. Ramses, David and Daoud will be at my side whenever I venture out to make discreet inquiries. As you yourself said, the presence of foreigners does not go unnoticed. Someone knows where Morgenstern is. It should not take us long to locate him, and when we do, he will lead us to Harun – and the queen.'

The conversation did not end in Harun's shop. We argued all the way to our hotel chamber, where our luggage awaited transfer to the railway station. The shouting may have disturbed guests in adjoining rooms, or even below in the lobby. My husband was torn between his commendable desire to keep me at his side and his obligations as an archaeologist. The site was vulnerable. I was less so, I pointed out, since I had my trio of bodyguards.

'You will send a telegram if you catch sight of Morgenstern,' Emerson said at last. 'I shall take the next train back here.' His manly arms encircled me into a tight embrace. 'Damn it, Peabody, what would I do without you to sew on my buttons and darn my socks?'

His choice of euphemisms made me smile.

FIVE

W

E ACCOMPANIED EMERSON to the railway station, where the usual chaos prevailed. Ramses, David and Daoud formed a protective perimeter around us as Emerson and I said farewell to each other. Since we were in public, we observed decorum, to the disappointment of the throng of busybodies openly staring at us.

'I don't like this, Peabody,' Emerson said. 'Those damnable Godwins could be on this very platform. Once they see that I have left, they may become even more aggressive.'

'Throwing a stick of dynamite at us qualifies as extremely aggressive, Emerson, as does barging into my bath chamber with the intent of throttling me. Attacking Ramses on the street was hardly a meek attempt at murder. I am hard pressed to conceive of any less aggressive behaviour from them. We have reduced their rank by two thus far. If the remaining brothers have any sense, they will retreat for the time being.'

He scowled at the crowd. 'You heard what Nefret said about them. They are crazed with hatred. You must take every precaution should you leave the hotel. I cannot bear the idea that – er – some harm might come to you.' His hands grasped my shoulders with such intensity that I had to suppress a wince, and his voice was gruff. 'Promise me, Peabody.'

I did so earnestly and eloquently. Our eyes remained locked until Ramses intervened, saying, 'Your train is about to depart, Father. I will take full responsibility for Mother's safety, with David and Daoud at my side. As soon as we have located Herr Morgenstern and Harun, I will send a telegram to Minya.'

Emerson boarded the train with visible reluctance. We waited on the platform until it laboriously departed the station on its journey south, and then made our way to the street. Ramses drew David aside for a hushed conversation; I did not attempt to eavesdrop since I knew I would find it distressing, if not alarming.

'Well, Daoud,' I said cheerfully, 'I think it's time to go shopping. This is a splendid opportunity to prepare for Christmas. Once we've begun to excavate in Amarna, it will be inconvenient to return to Cairo.'

Ramses was not above eavesdropping. He appeared beside me and said, 'We shall come with you.'

'I am shopping for you and David, among others. I can hardly have you hovering over my shoulder. Daoud will escort me. I have my little gun in my handbag and my parasol, should anyone dare to accost us.'

'Please do me one favour, Mother. Stay out of the bowels of the Khan el-Khalili and confine your shopping to the Muski, although even that is not very safe if the events of yesterday are any indication.'

'I suppose I could do that,' I said. 'We shall meet you at the hotel for tea.'

A cab took us to the edge of the neighbourhood. As Daoud and I made our way through the narrow streets, I could hear him behind me, humming tunelessly. I knew his eyes were moving constantly from side to side, watching for possible danger (and perhaps taking note of the wares on display, with an eye to gifts to be given during Ramadan. Daoud has several wives and a number of children.)

We went directly to Mayer's, where I meant to do most of my shopping. He had the best selection of knives in Cairo. I was able to select a new one for Ramses (I had noticed a few notches along the edge of his), and a very nice one for Nefret, whose hand was smaller than those of the men. It is essential that the shaft fits snugly and comfortably into the hand. Those made for the tourist trade, studded with false gems and wrapped with gold wire, would lacerate the user's palms before they could strike a stout blow.

For David, I purchased an eighteenth-century map of ancient Egypt with minutely detailed drawings of temples and palaces along the Nile. I smiled fondly at the depiction of the great Temple of Karnak next to the Winter Palace (our favourite hotel in all of Egypt), where Emerson and I had enjoyed a suite with a balcony overlooking the corniche, and watched the sun set over the Nile. Further down, the colossal statues of Ramses II, wearing the double crown of Upper and Lower Egypt, guarded the entrance of the complex at Abu Simbel in Nubia. We had regarded it in the golden hues of moonlight.

Shopping for Emerson presented a challenge. He abhorred what he considered to be clutter, which included almost everything that was not of utility at an excavation. I finally chanced upon a compass with a silver case inlaid with mother-of-pearl from the molluscs found in the Blue Nile. The iridescent hues reminded me of his eyes.

I selected a variety of scarves, jewellery, tobacco and sweets for our staff, who do not celebrate Christian holidays but always enjoy receiving gifts, and was pleased with the delightfully glazed ceramic serving bowl that I found for our dear friends Cyrus and Katherine Vandergelt, who would join us on Christmas Day. This season Cyrus was excavating on the west bank at Luxor, not far from the Valley of the Kings. Katherine was my closest confidante; she had watched over Ramses since his birth and was as bemused as I by his eccentric nature.

I was examining a set of pearl earrings when a British female voice caught my attention. 'Are you quite sure this scarab ring is genuine?' she was asking a clerk.

'Very sure, madam.'

'Which is what you would say, even if it had been carved in your back room yesterday,' she replied with a sniff. When she turned away, she saw me and let out a genteel gasp. 'Mrs Emerson, oh dear, please allow me to present myself.' She fumbled through her handbag. 'Here is my card.'

'Ermintrude de Vere Smith,' I read aloud, and then frowned. 'The name is familiar . . .'

Miss Smith was a lady of middle age; her attempts to conceal this with a profusion of cosmetics gave her a somewhat clownish appearance. The lip rouge extended beyond the natural shape of her mouth, and the red on her cheeks formed perfect circles. Under a bright pink dress, her body was pear-shaped and substantial.

'I am a novelist,' she admitted humbly.

'Yes, I remember now. *The Tent of the Sheikh, The Courage of the Sheikh, The Revenge of the Sheikh* and others.' These were among the books Emerson held in contempt, but I found them to be charming (and mindless) escapes into romance, although riddled with misinformation.

'The sheikh is a busy fellow,' Miss Smith said with a coy smile. 'I have heard so much about you, Mrs Emerson, and your estimable exploits. If only I could find the courage to venture out of my quaint little office to go into the desert in search of the tempestuous skies and the treacherous dunes, the blistering heat, the scorpions and snakes. I've never so much as sat on a camel!'

'It can be a trifle uncomfortable,' I said, edging backward to escape her aura of passion (and flecks of spittle). Daoud, who had half a dozen translucent scarves in each hand, was looking at me as if awaiting the signal to tackle Miss Smith. I discreetly shook my head at him. 'It was very nice to meet you,' I murmured.

'Are you staying at Shepheard's? Might we have tea? I can imagine nothing more invigorating than listening to your stories. You are a true heroine, an inspiration to women around the world. Your courage and resilience are legendary. Many of the young women in my books are pale and timorous, easily infatuated and eager to please the sheikh. I find myself clenching my teeth and telling them to defy their master, to risk death by fleeing into the desert. With a few exceptions, the ninnies simply swoon.' She put her hand on her bosom as she took a wheezy breath. 'Please forgive me for intruding on you, Mrs Emerson. I know how annoying it is to be pestered by admirers. I will leave you to your shopping.'

I must admit that I am not immune to flattery. 'I am not available for tea this afternoon, Miss Smith, but I have no plans for tomorrow, should that suit you.'

She clasped her hands together, beaming like a child on a new pony. 'Oh yes, Mrs Emerson! Thank you so very much. I shall look for you on the terrace at four.' She gestured at a young boy laden with parcels. 'Come along, Jamil. We must not bother Mrs Emerson any further.' She hobbled out of the store, the boy trailing after her.

'Was that wise?' Daoud demanded.

'The worst she can do is bore me to death.' I reviewed my selection of gifts, added a few more scarves and the pearl earrings and settled the bill with Mr Mayer, who urged me to linger for tea. I declined and allowed Daoud to carry my parcels. 'I think,' I said as we went out into the street, 'we might as well stroll by Harun's shop on our way to the hotel.'

'It is in the opposite direction – and you promised your son that you would stay away from the Khan el-Khalili.' He stepped in front of me, as obdurate as a stone-hewn pharaoh.

'It is but a minor detour,' I said firmly. 'I will not approach the shop, but merely keep an eye out for anyone who might be maintaining surveillance in hopes of Harun's reappearance. Herr Morgenstern comes to mind.' I did not add that Sethos was as likely a candidate, although identifying him would be a challenge. I had little doubt that he was aware of the Nefertiti sculpture and had every intention of stealing it from under our noses.

Ignoring Daoud's protests, I stepped around him and briskly set off for Harun's shop. As I walked past the alley where the dynamite had caused destruction and the death of Guy Godwin, I felt a shiver. The shops that had taken the worst of the explosion were already under repair, but many of the owners had lost their wares – and their paltry incomes.

Harun's shop was nearby. When we turned onto the narrow street, I caught a glimpse of pink in the multitude of pedestrians. I did my best to make my way with all due haste, but by the time we were across the street from the shop, I saw no one clad in that hue. I reminded myself that many Egyptian women wore brightly coloured robes. Others wore black robes and scarves, while the most conservative wore burkas that covered them from head to toe, with only a mesh rectangle that obscured their eyes. Which meant Sethos could be standing within arm's reach, smiling impudently at me.

Having observed that the shop was padlocked and dark, I scanned the faces of those at the tiny tables outside cafés for Herr Morgenstern. He would not have been in disguise; his Teutonic character precluded wiles and whimsy. I might have gone into the shops to look for him had Daoud not been rumbling like a mighty volcano, his expression so dour that I knew an eruption was imminent.

We departed the Khan el-Khalili and hailed a cab for Shepheard's.

From Manuscript H

'I SAY, OLD chap, are you sure you're up for this?' Ramses said, brushing lint off the lapels of his dark jacket. 'Tally ho and what not.'

David looked much more at ease in his suit and muted tie, as if he were a law clerk at Gray's Inn. 'As long as I don't have to sound like an upper-class twit. Not that I intend to say much, since my accent is perceptible. As your humble assistant's assistant, I shall remain respectfully silent.'

Ramses laughed. 'When have you ever been respectfully anything? Just don't snigger and expose our cover.'

They crossed the busy street and went to the gates of the German embassy. A guard demanded to know their business. Ramses pretended not to understand and said, 'I am Lord Cavendish, here to see

the ambassador.' His emphatic tone and imperious stare were adequate
to induce the guard to open the gate.

'Lord Cavendish?' whispered David as they approached the front
entrance. 'Why not the Prince of Wales or, better yet, William the
Conqueror?'

'No sniggering,' Ramses whispered back. He stuck out his chin as
the door opened and a grey-haired man gazed questioningly at them.

'*Guten Tag. Kann ich dir helfen?*' he said in a gravelly voice.

'Please tell the ambassador that Lord Cavendish of Devonshire
wishes to call upon him,' Ramses replied.

The man beckoned them into an entry hall and led them to a
small sitting room. '*Warten hier, bitte.*' They did as instructed and sat
in silence, although Ramses could almost hear David's highly amused
thoughts. After fifteen minutes, a young man with slick black hair and
a pencil-thin moustache entered the room.

'I apologise for the delay,' he said in accented English. 'The troubles
in Europe and the Middle East keep us very busy. The ambassador is in
a meeting at the present. I am Helmut Gunter. May I be of assistance?'

Ramses shrugged. 'Ah yes, I've heard there's a bit of a bother these
days, although it's damned hard to remember the details. Actually, I'm
looking for a friend of mine named Morgenstern. We met when he was
excavating in Syria several years ago, and had some bloody exciting
chess games. My assistant' – he tilted his head in David's direction –
'learned that Morgenstern is at a remote place called Amarna. I thought
I'd pop in and surprise him, so I hired a boat to take us to the spot, but
damned if the chap wasn't there. I was told that he's been in Cairo for
several weeks. Do you have any idea where he's staying?'

'We are aware of his presence in Egypt, but he is with the Deutsche
Orient-Gesellschaft. The ambassador has no knowledge of Herr Morgenstern's current whereabouts. If that is all, gentlemen . . .' Gunter
stepped back and opened the door to the foyer.

'Jolly good of you to see us, old boy,' Ramses said, shaking the man's
hand vigorously. 'We're staying at Shepheard's. Please let us know if

Morgenstern comes by the embassy. Come along, Arbaaz, we must get back in time for tea. There's a delightful young French mademoiselle who winked at me several times in the dining room last night.'

'She also winked at me, the waiters, the wine steward and her elderly chaperone,' David said. 'Her excessive nictitation may be the symptom of a serious medical condition.'

Ramses punched him on shoulder. 'Arbaaz, you scoundrel! You have shattered my fantasy of spending the evening in the arms of *la très belle mademoiselle*. We must find a watering hole where I can heal my broken heart with gin and tonic.' He looked at Gunter. 'Can you recommend a place hereabouts, Helmut?'

'I find the bar at Shepheard's to be satisfactory; there is nothing closer than that,' Gunter replied stiffly.

'A jolly good idea,' Ramses said. 'Thank you for your time. Come along and step lively, Arbaaz. I intend to be totally potted by dinner time.'

They remained silent as they walked across the gravel to the gate, and ignored the guard's *'Guten Tag'* as they continued down the street. Once they were around the corner and safely out of sight, they both began to laugh.

'Excessive nictitation?' chortled Ramses. 'It sounds like a contagious disease. Poor Helmut looked as though he wanted to flee to his office and barricade the door.'

David leaned against a wall and took out his pipe. 'I was getting bored. Gunter wasn't going to tell us anything useful. I did notice his carefully worded statement that the ambassador has no knowledge of Morgenstern's whereabouts.'

'As did I,' Ramses said thoughtfully.

DAOUD WAS STILL peevish as he joined me at a table on the hotel terrace, although he looked splendid in his scarlet turban and embroidered robe. I commented on the weather and the motorcars that drove by, but he remained mute with the exception of an occasional grunt. When the waiter appeared, I ordered tea for four. A few of the priggish English ladies stared at us, appalled that I would sit with a 'native' dark-skinned Egyptian man who was not of the same class. I returned their stares with a frigid smile. Miss Smith did not appear, to my relief; she was the sort to assume an empty chair was an invitation, despite my previous assertion that I would not be available.

I was taken aback when Ramses and David arrived, both clad in suits and ties. 'We don't normally dress for tea,' I said as they took their seats. 'Is that your father's suit, Ramses? It is ill-fitting on your slighter frame. Furthermore, I am quite certain I gave him that tie last year on his birthday.'

'Yes, it is his,' Ramses said. 'He took it out of his suitcase before he left for Amarna.' He leaned back, as if he'd explained everything to my satisfaction. I can assure my Readers that I was far from satisfied.

I turned to David. 'And you?'

'I borrowed this from an old friend who works at a bank. We were in school together for many years.'

I poured tea for them and waited while they took sandwiches and slices of cake from the platters. 'My shopping expedition went nicely, although I met a woman who may become a nuisance. Her name is Er-mintrude de Vere Smith. She's the author of those silly novels about a sheikh who keeps rescuing hapless maidens from whatever calamitous circumstances they happen to be in. They all fall madly in love with him, but he is a gentleman above reproach. Unbeknownst to them, he is the younger son of a baron who was cast out of his home upon the death of his father. His brother, a scoundrel and a womaniser, framed him for the murder of a beautiful young parlour maid who—'

'Shall I tell you where we went this afternoon?' Ramses said, unable to bear my cheerful prattle. It is a trait (or a weakness) inherited from his father. I have been known to take advantage of it when warranted.

'If you must,' I said in a pained voice.

'Well done, Aunt Amelia,' murmured David.

'Hmph,' Ramses said. 'We decided to find out if the German embassy might have knowledge of Morgenstern's lodgings. An attaché claimed not.'

'There was something odd about him,' added David. He repeated Helmut Gunter's response. 'We lingered in the area until half an hour ago. I watched the entrance and Ramses concealed himself in the alley behind the grounds. The only person to visit was a white-haired man with a briefcase. He arrived by carriage and had not emerged by the time we left.'

Ramses swallowed the last bite of cake. 'If Gunter has access to a copy of *Burke's Peerage*, he may be suspicious. The current Lord Cavendish is elderly, but he does have two sons. There are also other families in the peerage with the same name.'

'You told him you were Lord Cavendish?' I asked, appalled.

David laughed. 'You should have heard his performance as an utter twit. I'm beginning to wonder where he learned the nuances . . .'

'If I may continue,' Ramses said, 'we suspect Gunter knows where Morgenstern is hiding. If we're lucky, tonight he'll either go to Morgenstern or send a message telling him to come to the embassy.'

'And you intend to be there,' I said. 'You are aware you can't seize him, I assume. There is no proof that he committed a crime. Harun did not specify that Herr Morgenstern brought him the statue, which has disappeared, along with Harun. We have no witness, no evidence.'

'If he approaches the embassy, we will persuade him to accompany us,' Ramses said. 'This may require deception. You are not opposed to deception, are you, Mother? I seem to recall that you have availed yourself of it in the past.' He raised an eyebrow as he gazed at me across the brim of his teacup.

It was not a topic I cared to discuss. 'Tomorrow morning I must call upon Mr Russell at his office. I have been remiss in sharing information with him about these horrid Godwins. Afterwards, I suppose I ought to tell M. Maspero what we suspect about Morgenstern's treachery.'

Daoud growled as he looked over my shoulder. I was somewhat perturbed that he was crouching, his hands on the arms of the chair, prepared to bound across the terrace without regard for anyone (including me) in his path. I took a peek and turned back. 'No. Daoud. Miss Smith is not an assassin. She is harmless, if a bit wearisome. She seems to have continued shopping; her helper resembles a beast of burden. Shall I order more sandwiches?'

'I think not, Mother,' Ramses said, already on his feet. He held out his hand to assist me. 'Let us retreat to our chambers for a conversation about the wisdom of acknowledging strangers who approach you in public.'

I pointedly ignored his hand as I rose. 'I am neither a child nor a dithery ingenue, Ramses, and I will not tolerate being scolded.' I turned on my heel and walked into the lobby, hoping dearly that I didn't run into the cause of the spat. To my relief, Miss Smith had continued on her way. I stopped at the front desk, wrote notes to Mr Russell and M. Maspero alerting them to my intentions the following day, and requested that the envelopes be delivered as soon as possible. Baksheesh exchanged hands, and I was assured the notes would be presented within the hour. Daoud, Ramses and David were doing their best to be inconspicuous behind a large potted plant; Daoud's turban resembled an enormous white rosebud atop the fronds. I granted them the petty triumph of thinking they had fooled me by heading upstairs without a glance in their direction.

All men, no matter their ages or nationalities, are boys at heart. Even Emerson, impeccably well-bred, brilliant and highly regarded by archaeologists throughout the world, has been known to strut about and crow in a manner not unlike that of Mr Barrie's Peter Pan. I smiled as I recalled Emerson's disquiet when we attended the stage production in 1904. It had taken me a great deal of persuasion to prevent him from bolting out of the theatre.

I changed into an appropriately modest dressing gown and settled down to write a letter to Katherine. I did not glance up as Ramses and David entered the sitting room, taking pertinacious pleasure in pretending to be offended. When Ramses offered to prepare a whisky and soda for me, I merely nodded.

Once libations had been distributed and the men were seated, I put aside my pretence and said, 'Is it possible that Herr Morgenstern has taken temporary residence at the Deutsche Orient-Gesellschaft villa? He is the director, after all.'

David shook his head. 'The first place we went this afternoon was Gezirah Island. The secretary, a timid, bespeckled man, swore he had been the sole resident for the last month and had received no communications from Morgenstern. After receiving generous baksheesh, the security guard was adamant that Morgenstern had not so much as entered the villa in several months. He agreed, motivated by the prospect of a substantial reward, to alert us immediately should he spot our prey.'

Ramses snorted. 'You make us sound like crocodiles on the sandbank, awaiting a tasty meal of bratwurst.'

'Have you made inquiries about the present whereabouts of Harun?' I asked.

'Not with any success,' Ramses admitted with a sigh. 'He and his apprentices seem to have disappeared as if they were vermin with an underground burrow. I have made it known to certain acquaintances that I will pay handsomely for information concerning the location of his current workshop.'

'Which could be anywhere,' David added, 'since he has a large family, as well as unsavoury associates. His tools were missing. All he requires is a room with adequate light.'

I shrugged. 'He could be anywhere in Cairo or the surrounding villages. Our best chance is to find Herr Morgenstern, although he may not know the location of Harun's burrow, either. I doubt Mr Russell's men will have more success, but I will encourage him in the morning.' I paused to reflect on the undeniable significance of the bust of Queen Nefertiti. Thutmose had created his masterpiece, and then buried it beneath his studio when Amarna was abruptly abandoned to the ravages of nature and time. He had done so deeply enough that a previous archaeologist, Sir Flinders Petrie, had failed to uncover it during his expedition two decades earlier. 'We cannot allow Herr Morgenstern or anyone else to deprive the world of her beauty!'

'No,' Ramses said grimly, 'we cannot. Let's go to our room, David. I feel as though I am wearing a noose around my neck. Mother, if you do not object to dining alone, we will return to the German embassy to continue our surveillance. I hired a lad to keep an eye out while we came here for tea, but he cannot watch both potential exits. Daoud will watch Harun's shop in case Morgenstern is hovering nearby, thus relieving you from slipping out with that very intention.'

'I am aware of the danger in the dark labyrinth of Khan el-Khalili, particularly for an unaccompanied lady.' I saw no reason to admit that the idea had crossed my mind. Daoud had encountered Herr Morgenstern during previous seasons and would recognise him. What he might do if he saw him was beyond my powers of speculation.

After they had taken their leave, I returned to my letter to Katherine, reminding her that she and Cyrus were coming on Christmas Day. I refrained from mentioning the Godwins, since the attempted assassinations might cast a pallor on our festivities, nor did I explain why we had been given permission to excavate at Amarna. Cyrus would demand details, but I would leave that up to Emerson.

I decided not to partake of dinner in the dining room. Although the idea of dining alone did not perturb me in the least, I was leery of being joined by Miss Smith. Ali, the *suffragi* who had been remiss during our initial stay, was on duty in the hallway nearby. I requested that a tray be brought to my quarters, trusting that he would be speedy to make up for his earlier inefficiency in the matter of Judas. I then resumed my seat and took out my journal to make a list of everyone we had encountered or had been referred to after our arrival in Cairo. Since I intended to share it with Emerson, I omitted the name of the individual likely to have a deleterious effect on my beloved's good nature.

The Godwin clan headed the list, needless to say. Simply gazing at their odious names gave me a feeling of queasiness. We had no way of learning where they were staying, so all we could do was protect ourselves when the next occasion arose. Judas had not wasted any time. I was not sure when Ramses encountered the knife-wielding villain in Alexandria, but it had happened soon after his arrival from Palestine. Guy had made his ill-fated attempt the previous day. I had to admit the Godwin brothers were diligent.

On our arrival in Amarna, we had first come upon Octavius Buddle. His failure to react to my warning based on the card in Judas's pocket was odd. Mr Dullard, upon whom Emerson had leapt, seemed to be nothing more ominous than a missionary. However, events in the past had proved that no one could be eliminated as a suspect. Von Raubritter, another victim of Emerson's impetuosity, fell into the same category. Ramses and David had nominated the German attaché for my list. Herr Morgenstern, in cahoots with Harun, was obviously up to no good.

That left Ermintrude de Vere Smith, prolific writer of dubious talent. Ramses's remark about acknowledging strangers in public had a degree of validity. Had I proffered an icy stare and turned away when she spoke to me in the shop, I would not have been avoiding her in the hotel. I was confident that she was not Sethos in one of his sillier disguises. For those of my Readers speculating about the possibility, let me note that Miss Smith was shorter than I and had pale blue eyes.

Ali arrived with my meal and a bottle of the wine Emerson and I usually ordered. He set the small table with linen and silverware and opened the wine. Having missed lunch and watched the men devour the sandwiches and cakes at tea, I had a robust appetite. After I had finished eating, I poured a second glass of wine and meandered to the window to gaze at the pedestrians, motorcars, carriages and numerous peddlers who lurked near the entrance of the hotel. I was still preoccupied with my list, so several minutes had passed before I noted a lone man hovering on the pavement across the street. He was pacing back and forth and glancing surreptitiously at the upper floors of the hotel.

Even from a distance, I could see the filth on his coat and his unshaven face. Despite the balmy evening air, he appeared to be trembling.

I changed into more suitable clothing and hurried downstairs to the lobby. Mr Baehler called out a tepid greeting, which I ignored as I went out the front entrance. The man cowered in a doorway when I came across the street to get a better look at him.

'Herr Morgenstern,' I said, confirming my suspicion, 'how good it is to see you again! We had hoped to meet you in Amarna and were disappointed to be informed you were not there.'

'Do you know where she is? *Lieber Gott*, I must find my beautiful queen!' His voice was a weak, raspy whine. Spittle dribbled from his lips as he clutched his hands together in supplication. He looked so fragile that had I poked him out of frustration, he would have fallen to the pavement.

'I cannot answer your question, but I do insist that you accompany me to my quarters so that I can offer you a more civilised environment and a hot meal. There appears to be a nasty cut on your hand that requires medical attention. I have antiseptic and bandages among my supplies.' I firmly gripped his sleeve and propelled him across the street and into the hotel lobby. Mr Baehler stared but said nothing as we passed by the front desk.

Ali, who was in the hallway, was equally speechless. I ordered a dinner tray to be brought for Herr Morgenstern, and we continued into my sitting room. In the light he looked much worse than I had first realised. His beard, his moustache and his clothes were coated with grime, and his shoes were scuffed. His eyes were unfocused and watery above his concave cheeks. He looked as though he had had little to eat in the last few weeks. I sent him into the bath chamber to wash while I took out the necessary accoutrements to treat the ragged cut on his hand.

When he emerged, he was damp but not perceptibly cleaner. He had not spoken a word since our encounter on the street. I led him to a chair, gently pushed him down and began my ministrations. 'This does not appear to be infected,' I said soothingly, 'but it must be painful. Whatever happened?' He looked blankly at me. 'I am sure you will feel better once I've tended to this,' I continued, 'and you have had a hot meal. Would you care for a glass of wine?'

I had had livelier conversations with a camel. I taped the bandage in place and urged him to take off his coat. When he failed to respond, I jostled him out of it and placed it by the door in hope that the odour might be less potent. There was no point in attempting to interrogate him about the location of Harun's current workshop until he was fed. My expectation that I would learn something of use was diminishing by the minute, based not only on his physical condition but also on his piteous plea to be reunited with the statue of Nefertiti. It was ironic that Ramses, David and Daoud were out searching for him in order to find the location of the workshop, while he had come to Shepheard's in anticipation that we might share that same information.

At least that was my theory, and I am rarely wrong.

SIX

IT WOULD NOT become me to gloat over my success in locating and isolating Herr Morgenstern, especially since I had no idea what to do with him. A hot meal might revive him, but I doubted it. He remained slumped in the chair, mumbling under his breath and twitching as if he was infested with fleas. The alleyways of Cairo provided cruel sanctuary for stray cats and dogs, and his wound might well have come from predators fighting for garbage behind a restaurant. I had never entertained warm feelings for him, but it was impossible to avoid feeling compassion for a colleague who has plummeted to his nadir. Compassion is not to be confused with partiality, even for the most devout Christian. Herr Morgenstern had stolen an invaluable discovery. I winced as I envisioned Emerson's likely response in the current situation.

I had come up with a plan of action when Ali arrived with the dinner tray. I waited until he readied the table, and then said, 'My guest requires a robe while his clothes are cleaned and pressed, and I am sure you can find something adequate in the hotel laundry room. When you go through the lobby, please inform Mr Baehler that I require the immediate services of the hotel doctor.'

Ali's expression indicated that I was sinking in his esteem, but he glumly accepted baksheesh and departed the room. I regarded Herr Morgenstern with little enthusiasm. I urged him to his feet and led him to the table. His eyes were vacant and he showed no awareness of the food before him. I placed the fork in his hand, but it fell from his limp fingers and bounced under the table. I picked it up, gave it a cursory wipe with a napkin, replaced it in his hand and guided it to a morsel of beef.

'You must eat,' I said sternly. 'If you do not regain your strength, you will never find the statue of Nefertiti. She will be lost to you for ever. Now eat!'

He blinked as my words entered his befogged consciousness. He jabbed the fork into the bite and unsteadily guided it to his mouth. When he had repeated the action a second time, I poured him a glass of wine and retreated from his omnipresent redolence.

It was unfortunate that I could not notify Ramses and David. They would remain outside the German embassy most of the night, disguised in some fashion and hoping Gunter might lead them to Herr Morgenstern. Daoud would keep watch at Harun's workshop until one of us appeared in person to tell him of the futility of his effort. I dared not leave Herr Morgenstern alone.

I was relieved when Ali arrived with a clean thobe, a long robe that was the length of an extended nightshirt but more elegant, followed by a pink-cheeked man, no older than Nefret, who identified himself as Dr Forbes (no relation to my dear Evelyn, apparently). Over the years there had been several medical persons connected with the hotel, some accommodating, some needing to be instructed as to their role. The young man who arrived was new to me, but he had obviously heard of me. His eyes widened to an alarming extent when I introduced myself.

'This gentleman is suffering from a psychological illness,' I explained. 'How well versed are you in such disorders?'

'Er,' said young Dr Forbes.

'As you can see, my guest is in need of medical attention. Please take him into the bath chamber, bathe him thoroughly and examine him for sores, wounds and infections. After that, he will require a physical and mental evaluation. I shall greatly appreciate your diagnosis.'

The doctor was visibly perturbed by my request, but his youth and limited experience (and perhaps my authoritative tone) prevented him from refusing to perform duties more commonly assigned to a nurse or an orderly. He coaxed Herr Morgenstern from the chair and took him into the bath chamber. Once I heard water running in the bathtub, I rewarded myself with the ultimate few drops of the wine. I also made a note to dispose of my loofah and bar of lavender-scented soap in the immediate future. I could trust the hotel staff to replace the towels and washcloths.

When Herr Morgenstern emerged from the bath chamber, dressed in the long white robe, he looked more civilised. He was still in need of the services of a barber and a manicurist, but his general appearance was no longer repugnant. The doctor steered him to a chair and forced him to sit.

'How is his physical health?' I inquired.

'His body is covered with scratches, scabs and insect bites. The cut on his hand does not appear to be infected. I did not see any symptoms to suggest that he is suffering from an illness like dysentery or malaria.' He removed a stethoscope from his bag, and after a nod from me, continued his examination. 'His heart and lungs are sound, and there has been no serious injury, external, nor as nearly as I can tell, internal. I would say he is suffering from neglect – inadequate food, water, personal hygiene. Before any more drastic measures are taken, I would recommend a long rest, with constant nursing care to make sure he takes food and water at regular intervals.'

'And mentally?'

'He was unable to answer my questions coherently, which is undoubtedly due to his weakened condition. If he is taken care of for the next several days, he should regain his mental faculties. Now I must take my leave, Mrs Emerson. Another guest at the hotel is suffering from a migraine headache and has requested my attention. I wish you the best of luck with this gentleman.'

The doctor fled with undue haste, leaving me to consider my guest, who was now my patient as well. I could not arrange another room for him because he might depart at any hour of the night in order to resume his ineffectual search for his painted queen. The hotel staff were trained not to interfere with a guest's wishes. Even if I could order the night *suffragi* to stand guard outside the door, I was not confident that he would prevent Herr Morgenstern from leaving. The very idea that I might sit in the hallway all night was preposterous. This left only one option, somewhat less preposterous but nevertheless annoying.

'Let me help you to your feet,' I said in a voice noticeably devoid of camaraderie. 'You will be sleeping in the bedroom for the night, while I remain here. Other arrangements will be made for you in the morning.'

He was incapable of an audible protest. After I had settled him in the bed and turned off the light, I returned to the sitting room. None of the furniture was designed for a comfortable night's sleep; the sofa was too short to accommodate me, and the chairs had upright backs and lumpy cushions. In the past, I had slept on the floors of tombs and in primitive tents, but always with Emerson at my side (and often inside my bedroll).

I jammed a chair under the doorknob of the bedroom to prevent Herr Morgenstern from attempting to leave. I removed the cushions and created a makeshift bed on the floor, aware that an uncomfortable night awaited me. I decided it would be prudent to remain in my clothes rather than risk being obliged to chase him down the hallway while dressed unsuitably.

Nearly an hour passed before I drifted into an uneasy sleep.

'MOTHER MUST STILL be asleep,' Ramses said in a subdued voice as he came into the sitting room from the hallway. 'Shall we order breakfast in our room or go down to the dining room?'

'I would much prefer to bathe and go to bed,' David said plaintively.

'You were the lucky one. I'm the one who was caught by hose spray and thoroughly drenched. Who would have guessed that the German embassy staff watered the flower beds and shrubbery behind the building?'

'Anyone who battled mosquitoes all night while crouched under prickly bushes.'

'We will need four breakfast trays,' I said as I struggled up from the cushions aligned in front of the sofa. Ramses, who mastered the art of impassivity at a young age, gaped at me. David clutched the doorframe as he recoiled. I must admit I found their expressions droll, but I did not allow myself to smile. 'Why four trays, you ask? We have a guest in the bedroom and we must provide hospitality. Please locate Ali and ask him to bring the trays quickly. I am in dire need of coffee.' Based on numerous experiences in the past, I was not surprised that they were dressed in tattered robes, their dirty feet shod in sandals, their faces sporting untrimmed beards and moustaches. 'You might want to change into more respectable clothing and remove the faux facial hair as soon as you have the opportunity,' I added. 'I am impressed that you managed to enter the hotel dressed as you are.'

David grinned. 'We did not come in through the lobby, Aunt Amelia. The basement is a maze, but we are familiar with it.'

'Might I inquire into the identity of this guest?' asked Ramses, refusing to be distracted.

'Herr Morgenstern, obviously,' I responded. 'As soon as we have finished breakfast, one of us must fetch Daoud before his feet are permanently embedded in the pavement across the street from Harun's workshop in Khan el-Khalili.'

David left to give Ali our breakfast order. Ramses mutely watched as I collected the cushions and replaced them in their proper locales. I went into the bath chamber to freshen up as best I could, careful to avoid the wet towels on the floor. I could not be certain that the doctor had not used my brush or comb on his patient's head, so I edged them aside and ran my fingers through my hair. My shopping list was growing longer, I thought as I returned to the sitting room.

Ramses was gazing at the chair wedged under the doorknob. He turned to me, one eyebrow raised, and said, 'Do you care to explain how Herr Morgenstern came to be in your bedroom, Mother?'

'I am disappointed in you. I was quite sure that you would reason it out for yourself, but I will be happy to elaborate after you have roused him and accompanied him to the bath chamber so that he can avail himself of the facilities. It is vital that he remains under our constant supervision until he comes to his senses.'

'Did you leave the hotel last night?' His tone was accusatory, as if he were a schoolmaster interrogating a mischievous pupil.

'For no more than a minute or two, and I was always within view of the doorman. He is not as reliable as Daoud, of course, but I presume he would not allow one of the guests to be molested in front of the hotel. Please see to Herr Morgenstern's needs in the bath chamber. He will eat better if his food is hot, and it should arrive shortly. He will have to wear the thobe until his clothing is returned from the cleaners. I would like to think he would not venture out of the hotel dressed as he is, but he is fanatical about finding the statute of Nefertiti and is capable of bizarre actions.'

Ramses stared at me, his lips pinched, and then went to the bedroom door, removed the chair and entered the room. A moment later I heard him speak curtly to Herr Morgenstern, urging him out of the bed. The two of them crossed the sitting room and went into the bath chamber. I sat down and began another list. At the top of the list was informing Daoud that he needed to come to the hotel, since he was more than capable of standing guard at Herr Morgenstern's newly assigned room. Next on the list was arranging for said room. One of us needed to send a telegram to Emerson to inform him of the current circumstances. I knew of a shop nearby where I could purchase new toiletries, which I intended to do immediately after breakfast. Ramses, David and Daoud would have to alternate guard duty until they caught up on their sleep; the three of them had been awake all night. I planned to indulge in a nap, but only after the bedroom had been thoroughly cleaned and the bed equipped with crisp, fresh linens. I made a notation to have the pillows replaced.

While Ramses and David ate breakfast with gusto, Herr Morgenstern swallowed a few small bites, and I gratefully sipped coffee and read aloud my newest list. David quickly volunteered to send the telegram to Emerson, possibly because the telegraph office was only two blocks away. Ramses agreed to fetch Daoud and bring him back to the hotel.

They finished their meal and departed for their assigned duties, leaving me to tend to Herr Morgenstern until they returned. He was not an attractive guest – or captive, to be more precise – in that the coddled eggs he had attempted to eat had dribbled down the front of his thobe. I clenched my teeth and cleaned him up as best I could.

'Well then,' I said cheerfully, 'are you feeling better now that you are clean, rested, and nourished?'

'Where did you take her?' he bleated.

'On the assumption that you are referring to the bust of Nefertiti, I can assure you that we have not taken her anywhere. That was Harun's doing. Have you any ideas where he might have set up his new workshop?' He shook his head numbly. I suspected he was telling the truth, since he would not have come looking for us were he in possession of that information. 'Did you make any arrangement with Harun to return the original and the copies after they were completed?'

'No, I don't think so . . . I cannot recall . . .' He rubbed his face as tears flooded his eyes. 'I must find her, my precious Nefertiti. Do you have her, whoever you are?'

'I am Amelia Peabody Emerson, wife and colleague of Radcliffe Emerson, the greatest archaeologist of the previous and current centuries, and I do not have the statue in my possession,' I said resolutely. 'You need to retire to the bedroom for further rest. I will awaken you when luncheon trays have been brought here.'

I stared at him until he arose and made his way into the bedroom. I saw no reason to prop the chair under the doorknob as I had done the previous night; I was alert and confident of my ability to control him should he endeavour to leave. Although he was larger than I, he was barely able to totter. Nevertheless, I made certain that my parasol was within reach.

After David returned from the telegraph office, he agreed to remain in the sitting room while I dealt with other items on my list. I stopped at the desk in the lobby and retained a room for Herr Morgenstern. Mr Baehler, who had doubtlessly received reports from the doctor and Ali, was clearly disgruntled but did as I requested. He must have real-ised that engaging in a shouting match with me would only result in gleeful speculation among his guests. I exited Shepheard's and went to the shop to purchase toiletries, looking forward to the opportunity to see to my exacting personal requirements. Once I was presentable, I would call on Mr Russell and M. Maspero as I had intended.

I was a bit aggrieved when I encountered Miss Smith upon my re-turn to the hotel. Her pink dress had been replaced with one of mari-gold yellow, and once again her makeup had been applied with a heavy hand. 'Good morning,' I murmured politely as I attempted to hurry past her.

'I do so hope you are still available to take tea with me this after-noon, Mrs Emerson,' she trilled. 'I am so excited at the prospect that I scarcely slept last night. To sit across from you and hear about your escapades shall be a great honour. I am shivering with anticipation at the—'

'Yes, at four on the terrace. I shall see you then.' I continued around her and went up the stairs, ignoring whatever else she might have been saying – and vowing to never again read about her silly sheikh. I was pleased to find Ramses and Daoud in my sitting room.

'Are you unharmed, Sitt Hakim?' Daoud shouted as he leapt to his feet. 'The Father of Curses would never forgive me if something bad had happened to you! I would never forgive myself! I vowed to protect you, but that man entered your quarters and slept in your bed. I will punish him harshly for his impertinence.'

I was quite sure that any punishment inflicted by Daoud would be unlikely to aid in Herr Morgenstern's recovery. 'I am fine, my faithful friend, and touched by your loyalty. However, it is vital that we assist Herr Morgenstern in regaining his health, so you must be gentle with him. That will please the Father of Curses.' I handed him the key that I had acquired at the desk. 'Herr Morgenstern needs to be moved to the room down the hall. Please escort him there and require him to rest. Under no circumstances can he be allowed to leave the hotel.'

'Oh yes, Sitt Hakim,' Daoud said. Before I could reiterate my instructions concerning the continual well-being of Herr Morgenstern, Daoud went into the bedroom and returned with a white-robed body draped over his shoulder. He was humming as he continued into the hallway with his burden.

'Then we are to consider ourselves nursemaids for the next few days,' Ramses said without inflection.

'Have you a better suggestion?' I asked.

'We can logically extrapolate that Herr Morgenstern has no knowledge of the location of Harun's workshop. Otherwise, he would not have sought us out for that very information.'

'I have already arrived at that conclusion,' I replied. 'We must hypothesise that he promised to pay Harun very handsomely to make the copies. If the money has not changed hands, Harun will be obliged to locate Herr Morgenstern in order to complete their arrangement. That is why all of us need to return to Amarna as soon as our guest is capable of travel.' I paused to think. 'You have not yet told me if you learned anything of significance while skulking outside the German embassy.'

'I am afraid not,' admitted Ramses. 'The elderly man we observed entering the embassy shortly before four o'clock this afternoon was still inside when we returned to resume our surveillance. He must have stayed for dinner. According to David, the visitor and the attaché exchanged affable words and handshakes on the top step before the gentleman came to the gate to await his carriage. David was dressed as

you saw, and approached him, begging for baksheesh. The guard inter-
ceded, so David caught no more than a brief glimpse of the gentleman
before he entered his carriage.'

'And that is suspicious? There are many Germans in Cairo these
days. One would assume the ambassador has friends among them and
might enjoy entertaining them.'

Ramses tugged at his chin in the same manner as his father. 'True,
but I am sure that Helmut Gunter is in some way involved. He may believe that he knows how to locate Herr Morgenstern, but he is woefully
wrong unless he has Ali or the doctor on his payroll. Germany must
maintain a strong presence in Egypt in the face of the upcoming political chaos. The unveiling of the statue of Nefertiti will enhance their
prestige as dedicated Egyptologists.'

A disturbing thought entered my mind. 'This white-haired man
whom you observed entering the embassy – could it have been Sethos?'

'David said the man's height did not rule out the supposition. Regrettably, we have no one on our payroll at the embassy who might
have overheard any conversations that could allow us to acquire more
information. The Egyptians employed there work in the kitchen and
are never allowed to go upstairs, I was informed by a departing scul-
lery maid. Bribery will be of no benefit.'

'Sethos may lack the desire to assist the Germans in their quest for
the statue of Nefertiti,' I commented slowly, 'but he is keenly aware of
its value. Keep in mind that Harun's apprentices were creating at least
two copies. It makes sense that Herr Morgenstern would require only
one of them in order to fool the Department of Antiquities. We need to
find out if he asked Harun to make the second one.'

Ramses templed his long fingers. 'He is a blithering idiot at the
moment, and not even Daoud can shake a lucid answer out of him.
We need to leave Cairo as quickly as possible. You will be much safer
in Amarna with Father to keep an eye on you. Based on what Nefret
told us about Geoffrey Godwin's brothers, three of them remain dedicated to causing our demise. Why don't you give Herr Morgenstern

a dose of laudanum, place him in a commodious trunk and take the night train?'

'That will not have a meretricious effect on his recuperation,' I said. 'I shall do my best to ease him back into a state of coherency so that we may question him. If I have no success by late tomorrow afternoon, I shall reconsider your plan. I happen to have laudanum in my first aid kit and will give him enough so that he will wake up in his dig house in Amarna. I shall now retreat to the bath chamber to prepare myself to call on Mr Russell and M. Maspero.'

'I shall accompany you on these visits,' Ramses announced. 'You cannot leave the hotel without protection.'

Having predicted precisely what he would say (and finding it quite reasonable), I fetched attire from the bedroom, gathered up my recent purchases, and went into the bath chamber. I may have dallied, luxuriating in a hot bubble bath after thoroughly scrubbing myself with my new loofah. No one seemed to be inclined to stagger into the room and mutter the word 'murder'.

I felt much more composed when I emerged. Ramses, for some inexplicable reason, was pacing impatiently within the confines of the sitting room. He did not offer me a compliment as we went to the lobby and allowed the day doorman to hail a cab. When we arrived at police headquarters, he insisted on exiting first in order to scan the stream of harmless pedestrians. I refrained from pointing out that we had no idea how to identify the remaining Godwin brothers. Judas had been a large brute; Guy had been short and thin. The only characteristic they shared was a propensity to wear monocles.

Mr Russell greeted us warmly and offered us coffee. Ramses did not respond, so I graciously accepted for both of us. I proceeded to describe the most recent attack in Khan el-Khalili, omitting the identity of the person who had deftly caught and thrown back the stick of dynamite.

'This is dreadful!' said Mr Russell, his face reddening. 'We must capture these villains before they make any more attempts to harm you, Mrs Emerson – and you too, Ramses. I have received no useful communiqués from the constabulary in Cornwall, and thus we have no clue to their whereabouts in Cairo. The wisest course of action is for you to leave the city.'

'It has been suggested,' Ramses said coolly.

'We plan to leave tomorrow night,' I said, 'although there is no reason to believe they will be unable to ascertain our destination, Amarna. By now, everyone in Cairo is aware that we are excavating there, including the thieves and rogues.'

'Your . . . activities do tend to attract attention, Mrs Emerson, in that mayhem of one sort or another is usually involved,' Mr Russell replied with a dry smile. 'There is a rumour afoot that you are holding a hostage in a room at Shepheard's Hotel. I find that incredulous, to put it mildly.'

Ramses snorted. I frowned at him and quickly said, 'I have no idea whence such scurrilous rumours originate, but I can assure you that the Emerson family does not hold innocent people against their will. I believe I have related all that we know about the Godwins. If I learn anything of even minor significance, I shall see that you have that information before our departure.' I stood up, obliging Mr Russell and Ramses to do the same. 'Thank you for your time. I am heartened to know that your men will make every effort to apprehend the Godwin brothers in Cairo. Come along, Ramses. We have many more errands to run today.'

Once we were in a cab, Ramses said, 'Hell and damnation! It seems as if each breath one of us takes is worthy of speculation. Should you sneeze in public, everyone will hear that you've been hospitalised with pneumonia.'

'Your father shares the sentiment,' I said, patting him on the knee. 'There is nothing we can do to quash the rumour that was undoubtedly started by Ali in the laundry room or kitchen at the hotel. I shall have a word with him when we return. Now we must visit M. Maspero to give him the unpleasant news about Herr Morgenstern's treachery.'

The director did not keep us waiting. He seemed a bit unnerved when Ramses promptly sat down in a corner chair and crossed his legs. After bowing over my hand, he asked how he might serve us.

'I am here to be of service to you, monsieur,' I replied with a smile. 'I felt you should receive a report on the activities of Herr Morgenstern, which, if you recall, you asked us to investigate.'

I gave him a succinct, well-organised account of recent events, beginning with our discovery at Harun's workshop and ending with my prognosis of Herr Morgenstern's physical and mental status.

'*Mais quel contretemps!*' Maspero exclaimed. 'I regret, *chère madame*, that you should have undergone such difficulties. Surely there must be another explanation for his behaviour. *Peut-être* he believed it necessary to make a replica of the statue should the original be inadvertently lost or destroyed. His reputation as an Egyptologist, although scarcely as *magnifique* as that of Professeur Emerson, is laudable. You have said that Herr Morgenstern is improving. Will he be able to continue with his duties safely and responsibly?'

'I am fairly confident of that. However, should there be a relapse, may we assume you authorise us to take over if we judge him incapable?'

Maspero's eyes shifted. 'You understand, Madame Emerson, that I can only request that you report your concerns to me. It is unfortunate that we have no proof that a crime has been committed. The D.O.G. has the firman for Amarna; they are a major institution in Egyptology and it is up to them to provide a successor for Herr Morgenstern if he is unable to resume his position. Does he not have a staff, including an assistant director? I have heard of a young man—'

'His name,' I said, 'is von Raubritter, or so he says. Is the name familiar to you? It is not to me. He cannot be a trained Egyptologist. He closed down the site and left it unguarded, which speaks poorly of his dedication.'

'Herr Morgenstern has the right to appoint his own staff, and we are not in the habit of questioning scholars of his distinction.'

'There is nothing to prevent me from questioning him, I presume.'

'I certainly cannot prevent you, Mrs Emerson,' Maspero said with a martyred sigh.

'I will of course report my findings to you,' I said.

'*Merci*, Madame Emerson.'

Ramses rose from the chair. 'Shall we depart, Mother? Since M. Maspero is unable to give us adequate authorisation to supervise the excavation at Amarna, he is of no use to us. Professor Emerson will be disappointed, I am sure.'

'*Au revoir*,' I said as I followed Ramses out of the office.

Neither of us spoke as the cab took us back to the hotel. We parted ways at my door without formulating any future plans. I went into the bedroom and made sure the linens and pillows had been changed, put on a dressing gown and lay down for a much-needed nap.

THE SUNLIGHT HAD shifted when I awoke several hours later. I had missed my midday meal, but I intended to indulge in a hearty tea – regrettably with Miss Smith. Contrary to her aspirations, I would not engage in a monologue that prevented me from devouring delicate sandwiches and pastries. A proper lady never speaks with vestiges of food in her mouth.

After I had freshened up and donned a suitable tea gown, I swept through the lobby to the terrace. I was not surprised that Miss Smith had already chosen a table and given her order to the waiter. She waved at me as if she had been stranded in a lifeboat and I were a passing freighter. This did not go unnoticed by the snobbish women at nearby tables, who all leaned forward to engage in their favourite pastime.

'Good afternoon,' I said as I sat down. 'I hope you are enjoying your stay in Cairo.'

'Oh yes, ever so much! Maybe it is nothing more than the relentless heat, but I feel the passion arising in me, threatening to inflame me. May I pour you a cup of tea, my dear Mrs Emerson?'

'Thank you, Miss Smith.' I produced a smile of sorts. The temperature was mild, as befitting the winter season, and would be a tad chilly at night. Miss Smith must have been highly sensitive to be fraught with passion despite the cardigan draped over her shoulders.

'You must tell me about the Lost Oasis,' she said. 'I can think of nothing more thrilling than discovering it in the middle of the desert!'

I gazed longingly at a cucumber sandwich, but refrained from shoving it in my mouth. 'It was quite an ordeal,' I began obediently. 'The last camel died at noon, leaving us without food or water in the desert west of the Nile. Had we not discovered the oasis, we surely would have perished.' I continued with an edited version, omitting our first encounter with dear Nefret but perhaps embellishing the peril in which we found ourselves.

Miss Smith fanned herself with a paperback book. 'How thrilling, Mrs Emerson! I fear I would have succumbed to the harsh desert had I been forced to follow your steadfast resolve. I do hope I am not being presumptuous when I offer you this small token of my admiration.' She thrust the book across the table. 'It is my latest novel, although it pales in comparison to your adventures. Please accept it with my greatest gratitude.'

I had no choice but to take the book from her hand. The cover art had the familiar depiction of the fair-skinned sheikh gazing at a buxom ingenue in the throes of a swoon, and was entitled *The Shadow of the Sheikh*. I examined it with minimal interest until I saw a photograph of Miss Smith on the back cover. She appeared younger, as authors often do in their publicity photographs, but her likeness was unmistakable. As my Readers are well aware, I have a suspicious nature and had idly considered the possibility that she was an imposter. She was not. I reminded myself to tell Daoud that he was in no circumstance to pounce upon her should he see her in the hallway. 'Pounce' was not the most accurate word to describe his prospective reaction; his height and bulkiness would most likely result in a move more befitting a wrestler. It would not bode well for Miss Smith – or anyone of a lesser stature.

'I do hope you will enjoy it,' she prattled on. 'The heroine is a spunky gal who is willing to defend herself. When one of the sheikh's rogue henchmen enters her tent, she throttles him with a scarf. It was most invigorating for me, her creator. My publisher attempted to re-dact the scene, but I was adamant that it remain. I modelled her on you, Mrs Emerson, for surely you would have done the same in that situation.' She gave me a steely look that unsettled me.

I was taken aback by her atypical demeanour. 'I have never throttled anyone, nor do I intend to do so in the future. You must look elsewhere for your inspiration. These cakes are delicious, are they not?'

After an hour in which she wheedled me for more stories, I thanked her for my gift and excused myself. I went upstairs, where I found Daoud guarding the door of Herr Morgenstern. I detoured into my quarters to rid myself of the sheikh's shadow and his callous heroine, inspect my attire for errant crumbs and gather up a potentially *utile objet*. I then emerged and sent Daoud away to rest. It required a great deal of assertiveness on my behalf before he agreed to nap on the sofa in my quarters. (We both knew he would hover just inside the doorway to listen for the tiniest hint of a disturbance.)

I eased open the door. The drapes were drawn, and only a sliver of sunlight pierced the dimness. Morgenstern's clothing had been cleaned and pressed, and was hung in an open wardrobe. I tiptoed to the bed to examine my patient. He remained quiescent, eyes closed, as I sat at his bedside, but he had obviously been aware of what was going on, for now his eyes opened and he said, 'What is going to happen to me?'

I took out the compass I had purchased for Emerson as a Christmas present. It glittered as it dangled from a cord. 'Only good things are going to happen,' I said soothingly. 'Look at this object. Watch as it captures the light. It is good to watch it while your mind rests.' I swung the compass gently to and fro. 'Your eyelids are heavy. You can hardly keep them open. They are closing. But you can still hear. You can hear me. You will sleep when I bid you sleep, but when you wake you will remember what I say to you now.'

David, presumably having noticed that Daoud was no longer in the hallway, entered the room. I put my finger to my lips and resumed my soft, mellifluous instructions, ending with a final 'sleep'. Herr Morgenstern had a faint smile on his face as he sank into unconsciousness.

'You told him—' David began.

'That we were his friends and that he was our friend. What is wrong with that?'

'It isn't exactly true,' he said doubtfully.

'But it is to our advantage if he believes it,' I said as I drew him out of the room and carefully closed the door. 'Post-hypnotic suggestion has proved very effective in such cases, and his reaction was along the lines I had anticipated. We are returning to Amarna tomorrow on the night train. Maspero seems to believe that Herr Morgenstern can resume his work in an exemplary fashion, despite his obsession with the statue of Nefertiti. I believe that Harun will follow us, demanding to be well compensated for his copies. That will give us our best opportunity to seize this forger and demand information from him.'

'You do amaze me, Aunt Amelia.'

'Thank you,' I replied modestly.

SEVEN

THE FOLLOWING MORNING I opted to abandon caution and had breakfast in the dining room, despite the potential peril of being captured by Miss Smith for a further recitation of my exploits while my eggs congealed. To my relief, she was not present. I was having a final cup of coffee when Ramses strode across the room and sat down across from me. From his expression (and by that I mean a minuscule tic in his jaw), I could see that he was agitated.

'Whatever is wrong?' I inquired.

'Is Herr Morgenstern in his room?' he demanded in a hushed voice.

'Yes, he is. I stopped by on my way down here. He and Daoud were eating breakfast in a reasonably amiable fashion. Herr Morgenstern addressed me by name, which I find encouraging. I shall have another session of hypnosis with him this afternoon. I believe we shall encounter no difficulty persuading him to accompany us to Amarna.'

'His presence may be irrelevant. The statue of Nefertiti has been spotted in a shop across from the museum. It behooves us to fetch it immediately.'

'What!' I exclaimed, nearly dropping the cup. 'How could that be? Is it the original?'

'Lower your voice, Mother. We are not the only persons frantic to gain possession of this unique object,' Ramses said, glancing at the patrons at nearby tables. Several young women fluttered their eyelashes and giggled; Ramses does seem to have that effect on them despite his often indifferent response. 'We won't know if it is the original until I – excuse me – we examine it. If you have finished your breakfast, I suggest we engage the services of a cab and be on our way.'

I placed my napkin on the table and stood up, my heart beating fiercely and my knees gelatinous. No one took particular notice of us as we went through the lobby to the front of the hotel, where the doorman beckoned a cab. Once we were settled in the backseat, I took a deep breath and said, 'How did you come to learn about this, Ramses? Did one of your – er – acquaintances share this information with you?'

'Yes, although it cost me a goodly sum. The shop is owned by a miscreant named Abubakar, and caters to the multitude of tourists who visit the museum. He claims that many of his pieces are originals, which may be true in that some members of his family are thieves and tomb robbers. He also deals with replicas. My source claims that Abubakar does not realise the significance of the Nefertiti head, and has priced it nominally.'

I leaned forward and poked the driver. 'You will receive a good baksheesh if we arrive at our destination within five minutes. An encounter with the police will only slow us down, so you must obey the law. Do you understand?'

He replied with a guttural mumble as he accelerated through a busy intersection, his hand pressed against the horn in an inharmonious warning. Horses pulling carriages reared, flinging their passengers against one another, and a panicky donkey crashed its cart into a street vendor's rack of rugs. When our driver veered onto the pavement to avoid a camel, fruits and vegetables flew through the air like multicoloured snowballs. Although my Arabic is of the more polite variety, I had no difficulty translating the profanities (and bruised produce) hurled at us as we sped through narrow backstreets. Ramses was slumped against the upholstery, his shoulders quivering as he struggled not to laugh aloud at my wide-eyed consternation.

'Well done, Mother,' he said as the cab braked to an abrupt stop and the driver turned around to give us a somewhat toothless grin. 'It seems as though we have arrived in a mere four minutes, give or take a few seconds. Please reward our driver as you promised while I observe those who are loitering in the vicinity.'

I dealt with the driver, receiving an even wider somewhat toothless grin, and then emerged from the cab. 'I doubt anyone was able to follow us, no matter how desperately he may have tried. Let us purchase the statue without haggling over the price and return to the hotel to make preparations to leave on the night train. As much as I would enjoy sending a telegram to your father with this astonishing news, I am loath to risk sharing the information with an employee at the telegraph office. You have your spies, but so does Sethos. This requires the utmost discretion.'

'It does indeed,' Ramses said as he took my arm and escorted me into a poorly lit shop crowded with shelves displaying pots, figurines, papyrus scrolls, hookahs and garish souvenirs. With only minimal regard for the tourists blithering over the wares, he forced our way to the counter.

Abubakar, who obviously recognised us, nodded warily. 'How kind of you to visit my lowly shop, Sitt Hakim, you and your son. I am honoured by your presence and will do everything within my power to please you. I have several fine pieces from the Twelfth Dynasty, if you should care to examine them.'

'It has been brought to my attention,' I said with a thin smile, 'that you have a statue – well, nothing more than a head – of some unknown Egyptian queen or consort. Even though it is only a copy, I would like to add it to my collection. I do not see it on display, so I assume it is in your back room.'

'We would like to see it *now*,' added Ramses. His tone made it clear that this was not a request.

'Of course,' Abubakar whined, and then hurried through the curtain behind him. I was congratulating myself on maintaining my composure despite the tightness of my throat and difficulty breathing when he reappeared and set down the statue of Nefertiti. 'It is very nice, this piece, and beautiful. I will be sorry to lose her, but I will make the sacrifice for you, Sitt Hakim.'

I heard Ramses inhale sharply as we stared at it. Before he could respond, and I was quite sure he would do so in a manner that would alarm other patrons in the shop, I said, 'Where did you acquire this, Abubakar?'

'I cannot say,' he said, his head lowered to avoid meeting our eyes.

Ramses leaned forward and grasped the front of the shopkeeper's thobe. 'I think you can say, and you will do so now unless you dare defy the Brother of Demons. It will not bode well for you should you lie to me.'

'Now ain't that pretty, Lucinda?' drawled a voice with a distinctively American accent. 'If these folks don't fancy it, I think it'll look real fine on our mantel next to that cute li'l statue of Buddha that we bought in Japan last year.'

'You are welcome to it!' Ramses snapped as he took my arm and led me out of the shop. 'Damnation! It is not even a decent copy! Did you see the bl— blasted crook in her nose?'

I insisted that we sit down at one of the tables in front of a café. I was as disappointed as he was, and struggling not to screech in frustration. After several deep breaths, I said, 'It is likely to have been sold to Abubakar by one of the less-skilled apprentices in Harun's workshop. The lad not only distorted her nose, he also chipped her earlobe. What is most disturbing is that it cannot be one of the pieces we saw only two days ago, which were in a preliminary stage.'

'Implying that Harun has been making copies for at least a month,' Ramses growled, his teeth bared. An approaching waiter abruptly veered around us to welcome a group of students. 'We have no further business here, so I suggest we return to the hotel to question Herr Morgenstern.'

'He might be more forthcoming in a hypnotic state,' I said optimis-

tically, although I had reservations about the outcome. 'There are carriages parked across the street, awaiting museum patrons.'

Ramses gave me a dry smile. 'Shall I find a driver who can deliver us
to Shepheard's Hotel in less than five minutes?'

'I do not believe that is necessary.' I was about to expound on the
prior necessity of expediency when I saw the American gentleman
emerge from the shop, clutching the bust of Nefertiti in his arms as if it
were an infant. He was wearing tight denim trousers, what I thought
was a cowboy hat, leather boots and a plaid shirt that strained to span
his substantial girth. I took a small degree of pleasure as he staggered
down the street with his forty-pound purchase. It would be very much
at home on his mantel next to the statue of Buddha, since both were
likely to be of minimal value and no artistic merit. His unseen wife,
Lucinda, must have remained in the shop to browse for more tasteless
souvenirs.

When we arrived at the hotel, Ramses informed me that he had
an errand to run but would return in a timely fashion to depart for
the train station. Ali was hovering in the hall should any guest require
his attention. Upon spotting me, he attempted to blend into the floral
wallpaper without success.

'I wish to have a word with you,' I said sternly.

'*Masa el-kheir*, Sitt Hakim. The weather is very nice, yes? It is a good
day to shop for beautiful things.'

He began to wither as I made my feelings known in regard to his
inability to refrain from gossiping with members of the hotel staff. I
felt a pang of sympathy for him, since I had known him for a long time
and had always found him to be a decent chap, but it was vital that our
imminent departure did not become common knowledge. I continued
to scold him until his eyes welled with tears and he begged my forgiveness. Satisfied that he would not risk further indiscretions, I rewarded
him with a pat on the shoulder.

I tapped on the door of Herr Morgenstern's room and entered, expecting to find Daoud seated in a chair between the bed and the sole

egress. Therefore, I was surprised when David arose from an armchair. 'Where is Daoud?' I inquired.

'I sent him away to rest. I hope that is all right with you, Aunt Amelia.'

'I have complete confidence in you, dear boy.'

'The – er – patient seems to be all right. Do you want to look at him?'

'He seems to have passed from the hypnotic state into ordinary sleep. Interesting. That does not always occur.' The volume of Herr Morgenstern's snores was an adequate assurance of repose. However, as any responsible physician would do, I made certain by carrying out a brief examination. Respiration and pulse were within normal ranges, and when I raised one of his eyelids, a placid eye seemed to return my gaze with vague interest.

I pulled David into a corner of the room and quietly told him about the copy of Nefertiti. 'We must establish the number of forgeries that Herr Morgenstern requested, so I am resolved to hypnotise him again. I have the compass in my handbag, having intended to have another session at some time today.'

'I have the utmost faith in you, Aunt Amelia. I am quite sure you could charm a cobra.'

I was less confident than he, since I am always uneasy in the presence of vipers. I sat down on the edge of the bed and gently shook Herr Morgenstern until he awoke. 'Look at this,' I murmured as the compass swung back and forth. 'See how the light glitters. How soothing its motion is, how pleasing to watch. You are feeling sleepy now, but your eyes will remain open and you will hear my voice.'

Once I was convinced he was in a hypnotic trance, I began to speak softly about his beloved Nefertiti. I asked him if he had instructed Harun to make more than one copy, and he shook his head. I then repeated what I had said to him in the previous session, which was that we were his dearest friends and he could trust us. I stressed that returning to Amarna was his only hope of regaining the statue. When he nodded in agreement, I bade him to sleep.

'All is well,' I said to David. 'Shall I find you some cotton wool with which to plug your ears?'

'No, thank you,' he responded, squaring his shoulders. 'If there is any change in his breathing, I should be aware of it.'

'You are a great comfort to me, David.' I gave him a hug. I could not resist adding, 'As you are to Lia.'

I left him with a blush on his face and retreated to my quarters to make preparations for our departure. The memory of what had taken place in Abubakar's shop weighed heavily on me. The gleeful anticipation of retrieving the bust of Nefertiti, accompanied by what I can only describe as a rather thrilling race across Cairo, only to result in devastating disappointment, overwhelmed me yet again and I was forced to lie down with a cool compress across my brow. I was imagining the look on Emerson's face when he heard what had taken place, fairly certain that he would erupt in fury. Had he been with us, the fake bust would have ended up on the floor in hundreds of pieces, thus depriving the American gentleman of his opportunity to enhance the decor in his parlour. Something concerning his departure disturbed me, but I could not put my finger on it. I had drifted into an uneasy sleep when I heard a knock at the door.

Assuming that Ramses had returned from his so-called errand, which most likely had to do with Abubakar's reticence to identify whoever had sold him the pathetic copy, I opened the door.

'Sitt Hakim,' gasped Ali, 'you must come quickly! I am hearing noises in the room at the end of the hallway, where your guest is staying. It sounds like there is a fight.'

I brushed past him and hurried to the room. The opening of the door displayed a singular tableau: Herr Morgenstern, now dressed in his own clothes, wrestling with David. They staggered back and forth, clinging to each other in a bizarre waltz. A table had been overturned, and pieces of a porcelain lamp were strewn on the floor.

'What the devil?' I cried out.

'He is trying to leave,' David said, panting from the ongoing exertion. 'I knew you would want to examine him first. He doesn't seem – er – quite himself.'

I could almost hear Emerson shouting, 'Yes, he is! Unpleasant, unreasonable, ungrateful!'

'Frau Emerson!' Herr Morgenstern bellowed. 'Is it you who is keeping me captive here?'

I gestured at David to release his opponent, which he did reluctantly. 'No one is keeping you here against your will, Herr Morgenstern. I found you wandering the streets, incoherent and unwashed. Now you have enjoyed our hospitality and have been given food and a warm bed. Do you know your full name?'

He did, and he answered my other questions about his age, position *und so weiter* (as he would have said) with a readiness that assured me my ministrations had restored him to his normal competence. I then told him he might go, and he departed with a pleasant nod in my general direction.

'Shall I follow him?' asked David.

'If you wish, but I suspect he will head to the Deutsche Orient-Gesellschaft to take sanctuary until he returns to Amarna. He believes this is his only hope of being reunited with Nefertiti.' I sighed as I thought this over. 'Oh bother! Emerson and I were planning to stay in the dig house, and I wasted an entire day making sure it was habitable. We cannot refuse him possession of it, since he is the person who ordered its construction – and paid the workers.'

'I know it will be painful for you to endure Fatima's hearty meals, elaborate teas and rose petals sprinkled on your bed,' David said with a grin. 'Did I fail to mention whisky and soda on the upper deck, with a splendid view of the sun setting behind the mountains in the desert?'

I tossed the discarded thobe at him and returned to my room to pack.

TO NO ONE'S surprise, the railway station was crowded with those anticipating the arrival of passengers on the train and those preparing to climb aboard it. Daoud's imposing stature provided us with a path to the boarding platform amid the jostling of elbows and the cacophony of jabbering, multilingual voices. Ramses kept a firm grip on my arm as we sought an adequate space in which to wait for however long was necessary. The railway authorities in Egypt are not obsessed with strict schedules; our particular train would appear, *inshallah*, when it appeared. David arranged our luggage as a barrier in front of us, and I sat down on a bench to rest, preferring it to the close confines of the Ladies Waiting Room.

That which ensued happened so rapidly that I could scarcely recall the events later. Ramses, who had been standing with his arms crossed in a menacing fashion, yelped and clasped his hand to his neck. A woman behind him screamed as she collapsed on the platform. I attempted to rise in order to offer assistance, but Daoud grabbed me with such vigour that my feet were dangling several inches above the concrete. At the same time, Ramses and David thrust their way through the frenetic crowd and disappeared. I shouted at them to stop to no avail; my words were drowned out by not only shrieks but also the imminent arrival of the train.

Despite my strident pleas to be released, Daoud carried me across the platform, and when the train shuddered to a halt, opened the door of the nearest passenger car and deposited me on the top step. 'I must protect you, Sitt Hakim. We will find the proper compartment after the train leaves the station.'

There was no point in arguing with him or attempting to elude him. The woman who had collapsed was now surrounded by family, friends, officials in khaki uniforms and gawkers. I could not see if she was able to stand up. I was struggling to peer over Daoud's shoulder for Ramses and David when they came running towards us. Daoud allowed them to join me, although he continued to block the door, to the indignation of our fellow passengers.

'What is happening?' I demanded as we entered the nearest compartment. 'Is that blood on your neck, Ramses? Are you wounded?'

Ramses's complexion was disturbingly pale. 'The projectile only grazed me. I felt nothing more than a momentary weakness in my neck and shoulder. Considering the status of the woman who was struck, I was most fortunate. There is a long and varied history of the utilisation of poison darts. Heracles and Odysseus used them to defeat their enemies, but Magellan, Alexander the Great and Lucullus all fell victim to them. In Africa, the most common poisons come from oleander and milkweed, although tribes in the Kalahari Desert often use the larvae and pupae of a particular species of beetle.'

I realised that the motive behind his lecture was not to illuminate me, but to give all of us the opportunity to regain our wits. 'Fascinating, my dear boy,' I said, 'but I insist on knowing what happened after you and David dashed through the crowd in what I must assume was to give pursuit to the perpetrator.'

Rather than complying, Ramses said, 'Let us locate our reserved compartment, where we might do well to have a sip of whisky before I continue.'

'Indeed,' said David, who was quite as pale as Ramses and shivering despite the stifling heat.

Daoud appeared at the door of the compartment, laden with our luggage. The train began to pull away from the station as we progressed through several carriages and eventually located our private compartment, where we collapsed in silence. After Daoud had taken the luggage to the proper storage carriage, he returned and positioned himself in front of the door with an ominous scowl.

I took the small flask from my handbag and offered it to Ramses. After he had taken a swallow, he passed it to David, who did the same. 'Well?' I demanded as I resisted a maternal urge to utilise my handkerchief to wipe away the droplets of blood on his neck. 'Was this another attempt by the Godwins to murder one of us?' I must acknowledge my voice was trembling. When David handed me the flask, I let the remaining whisky dribble down my throat.

Ramses took a bent card from his pocket and handed it to me. 'He threw this at me before he made a bold endeavour to escape by leaping across the train tracks. His foot caught the rail and he fell prone only inches away from the train's engine. I am reluctant to relate the gruesome details, Mother, but I can assure you that neither he nor his monocle survived.'

I stared at David until, with pained reluctance, he said, 'Cromwell's head was severed as we watched in horror. There was no possibility of saving him from his folly.'

'How utterly dreadful,' I said, willing myself not to envision the scene. 'I could not wish this on anyone, even my most dedicated assassins. It is ironic that he should come to such an unsavoury demise. The original Cromwell supported the beheading of Charles I, but then suffered the same fate after the Royalists regained power and dug up his corpse in 1660. Ramses, are you quite certain that you are feeling no ill effects from the dart?'

'I am fine,' he said. 'I am more concerned about the innocent woman who was the victim of Cromwell's vicious attack. These Godwins must be stopped before they do further damage, curse them! Do they believe they can hide behind their absurd monocles?!'

'There are only two brothers remaining,' I commented. 'Absalom and the oddly named Flitworthy. Let us pray it takes them a lengthy amount of time to determine where we are and follow us. I have no doubt that they will, but we shall be prepared to put a stop to this vendetta. Poor Nefret must be riddled with regret for having been lured into marriage by Geoffrey.'

Ramses did not respond.

THE TRAIN WAS a mere two hours late as it arrived at the non-designated stop convenient to our dahabeeyah. When I appeared at the bottom of the steps, Emerson clasped me to his manly chest. Ignoring the grins of Selim and members of our crew, he said, 'I missed you dreadfully, Peabody! I should not have left you in Cairo. Please assure me that you are safe and well.'

I wiggled out of his embrace so that my feet reached firm ground. 'You should know by now that I am more than capable of taking care of myself. I will admit that much has taken place since you received the telegram, some of it quite unpleasant. I should prefer to describe these events after I have had the opportunity to freshen myself and have breakfast or lunch, as Fatima chooses. The offerings on the train have not improved.'

Emerson looked at Ramses, who had fashioned a scarf around his neck to resemble an ascot (and coincidentally cover the wound on his neck). 'Hmph!' he said, his eyes narrowed in suspicion. Daoud's face was stony, and David's was concealed by smoke from his pipe. Rather than demand explanations, Emerson offered me his arm and we climbed into the small boat to cross to the *Amelia*. Daoud went on to join the rest of our team.

Fatima was hopping about excitedly when we came aboard. She hugged me and then enveloped Ramses in a motherly embrace that caused his ears to pinken with embarrassment. 'I must prepare a meal immediately! You must eat, all of you. The food in Cairo is not healthy.' She disappeared into the galley and began issuing shrill orders to her staff.

Emerson tried to accompany me to our cabin, but I placed my hand on his broad chest and told him I would join him shortly on the upper deck. It was heartwarming to be back in the comfort of our nautical home (and marital chambers). Fatima had adorned the washbasin with flower petals and added a few drops of aromatic oil. I was exhausted but resisted the temptation to sprawl across the bed, and instead changed into a frock suitable for the upcoming inquisition – and Emerson's inevitable explosion of curses when he heard the story.

When I appeared on the deck, I found him, Ramses and David partaking of whisky and soda. 'It is a bit early in the day for this, is it not?' I said with a facetious frown.

'If I am correct,' Ramses said, 'it is five o'clock in Mongolia. In any case, this is well deserved. May I offer you one, Mother?'

'A small glass of sherry will suffice,' I said as I sat down next to Emerson and put my hand on his. 'You're looking weary, my dear. Is all going well at the excavation site?'

'Do not endeavour to distract me,' he replied in a chilly voice, his brow lowered above his eyes. 'To begin, where is Herr Morgenstern? Why did he not arrive with you on the train from Cairo?'

I took a sip of sherry and related in detail my discovery of Herr Morgenstern outside the hotel, the doctor's diagnosis and instructions and my success with hypnosis. 'We could not in good conscience compel him to remain at the hotel after he had come to his senses and achieved a modicum of health. He will, I believe, return here in the next day or two to resume his duties. You and he will have to come to an agreement concerning the city site.'

Ramses cleared his throat. 'Shall you tell him about the copy we encountered in Abubakar's shop across the street from the museum, or shall I?'

I motioned at him to enlighten Emerson and sat back in preparation for a lengthy diatribe, interrupted by choice curses and threats. It would only worsen when he learned what had taken place at the train station, I mused. And it did. Emerson's voice could have been heard as far away as Luxor, and must have been painfully audible to the tourists disembarking less than a mile away in order to view the remains of Amarna from beneath their wide-brimmed bonnets and bowlers.

He broke off in the midst of an especially profanity-laden rant when Fatima appeared to announce that luncheon was served. I smiled gratefully at her as we went to the dining room. Although all the members of our staff are inured to Emerson's outbursts, he does make an effort to moderate his language in the presence of ladies. However, he was still harrumphing under his breath as we took our places at the table.

'Have you heard from Nefret?' I asked.

Emerson smiled for the first time in a long while. 'After I received your telegram, I sent one to her informing her of what I believed was your accomplishment in – er – providing hospitality to Herr Morgenstern. Her reply stated that she would arrive here this afternoon.'

We finished the meal without further conversation, interrupted only by Fatima's periodic entreaties to refill our plates. Emerson put down his napkin and asked me if I intended to accompany him to the site to evaluate the progress that had been made in the last few days. His tone of voice and general demeanour indicated little enthusiasm but even less doubt that I would respond affirmatively.

'Of course, Emerson,' I said briskly. 'Allow me to change into more practical clothing. I shall return in no more than a few minutes. Ramses, I suspect you are still feeling the effects of the poison from that dart. You need to rest, my dear boy.'

David, who probably knew Ramses better than anyone, said, 'His gait is unsteady. I will remain here in order to monitor him, unless you think my presence is necessary.'

'I am capable of protecting Peabody,' Emerson said with a grim look.

I knew he was remembering the note that Sethos had slipped under the door at the hotel. 'Yes, you are. We shall see the both of you at tea time, and Nefret as well if the train arrives in a timely fashion.'

IN THEORY THERE is no reason why two excavators cannot share a single site. In practice it is a recipe for disaster except in rare circumstances. At Giza, for instance, the mastaba fields surrounding the pyramids are so extensive no reasonable man could object to a division at certain times.

Often there were several different expeditions working there, more or less amenably.

Amarna was a much smaller site but the archaeological features there were of so diverse a nature that a *reasonable man* would be willing to share, especially when a particular task was beyond his resources. The nobles' tombs, wonderfully decorated and inscribed, required skilled copyists. The boundary stelae, inconveniently located high in the cliffs, were badly battered and difficult to reach; Herr Morgenstern had not attempted to access them. The city site itself stretched for several miles, a complex mixture of temples, elegant villas and smaller dwellings.

The Workmen's Village, which was of no interest to him, often contained material that shed light on the customs and living conditions of ordinary working Egyptians, a subject that has not been studied as intensively as has the habits of their superiors. But these humble homes did not produce elegant sculptures or troves of jewellery. It was such discoveries that brought journalists to interview the excavators who found them, and I am sorry to say that archaeologists are no more averse to public acclaim than are ordinary men. Emerson is an exception to this general rule. As he once put it, 'We have had to curse attention from the press.' He would have liked to blame this on my habit of poking my nose into criminous activities – as he called it – but was forced to admit that his own habits, such as the time he kicked a journalist down the stairs at the Winter Palace in Luxor, had attracted at least as much interest from the press.

But I digress.

The Reader will have noted my emphasis on the words 'reasonable man'. I had no reason to suppose that Herr Morgenstern would be reasonable about his site, and to be honest, I doubt many excavators would have been. They are as possessive about their concessions as people are about their homes. One can hardly imagine Mr X inviting Mr Y to move into his living room. For Herr Morgenstern to invite Emerson to join him in excavating the city site would have been equally unimaginable.

And for Emerson to confine his activities to the Workmen's Village was, if not unimaginable, decidedly unlikely. My admonishment that he and Herr Morgenstern needed to come to an agreement had been lost in the breeze.

AS I HAD expected, Emerson struck out straight across the desert towards the city site. I had not thought of a way to deter him, so I could only slow him down a bit while I continued to cogitate.

'Please don't walk so quickly,' I said, catching hold of his arm. 'I am quite out of breath.'

He immediately slackened his pace, but looked at me in surprise. 'Quite well, are you, Peabody?'

'A momentary shortness,' I said. 'Where are you going, Emerson? The shortest way to the Workmen's Village is—'

'Confound it, I know the location of every structure in Amarna as well as I know the scars on my body. Maspero authorised us to take over the site, should we find it necessary. Clearly, Herr Morgenstern abandoned it, and there has been no sign of activity since we departed for Cairo. We have an obligation to make sure none of the local thieves are disturbing his excavation.'

'No one could quarrel with that intention,' I admitted, 'if you are sure that is all you intend.'

'I also intend to interrogate that chap von Raubritter,' Emerson said. 'Who the devil is he, anyhow? For all we know, he may have usurped Morgenstern's authority and is making off with valuable discoveries.'

When we reached the area where Herr Morgenstern had been working, we found it deserted except for a few goats and an indolent fellah dozing in the shade of a spindly tamarisk tree. After he had been shaken awake by Emerson, this individual claimed he had come to the site in hopes of being hired. However, he departed with such celerity that might lead one to question this intent when von Raubritter appeared, out of breath and dishevelled.

'Good heavens,' I said. 'Are you all right, Herr von Raubritter? Has something happened?'

'No, no. That is—yes, I am well. Nothing has happened to me. I was in haste, hoping to have a word with you, Mrs Emerson. I have been told that you encountered Herr Morgenstern in Cairo and that he was not in his right mind. Based on what I have been told about him, I have a theory that might explain his symptoms. I am frantic to share this with you before more calamities befall him.'

Emerson, who had been investigating a concavity behind a ruined wall, suddenly stood up, glowering like a disagreeable incarnation of Ra, the sun god. Von Raubritter let out a strangled German swear word. 'Mrs Emerson is not to be accosted so unceremoniously!' Emerson snapped. 'If you wish to speak with her, you must make an appointment with both of us.'

'Yes, sir, of course. That would be better. I don't want to keep Mrs Emerson standing in the sun. I apologise. When—'

Emerson made a great show of consulting his nonexistent watch.

'You are welcome to join us for tea if you like,' I said, before Emerson could put the poor fellow off.

'Thank you, that is most kind.' The polite young man's face was ashen.

'Come along, Peabody,' said Emerson. And off he went, clasping my arm and leaving von Raubritter staring after us.

'How rude you were, Emerson,' I scolded.

'Not at all. You must not encourage these fellows, Peabody. They are likely to mistake your courtesy for – er – something warmer.'

It is a delusion of Emerson's that every male person I meet develops amorous feelings towards me. It is rather an endearing delusion, though, so I have given up trying to convince him that he is mistaken.

'I am sure Herr von Raubritter's intentions are completely

honorable. He seemed extremely perturbed about Herr Morgenstern's condition. Germans tend to be stoic. Do you not find that ominous, Emerson?'

'I do not even find it interesting,' he replied blandly.

I did not believe him for an instant.

EIGHT

VON RAUBRITTER DID not turn up for tea. I assumed Emerson's rudeness had frightened him away, and since we were fully occupied (with one thing and another) for the remainder of the evening, I did not give him another thought.

I was, therefore, surprised when after we had sought the marital couch Emerson suddenly burst out, 'What the devil do you suppose happened to von Raubritter? It is time I had a talk with that young man.'

'He is not so young. I would estimate his age—'

'It is not his age, but his credentials and his motives that I question. Curse it, Egyptology is becoming an unsupervised game! People pop up out of nowhere and begin digging. That fellow Biddle—'

'Buddle, Emerson.'

'Biddle, Baddle, Buddle, whatever his name! Who the hell is he, anyhow? And the hairy fellow—'

'He is a missionary.'

'So he says. Have you ever heard of the Church of the Enlightened whatever it was?'

'No,' I said, 'but there are a number of odd religious sects wandering around the English countryside. I have been told that in America one can find them on corners with signs that proclaim the imminent destruction of the world. As far as I can tell, it has yet to happen. Apocalyptic fear has gripped many ancient cultures, including Rome. They made numerous predictions going back to 753 BC. The Essenes, a sect of Jewish ascetics—'

'Do not lecture me, Peabody! I am well aware of such religious twaddle. Our concern is Amarna. There are too many unidentified persons roaming about. First thing tomorrow I will catch up with von Raubritter and interrogate him. I have an uneasy feeling about him.'

'Why, Emerson!' I exclaimed. 'Are you having a premonition?'

'I never have premonitions,' he said emphatically.

Naturally, I did not contradict him.

I DREAMED OF Abdullah that night. The old man and I had developed a strange yet strangely satisfying relationship over the years he had served as our *reis*. Some might say I dreamed of him because I was reluctant to admit he had left my life for ever. He was not sorry to go, I believe. His health was bad, and he had grumbled about sitting in the sun like other useless old men. He would have preferred to go out in a glorious gesture of heroism, as he did when he took in his own body the bullet meant for me.

Yet those dreams were not like the amorphous, half-remembered visions that usually come in sleep. They were sharp and as vivid as life, and the setting was always the same – the cliff behind Deir el-Bahari, where we had so often stood together watching the sunlight spread across the valley of the Nile. And Abdullah was not like the ageing man he had been at the end. He was tall and strong and black-bearded, and he came striding towards me with the free steps of a man in the prime of life.

I laughed aloud as he approached, in part from the joy of seeing him and in part because his face was set in a familiar scowl. Abdullah had never thought highly of my common sense. I was due for a lecture.

I did not hold out my hands or embrace him as I would have done in life. Something told me it would not be permitted.

'It is good to see you again,' I said, and laughed again because the words were so banal, so inexpressive.

I thought I saw a spark of amusement in his dark eyes, but he spoke to me as sternly as he had always done.

'When will you learn to be sensible, Sitt? You face an enemy like none you have ever known, and you laugh like a schoolgirl.'

'Then you must make me be sensible, Abdullah. Tell me how to know my enemy.'

Abdullah shook his head. 'You know I cannot do that, Sitt. Fix your mind on the problem at hand. You are too easily distracted by other matters.'

'But there are too many matters going on. The man who attacked in my bath, the would-be bomber, the horrific decapitation at the train station, as well as the strange events at Amarna. Herr Morgenstern, who has disappeared yet again, leaving the site unguarded. But you know that, I suppose.'

'There is nothing mysterious about his absence,' Abdullah said in exasperation. 'Put together what you know of his activities and ask yourself why he was clad in filthy clothes and ranting like a madman in Cairo.'

'Oh,' I said. After pondering for a few moments I said slowly, 'He had come upon the bust of Nefertiti and was enamoured of it. He knew that in the final division the antiquities people would not let him keep it, so he concealed it and went to the most renowned forger in all of Egypt. I suppose he desired to keep his scheme a secret, which is why he did not choose to stay at the Deutsche Orient-Gesellschaft. However, I am sure he had funds to reside in a nondescript hotel where he would not be—'

'Sitt.'

'Yes, Abdullah?'

'Three men recently tried to murder you. Not an unusual happening,' said Abdullah with heavy sarcasm, 'but one that deserves your attention. Or do you not believe these attempts to assassinate you are important?'

'It wouldn't be the first time,' I said, trying to lighten the mood. It did not succeed. His scowl darkened even more. 'Abdullah, don't reprimand me,' I said. 'Emerson will look after me as he always does. Furthermore, I am not incapable of defending myself.'

Abdullah sighed. 'My time here is over for now. Sometimes I don't know why I bother. You will soon go on your merry way without taking even normal precautions. Emerson cannot protect you if you engage in reckless behaviour. You must keep a constant vigilance for those who wish you harm. They are very close at hand.'

It seemed an extraordinary thing for him to say. Then I realised I was awake and the voice I heard was not that of Abdullah but that of Emerson, mumbling in his sleep as he sometimes did.

WHEN WE LEFT the boat the following morning, we found an old acquaintance waiting: Reis Abdul Azim, Herr Morgenstern's long-time assistant.

'Good to see you,' said Emerson, shaking hands. (Egyptians had resigned themselves to this habit of Emerson's.) 'Where the devil have you been? What are you doing out here?'

'Waiting.'

'For what?' I asked.

'For Morgenstern Effendi. Or you. Someone who knows what to do.' The old man's untamed white eyebrows fluttered alarmingly, and he went on with mounting passion, 'Who is this von Raubritter? He knows nothing of excavation!'

'You don't know who he is?' I said, taken aback.

'No, and I will not take orders from him. He came here after Morgenstern Effendi went to Cairo, and stumbled around with a baffled look on his face.' Abdul Azim frowned like an ill-tempered camel. As my Readers know, the majority of camels are sulky and uncooperative, as are some members of my family. I keep a variety of powders for headaches and indigestion in my first aid box, and restock it every season.

'Nor should you,' I replied. 'Herr Morgenstern has been ill. He is much better now and will soon be able to resume work. What do you know about his departure for Cairo so early in the season?'

'Nothing. It was not my place to seek an explanation.'

I gave him a fierce stare. 'So you were not there when he uncovered the bust of Nefertiti? Were you taking a nap?'

Reis Abdul Azim appeared to be shrinking as he hunched his shoulders and lowered his head. 'No, Sitt, I was not there. He announced that he was closing the site for the day and sent all of us away, even though there remained several hours of daylight. The next day he was gone. I could see that an object had been removed and the space filled with sand; I did not know what it was.'

Emerson uttered a colourful profanity, but I cut him off before he could launch into a torrent. 'In any case, Herr Morgenstern has recovered. I expected to find him here, back at work.'

'He has not come. This man von Raubritter—'

'We are going to speak with him now,' Emerson said. 'Come with us if you like. We have been authorised by Maspero to make sure the work is continuing.'

It did not occur to the *reis* to ask if Herr Morgenstern had approved this. If I may say so, our reputations were so high (and Emerson's command of Arabic invectives so extensive) that no one dared question our authority.

There was usually a small crowd around any excavation area, some hoping for work, others with nothing better to do. This morning not a soul was in sight.

I turned to Reis Abdul Azim. 'What is going on?'

He shrugged and spread his hands wide to indicate ignorance, but there was fear in his eyes as he began to back away from us.

Emerson let out a reverberant oath and broke into a run. Following, I soon saw what he had seen – an object protruding from the sand like a stick marking a particular spot. It was not a stick. It was a human forearm.

The body had not been buried deep. It took Emerson only seconds to uncover the face and neck of the person of whom we had been speaking moments earlier. 'Sit down, my dear, and have a sip of water,' he ordered. 'You appear a trifle upset.'

I took his advice, for the sight was disturbing. I handed him the flask. He emptied it in one gulp and said, 'Von Raubritter was a civilised young man, even if he was not a trained archaeologist. Who could have done such a thing? A Godwin, do you suppose?'

'That makes no sense, Emerson. What connection could he have had with the Godwins?'

'The five brothers appear to be possessed by revenge, but there is method in madness, as the saying goes. What arcane meaning can this peculiar tableau have?'

'The extended arm may not have been deliberate,' I commented. 'There is a phenomenon known as cadaveric spasm – instantaneous rigor mortis. It sometimes follows a violent struggle.'

The evidence of that was indisputable. Rusty patches of dried blood covered the dead man's shirt and his battered head and face.

'He was stabbed in the neck,' Emerson went on, 'and then struck or kicked in the head while he lay on the ground. After I collect his wallet and whatever else he has in his pockets, I suppose we had better cover him up again.' It did not take him long to find a leather wallet and a few oddments of no prospective significance. I intended to analyse them all the same. As my Readers know, the devil is in the details.

'Wait,' I said. 'Tell Selim to bring the camera.'

Emerson shouted at Selim, who trotted over and took several photographs. I handed Emerson one of my large handkerchiefs. He placed it carefully over the dead man's face and began to scoop the sand back in place.

'He asked to speak with us,' I mused, 'but he did not come. He was killed in order to prevent him from telling us . . . what? We may never know.'

'Do not be melodramatic, Peabody. This is not one of those as-inine Gothic novels you hide on the top shelf of the linen closet. I presume that you have in one of your innumerable pockets a note-pad and pen. We must send a telegram to Russell.' I located such objects. He scribbled a message and asked Selim to have it sent from the telegraph office in Minya. 'What the blazes are we to do with von Raubritter? We cannot just leave him lying in the ground in that grotesque position.'

'I do not see what else we can do, Emerson. Sand is the best preser-vative we have. Rigor is fully advanced and will last at least two more days. He will not be disturbed, since you know how the men feel about what Abdullah called "fresh dead bodies".'

'We ought to do something to mark the place in case jackals are – er – drawn to his arm. Ah, I have it. Not only an appropriate marker, but effective protection.'

'From jackals?' I said.

'Hmph,' Emerson replied. 'We could break his arm in order to bury him more efficiently, but I am loath to do so. Unless you . . . ?'

When we left von Raubritter to his (temporary) rest, my second-best parasol was firmly anchored by a large rock, sheltering the spot. I was not convinced that jackals would be intimidated by my scent, but I had no other suggestions.

AFTER THE PHOTOGRAPHS had been developed, Selim set off for Cairo with copies of them. We had instructed him to show them to the police in Minya in case they desired to investigate, but apparently they did not feel any urgency.

Nefret arrived in the late afternoon. I greeted her with a warm hug, as did Emerson, and I suggested that he enlighten her as to the previous events in Cairo and the fatal attack on von Raubritter. Her eyes were round at his conclusion. 'How dreadful for you, Aunt Amelia!' she cried out. 'Only someone with your fortitude could have survived such calamitous doings. I am so sorry that I allowed myself to put you in peril from the Godwins.' Tears began to streak her rosy cheeks. 'Can you ever forgive me?'

'This is not your fault,' I said gently. 'Come sit next to me and tell us about your clinic. Is all well with your physicians and midwives?'

'Yes, and they took pleasure in showing me the new maternity ward. A dozen newborn babies were thriving happily, if loudly. I spent an afternoon in a rocking chair, getting acquainted with them. I over-saw several surgeries, all of which were performed to my standards.' She clutched my hand tightly. 'But I feel so dreadful that I did not insist on accompanying you to Cairo.'

'I must admit there were moments when I wished you were there. However, we all survived and are here to welcome you home.'

'Indeed,' inserted Emerson, gazing at her with deep paternal affec-tion. 'This is worthy of a celebration. Shall we have drinks on the upper deck before dinner? Peabody, have you checked on Ramses and David?'

Nefret rose to her feet. 'Is Ramses still feeling adverse effects from the poisoned dart at the train station? I am not sure what medication might help him, but I can experiment with what I have available.'

'I will go to their cabin now,' I said hastily, 'and meet you on the deck to enjoy a blissful view of the setting sun.' My tone, although lacking Emerson's authoritarianism, settled the matter. Ramses, who appeared to have no lingering symptoms, was deep in conversation with David when I entered their cabin. Rather than inquire into whatever scheme they had concocted (which would force them into equivocation, if not prevarication), I told them about Nefret's timely arrival and von Raubritter's untimely departure. We joined Emerson and Nefret for a leisurely drink before Fatima beckoned us to dinner. The subsequent conversation centred on potential archaeological discoveries in both the Workmen's Village and Thutmose's studio. The recent deaths were not commented upon by anyone, including me.

THANKS TO MY spouse's sluggish habits in the morning, we were still sitting over breakfast the next day when who should appear but Herr Morgenstern himself. His hair had been trimmed and his fingernails manicured, and his clothes were pristine. I awaited his first words with some curiosity. He began with a friendly salutation ('*Guten Morgen*') and went on to apologise for intruding. Emerson was left speechless by this unexpected cordiality; I, who had hoped for such a reaction to my hypnotic treatment, responded with matching amiability.

'Do join us for breakfast, Herr Morgenstern,' I said. 'It is good to see you on your feet again.'

'I believe I must give you some of the credit, Frau Emerson.' He took a seat and eyed appreciatively the plate of eggs that Fatima placed in front of him. After he had been supplied with coffee and toast, he tucked into his breakfast with a true Teutonic appetite.

When he had finished, he let out a sigh of satisfied repletion, applied his napkin to his moustache and said, 'It is not good for the digestion to discuss unpleasant subjects while eating, but I believe we must deal with one of them now. I am told you found a dead body at the site of my excavation.' He waggled his finger at me. 'It is a very naughty habit of yours, Frau Emerson.'

The note of levity was not only inappropriate, but quite unlike him. I responded severely, 'Not only dead but foully murdered.'

'Murdered? Are you certain?'

'He did not cut his own throat and then bury himself,' Emerson said, resenting the implication that I had invented or imagined a crime. 'Weren't you curious enough to examine the body?'

'Seeing that Frau Emerson's notorious – famous, I mean – parasol had been left to mark the spot, I took it for granted that she had conducted her usual thorough examination.' Herr Morgenstern took a deep draught of coffee, applied his napkin again and went on, 'I trust you will be removing the remains as soon as is possible. They were buried in an area where I had been discovering interesting material.'

'Oh?' Emerson's eyes brightened. 'What—'

'Emerson,' I said sharply, 'do not allow yourself to be distracted. We cannot disturb the remains until we have heard from the author-ities in Cairo. Selim has gone there with copies of the photographs he took of von Raubritter, but it will be a while before we receive a response.'

'You ordered your reis to take photographs of the dead man?' Herr Morgenstern's tone was a blend of admiration and disapproval. 'Your aplomb amazes me, my dear lady.'

'No doubt you consider it unwomanly, but you should be accus-tomed to my habits by now.'

'I should,' he said with a sigh, 'but I doubt I ever will. Do you have copies of the photographs?'

I did, of course. Herr Morgenstern took a long time inspecting them and then finally shook his head. 'He reminds me of someone. I cannot think who.'

Emerson stared at him. 'You do not recognise this man who claimed to have been left in charge when you – er – went to Cairo?'

'I cannot be sure,' he mumbled, rubbing his temples. 'It is all very confusing.'

'I have examined the contents of the man's wallet,' Emerson said flatly. 'He is – was – twenty-seven years of age and lived in Darmstadt, which is in the southern part of Germany. Quite recently, he was a student at the university, which has a department of archaeology. If you employed him, he might have had adequate academic credentials but obviously no experience in the field. It is curious that you burdened him with the supervision of the excavation in your absence.'

'Did I?' Herr Morgenstern re-examined the photographs. 'Are you sure?'

'That is for you to tell us.'

I stared at Emerson, amazed by his tact. It is a virtue he rarely employs. 'Do not distress yourself, Herr Morgenstern,' I said. 'It can be difficult to tell, given the circumstances.'

'*Aber natürlich*. Thank you for an excellent breakfast. I hope you will stop by my excavation at any time.'

After he had gone, Emerson looked at me in unconcealed awe. 'Good Gad, Peabody, what did you do to him? The old curmudgeon is as mild as a lamb, if noticeably muddled.'

'I must say,' I acknowledged, 'that I did not expect such a thorough-going reformation. Perhaps the hypnotic process has brought out his true nature, hidden for all these—'

'We are well acquainted with his true nature, which is that of a stiff Prussian pedant. This hypnosis of yours . . . Are you sure you ought to be messing about with people's minds?'

'We all "mess with" people's minds every day, Emerson. We seek to influence them with words and acts of varying effectiveness. Some methods are more effective than others.' I had no intention of elaborating on them.

'Hmph.'

'If you doubt the legitimacy of my methods, you will ignore Herr Morgenstern's invitation to visit his excavation.'

He burst into laughter. 'Touché, Peabody. Game and match to you.' He tossed his napkin onto the table and rose.

'Where are you going?' I asked.

'To visit the excavation. Did you think I was going to Luxor to rock babies at Nefret's clinic?'

'You might at least wait until this afternoon. Herr Morgenstern may be willing to have you visit him, but I doubt he will meekly hand over his concession to you.'

'Such an idea never entered my mind,' said Emerson.

He was easier to read than one of Miss Smith's novels, and far more entertaining.

'DO REMEMBER, EMERSON,' I said with a trace of tartness, 'what M. Maspero told Ramses and me when we were most recently in his office. On our previous visit, he implied that he would authorise us to take over the concession if we found cause. Now he has backed away from that assertion.'

We were walking towards the Workmen's Village, trailed by Ramses and David. Nefret had begged off in order to unpack her suitcase and enjoy a few hours of solitude.

'Maspero is an idiot,' Emerson said dismissively. 'We shall assess the situation and do what is necessary to ensure the integrity of the excavation. Herr Morgenstern already has stolen the Nefertiti bust in order to replace it with a forgery meant to fool the Service des Antiquités. He is not to be trusted, Peabody.'

'I agree that his motive was not exemplary, but until we have proof we must maintain a civilised agreement about his firman. It is his, Emerson. You cannot use physical force to compel him to concede authority to you.'

'Balderdash!'

I was filled with apprehension when we arrived at the Workmen's Village, since I had little hope that it would prove to be our ultimate destination. Emerson does not allow anyone to thwart him when he has made up his mind. Therefore, I was relieved when he greeted Selim (with a vigorous handshake, of course) and began to issue orders to commence work in a partially upright structure. I could sense that Ramses and David were bemused, but they were wise enough not to comment. As was I.

We remained at the site beyond tea time, despite the gathering grey clouds. I was preparing to suggest that we return to the dahabeeyah when Emerson said, 'It is time to call upon Herr Morgenstern. He has had an entire afternoon to gather his crew and resume work. We should applaud his efforts in order to encourage him.'

'I have never known you to express such an altruistic gesture,' I said drily.

'Do you find me incapable of altruism?'

'Heavens no, my dear Emerson. You are the embodiment of generosity for your fellow man – and woman.' I had already prepared myself for the previous exchange, since I knew it was inevitable. I slipped my arm through his and we set off for the city site.

No one was there. Emerson rumbled ominously as he looked at the floor of Thutmose's studio, still covered with a thick layer of sand. 'This is incompetence of the highest level!' he shouted. 'There is no one standing guard! I must speak to Morgenstern immediately.'

'He is likely to have resumed residency in the dig house. I prefer to wait here while the two of you discuss the matter, I am sure at great length. Please bear in mind that the sun will be setting soon, and the walk back will be more arduous in the dark.'

After Emerson strode away in the direction of the dig house, his expression formidable, I ascertained that von Raubritter's body had not been disturbed by man nor beast. I repositioned my second-best parasol, which had toppled, with a few more rocks. Satisfied that I had done my best, I opted to explore for structures of potential interest in the future. I strolled along the once-grand Siket es-Sultan, gazing with great curiosity at what had been discovered by previous archaeologists. It had first been mapped by Napoleon's corps de savants in 1798, and had been a source of intense interest to Egyptologists from numerous countries.

I turned to gaze at the cliffs, where Alessandro Barsasti had discovered the king's tomb twenty years ago. This is when I first saw a woman against a backdrop of gunmetal clouds rimmed with gold by the sun. She moved like a wounded bird, her black draperies flapping about her. I called to her to stop. Either the rising wind carried my voice away, or she would not heed it. I went after her as fast as I dared on the uneven terrain, but somehow she managed to keep ahead of me as she limped along the wadi at the base of the cliffs.

I have already mentioned that towards the middle of the afternoon the sky had darkened but we had hardly noticed. Rain is so rare in this part of the world that I was astounded when it was loosed in a hammering downpour. Muttering under my breath, I opened my parasol and continued in pursuit. The rocks beneath my feet grew slippery as the water rose. The anonymous woman seemed to have difficulty as well. I shrieked at her but she did not look back.

A trickle of water dampened my boots as I persevered. The trickle rose rapidly to a stream. I knew from past experience the water would continue to rise and it would carry with it boulders and other objects that would threaten my safety. I would have to reach higher ground, and soon. The walls of the wadi rose steeply, and rivulets of water precluded any hope of scrambling up them. There was, if memory served, an abandoned tomb in the cliff nearby, but I lacked the means to take sanctuary there. I began to panic as I struggled to keep my balance in the treacherous stream.

Then I heard a cry like that of a falcon – but it pronounced the syllables of my name. Looking up, I beheld a human form perched on a ledge. The darkening sky prevented identification, but I had a very good idea as to who it might be.

A rope dropped down. It was a sufficient message in itself, and I knotted it firmly around my waist. I had time only to close my parasol before I was drawn upward with such velocity that certain parts of my anatomy came into painful contact with the cliff face.

Sethos – my presentiment had been correct – hauled me up onto the ledge of the tomb. He was dressed in a blue robe and a red and white checkered kaffiyeh, his tinted face obscured by wire-rimmed eyeglasses, an outrageously large moustache, a variety of artistic warts and a singular black beetle brow. 'You are exceedingly damp above the knees,' he said. 'Would you care to remove—'

'No,' I gasped. Dangling from a rope high above roiling water has always had a deleterious effect on my composure.

'Ah well. Sit down then, and enjoy the view. I doubt the water will rise any higher.'

I came to my senses and peered down at the wadi. 'The woman!'

I exclaimed. 'I do not see her. What became of her? She was heading straight for the deeper water.'

'A woman in distress? And you followed her? Will you never learn?'

'She may have been swept away. The flood—'

'Was an act of Providence,' Sethos interrupted. 'If you had followed her a little farther you would have found yourself confronting not a woman, but a man armed with deadly weapons. He would probably have used a knife, but a pistol could have been a viable option. He would have been up the cliff and away before Emerson arrived. How the devil did you elude Emerson? He is supposed to be watching over you.'

'He went to speak with Herr Morgenstern.'

'And you went dashing off without a word to anyone?'

I felt certain I would hear a repetition (and more than once) of this criticism from Emerson, so I deliberated briefly over my response. Not that I felt obliged to make excuses, or even explanations, for my behaviour, but it would save time and energy if Emerson accepted my reasons without excessive debate. I decided to ascertain how Sethos would respond to them.

'It was necessary to act immediately,' I said. 'I believed the woman to be in imminent danger.'

'Amelia, kindly do me and your much-harried husband the favour of stopping to think before you act. It seems to require at least two of us to keep you out of trouble, and I cannot spend all my time here. My business is suffering.'

'That hardly elicits sympathy from me, since your business is tomb robbing, forgery, fraud and murder.'

Sethos let out a peal of hearty laughter. 'If you intended that as an insult, dear Amelia, you have missed the mark. It is a relatively accurate description.'

We sat in oddly companionable silence for a time, watching the torrent of stones and foaming water below. Once again Sethos had come to my rescue – the phrase is trite but accurate – in the nick of time, yet

I was annoyed with him. I had been in his presence on several memorable occasions, but I could only describe his general features. His height, almost as great as Emerson's six feet and a bit, could not be concealed, but stooped shoulders and a general air of . . . What shall I call it? A posture of ineptitude, incompetence, helplessness can create an impression of smaller size. Arrogance and scorn have the opposite effect, which is why most Egyptians would claim that Emerson is at least seven feet tall.

I was pondering my chances of yanking off Sethos's moustache when he said, 'Have you ascertained what the problem here in Amarna is?'

'Problem? Oh, so it was you who left the damaged ushebti?'

'Who else? I knew you would be clever enough to understand its meaning.'

'So did Emerson.' I hoped this would irritate him, but he only smiled.

'I have never underestimated Emerson's intelligence. His weakness is that he allows his outrageous temper to overrule his common sense.'

'What about you?' I asked. 'Have you no clue as to what is going on here? You would not have brought the ushebti to us if you were not suspicious.'

'Herr Morgenstern's behaviour was peculiar. He left Amarna in the middle of the night, carrying a large canvas bag. An acquaintance of mine followed him to Cairo, but lost him at the train station. I was, shall we say, intrigued.'

I glared at him. 'And when you could not find him, you chose to follow us. Did our visit to Harun's shop offer you some enlightenment?'

'Harun is an old friend of mine,' Sethos said, 'although I wish he would comb his beard every few months. He always seems so dusty.'

'Indeed,' I said distractedly. If I were to believe him, he had not made a deal with Harun for a copy of Nefertiti's bust. I experienced some enlightenment of my own. 'Is Lucinda enjoying her trip to Cairo and delighted by your recent purchase at the shop across from the museum?'

'I realised from your and Ramses's reaction that it was a fake, but I felt it warranted closer examination. One never knows when one might need a facsimile of a masterpiece.' He smirked for a moment, and then said in a sober voice, 'But something is awry here. I suspect that the man who calls himself von Raubritter is involved. He is not one of my usual suspects, so I have not been able to get a line on him.'

'He is dead. We found his body yesterday. We are sending photographs to Cairo to have him identified.' I did not mention Herr Morgenstern's failure to recognise him.

'Alas, we must end this delightful encounter. I believe I hear Emerson approaching.'

There was no doubt about it. Emerson's stentorian shouts echoed from cliff to cliff. 'Peabody! Where have you gone? Answer me! Peeaaabody . . .'

'You had better respond,' Sethos said, rising to his feet. 'Please excuse me. I prefer to avoid him when he is in this frame of mind.'

'Where are you going?'

'Up,' he said succinctly. And up he went, climbing with the expertise of a mountaineer. He was out of sight when Emerson appeared, forcing his way through the fierce stream.

I raised my voice to the pitch that has been known to quell rioting mobs and family arguments. 'Up here, Emerson!'

Emerson stopped, planting his feet firmly against the torrent and bracing himself against the wall. Only a man of enormous strength could progress so far, but although the water level was beginning to recede, Emerson was being battered by stones of various sizes.

'What are you doing up there?' he bellowed. 'Curse it, Peabody—'

'Calm yourself. As you can see, I am perfectly safe. You are the one in danger. Please join me.'

'That seems sensible,' Emerson admitted. He began to climb. Several times his foot slipped, but his grip on the rock face kept him from falling and he was soon at my side. His first act was to seize me in an embrace that squeezed the air out of my lungs. His second was to commence a diatribe, interspersing it with endearments and profanities, which I shall not reproduce out of courtesy to my more genteel Readers. Once he had run out of breath, he sat down next to me. I took out my handkerchief and wiped blood off his cheek.

'Oh dear,' I said. 'We must get back to camp so that I can tend to your injuries.'

'Another shirt ruined,' grumbled Emerson.

I nodded. 'It certainly is. Most of the buttons are missing, and there are innumerable rents and tears, not to mention quite a few bloodstains. I suppose I should have purchased more shirts for you in Cairo. You seem to go through them in short order. It might be more economical to purchase them by the gross.'

'You cannot divert me so easily, Peabody. Why did you go off without announcing your intentions?'

'There was a woman in the distance—'

'Or a figure swathed in anonymous black drape. Will you never learn?'

'That is what Sethos said.' I regretted the words as soon as they came out of my mouth, but to my surprise Emerson did not react as he usually did to the mention of that name.

'I suppose it was he who got you up here,' he said, looking at the coil of rope. I opened my mouth to reply, but he waved me to silence with a magisterial gesture. 'I beg you to say no more, Peabody. I know only too well what Sethos's motives were. They have not changed since that day he imprisoned you in his seraglio and wooed you with whimsical speeches and voluptuous surroundings.'

'They made no impression on me, Emerson. I was and am always yours alone.'

'I know that, but I also know you have a certain weakness for the fellow, since he did not take advantage of you – or had not done so before I arrived on the scene. Do not forget that you had not been with him long.'

'How can I ever forget? The site of you bursting through the door, an unsheathed blade in each hand . . . The duel that followed, as you fought for me like a gallant knight of olden times. I confess, it made my heart beat faster and filled me with pride to have you as my champion.'

'Hmph,' said Emerson, giving me a meaningful look. 'Keep hold of that thought, Peabody. Let us descend now, before the light fails.'

NINE

B Y THE TIME I had seen to Emerson's cuts and bruises in our
cabin, we were late to dinner. When we sat down at the table,
we found that Mahmoud had burned the roast. He always did it
deliberately, in order to punish us for our tardiness, though he would
have denied this with his last breath. He was as temperamental as a
French chef, and there was no use reprimanding him since his response
was to subside onto the floor, looking mournful and declaring himself
unable to ever cook again.

Emerson's brow furrowed when he beheld the charred meat. 'Tell
Mahmoud he is dismissed! Now, and without a character reference!'

Since this scene occurred every few weeks, Fatima reacted without
undue alarm. 'Yes, Father of Curses. It is not as bad as it looks.' She
seized a large knife and sawed the roast in half. There was a suggestion
of pink in the middle of it. After she had carved and served it, Emerson
calmed down a bit and we passed the remainder of the meal in congenial
companionship with Ramses, David and Nefret.

Once we had retired to the lounge, I began to describe my encounter with Sethos on the ledge of the cliff. The atmosphere plummeted as
if we were in England on a wintry day (in this case, an ice storm).

'You chased after a dark figure?' Ramses said, clearly appalled. 'It did
not occur to you that you were putting yourself in peril? Von Raubritter was murdered only a day ago. How could you, Mother?'

Nefret frowned at me. 'Have you forgotten there are still two God-win brothers in Egypt? How many attempted assassinations will it take to get your attention, Aunt Amelia?'

'Those beastly Godwins will never give up,' added David as he passed the brandy decanter. 'You must be more aware of the danger.'

I do not care to be criticised for acts of Christian duty, and this certainly qualified. 'And what if the woman was from the village and flee-ing from abuse? I was attempting to save her life, as any of you would have done. It is a matter of altruism, Emerson. You are familiar with that concept, are you not?'

'Hmph.'

'So I suggest,' I said, 'we analyse Sethos's story. He claimed to have no knowledge of Herr Morgenstern's whereabouts in Cairo, and fol-lowed us to Harun's workplace. This implies he did not arrange to have a copy made of the Nĕfertiti statue, and only realised its significance in Abubakar's shop.'

'He is a bl— blasted liar!' Emerson said hotly. 'He would not have hired spies to watch Morgenstern if he was not up to his old tricks.'

'I agree,' said Nefret. 'He must have heard rumours. The crews chatter like old women sitting in the shade, and there are always shift-less bystanders who are amenable to bribery.'

'Von Raubritter might have been equally amenable,' Ramses said, 'but that does not explain his murder.'

'Sethos had no motive to kill him,' I said, keeping an eye on Em-erson, who has been known to lose his temper whenever I have been obliged to come to Sethos's defence, no matter how mildly. When his eyes narrowed, I stood up and said, 'I am exhausted from the ordeal. Emerson, please do me the honour of escorting me to our cabin. Good night, dear children.'

It was possible that I had ruffled Emerson's feathers, so I went about soothing them with womanly zeal.

EMERSON, WHO HAD slept soundly, preceded me to breakfast. When I entered the dining room, Ramses gave me a baleful look as he seated me at the end of the table. 'We have been discussing the Godwin brothers,' he said (as if I hadn't anticipated as much). 'Judas, Guy and Cromwell are no longer threats due to their impulsive attempts to cause us harm. You must keep in mind, Mother, that two of them remain at large – Absalom and the oddly named Flitworthy.'

'So who was Absalom?' Nefret inquired as she buttered a slice of toast. 'From the Bible, I seem to recall, but I do not know the details.'

I refilled Emerson's coffee cup (he was not yet adequately caffeinated to engage in polite discourse), and then said, 'Absalom was the third son of King David and renowned for his handsomeness, charm and love of pomp and royal pretensions. Eventually he declared himself to be the king, raping his father's concubines as a loathsome gesture of superiority. He fomented a rebellion that concluded with his death at the battle of the Wood of Ephraim.' I winced as I took a sip of coffee. 'A most undignified death, one might say.'

'You must tell me what happened to him,' Nefret wheedled with an impish grin.

'He was caught by his head in the boughs of an oak tree and dangled there, still alive. Despite receiving orders to the contrary from King David, Joab pierced Absalom in the heart. There were very few happy families in the Old Testament.'

'There are no oak trees in Egypt,' David said, 'and it is challenging to imagine anyone being caught by his head in a palm tree.'

I grimaced. 'That is true. However, we cannot ignore the irony of the way the first three Godwin brothers met their fate. Judas was stabbed in the back and Guy was killed by a stick of dynamite. Cromwell was beheaded by the train.'

'We don't have time for irony,' Emerson interjected loudly. 'We are here to work, and also to monitor Herr Morgenstern's mental status. He assured me that he would post guards at the site to ensure that no one could steal so much as a shard from Thutmoses's studio.'

'Which I find rather ironical,' I said. 'The Americans have a saying about the futility of locking the barn door after the horses have been stolen.'

'Bah!'

'David and I plan to return to Cairo tonight,' said Ramses, looking directly at his father.

Emerson's scowl was fierce enough to send Fatima back into the kitchen. 'I need both of you, and Nefret, at the excavation. We are here to concentrate on our concession, not go running off to Cairo with some harebrained idea.'

'We will be gone only a day or two.'

'Absurd! Your mother needs to be protected by all of us. Who knows what she might do if left on her own?'

'Excuse me,' I said sharply, 'but I am quite capable of looking out for myself and will not tolerate being treated as a recalcitrant child. Ramses, why do you and David feel the need to go to Cairo? Are you still obsessed with the German embassy?'

'I would not describe it as an obsession, Mother.'

I tried a few more questions, and then acknowledged to myself that I would get no more information from him or David. Nefret remained silent, perhaps envisioning the biblical Absalom's demise. Emerson finished his coffee and announced that we were leaving immediately for the site, which obliged me to point out that I was clad in an embroidered dressing gown and slippers. He commented that I seemed to waste a lot of time changing clothes. I asked if he preferred me to sleep in my khaki trousers and belt. The exchange went back and forth until Emerson threw up his hands, literally.

'Whenever you are ready, Peabody,' he said. 'I think I need another cup of coffee.'

SELIM WAS WAITING for us on the river bank. 'Chief Detective Russell sends his regards,' he began. 'He did not recognise the man in the photographs, nor did any of his officers. He made inquiries at the German embassy and the Deutsche Orient-Gesellschaft, but no one knew anything about a man named von Raubritter.'

'Did he have any suggestions about what we are to do with the body?' I asked. 'We cannot ignore it. I feel so badly that he was assaulted with such violence. He may not have been an adept archaeologist, but he was a very courteous and well-spoken young man.'

Emerson winced. 'Yes, he was. Selim, what did Russell suggest?'

'He said he would send a telegram to the police in Minya with instructions to investigate.'

'We are here to excavate, not keep a vigil around a grave! If the police do not appear by noon, I will go to their headquarters and drag them back here by their heels!'

I did not question the sincerity of his threat. Emerson is seldom impressed (and never intimidated) by those who assume they possess authority – or dare to disagree with him. He does not tolerate incompetence or laziness, both characteristics of small-town policemen. I could only pray they arrived soon.

We continued to the Workmen's Village and commenced work. I was measuring bits and pieces when I heard voices. I looked up with the expectation of seeing uniformed policemen, but was irritated to see tourists.

Amarna is a popular stop for the Cook steamers; the more lethargic visitors (made even more lethargic by the enormous English breakfast served on board) sit on the deck, watching their more energetic fellow passengers riding donkeys towards the cliff tombs. Luckily, few of them bother with what they are told are dull sites, which was all to the good. As we had learned from past experience, most of the ones who did approach asked idiotic questions or handled the artifacts – or tried to steal a few as souvenirs. Emerson has been known to demand that certain of them empty their bags and pockets for his inspection. He has an acute eye for petty thieves.

We worked until noon. Emerson, who seldom wears a watch because he can determine the time as if he were a sundial, called a break so that we could have our luncheon meal on the dahabeeyah. To my relief, we encountered two police officers embarking from a boat; I had no doubt that Emerson would have carried through with his avowal had they not arrived in a timely fashion. They recognised him, naturally, and began begging his forgiveness for their tardiness and promising to investigate the murder. Rather than lecture them on the finer points of forensic analysis, he sent them on their way with only a perfunctory profanity.

The afternoon passed uneventfully. There was only a minute chance we might come upon an artifact of astounding significance, and we did not. I expected Emerson to suggest a visit to Herr Morgenstern's site either to confirm that it was under guard or to grill the policemen, but he said nothing. When Ramses and David volunteered to check on the site, Emerson nodded curtly.

Fatima had prepared a particularly lavish tea, to which we had invited Selim and Daoud. Daoud had taken to the English custom of afternoon tea (with the concomitant sandwiches, cakes and biscuits) with great enthusiasm. As a large man, he required considerable nourishment, and he nodded in agreement when Emerson remarked, 'I don't see why Fatima bothers with these little sandwiches. They are only a mouthful. Why not a hearty slab of meat or cheese between two thick slices of bread?'

I smiled indulgently but did not bother to reply to what was clearly a rhetorical question. 'If you remember, Emerson, we had a reason for inviting our friends here this afternoon. Would you care to explain the situation, or shall I do so?' Emerson tried to speak, but his mouth was full of sandwich (I confess I had taken this into account). 'Very well, my dear, I will take this task upon myself.'

'I will do it,' Nefret said.

I looked at her with some surprise, for it was not like her to put herself forward. 'By all means, if you wish. I had thought you might not want to recall—'

'It is not a question of what I want, Aunt Amelia, but of what is necessary. We had agreed, you remember, that Selim and the others should be apprised of the situation so that they can take steps to protect you.'

She covered it all quite well, so I did not interrupt. Selim listened with the keen attention he always demonstrated, Daoud with his usual placid look. He understood the situation perfectly well: keep strangers away from the Sitt. Everything else was unimportant.

'So,' said Selim, 'these people mean you harm. How are we to know them?'

'Well, they are English,' Nefret said. 'Unlike ordinary English tourists, who usually travel with a group, they will be unaccompanied.'

'That is a help,' he said doubtfully, 'but what is to prevent them from joining such a group? You cannot describe their appearance? Colour of hair, height? Anything?'

'I'm afraid not,' Nefret murmured. 'Oh, Selim, I am sorry to be of such little use. The only thing the Godwins have in common is an eccentric fondness for monocles.'

Like all our people, Selim adored Nefret. 'We will find these people, Nur Misur, no matter how they appear.'

Daoud nodded again, his cheeks bulging with cake.

AFTER THEY HAD gone and Nefret indicated that she did not desire further conversation, I went to our cabin and changed into my embroidered gown. I was very fond of it because it allowed a pleasing circulation of air and a sense of freedom. I have always been appalled at the concept of corsets because they contort a woman's body and endanger internal organs. Many of my friends in England submit themselves to tightly laced bodices in orders to achieve hourglass figures. Life is too short for such nonsense, especially with a husband whose fingers tend to fumble in moments of passion.

I went to the upper deck, where I found Emerson ensconced in his favourite chair, smoking his pipe and reading.

'Why, Emerson!' I exclaimed. 'Are you reading the Bible?'

'I wanted to refresh my memory as to the activities of that band of villains,' he said, slamming the book shut. 'What a repellent lot they were! Adulterers, murderers, rapists, guilty of incest, treason and worse! King David coveted Bathsheba, who was another man's wife, and sent that man out to certain death. That violated at least two of the so-called Ten Commandments, supposedly written in stone. God turned a blind eye.'

'We do not always understand His ways.'

He brought his fist down on the book. 'This is nothing but an oral tradition of a tribe of barbarians who had somehow got the notion that a single all-powerful god was in charge of them and the universe. That would have been harmless enough except that the corollary was that since he was the only god, everyone else had to acknowledge him – or die. Thus did monotheism come into existence. It has been called a great gift to the world; rather, it is a curse that has been responsible for some of the most heinous crimes committed against humanity.'

Every now and then Emerson carries on like this. I have become accustomed to his outbursts, although they are heretical in the extreme. I have found that it does not do to question the Scriptures literally, for most of the Old Testament is either distasteful or unbelievable. The self-appointed interpreters of the divine commands often did not hear His words clearly.

'Why don't you read the New Testament?' I suggested.

'Well,' said Emerson, looking a trifle sheepish, 'I admit that fellow's speeches make sense from a moral standpoint.'

'They are the standards we all live by, including you, Emerson. And you succeed far better than the ranting preachers. "In my Father's house are many mansions." I am certain one is reserved for you.'

'You must confess, Peabody,' said Emerson, giving me one of his sly sidelong glances, 'that the other place has its attractions. Far more interesting company there. All the pagans – Socrates, Plato, Genghis Khan, Confucius, the pharaohs . . .'

Entering into the spirit of the thing, I replied, 'How do you know they will be there? The Redeemer can forgive worthy pagans and welcome them into Paradise.'

'I won't go anywhere unless you are there, too. Would you consider committing a few minor sins in order to be eligible for Hades?'

'You will have your little joke, Emerson.'

'It was not a joke. But if you will put in a good word for me, I may squeeze into heaven after all. What I am about to propose,' he added, looking meaningfully at me, 'is not a sin. Even that old stick St Paul said—'

'I am familiar with that passage, Emerson.'

'I am pleased to hear it, Peabody. Shall we . . . ?'

'An excellent idea,' I said.

RAMSES AND DAVID had left after dinner, laden with a parcel of sandwiches and pieces of baklava and basbousa that Fatima had forced upon them with numerous admonishments to be wary of the food in Cairo. Daoud had taken up residence on the upper deck, equipped with a blanket, a rifle, his prayer rug and a hefty plate of leftovers from dinner.

After breakfast, Emerson, Nefret and I set off for our site. Selim endured a handshake and told us that he had spoken to the crew, and all of them would be on the lookout for strangers. When I asked him if he had mentioned monocles, he laughed.

'If a monocle is meant to be a disguise,' he said, 'it is not effective. What is more, all the assassin needs to do is remove it. That would not be difficult, Sitt Hakim.'

'True,' I admitted.

Emerson harrumphed and began to issue orders. I resumed measuring oddments, mainly faience beads and some small broken pottery figurines, while Nefret and Selim took photographs of whatever Emerson indicated. Towards the end of the morning, he announced it was time to call upon Herr Morgenstern.

'I did not think you would wait this long, Emerson,' I said as we walked along the path through the cultivation to the city proper.

'Have to give the man an opportunity to resume excavating,' he said grudgingly. 'However, if we find the site vacant and without guards, we shall seize control until the D.O.G. assigns it to someone more competent.' He looked at me, his eyes glittering dangerously. 'And please don't repeat what Maspero told you, Peabody. The excavation is too important to be sacrificed by incompetent bureaucracy.'

'Yes, dear,' I said. Argument was futile. Furthermore, I agreed with him wholeheartedly, even though I was not confident that Herr Morgenstern would consent with no more than a shrug. 'It occurs to me that something was amiss in the dig house. It is customary for an Egyptologist's assistant to stay as well. When we were there, there was no indication that anyone but Herr Morgenstern had been residing in the house. Where do you suppose Mr Buddle and von Raubritter were staying?'

'That had not occurred to me, Peabody. Buddle claims he is here as a representative of someone named Ridgemont, who must be underwriting a goodly part of the cost of the excavation. I don't know about von Raubritter, but one would think that Herr Morgenstern was obligated to offer hospitality to Buddle.'

'Whose name was on the card we found in Judas's pocket,' I replied. 'He was blasé when I warned him that he was in danger. All of this is perplexing, Emerson.'

'Damned perplexing,' he muttered.

When we arrived at the location where we had uncovered von Raubritter's body, I was relieved to see that it had been removed by the police. My parasol remained open but askew. Pragmatism indicated that I retrieve it.

'Herr Morgenstern!' shouted Emerson, waving his arm. 'We have accepted your invitation to visit the site.'

'*Guten Tag,*' he responded as we joined him. He was standing at the perimeter of Thutmose's studio; his workmen were on their knees, carefully brushing sand into buckets. 'We are near the level we had previously achieved when I left for Cairo.'

Emerson, his arms akimbo, observed the scene without expression. 'Hoping to find something that rivals Nefertiti's statue?'

'I do not understand you,' Herr Morgenstern said, staring in bewilderment. 'But, yes, I do have expectations. Thutmose did his best to secure his work after Amarna was abandoned and left to looters.'

I was about to say that he could hardly claim ignorance of the statue when I heard my name shrieked in the distance. I shaded my eyes and saw a most peculiar and unwelcome figure dressed in a voluminous lavender robe and purple veil, perched precariously atop a camel. Precariously, because she (I had no uncertainty as to her identity) was being jolted back and forth as the camel plodded unhurriedly, its reins held by an exasperated camel driver.

'What the blazes!' Emerson exclaimed. 'You seem to attract the weirdest people, Peabody.'

'I gather that is not a compliment,' I replied, unable to refute his allegation.

The camel was brought to a halt nearby. Getting on and off said beast can be startling. One end drops abruptly, causing a forty-five-degree angle, and before its passenger can catch a breath, the other end drops as abruptly. Miss Smith's face was ashen as the camel driver grabbed her around the waist and yanked her off the saddle.

'Mrs Emerson,' she said, struggling to regain her balance, 'isn't this exciting! It is my very first time upon a camel, and likely to be my last. What rambunctious animals they are! Stubborn, vicious, flea-bitten, and smelly. I could have hired a donkey, but I felt this was a golden opportunity.'

'Ah yes,' I said. 'Allow me to present Herr Morgenstern, who is in charge of the excavation, and my husband, Radcliffe Emerson. Gentlemen, this is Miss Ermintrude de Vere Smith.'

'I am thrilled to meet you,' she simpered. 'I have heard so much about you, Professor Emerson. Many characteristics of my fictional sheikh are modelled after your legendary personage. You are known as the Father of Curses. I pray I am not to be the subject of one.'

'*Es ist eine Ehre*, Fraulein Smith,' said Herr Morgenstern as he bowed and kissed her hand.

She glanced at Emerson, perhaps in anticipation that he would do the same. He produced a chilly smile. 'I hope I am not interrupting you,' she went on valiantly. 'When I heard on the boat that you and Mrs Emerson were excavating in this locale, I fear I gave in to one of my silly impulses and had my luggage removed and transported to Minya. Once on shore I realised there were no hotels. It was daunting, to say the least, but I decided to rent a little mud house in the village so that I could experience Egypt to the utmost. I am planning to keep a journal that details every moment of my stay.' She giggled, batting her eyelashes at the men. 'Now all I must do is find a dashing sheikh. Do either of you happen to know one nearby?'

Emerson's face was stony. 'No, Miss Smith, I do not. I suggest you continue farther into the Eastern Desert, where sheikhs frolic in the dunes by day and their harems by night. They always are on the lookout for more wives and concubines.'

'Sir, you make me blush,' she said coyly. 'You must not tease me now that we are to be neighbours.'

I intervened before Emerson could respond, in that I knew he was less than charmed with the situation. 'Are you sure this is wise, Miss Smith? The majority of the villagers are gentle and considerate, but there are some scalawags who do not hold unmarried women in high esteem. The houses are not secure. I do think you should reconsider your decision, and inquire at Minya about the possibility of hiring a motorcar so that you can reboard the Cook's steamer upstream.'

'When I saw the primitive and unsanitary living conditions, I felt some amount of trepidation,' she replied. 'However, I cannot live my life through fictional characters and imaginary settings while I write in my cottage, with my cat in my lap. Your courage, Mrs Emerson, has empowered me. Surely you of all people understand my thirst for adventure, even if there is danger afoot.'

'I do understand—' I broke off as I spotted a figure coming rapidly towards us. 'I believe that is Mr Dullard, Emerson. Please remember that you have already attempted to rip off his beard.'

'Hmph,' Emerson said, frowning. 'Even if he is who he claims to be, I have no use for him or any other missionaries. I assume you remember what happened at Dahshur, Peabody. That fellow went quite insane after we found the Coptic manuscript in a mummy case that referred to "the son of Jesus". He murdered an antiques dealer and attempted to do the same to you, all because of his avowed religious beliefs.'

'You must tell me all about it,' Miss Smith said, and then gasped as she caught a better view of Dullard. 'My goodness, he seems to possess a great deal of hair . . .'

'*Das ist wahr,*' Herr Morgenstern murmured. 'Let me assure you that he is harmless. He has come to this site many times in the past because he is curious about the process of archaeological excavation. I gladly have answered his questions, invited him for drinks and meals, and even made a small donation to his church. We are all fellow Christians, are we not?'

I discreetly stepped on Emerson's foot to prevent him from exploding with a stream of invectives.

Dullard was panting as he drew near. 'Good morning, Professor and Mrs Emerson, and you as well, Herr Morgenstern.' His eyes widened as he gazed at Miss Smith. In his high-pitched and squeaky voice, he said, 'I don't believe we have been introduced, madam.'

I performed the obligatory social task of making proper introductions, and was stunned as the two stared at each other with what might be described as profound intensity. Neither of them seemed capable of speech. I finally said, 'What brings you here today, Mr Dullard?'

'I heard that my friend Herr Morgenstern was back,' he said distractedly. 'And you, Miss Smith? Do you have an interest in Egyptology?'

'Oh yes indeed,' she replied, her eyes locked on his as if they were communicating wordlessly. 'I am the author of a series of books set in the very recent past, in nineteenth-century Egypt, and I am here to experience it for myself.'

'An author?' Dullard gaped at her as if she had declared herself to be a trapeze artist. 'You write books?'

'That is what authors do,' I commented.

He bit his lip as he pondered this. 'Might you wish to visit a Coptic village? I shall be happy to escort you. The Copts in Egypt date back to the first century and have a fascinating history of persecution and acceptance.'

'How terribly kind of you, sir,' she said.

Emerson slapped Dullard on the back. 'An excellent idea, old boy! Miss Smith is eager to experience it for herself, as she just stated. Please do not allow us to detain you any further.' He turned his back to continue observing the workmen. 'Morgenstern, come have a look at this. You, too, Peabody. I believe we are about to uncover another sculpture by Thutmose.'

I was flabbergasted when Miss Smith offered her arm to Mr Dullard, who was goggling at her as if he were intoxicated. They made an odd couple; he was at least a foot taller than she and coated with copious dark hair, while she was fair-skinned and as plump and rosy as a pomegranate. I watched them walk in the direction of the Nile, where presumably he had a mode of transport to the far shore. They toddled away amid squeaks and giggles.

'Emerson,' I said, 'I believe I shall return to the dahabeeyah now. Do remember that Fatima can be a trifle belligerent when we are late for a meal. Good day to you, Herr Morgenstern.'

'*Guten Tag*, Frau Emerson.'

I knew perfectly well that my pronouncement left Emerson in a painful dilemma. He had sworn to stay at my side to protect me, but he had caught a glimpse of something that might prove to be of archaeological value. The decision was his, of course, but he needed to be reminded that Herr Morgenstern was in charge. I did not look back as I walked towards the village site.

'Peabody!' he called in a rather pathetic voice.

I held up my hand and wiggled my fingers in farewell. When I arrived at our site, I found Nefret and Selim in the midst of a minor dispute over the placement of the tripod. I gathered Nefret up and we walked through the scattered huts alongside the shore. After I related the unexpected arrival of Miss Smith and her equally unexpected departure on the arm of the missionary, I said, 'I am concerned about her safety, but she is determined.'

'Maybe she was expecting you to offer her a cabin on the *Amelia*,' said Nefret with a wicked smile. 'That might incur the wrath of the Father of Curses.'

'One shudders to imagine Emerson's reaction to such an invitation. In any case, we do not have room for her. I suppose I ought to invite her for tea or even dinner, but that is the extent of my Christian duty. She has made a decision, and she must endure the consequences. If we can figure out which hut is to be her temporary home, I will ask Selim to have the night guard keep his ears open for sounds of distress.'

'Not a problem, Aunt Amelia.' She went to the nearest hut and engaged in conversation with its occupants. After a rapid exchange in Arabic, Nefret returned to the path. 'There has been a great deal of chatter about the appearance of the English woman. It took three men to transport her trunk, suitcases and hatboxes from Minya to this location, and over an hour to force the trunk through the doorway. Shall we have a look?'

'I think we should, if only to be neighborly,' I said.

Nefret led the way to a small structure built of clay bricks. It looked as though it had somewhat melted from the recent rainfall, but the roof had survived. 'The family that was living here accepted a great sum of money to move out for an unspecified amount of time, and they did so cheerfully.'

'I can understand why,' I said as we entered the hut. It contained one room that served as bedroom, kitchen and parlour. A cauldron hung above a pile of charred wood in a small fireplace. The furnishings comprised sleeping mats, a crude table with benches, random cookware and a lantern. The quantity of luggage was extraordinary. Miss Smith would find it challenging to unpack in a room that lacked closets, but clearly she was prepared to be presentable in all elegant social affairs. She would find none in Amarna.

A large group of villagers were waiting outside, chattering like magpies. After they bestowed the usual greetings and extravagant compliments, they swarmed around Nefret and inundated her with questions, which consisted of several including the Arabic words for 'who' and 'why'.

I rescued her and we resumed walking toward the shore, where one of our men was waiting to escort us onto the dahabeeyah. 'Miss Smith has truly lost her mind,' I said. 'That can be the only explanation for her behaviour. I regret that you did not have the opportunity to observe her and Mr Dullard when I introduced them. If I believed in such nonsense, which I don't, I would describe it as love at first sight.'

'So she has found her sheikh. Good for her!'

I smiled indulgently at Nefret. 'Possibly, but you have not met Mr Dullard. I will describe him while we have luncheon, with or without Emerson.'

EMERSON ARRIVED WHILE we were lingering over dessert and coffee. He offered a halfhearted apology, and merely flinched when Fatima banged down a plate of cold food. 'Herr Morgenstern's crew uncovered a statue, likely to be of one of Akhenaten's daughters. It is broken but salvageable.'

'Did you think to ask him why neither Buddle nor von Raubritter was staying in the dig house?' I asked.

'He said he did not know,' Emerson said. 'His cognisance seems to come and go – or he is a consummate liar. I made a reference to the Nefertiti bust and he again claimed to have no knowledge of it. When I asked him why he had gone to Cairo, he mumbled something about purchasing supplies. The next moment he began describing the makeup of Akhenaten's household and lineage with great clarity. Then, without reason or provocation, he burst into tears and ran in the direction of his house. Could this be the result of your attempts at hypnosis, Peabody?'

'Absolutely not,' I said.

Nefret frowned. 'His symptoms suggest psychotic episodes. I wonder if he is taking some sort of drug that causes these severe fluctuations in lucidity. If you will excuse me, I would like to consult my medical journals.' As she left the dining room, she paused briefly in the doorway to rearrange the flowers in a vase.

'Have you noticed,' I said to Emerson, 'a tension between her and Ramses? They have not really spoken to each other with the exception of the necessary civilities.'

'I'm sure they have, Peabody, but not within your hearing. They are adults and beyond your desire to meddle. The last time they were together resulted in a nightmare for all of us. Nefret saw her husband fall to his death despite Ramses's effort to save him. Ramses may not have been fond of Geoffrey, but he never disparaged him.'

'Because he was reared to be a gentleman,' I said, 'and he thinks of Nefret as a beloved little sister. At least he used to . . .'

'Allow me to repeat that they are adults.' His voice rose. 'Fatima, am I allowed dessert?'

There was no reply from the kitchen.

TEN

From Manuscript H

WHEN THE TRAIN arrived in Cairo, only two hours late, David and Ramses exited the station without glancing at whatever bloodstains might still be visible on the tracks. They had changed into grimy thobes and kaffiyehs during the trip, and went directly to a café, where they were greeted in a friendly but uneasy fashion.

After they had eaten, David lit his pipe and said, 'How long do you think it will take before your spies wander in, their palms itching for payment?'

'I am confident that our arrival has been noted.' Ramses gestured for another cup of coffee. 'Would you like to make a wager?'

'I'll risk a quid that no one appears within an hour, starting now.'

'Pull out your wallet,' Ramses said with a smirk. 'Latif is watching us from the pavement. Surely he can find the courage to approach us before an hour has passed. Look, here he comes.'

Latif, a clever lad of no more than twelve years old, was fairly fluent in English from his encounters with gullible tourists, lived on the streets and relied on his wits to survive. Ramses sympathised with his plight and always rewarded him generously when he provided information.

Ramses told him to sit down with them and order whatever he liked from the menu. Latif did so with haste, and then gobbled down the meal. Once he had finished, he leaned forward and whispered,

'I have heard a most amazing statue from Amarna is on the market in Cairo. I can show you the shop, Brother of Demons. It will be a great honour.'

'And please allow me to have the great honour of paying the bill,' David said with a facetious smile.

Shortly thereafter, they entered the narrow streets of the Khan el-Khalili and went past Harun's workshop (dark and vacant) to the shop of a notorious antiques dealer. Ramses placed a liberal sum in Latif's hand and sent him on his way. He and David went inside and examined the wares on shelves and in display cabinets, speaking to each other in Arabic.

'Is this all you have?' Ramses said to the proprietor. 'Trash?'

'Be away with yourselves,' the man said dismissively. 'I have nothing you beggars can afford. If you do not leave immediately, I will throw you out the door. Everyone will laugh when you sprawl in the street.'

'Is this how you address the Brother of Demons?' said David.

The proprietor gasped, his eyes flickering with fright. 'Oh no! I did not realise it was you. You must forgive me for my impudence, but I did not recognise you dressed like this. I am overcome with shame, Brother of Demons!'

Ramses regarded him with icy disdain. 'I have been told that you have a rare find from Amarna. Show it to me.'

'Of course, of course. I acquired it only yesterday and have kept it back until I can appraise it, but I will fetch it for you. May I offer you tea?'

'Show it to me,' Ramses repeated flatly.

David was stifling laughter, his shoulders quivering. 'You sound remarkably similar to someone whose name I need not mention.'

'Do you think there is any chance he has the original?'

'We shall find out in a minute,' David said, 'unless Sethos arrives in disguise and snatches it from under our noses. The last time he pretended to be an American in cowboy apparel.'

'I will be on the lookout for pregnant women in burkas, Italian counts, British lords or ladies, Turkish pashas and Chinese art dealers. You stay on the lookout for everyone else.'

'Of course, of course,' David replied, mimicking the proprietor. 'Anything I can do for the Brother of Demons.'

The proprietor returned from his back room and placed the statue of Nefertiti on the counter. 'It is most beautiful. As I said, I have not yet appraised its value, but I will give you an excellent price. Please examine it to your satisfaction.'

'Damn,' Ramses muttered quietly, 'another forgery. They are beginning to pop up like weeds. We must stop Harun before he makes more copies and scatters them across Cairo.'

'A forgery?' said the proprietor. 'That cannot be. I was assured that it is original and worth much money.' He paused for a long moment and then said, 'This very day I planned to take it to the museum and give it to them, since I do not deal with thieves. You must take it, Brother of Demons, and tell the authorities of my good intention.'

Ramses ignored him. 'What a fool this apprentice must be to have replaced the missing black iris in her left eye. Father had noted its curious absence most particularly. Yes, we will take it with us after you tell us who sold it to you.'

'A boy, he did not tell me his name. He was very nervous and afraid that he was followed. After I paid him, I let him leave through the back door. I am so sorry I cannot be of more assistance.' He clumsily wrapped the bust in brown paper and string, all the while reasserting his 'good intention' and stressing that he would accept no payment for that which deserved to be placed in the Egyptian Museum.

Once they were on the street, David said, 'So what are we to do with this blasted forgery? I don't fancy hauling it around all day. Sethos is sure to be nearby, watching us. He might appreciate an early Christmas gift.'

'That he can sell as the original to some greedy collector,' said Ramses as he shifted the heavy parcel to his other arm. 'I would prefer to smash it to pieces, but I think we should keep it until circumstances dictate otherwise. Sethos does not know it is just the work of another inept apprentice from Harun's workshop. That may prove useful, somehow. Let's find a hotel where we will not be recognised and consider our next move.'

'Lord Cavendish, I presume.'

'And as my lowly assistant, you get to carry this damnable thing.'

'The honour should be yours, sire.'

'Bugger,' Ramses said, laughing.

The hotel they chose would not meet the standards required of anyone with a distaste for strange odours, insects and rodents, questionable hygiene or a modicum of security. The lock on the hotel room door consisted of an interior deadbolt to prevent intrusion when guests were present, although a strong kick would thwart it. The minimal furnishings did not offer an adequate hiding place for Nefertiti in their absence.

'I suppose we could ask the hotel clerk to store it in a locked room,' David said dubiously, 'but he is susceptible to bribes like his brethren in the same trade.'

'Why couldn't it have been an ushebti?'

When they left the hotel, dressed in gentlemen's apparel, David was carrying a lumpy canvas bag. The clerk's eyebrows were raised as he called a faint farewell. They hailed a carriage to take them to the German embassy, and were greeted by the guard. Ramses brushed him aside with a curt word in German, and they walked up the drive to the front door.

'We are here to see the ambassador,' he said to the elderly butler. 'Inform Herr Gunter that we will wait as long as necessary.'

'Herr Gunter is not here at this moment. The ambassador left several weeks ago for a conference in Berlin.'

'In that case, we will have a spot of whisky while we wait in the drawing room,' Ramses said as he and David went inside, ignoring the butler's protest. 'Might there be a chessboard or a deck of cards with which we can amuse ourselves until Herr Gunter returns? The afternoon is at our disposal.'

The butler showed them into the room in which they had waited previously, mutely pointed at a tray with decanters and glasses, and then shuffled away, mumbling to himself. They helped themselves to a modest quantity of whisky diluted with water.

'What now, Lord Cavendish?' David asked as he meandered around the room, opening drawers and cabinets. 'No chessboard, no cards. Your lordship will be dreadfully bored, I fear.'

Ramses opened the door and peered at the entry hall. 'That pesky fellow has disappeared. Let's have a look around the place while we can. Gunter lied about the ambassador's whereabouts when we were last here. If he returns while we are prowling, I shall point this out and claim we are confused and wanted to see for ourselves. A feeble excuse, I know, but in character.'

'The offices are likely to be here on the ground floor, but they will be locked.'

'That has never deterred us before,' Ramses said as he eased into the hall. 'Don't forget the bag. If Gunter turns belligerent, we may be forced to leave with alacrity.'

The embassy was spacious, but not palatial. They looked into a large drawing room suitable for social gatherings, a library and a dining room with an expansive table set with silverware, fine crystal and withered flower arrangements. They heard no voices or footsteps as they continued onward. The butler, Ramses thought, must have retreated downstairs for a shot of Jägermeister to recover from David and Ramses's brash display of impropriety.

The ambassador's office was in impeccable order but slightly dusty. In contrast, Gunter's desk and file cabinets held untidy stacks of folders and unopened mail. The walls were covered with maps of Europe, Egypt and the Middle East.

David crouched in front of a cabinet and utilised a small tool to unlock it. 'Oh my God,' he said, forgetting to whisper. When he arose, he was clutching a bust of Nefertiti. 'Unbelievable.'

'Was the white-haired man we saw the other night carrying anything when he entered the embassy?'

'We both saw his briefcase, which could not have contained any-thing this large. Do you think it could be the original?'

Ramses frowned. 'I do not see any glaring flaws, but I will need to examine it more carefully. This is not the best place to do so. Relock the cabinet and the door as we leave. I recall there is an exit at the end of the hall, and I suggest we use it immediately.' He picked up the canvas bag and the bust, peeked out the door and motioned David to join him. 'This will be most awkward if Gunter appears about now. On the other hand, he can hardly have us arrested without explaining why he is in possession of a valuable antiquity.'

'Shall we ponder his options or get the hell out of here?'

'Is that the way to speak to Lord Cavendish, you dismal minion? For your impertinence, you can carry one of the Queen Nefertitis. How many of the bloody things are there? We may need to purchase a steamer trunk to take them back to Amarna with us.'

They left through the door at the end of the hall, and were crossing the backyard when a male voice shouted, 'Duck!' They reacted instinc-tively. A bullet fired from the door behind them splintered against the wooden gate, followed by a shot fired from the alley. 'Now run, dam-mit!' the voice ordered.

Ramses and David complied, keeping low and zigzagging until they reached the sanctuary of the alley. Another bullet hit the gate. '*Stoppen, Diebe!*' screeched a more familiar voice, that of an enraged Helmut Gunter.

As they ran towards the nearest street, Ramses said, 'Take my coat and wrap it around the statue. Helmut most likely will come after us, and we know he is armed. I do believe it might be prudent to stay at Shepheard's Hotel for the night.'

'And leave Cairo in the morning?' asked David.

'Well, no,' Ramses said with a scowl. 'We must uncover the link between Herr Morgenstern and Helmut Gunter. Maybe we should ask Sethos; he seems to be dogging our footsteps and looking out for us.'

David flagged down a taxi. Once he had instructed the driver to take them to Shepheard's, he said, 'Only because of his devotion to your mother. Otherwise, he would have disabled or shot us in order to get his hands on Nefertiti. He might have been nonplussed when he ended up with two of them.'

'A total of three, thus far.' Ramses examined the statue they had taken from the embassy. 'Another forgery, blast it! We have to find Harun's workshop before copies of Nefertiti start showing up in all the shops in Cairo. As disinclined as I am to physical violence, I would really like to throttle him.'

ELEVEN

MY BELOVED EMERSON was attempting to quell a rebellion. He was surrounded by a throng of workmen airing their complaints vociferously, while Mr Dullard restrained Herr Morgenstern in a bear hug. Reis Abdul Azim squatted in a shaded spot, his hands covering his face. Mr Buddle stood at a judicious distance, radiating displeasure. An audience had gathered to enjoy the spectacle.

I spotted Nefret in the melee and pushed my way to her side. 'What on earth is going on?' I said, obliged to raise my voice to be heard.

'I have taken charge of this excavation!' Emerson roared. 'Do you dare defy the Father of Curses?'

The workmen may have lacked the courage to defy him, but they were determined to protest their treatment. They sounded, I thought wearily, like a herd of recalcitrant donkeys. Emerson was enraged, as to be expected, but unable to shout them into submission. This was surprising. My husband is more than capable of intimidating a battalion into a frenzied retreat. Whatever Herr Morgenstern had done to enrage the workmen must have been horrendous.

Nefret leaned forward to be better heard. 'Herr Morgenstern is overcome with affection and enthusiasm. Selim told me what provoked this unpleasantness. Herr Morgenstern has been embracing and even kissing his workmen, and to make it worse, bestowing baksheesh at random. Those wailing most loudly are the ones who received only a coin or nothing at all.'

'Do you have a diagnosis?' I asked.

She shook her head. 'I have no inkling, Aunt Amelia. I would like to interview him in a calmer environment.'

'Say no more,' I said emphatically as I gripped my parasol and utilised its tip to force my way through sweaty bodies to Herr Morgenstern and Mr Dullard. 'I think it might be wise to allow Emerson to deal with the situation. Shall we withdraw to the dig house?'

'Mrs Emerson!' Herr Morgenstern exclaimed, kicking up sand as he tried to free himself. 'I am so delighted to see you again after our lovely time in Cairo! We must go again, you and I, so we can dine and then dance until dawn. You are the most divinely wonderful—'

'Now!' I shouted at Mr Dullard. 'Follow me and do your best not to step on anyone's foot. This cannot be allowed to degenerate into a tasteless brawl.'

Mr Dullard lifted Herr Morgenstern a few inches and carried him through the agitated workmen, knocking several of them to the ground. Once we were more safely ensconced under a palm tree, he said, 'Good morning, Mrs Emerson. How are you today?'

'Lovely,' I said acerbically. 'Do you have any idea why Herr Morgenstern is behaving oddly?'

He shook his head with such vehemence that his beard flung itself about like a pendulous furry animal. 'He was fine last night when I visited him, although he was drinking peppermint schnapps to the point of inebriation. Since I myself do not indulge in alcoholic beverages, I discouraged him as best I could and eventually helped him to bed.'

I looked over at Emerson, whose bellowing had grown so loud that it echoed off the cliffs in the distance, and determined that he would soon have the disturbance under control. 'Herr Morgenstern, we are going to your dig house so that we can all enjoy a nice cup of tea.'

'What a splendid idea, Mrs Emerson! There is nothing more agreeable than a midmorning cup of tea. You will forgive me if I cannot offer biscuits, but my pantry is meagre.'

'You have no reason to apologise,' I replied. Once Mr Dullard set him down, I took his arm and propelled him in the proper direction. Nefret followed us, her brow crinkled. Mr Dullard did as well, but unceremoniously deserted us when he saw Miss Smith emerge from the cultivation and wave vigorously at us. Or, more probably, at him.

Nefret grabbed Herr Morgenstern's other arm. She leaned forward so that I could see her eyes rolling incredulously, her elegant eyebrows raised nearly to her hairline. I had given her an account of the previous day's peculiar encounter between the two of them, but I had struggled to assimilate it myself. I could not fault her for scepticism.

The dig house was no tidier than Emerson and I had found it previously. It was less dusty, but the odour of garbage was almost as pungent and dirty dishes and bottles cluttered the counter. Herr Morgenstern had either returned from Cairo with a copious supply of schnapps and whisky, or he had hidden his cache in the locked room. Unable to contain my natural affinity to restore decorum, I gestured at Nefret to watch Herr Morgenstern and utilised a filthy dishtowel to gather up the scraps of fetid meat and vegetables. I piled everything on a stack of plates and carried it outside, my nose wrinkled. It is one thing to be confronted with the redolence of a foul, musty, heretofore unopened tomb; it is a most exhilarating experience, laden with anticipation and reveries of treasures to be uncovered. Foodstuffs infested with maggots hold no appeal. I had some experience with such matters, since Ramses's boyhood bedroom had been littered with dishes containing the remains of half-eaten fruit and sandwiches. When I had lectured him about the matter, he had patiently explained that he was conducting scientific research that would revolutionise theories about the decomposition of human flesh. By that, he meant the appearance of maggots. He was, if I recall accurately, no more than six years old. Emerson gave him a microscope for his next birthday.

Nefret was making tea when I returned. 'Herr Morgenstern went to his bedroom to put on a clean shirt in honour of the occasion. I don't know what to think about him, Aunt Amelia. One moment he is docile, the next exuberant.'

'It is curious that he is not exhibiting the symptoms associated with the aftermath of an excess of alcohol. Beverages like peppermint schnapps have a high level of sugar as well, which can result in a pounding headache that can persist all day.' I held up a hand. 'No, dear girl, I do not know this from personal experience. Ramses has tested various potent beverages in the name of advancing knowledge of mental incapacitation, or so he says.'

I realised that my thoughts kept returning to Ramses because I was worried about him and David. I shared my concern with Nefret, who responded with only a shrug. She had always been headstrong and insistent on joining the two on their perilous forays, and often wore them down until they reluctantly acquiesced. I cannot explain the source of her wily persistence, so I must presume it developed during her childhood in the remote oasis. This time she had remained silent. 'Nefret,' I said hesitantly, 'I have noticed that you and Ramses seldom speak to each other. Is there a problem?'

She gave me an indignant look. 'I do not know why you say that, Aunt Amelia. There is no problem. Ramses is rightfully distracted by the idea that those insidious Godwin brothers have vowed to harm you.' She paused, frowning, and then said, 'Unless he blames me, which is not unreasonable. I chose to marry Geoffrey. I shall regret that decision the rest of my life, since it has caused so much pain to all of us.'

'No one blames you, as we have told you innumerable times. None of us was aware of his true nature. Even I, with my superior ability to judge human nature, failed to recognise the depth of his wickedness.'

'That does not absolve me, Aunt Amelia, but let us speak no more of this. Herr Morgenstern has been in his bedroom for a long while. If you will search for clean tea cups, I will tap on his door.'

I had scarcely taken a step when she returned, a perturbed look on her face. 'What's wrong?' I demanded. 'Was he in a state of partial or full nudity? Did he make vulgar remarks?' I picked up my parasol. 'This is completely improper and I shall make that clear to him.'

'He wasn't there.'

'Are you sure?' I blurted out as several of Emerson's choicest profanities flooded my mind. 'Did you look under the bed?'

Nefret ignored my inane questions. 'There is a door at the back of the house to give the occupants easier access to a primitive privy. I suppose he could have availed himself of the opportunity to deal with a natural imperative, but I am not confident. If he has returned to the site, the Professor will be livid.'

'Quite livid, indeed,' I muttered. Nefret and I located an open door at the back of the house, and approached the privy. I halted at a polite distance and called, 'Herr Morgenstern! Are you there?'

We heard no reply. After several more attempts to elicit a response, I clenched my teeth, approached and rapped forcefully on the door. 'Please avert your eyes, Nefret; this may prove to be a scene that neither of us desires to have etched in our memory.'

I flung open the door to expose the interior. I will not describe it, out of regard for my more delicate Readers, but I immediately determined that it was uninhabited. My reaction was ambiguous. Pragmatically, I had hoped to find Herr Morgenstern and order him to return to the house. Then again, I had no desire to find him with his trousers around his ankles.

'Over here, Aunt Amelia,' Nefret said. 'I am not a well-schooled Egyptologist, but I do not think these clothes date from the Eighteenth Dynasty, unless Akhenaten wore trousers, a tweed coat, boots and unterhosen.'

I scanned the bleak terrain. 'That blasted man! Not only has he fled, but he has done so with no thought of propriety. We must stop him before he tries to find a nubile dance partner in the village. Egyptian women are modest, and their male relatives are protective – and easily incensed. Should Herr Morgenstern appear in his current – er – lack of attire, he will be beaten senseless, if not killed. I will go there immediately, and then to the city site. Find Mahmoud and tell him to gather a search party. We must hope that Herr Morgenstern is nearby, happily building a sand castle.'

'Or a sand temple for Nefertiti.'

We parted ways. I took the path through the village, listening for shrieks of outrage, but all seemed peaceful. I continued to the city site. As anticipated, Emerson had taken control and was issuing orders to the crew. Mr Buddle stood at the periphery, scribbling notes on a pad of paper; Mr Dullard and Miss Smith were not to be seen. A vast sense of relief swept over me, but only for a moment. Herr Morgenstern had gone elsewhere, and was either hiding in the remains of crumbling structures or capering in the perilous desert. He would be relatively safe until darkness fell (unless he stepped on a scorpion or viper). After that, he might inadvertently tumble down an embankment and arouse the interest of jackals. It is always depressing to hear them snarling at night and then see vultures circling at dawn.

Nefret, Mahmoud and half a dozen men were waiting outside the dig house. I warned them of Herr Morgenstern's state of undress, divided them into teams, and sent them in varied directions. The visible topography was a semicircle, defined by the cliffs. Unless he was a skilled mountaineer, he had few escape routes available. I winced at the image of a pudgy, wrinkled and most unfortunately naked body, buttocks undulating as he attempted to scale the rocks. Had I been of less stalwart character, I would have recalled the search parties and made myself a cup of tea.

As it was, I took a swallow of water, squared my shoulders and set off in the direction of a village to the south, Hag Kandil.

From Manuscript H

AFTER SEVERAL HOURS, Ramses began to worry about David, who had left for the hotel in which they had previously changed clothes to collect their belongings. It was on the far side of Cairo, near the train station, but David was carrying ample funds to take a taxi there and back. Utilising shortcuts and alleys, one could complete the round trip on foot in little more than an hour.

Ramses would have kept watch out the window had it given him a view of the street, but the modest hotel room offered only a view of the back of a building. He wanted to leave Shepheard's and follow the route that David had most likely taken. It did not seem wise, however, since Sethos was quite capable of assuming a disguise that would allow him access to the hotel and stealing the two forgeries of Nefertiti.

It was a most irksome dilemma, he thought as he paced back and forth in the small confines. Had Sethos found a way to detain David, knowing that Ramses's first impulse would be to go to the shabby hotel? Or, more ominously, had Gunter been waiting outside Shepheard's, accompanied by a pair of brawny, Teutonic thugs?

When he banged his shin on the foot of the bed for the third time, Ramses ceased pacing and opened the door. The corridor was empty. Ali was assigned to the luxurious suites at the front of the building; he had only come to their room as a courtesy – and to blather about the highly esteemed Mrs Amelia Peabody Emerson.

Ramses left the door slightly ajar so that he could hear footsteps should anyone approach. A group of students passed by, speaking boisterous Italian, and went into rooms at the end of the hallway. A few minutes later, a thin young woman came pushing a wheelchair. Its occupant, a frail dowager with only a few tufts of white hair, glared suspiciously at him until he eased the door shut. Not even Sethos, the Master of Disguise, could have assumed the identity of a shiny-faced student or a diminutive lady whose head was lower than the back of the wheelchair.

'Damnation!' Ramses said to himself as he sat down on the bed and gazed at the two forgeries. The apprentices were becoming more skilled, he thought unhappily, and Harun had lost control of them – however many there were at the secret workshop.

The late afternoon light was fading. Soon the muezzins would climb the stairs to the tops of their minarets to chant the adhan and hasten the pious to prayer. It was infuriating to feel as if he were a captive in the hotel room, unable to leave the premises and search for David.

He sprawled across the bed and was contemplating what his father would do (lay siege against the city of Cairo) and what his mother would do (make a list of the obvious suspects) when he heard a creak in the corridor. He leapt to his feet and threw open the door in time to see the flutter of a robe at the stairwell. By the time he reached the top step, he saw no one. Cursing handily, he returned to the room and discovered that his unseen visitor had slipped a folded piece of paper under the door. He snatched it up and read, 'Keller'. It was the German word for 'basement'. It took only a second to deduce that it referred to the grand house from which he and David had retreated that morning.

It could be one of two things: Sethos was informing him of David's whereabouts as a favour, or Gunter was setting a trap. Both scenarios required Ramses to leave the hotel, with or without an eighty-pound burden. Although he did not trust Mr Baehler, he realised that he had little choice but to leave the forgeries in the hotel safe. He placed one in the canvas bag and rewrapped the other in the brown paper, locked the door behind him and went down to the desk.

'Good afternoon,' Baehler said, barely glancing up. 'Going out, sir?'

'Yes, and I need these to be placed in the safe.'

'I fear that is impossible. This is our high season, and many of the ladies insist that their jewellery be secured.'

Ramses restrained himself from pointing out the folly of dim-witted tourists who travelled with diamonds and pearls only to impress one another at dinner. 'That is unacceptable. Please make room for these in the safe.'

Baehler smirked. 'Even if I were to remove the jewellery boxes, I could not make your . . . parcels fit inside the safe. May I suggest you leave them in your room?'

'Indeed you may suggest it, but that is quite impossible as it is not sufficiently secure, as I am sure you will agree, otherwise there would be no need of hotel safes,' Ramses responded caustically. 'These are extremely important and my mother would be most displeased if anything untoward were to happen to them. They belong to her. I should hate to have to tell her that these were left in my room after she expressly asked me to put them in your safe, Mr Baehler.' The veiled threat of Ramses's mother worked.

Beads of sweat appeared on the manager's forehead. 'I am most upset that I cannot accommodate you, but I will do all that I can to protect your – er – Mrs Emerson's parcels. There is a closet in the office that is used for the storage of supplies. It does not have a lock, but no one is allowed in the room except myself and the night clerk.'

Ramses knew that it would soon be dark. David had been gone for six hours, and the only explanation could be that he was tied to a chair in the embassy basement. Ramses refused to acknowledge any alternatives. 'Show me this closet.'

It proved to be a standard closet with shelves to hold stacks of paperwork, along with Mr Baehler's hat, an extra jacket, a pair of dress shoes and a large box of tiger nut cakes. Once the parcels had been stored on the floor of the closet, Ramses instructed the manager to call the maintenance man to bring a hammer and nails. 'If you need anything from the shelves, you best retrieve it now.'

Although his sigh was audible, Baehler had the sense to shake his head. 'No, Mr Emerson. I shall remain vigilant until you return. Please tell Mrs Emerson that her items are safe from the clutches of thieves. I will work the night shift as well.'

Ramses pounded a dozen nails in the closet door, and then exited the hotel through the door in the basement that he and David utilised more often than the main entrance. The alley was populated only by dogs, cats and rats, all amicably foraging through garbage bins. He spotted a clothesline behind a house and deftly scaled the wall. He took a thobe and ghutra, used a clothespeg to leave an ample sum in exchange and donned the garments over his clothes once he was back in the alley. It was tempting to proceed to the German embassy, but imprudent until he possessed further information.

He headed for the Khan el-Khalili, and roamed the claustrophobic alleys and streets until he was certain that he was not being followed, and then went to the miserable hotel by the train station. The clerk eyed him curiously as he walked by the desk and continued upstairs to the room. Their suitcases appeared to be undisturbed, and there was no sign of anything amiss. After rolling the Arab clothes in a tight bundle, he carried the suitcases downstairs and dropped them in the lobby.

'Take care of these until I return,' Ramses said in Arabic to the clerk. 'Has anyone made inquiries about my companion and me?'

'*La, effendi.*'

'No one?'

The clerk shook his head. 'I have been here all day.'

Ramses went out to the street and glowered at the passing pedestrians with such fury that several of them abruptly turned around and fled. He had no reason to believe the clerk (or to believe the suitcases would ever be seen again), but he knew that David's abduction had taken place en route from Shepheard's – and in broad daylight. Regrettably, Ramses encountered nothing suggesting a disruption.

Baehler waved as Ramses came into the lobby. 'All is well, Mr Emerson. A white-haired gentleman requested that you join him in the bar. He did not offer his name.'

Ramses had no doubt as to the gentleman's identity, if anyone could consider him to be a gentleman. Ramses did not. He went into the bar and sat down across from a man who could easily pass as an Oxford don well past his prime. His complexion was sickly pale and dotted with liver spots and warts; his thick moustache and beard dominated his features.

'Whisky and soda,' Ramses said to the waiter.

'I understand that your friend David is in distress,' Sethos began mildly.

'One might think so. Did you slide the paper under the door, or did Gunter?'

'Gunter seems to believe that you are now in possession of the original Nefertiti bust. Are you?'

'I am more concerned about my friend. Was the message from you?'

'You do so remind me of your dear mother. I can't remember when she last answered a question, but I will answer yours. Yes, I was outside the hotel when David emerged and was surrounded by several men, one of whom was wielding a hypodermic needle. He succumbed to the injection and was hustled into a private car with a special licence plate for foreign dignitaries. Although he has many enemies here and in the Middle East, I think we can presume the car came from the German embassy.'

'And therefore he is in the basement?' Ramses asked, scowling.

'A logical conclusion. Where else would you keep a hostage? In a spacious guestroom?' Sethos beckoned a waiter and ordered another round of drinks. Once they arrived, he said, 'I do not believe you will succeed in rescuing David without assistance. By now Gunter has assigned guards inside the embassy and on the grounds, all warned to watch for you. I believe our best opportunity is to create a diversion of such magnitude that the guards are distracted long enough for you to get down to the basement and fetch your friend. It will, I admit, take more than the two of us.'

Ramses leaned back and thought for several minutes. 'As loath as I am to accept your cooperation, I feel I must. What do you suggest?'

'A heart attack.'

WHEN I REACHED Hag Kandil, my worst fear was met. The fellahin were gathered near the community well, their voices shrill as they scolded a youth on his knees in the sand. He was without clothing. I had a very good idea about what had happened, but I nodded politely at an elder and inquired as best I could in Arabic. The response was difficult to understand, although I deduced that a camel was the source of the displeasure. I turned my attention to the boy, who was clearly distraught by my presence and humiliated into shuddering sobs.

'Which way?' I asked him, gesturing in different directions.

He was unable to meet my gaze, but lifted his arm and pointed towards the Eastern Desert. I thanked him and, my own eyes averted to spare him any further embarrassment, said, 'I need a camel.'

After a lengthy debate among themselves, the eldest of the elders named a sum. I shook my head and offered a lesser sum (to accept the initial price would be an insult to both of us, since haggling is a requisite custom in Egypt). It took us only a few minutes to arrive at an acceptable compromise. Shortly thereafter, I was mounted on a camel and plodding along a route towards a schism in the formidable mountains. Herr Morgenstern could be no more than an hour ahead of me, blessedly covered with the boy's white robe and ghutra, and plodding at the same rate on a stolen camel.

I arrived at the crest and paused to take in the vast expanse of the sandy highland. The dunes rolled endlessly, aglitter with sunlight. Jagged mountains and deep wadis made for few opportunities to transverse the terrain to the Red Sea. There were no oases to offer comfort to travellers. The only inhabitants were nomadic Bedouin tribes that had learned over the centuries how to locate water for their herds of sheep, goats and camels. I wished I knew how to locate Herr Morgenstern with the same acumen.

I nudged the camel with my boots to encourage him to move more quickly, but he ignored me with an indifferent snort. We ambled along for quite some time until I saw a group of tents and human activity. My camel, for reasons known only to himself, began to trot. My pith helmet flew off my head. I clung to the saddle as I was jolted most unpleasantly (and painfully), and was relieved when we reached the Bedouin camp. Based on the number of tents, I inferred that the tribe was composed of thirty or forty men and their multiple wives and children. A large number of them had congregated to stare at me. I was not apprehensive; Emerson and I were acquainted with several sheikhs, and Ramses (at his own insistence) had spent a long while living among a particular tribe in order to learn their survival skills. I had worried that he had also learned some manly skills, but it was a topic that both of us had avoided.

'*As-salaamu-alaykum!*' I called in a friendly fashion.

'*Wa 'alaykum-salam wa rehmat-allah wa barakat ahu!*' responded several of the men. The women, of course, said nothing, but their kohl-ringed eyes were rounded with astonishment. It was likely that I was the first fair-skinned person they had ever seen, as well as being an unescorted woman – and astride a camel in my divided skirt.

'Sitt Hakim,' a young man said with a gasp. The other men gathered around him and pelted him with questions. I was unable to understand their Bedouin dialect, but their gestures and glances at me suggested my reputation was not unknown to even the most remote tribes. A woman in a red robe and scarf approached cautiously and took the camel's reins. The beast thudded to his knees, propelling me forward, and then dropped its haunches, propelling me backward. I had learned long ago to grab the saddle and hope for the best.

An octogenarian with a white beard that hung to his waist beckoned to me. 'Sitt Hakim?' he said, his voice imbued with awe.

'*Aywa,*' I murmured modestly to the sheikh, then turned to smile at the giggling women and children. Had Emerson appeared in my stead, the women would have been flattening tents and gathering up cookware. The men would have been too petrified to meet his steely glare. 'I am looking for a traveller, a grey-haired German. Have you seen him?' I said this in Arabic, but their perplexed frowns intimated that they did not understand me. My Arabic is passable, so I could only assume the tribe had its unique dialect and little contact with the rest of the world.

'May I be of help to you?' said a youth with a nascent wisp of a beard. 'I speak English.'

'I am delighted by your kind offer. Where did you learn English?'

'It is a very sad story, Sitt Hakim. My name is Omar Hassan el-Tayeb, if it pleases you. I was seven years old and was tending to our flock of sheep when a ewe slipped down the side of a wadi and I went after her. I encountered a band of Turks, who beat me and took me captive. When we reached Cairo, they sold me to a British family to work as a houseboy. The master was a kind man and allowed me to accompany his children to their classroom to be tutored. I learned many things, but all I dreamed about was reuniting with my tribe and family. After eight years, I slipped out and searched the desert until I found them.'

I blinked until I could trust myself to maintain my composure. 'A very sad story, I agree. I am appalled that a British family would have anything to do with slavery. You must tell me their name.'

'I cannot do that. They were good to me. I met other boys in my situation who slept on blankets in the basement, worked sixteen hours a day and lived on scraps from the kitchen.'

'Then I should have the opportunity to praise them for their generosity.'

He gave me a wry smile. 'I think not, Sitt Hakim. You said that you are searching for a German man?' When I nodded, he continued. 'He brought himself here perhaps an hour ago, barely managing to stay atop the camel. He was singing loudly in a language I do not know. It could have been German – or gibberish. Once he regained his balance on the sand, he threw his arms around Sheikh Nasir el-Din and kissed him on the lips.' Omar shuddered at the memory. 'He then lunged at the nearest woman, who is one of the sheikh's granddaughters. His throat would have been slit had he not been burning with fever. My own mother took him to our tent and has been bathing his face with water, but he is still delirious. We are not sure what to do with him.'

'Please tell Sheikh Nasir el-Din that Professor Emerson and I are gratified by his benevolence. This German man is an archaeologist and a friend. His recent behaviour is contemptible, but we believe that he is ill. If the Sheikh has no objections' – I smiled warmly at the old man, who was scowling at us – 'I will take Herr Morgenstern back to Amarna so that he can receive medical attention.'

Omar shrugged. 'I will tell him what you have told me, but do not be surprised if he wishes to think about this. His reputation has been blackened by this German man's disrespect.'

'Remind him that Professor Emerson has ever been a friend to his people, as have I. We deeply respect his need for dignity, and understand his outrage, but also know that he is a merciful man who would not punish someone who is ill for deeds beyond that person's will.'

'I will do my best,' he replied morosely.

'I am quite sure your best will be adequate. In the meantime, I would like to see Herr Morgenstern to assess his physical condition. It is a long ride back to Amarna and the sun is harsh.'

Omar nodded. 'Of course, Sitt Hakim. *Inshallah*, this can all be over soon and without ill feelings.'

The tents were in rows, decorated with colourful wall panels and rugs woven with camel hair. At least two dozen children followed us, whispering and snickering. A goodly number of women were behind them, doing much the same thing. I felt as though I was leading a parade to Buckingham Palace to call upon King George V, albeit without the pomp associated with proper protocol.

'This is my mother's tent,' Omar said with a gesture. 'I shall return to speak to Sheikh Nasir. I hope you will accept food and water, and rest until the sun has moved on and is less punishing. It would not be wise to leave before then. The desert is cruel. There are no oases in which to take shelter, which is why there are no trade routes to the Suez – only the bones of those who overestimated their shrewdness and expertise.'

'I would like to think that I have never done so,' I said primly. An image of Emerson appeared in my mind. He was laughing uproariously and slapping his thighs. I had a premonition that he would not be laughing when he learned about my solo trek to the Bedouin camp. He would be more inclined to scold me at length for breaking my word and behaving recklessly, as well as overestimating my shrewdness and expertise. 'Please return here after you have spoken to the sheikh.'

Omar's mother hovered in the doorway. I smiled warmly as I introduced myself and then inquired about her name. She spoke Arabic, and shyly admitted that her name was Ikram, which I recognised as an Arabic derivative for hospitality and generosity.

'May I see the German man?' I said in Arabic, careful to enunciate and speak slowly. She nodded and led me behind a woven cloth. Herr Morgenstern was sprawled across a rug, snoring like an asthmatic bull. A bowl of water and a small cloth were nearby, but prudently out of his reach. His face was disturbingly red and dry. I recognised the symptoms of heatstroke, a serious condition that required immediate medical attention. Ikram pointed at the bowl of water and shrugged; I had no difficulty understanding her.

I was frowning at the patient when I realised the light had taken on a peculiar intensity. The patterns in the panels began to throb in a kaleidoscopic swirl. I felt Ikram's hand on my arm as I lost consciousness.

TWELVE

DAMP ANIMAL SLITHERED across my face. I attempted to
knock it off, but my arms were pinned down firmly and voices
admonished me. Panic overwhelmed me with the ferocious-
ness of a sandstorm, sucking away my breath and causing my heart
to thump erratically. I jerked my arms free, rolled onto my side, and
shouted, 'Where am I? Who are you?'

I could not understand the babbled replies. I forced my eyes open
and saw patterns of bright colours on the wall and women hovering
around me. A washcloth, rather than a drowned jerboa (a long-eared
desert rodent, as most of my Readers know), was draped across my
forehead. After a lengthy moment to think this over, I sat up. I knew
where I was (the Bedouin camp) and who the women were (Bedouin
wives, widows and maidens), but I could not come up with an adequate explanation for why I was lying on a mat. 'What happened?' I
demanded.

'Too much sun,' Omar answered from a polite distance. 'My
mother begs you to stay on the mat and drink water until you feel
stronger. My sister has a bowl of broth for you. We were all very
worried, Sitt Hakim, even though you have a reputation for fortitude
and bravery.'

'Thank you.' I accepted a cup of water and sipped it until my memory reorganised itself. 'I suppose I must have fainted, which I rarely do.

One must acknowledge the intensity of the desert sun at its pinnacle, but I was frantic to find Herr Morgenstern before he became hopelessly lost. Is he doing better?' My question was perfunctory, since I knew he was in grave danger from the heatstroke. I rather wished Nefret was on hand to offer medical advice, but I would have been furious had she followed me on my foolish trek into the desert.

Omar winced. 'I am sorry that I cannot tell you that his condition has improved. He is in and out of craziness, at times allowing my mother to bathe his face in water, and then trying to shove her aside and stagger to his feet. Sheikh Nasir el-Din has not yet decided what to do with him.'

I drank another cup of water and then held out my hands to allow the women to help me stand. After a bit of wobbling, I sat down on a stool. A pretty young woman with the round eyes of a doe placed a bowl in my hands and then backed away as if she had made an offering to one of the myriad gods and goddesses of antiquity. '*Shukran*,' I said warmly and forced myself to take a small swallow. I was not at all in the mood for a hot beverage, but I had no expectation of a whisky and soda – especially one served to me by my beloved Emerson. Were he present, he would fling Herr Morgenstern over his shoulder, summon clouds to cover the sun and staunchly trudge back to Amarna in short order. Regrettably, I lacked the strength to do so – but I did have two camels.

I took a second swallow of the broth to be polite, put aside the bowl and went behind the wall panel to evaluate Herr Morgenstern's status. He was supine on a mat and disturbingly silent. A woman knelt next to him, moistening his lips with a cloth. He did not respond when I nudged him with my foot, forcing me to bend over and ascertain that he had a thready pulse. 'Herr Morgenstern! You must open your eyes now! I have come to take you back to Amarna for medical help.' I did not threaten to stuff a jerboa in his mouth, although I must admit the idea crossed my mind. Had he behaved like a proper archaeologist from the beginning, none of the subsequent calamities would have taken place. He would have uncovered the bust of Nefertiti, alerted M. Maspero at the Service des Antiquités and basked in the publicity that he rightfully deserved. I nudged him once again with my foot, perhaps with more vigour than necessary. 'Open your eyes, you sorry excuse for an Egyptologist!'

He emitted a soft groan.

Sighing, I brushed sandy residue off my clothing, patted my hair, retrieved my parasol and said to Omar, 'I would like to speak to the sheikh. Please escort me to him.'

'As you wish, Sitt Hakim,' he said without enthusiasm.

There were few people visible as we walked along the rows of tents. Despite my years (well, decades) of experience excavating in the deserts, I grimaced as the sun bore down on me. I have always insisted that work cease during the worst of the heat in adherence to the admonishment that only mad dogs and Englishmen go out in the midday sun. Emerson was known to object, claiming that I was as overprotective as a mother hen, but he rarely attempted to counteract my order. The workmen from other sites expected to work from dawn to dusk with only nominal breaks for water and food to earn a pittance for their backbreaking labour. We have always treated our workmen with respect and paid them well enough to maintain their loyalty. This is not meant to imply that they were not unsettled by Emerson's periodic outbursts of aggravation and ensuing streams of profanities. Most people were.

Sheikh Nasir el-Din was seated on a rug in a large tent, puffing on a hookah and watching babies drool and toddlers careen about the room. When he saw me, his lips twitched but he did not speak.

'Shukran,' I said as I sat down near him, uninvited but resolved to gain his permission to take Herr Morgenstern back to Amarna. I glanced at Omar. 'Please tell the sheikh that I am very grateful for his hospitality. I am sure that Professor Emerson will think kindly of you for providing me with water and shade.' I waited until Omar had translated my words, and then continued. 'Herr Morgenstern behaved very badly, very badly indeed, but he did not know what he was doing and would never have done this dreadful thing had he been in his right mind. I am sure that the sheikh is familiar with the idiosyncrasies of those suffering from the formidable heat, and has shown them compassion. I hope he will do so in this instance.'

He sombrely listened to Omar's recitation, and then muttered something. I did not wait for Omar to interpret it, and moved on to my next ploy. During the walk, I had taken a mental inventory of my tool belt. I retrieved my electric torch from one of my pockets. 'Perhaps this gift may soften the sheikh's justified indignation.' I switched it on and let its beam flutter around the ceiling of the tent, and then handed it to him. 'It is a useful tool.'

After half an hour of haggling, he was the proud possessor of the torch, a collapsible cup, a small pair of scissors and a notepad (should he wish to make a little list). I had his consent to take Herr Morgenstern out of his sight – for ever.

Omar was grinning as we walked back to his mother's tent. 'Nicely done, Sitt Hakim. Sheikh Nasir el-Din can be obstinate, especially when he has been treated disrespectfully.'

'I cannot fault him for that. I have spent many seasons in the Middle East and am aware of the customs and traditions of the Arab people. The British are equally reserved in matters of familiarity. One does not wink at the king or offer one's hand to the queen. Queen Victoria, in particular, was not amused by informality.' I opened my parasol as I felt the sunshine on my neck. 'You and I, Omar, must figure out how to transport Herr Morgenstern to Amarna as quickly as possible so that he can receive proper treatment. Now that I no longer have an electric torch or a notebook with which to barter, may I offer you a camel?'

I would have preferred to wait until the sun had begun to retreat, but I knew very well that my absence had been noted not only by Nefret, but also by Emerson, Selim, Daoud and no doubt Fatima. I did not anticipate what might be categorised as a warm welcome back, particularly from my beloved husband, who can be irritable (and irritating) when he believes I have behaved recklessly.

Half an hour later Omar and I left the Bedouin camp. Herr Morgenstern, loosely wrapped in a sodden robe and kaffiyeh, was draped over the camel, and my parasol was open and secured to the saddle to provide shade. I had covered my head and neck as best I could with wet scarves. Omar, on foot, held the reins of both camels, utilising verbal cues, untranslatable invectives and a switch (most likely made of camel hair) to encourage them to move at a brisk walk. My head ached too severely to attempt congenial conversation. I sipped water and clung to the saddle. Less than a mile from the camp, Omar found my pith helmet and returned it to me with a cheery smile that I was unable to reciprocate. I did insist that we stop every now and then to sprinkle Herr Morgenstern's inert body with water that Sheikh Nasir el-Din had generously provided us.

The sun was in my face as we approached Hag Kandil. The residents were moving about, conducting business and behaving in an ordinary fashion – with one exception. As in most villages, the well serves as a communal centre for the exchange of gossip, arbitration by the elders and negotiations regarding the purchase of wives and livestock. One expects to see a modicum of activity at any given moment. A lone figure stood next to the well, arms crossed.

'Oh dear,' I murmured. 'I do believe Emerson has ascertained that I was here this morning, and has learned of my Christian endeavour to rescue Herr Morgenstern. I suspect he is not pleased.'

Omar gulped. 'This is not the way I had hoped to encounter the Father of Curses. Have you any suggestions, Sitt Hakim?'

Had he been capable of flapping his wings and soaring away, I would have suggested it. 'Help me off the camel, and then mount it and ride back to your camp. Do not look over your shoulder. Emerson's eyesight is remarkably acute, but he may not be able to make out your features at this distance.'

'I am reluctant to desert you, my lady. Are you confident that you are able to walk this final distance?'

'Help me off the camel,' I repeated grimly. 'If I cannot walk, I will crawl. You had best stop bleating and follow my directive before my husband takes it upon himself to race towards us in a maelstrom of fire and brimstone.'

Moments later, Omar was astride the camel and galloping in an easterly direction. I paused to readjust the scarves around my neck, straighten my pith helmet and prepare my defence. Rather than come to my aid, Emerson did not so much as blink as I led the camel to the well. Perhaps I imagined the faint whiff of brimstone emanating from his ears.

'Thank God you're here!' I exclaimed. 'Herr Morgenstern is in dire need of medical assistance. When he fled into the desert, he was stricken by heatstroke. I do hope Nefret will be able to save him before he succumbs.' It seemed like a reasonable beginning.

'And you followed him,' Emerson said flatly.

'I could not allow him to perish. Despite your steely demeanour, you are a man of great compassion, as you have told me often. You would not have dallied here, waiting for others to join your mission of mercy; you would have done precisely what I did.' He opened his mouth, but I continued before I could be treated to an interminable lecture. 'We really must take Herr Morgenstern to the dahabeeyah to continue to hydrate him in an effort to lower his body temperature.'

'Were you not concerned about the as-yet-unidentified assassins determined to kill you?'

To be quite honest, I had forgotten about them. 'Of course I was, and I took precautions. However, I could not allow timidity to override my Christian duty to a fellow human being who is now hovering on the brink of death.'

Emerson seemed to recognise the futility of further discussion (at that moment, anyway) that focused on my irresponsible behaviour and disregard of his words of warning. 'Are you quite certain this is the German fellow and not a newly wrapped mummy? The villagers are disconcerted.'

I noted that we had drawn a crowd of busybodies, children and men with beards. 'If there are tomb robbers among them, the only mummy they might have seen would be brown, desiccated and liable to crumble if disturbed. How do you suggest we best transport Herr Morgenstern?'

'You seem to have devised a reasonably efficient method, Peabody,' Emerson said with a very slight undertone of admiration. He shouted at one of the villagers, who dashed away and quickly returned holding the bridle of a sturdy black steed. Once my husband had deposited me on the saddle, he took the reins of the camel and swung himself behind me. Our small and peculiar processional headed for Amarna.

I felt his breath on my neck as he said, 'When I deduced where you had gone, I nearly went mad from worry. I was waiting for my horse to be watered before coming to find you, even if I had to scour every inch of this bloody awful desert from here to the Suez Canal. I am willing to sacrifice my life for you, Peabody, but less eager to sacrifice my sanity. Is there any hope that you are capable of paying the slightest bit of attention to me when I beg you to resist these ridiculous impulses and protect yourself?'

'There is always hope, Emerson.'

WE HAD A reception party awaiting us when we arrived at the dock, although no one was cheering. Selim's arms were akimbo as he glowered at me. The workmen dared not do more than grumble (Emerson does have that effect on them). Daoud loomed behind them, his jaw clamped.

'I'm relieved to see my search parties have returned safely,' I said, resolved not to allow myself to be intimidated further. 'This body draped over the camel is Herr Morgenstern, who was incapacitated by heatstroke. We must convey him to the boat and do what we can to help him recover.'

Emerson set me down on the ground as Selim and the crew pulled Herr Morgenstern off the camel. They did not do so gently, I regret to say, but I could hardly reproach them – nor could Emerson. 'We shall stop work for the day,' he announced, 'and after I have seen to our undesirable guest, I will return to reward you for helping search for him. There will be additional baksheesh for whoever volunteers to return the camel to its rightful owner in Hag Kandil.'

I could feel the aura of disapproval begin to dissipate, or so I thought until Nefret appeared from behind Daoud. Her scowl was fierce, her eyes flickering like those of an incensed cobra.

'Aunt Amelia! What is wrong with you? How could you take this – this inexplicably bizarre risk?' she began in a strident voice that ricocheted off the cliffs and might have sent crocodiles slithering into the water. I permitted her to scold me (which she did in no uncertain terms, replete with some of Emerson's choicest profanities regarding the cause of my adventures) until she paused to catch her breath.

'Yes, dear girl, you are absolutely right, but we cannot remain here while Herr Morgenstern battles for his life. You may resume your meticulously detailed analysis of my rash foray later this afternoon. Have you ever treated a patient for heatstroke?'

'No, but I have read about it.' She bent down and uncovered Herr Morgenstern's florid face. 'He is not sweating – a bad sign. The only reason he has survived thus far is that his skin has been kept moistened. We must get him on board and in the tin bathtub immediately.' She began to issue orders with such authority that no one hesitated. As her patient was transported along the plank, she looked back at me with a grimace of frustration. Luckily, I have had extensive practice calming tousled emotions. It is an essential skill in dealing with my family members.

After a spirited protest, Fatima allowed Daoud to place the tin bathtub in the cabin utilised by Ramses and David. Once it was filled with tepid water, Nefret and I unwrapped Herr Morgenstern and supervised as he was lowered into the bathtub by the crew members. I dunked the kaffiyeh and draped it over his face, then abruptly sat down on the edge of the bed as my knees folded.

'Peabody!' exclaimed Emerson, who had been pacing in the background. 'Are you ill?'

Nefret spun around. 'Aunt Amelia, are you feeling faint? Shall we assist you to your cabin so you can rest?'

I forced myself to sit upright. 'I am not in need of rest at this moment. I am in need of a whisky and soda on the top deck, where the breeze will be restorative. Emerson, your arm, please.'

'But I have prepared tea,' Fatima objected. She may have intended to elaborate, but caught Emerson's glare and scurried to relative safety near the door. 'I will send up a platter of sandwiches and scones.'

Nefret appraised me. 'Before you go up to the deck, you must change into a robe that allows better ventilation.' She held out her hand. 'Come along, Aunt Amelia.' It was not an invitation.

I took her proffered hand and squeezed it. We went into the cabin, and I meekly allowed her to help me out of my dusty and odiferous clothes. I would prefer to claim that I had perspired delicately during the journey to and from the Bedouin village, but I could not deny the wet patches that afflicted various areas of my person. Furthermore, I had been in close proximity to a camel for several hours. There is a reason why Eau de Camel is not sold in the finest shops in London.

After I had utilised soap, water and a towel, Nefret helped me put on my dressing gown and slippers. I emerged from the cabin and almost bumped into Emerson, who was lurking outside the door. He offered me his muscular arm. I accepted his assistance as we went up the steps to the deck, and I allowed him to settle me into a chair as if I were a frail dowager. Fatima had provided an abundance of tea sandwiches, as well as slices of cake, fresh scones and a pot of strawberry jam.

'Your whisky and soda, Peabody,' he said as he set a drink on the small table. 'I have made amends with the crew and sent the camel back to its owner. I will wait until you have availed yourself of adequate nourishment before we continue our previous conversation.'

'Conversation? That is not the word I would use to describe your irrational diatribe, Emerson. Do try the smoked salmon sandwiches with cream cheese. They are quite tasty.' I took a swallow of my drink and closed my eyes, wishing the whisky could soften my memory of the recent events.

'I lost my appetite hours ago when I deduced where you had gone.' He stuffed three or four of the delicate little sandwiches in his mouth and masticated grimly, as if he were enduring a punishment. 'I will restrain myself from further irrational diatribes, but we must come to an agreement. You are driving your family crazy with your disregard for your personal safety. I would like nothing better than to order Daoud to stay within a foot of you from the moment you finish breakfast until we have retired to the marital chamber for the night. I cannot lose you, Peabody. You are my life, my raison d'être, despite the fact that you are more headstrong than an elephant and more fearless than a jackal.'

'I do seem to have that reputation,' I acknowledged as I took a bite of sesame seed cake. 'I should not have gone after Herr Morgenstern, but I felt I had no choice. Yes, it was my Christian duty – and also my moral imperative to rescue a fellow human being who was mentally incapacitated. We cannot cast aside those who are "the least of these, our brethren".'

'Does that include the Godwin brothers?'

I thought this over. 'In the sense that they are mentally incapacitated by their deranged desire for revenge, I suppose so. I would never wish such gruesome deaths on anyone, including my most evil enemies. Even worse are the cold-blooded executions orchestrated by the judicial system. The Ten Commandments include the dictate "Thou shalt not kill." There are no exceptions in a footnote at the bottom of the page'.

Emerson snorted. 'Then what should we do with them? Send them to a seaside resort for rehabilitation? Force them to take up hobbies that do not include mayhem and murder? We must do what is in the best interest of society.'

'A civilised society does not condone violence. We no longer throw virgins into volcanoes or sacrifice children on a bloodstained altar. We do not haul those who displease us to a scaffold to be beheaded by a hooded executioner.'

Nefret came up the steps in time to hear my last few words. 'Goodness, I hope we are not discussing Herr Morgenstern's future.'

'Then he will survive?' I asked.

'I cannot say for certain, but his body temperature has fallen a few degrees.' She sank into a chair and nodded at Emerson as he handed her a drink. 'What a bloody awful day this has been for all of us. A bloody awful week, for that matter. I think we should pack up and set sail for Cairo or Luxor – I do not care whether we go north or south.'

'We cannot leave Amarna under these circumstances,' Emerson replied with surprising mildness. Had I made the same suggestion, I would have been treated to a tedious sermon about the site, its history, its significance, its magnificence, its vulnerability, its venerability and every single discovery since the late eighteenth century, all of which were more than familiar to me. The thought made my eyelids heavy.

'Yes, I realise that,' said Nefret as she reached for a sandwich, 'but what are we to do about Aunt Amelia?'

I cleared my throat in a genteel fashion. 'Excuse me, but have you forgotten that I am present? I am quite sure that if I pinch myself, I will feel a distinct sensation of pain – as would you, Emerson, were I to pinch you. I may be exhausted, but I am far from feebleminded. If the two of you care to discuss me as if I were a forged copy of Nefertiti, I will retreat to the lounge and begin a new list of suspects. I no longer have my notebook, but I do have stationery.'

Nefret opened her mouth, then closed it.

Tact is not prominent among Emerson's virtues. 'Really, Peabody! All of us are dedicated to protecting you until those abominable Godwin brothers are no longer a threat. I am equally opposed to state-sanctioned executions, but I would be satisfied if they were incarcerated for the rest of their sorry lives. In the meantime, we must come to an agreement.'

I raised my hand to display its palm. 'I promise not to leap astride a camel and gallop into the desert without informing you in advance. I will permit Daoud to remain near me whenever I am ashore. Now let us move on to other issues. Did we receive a response from Chief Russell concerning the murder of von Raubritter?'

Emerson was not pleased by my artful endeavour to change the subject, but after a rumble of displeasure he said, 'We received a telegram this morning. Von Raubritter entered Egypt on a tourist visa several weeks ago, about the time Herr Morgenstern went to Cairo with the bust of Nefertiti. Russell sent one of his men to the Deutsche Orient-Gesellschaft and was informed they had no knowledge of von Raubritter, nor did the German embassy. Authorities in Darmstadt confirmed that he was a resident and had never been arrested or involved in an official police investigation. He lived alone in an apartment, and according to his landlord, paid his rent promptly.'

Nefret feigned a yawn. 'Did the police question his pets?'

'What is curious,' I mused, 'is his appearance here. Could he have come to visit Herr Morgenstern and been surprised by his friend's inexplicable absence? It may be that he was the sort who cannot tolerate idleness. He might have taken it upon himself to put the crew back to work.'

'Despite the presence of Biddle?' commented Emerson.

'Buddle,' I said. 'We know that Mr Buddle has no qualifications in the field of Egyptology. He claims to be here to represent the proprietary interests of Ridgemont but has proffered no proof. We must interview him as soon as possible.'

Emerson nodded. 'We know that he has rented chambers in a private house north of Minya. Rather than spend the evening knocking on doors, I think it might be less burdensome to interview him tomorrow morning at the city site.'

'He does tend to skulk in the shade and scribble notes,' Nefret said.

'Octavius Buddle is a cocky little man with an elevated sense of self-importance,' I said.

'His presence is insignificant but potentially bothersome if he comes to harm, though he has shown no alarm about Herr Morgenstern's noticeably peculiar behaviour,' Emerson pointed out, anger beginning to creep into his voice. 'If he is so dedicated to protecting and maintaining the integrity of the site, he is the one who should have demanded that Maspero find an adequate substitute to continue the dig.' His expression left no doubt as to identity of the most obvious candidate.

'Which is why M. Maspero invited you to his office as soon as we arrived in Cairo, if you recall.'

Nefret put down a half-eaten sandwich. 'Are you forgetting about the slip of paper you came across in Judas's pocket after he expired in your bath chamber? What on earth can be the link between the Godwin brothers and Mr Buddle? If they intend to assassinate him, they are doing a very poor job of it.'

'Buddle could not defend himself against a dust devil,' said Emerson.

'Or a jerboa,' I added. 'If Mr Buddle is not an intended victim, I am at a loss to come up with an alternative theory as to his involvement. I cannot envision him socialising with a lower-class family of murderous thugs.'

'A jerboa?'

THIRTEEN

From Manuscript H

AS LOATHSOME AS the concept was, Ramses forced himself to acknowledge that his best expectation of rescuing David lay in an alliance with Sethos. They remained in the hotel lounge for a long while, mulling over options until they finalised their scheme.

'I am still worried that Gunter will recognise me,' Ramses said.

Sethos scoffed. 'You have your soubriquet, my dear boy, but do not forget that one of mine is Master of Disguises. You need to go to the weaver's shop and instruct him how to make the item we discussed. I must organise some of my less scrupulous associates, ascertain the location of the hospital nearest the German embassy and purchase a few items. I suggest we meet in your room in an hour.'

'How do I know that you will not break into my room as soon as I leave the hotel?'

'It crossed my mind,' Sethos said blandly, 'but I am quite sure you have found a place to stash the two forgeries of Nefertiti's bust.'

Ramses raised an eyebrow. 'What makes you think they are both forgeries?'

'Had you stumbled across the original, you and David would be on the train to Minya.'

'Unless Gunter kidnapped him before we could leave. He would not have done that unless he believes that the bust we – er – relocated from his office is the original. He denied any knowledge of Morgenstern's whereabouts in Cairo, but he was lying.'

'Interesting,' murmured Sethos. 'Run along to the shop I recommended and utilise my name should Shamal quibble. I will see you in an hour.'

Ramses was not pleased to be treated like an errand boy, but he walked out of the hotel and hailed a cab to take him to the edge of the Khan el-Khalili. He instinctively took precautions from being followed as he made his way through alleys and narrow streets to arrive at the weaver's shop. Shamal, a particularly dark-skinned elderly man, began to squawk when Ramses explained the required expediency of the mission.

'It cannot be done today! Come back tomorrow or the next day. Macramé requires nimble fingers and artful configurations, which take time. I may be the best in Egypt, but what you desire is not easy. I must think on it.'

'You may know me better as the Brother of Demons,' Ramses said in an ominous voice, damned if he would utilise Sethos's name to intimidate the weaver. 'I do not care to listen to you whine. We will go to the back room and I will draw a sketch for you.' He narrowed his eyes. 'Now, Shamal.'

Shamal's fingers proved to be nimble enough to translate the crude drawing into jute, twine and leather. Ramses paid him generously, accepted the parcel and took a cab back to Shepheard's Hotel. He was not surprised to find Sethos seated in his room.

'Find anything of interest?' Ramses asked with mock curiosity.

'I did not bother to search under the bed or in the closet,' Sethos said with a shrug. 'I have better things to do – and so do you. Change into these clothes and then sit down so I can alter your appearance.'

His jaw clenched, Ramses complied.

WHEN THEY BECKONED a carriage at the kerb outside the hotel, the driver merely glanced at the white-haired old man and his exceedingly plump assistant with a crooked nose, red ears resembling rose petals, a complexion riddled with acne and neglected teeth. Sethos's suit and tie were reminiscent of the Victorian era; Ramses's attire was cheap and ill-fitting.

'To the German embassy,' Ramses simpered to the driver, 'and be quick about it. Well, as quick as you can. Don't run over anybody. Moderation, dear chap, and self-discipline. These are the keys to a harmonious life.'

Sethos snorted. 'Please do what you can to minimalise intercourse with Gunter. He will not recognise you, but he may become so annoyed that he shoots you anyway. If he doesn't, I might.'

'And risk my mother's wrath?'

'She does have a temper, at times more rabid than your father's. I will be careful to shoot you in a nonessential body part.'

'How comforting,' Ramses said drily, 'but all of my body parts are essential to me. I cannot return to Amarna missing so much as my little finger. I am planning to learn to play the kanun, which requires all my digits to pluck the strings in a melodious fashion. Furthermore, my toes will be indispensable when I take up ballet.'

The carriage stopped at the kerb in front of the embassy, and the guard allowed them to continue to the porch. Ramses steeled himself not to react when the butler opened the door and muttered, '*Guten Abend.*'

'Good evening to you,' Sethos said. 'I am here to see Herr Gunter once again. Tell him it is of the utmost importance. My name, if you have forgotten, is Professor Ambrose Doyle. This is my secretary, Higginsnort.'

The butler gestured for them to enter. He led them to the front room and pointed at the decanters. '*Machen Sie es sich bequem,*' he said in the same dour voice as he left the room.

'If we are to make ourselves comfortable, we should have a drink,' Ramses said. 'What do you prefer?'

'Whisky and soda. Is that not your parents' preference?'

'Hardly any of your business, is it?' Ramses poured a scant amount of whisky into two glasses and topped them with soda. He delivered one to Sethos, and then sat down across from him. 'How many guards did you see in the courtyard?'

'Three concealed in the bushes, and the one at the gate. I presume they are all armed.'

'You overlooked the one on the roof,' Ramses commented as he tasted his drink, 'and there are likely to be more behind the house. What was your story when you came here several days ago? It must have been credible, since you stayed so long.'

'I told Gunter that I was an old acquaintance of the ambassador and enjoyed his hospitality when I was in Berlin on sabbatical. I also mentioned that I was a professor of ancient history at Cambridge and familiar with the Egyptian dynasties. Gunter insisted that I stay for dinner and peppered me with rather naive questions about current archaeological activity – including Amarna. He did not mention Nefertiti, nor did I.' He glanced at the door. 'Kindly remember that you are a pathetic pretext for a secretary – with a Welsh accent.'

Gunter entered the room and bowed. 'Good evening, Professor Doyle. The manservant informs me that you claim to be here on an important mission.' He glanced at Ramses, curled his lip and turned his attention back to Sethos. 'Please enlighten me, sir.'

'I am eager to do so, but I am feeling queasy. I was at an excavation at Giza for the day and may have overestimated my stamina. When you are my age, son, you will learn the necessity of taking precautions against the stultifying heat of the desert.' He fanned himself with his hand. 'Higginsnort, my pills are in a small brown bottle in my briefcase. Find them and be quick about it!'

'At once,' Ramses responded in the voice of a tremulous tenor (with a Welsh accent, of course). 'Do you need a glass of water?'

'No, you ass, I simply want to have them nearby.' Sethos loosened his necktie and collar. 'I am finding this room to be intolerably stuffy,

Herr Gunter. I suggest we relocate to the dining room to enjoy the evening breeze. Higginsnort, help me to my feet.'

Gunter had no choice but to trail after them as Sethos staggered down the hall and into the dining room. 'I am most concerned about your well-being, Professor. The ambassador has a private physician on call day and night. Shall I send for him?'

'No, but I appreciate your offer. I am confident I will feel better once the windows have been opened.' Sethos sank down on a dining room chair and cradled his face in his hands. 'I must relate the gossip from the archaeologists at Giza. It involves a bust of Nefertiti, found at Amarna and in exceptional condition. It is rumoured to be quite beautiful.'

Gunter sat down across from him, visibly salivating. 'Please tell me more, Professor Doyle. I am ignorant in such matters, but I find the field to be of great fascination. Were you told what happened to this bust? Is it under the control of the Deutsche Orient-Gesellschaft or the Service des Antiquités?'

'Not precisely,' Sethos said as he began to tremble. He blotted his forehead with a pristine handkerchief. 'I need to go to the nearest lavatory. Higginsnort, do not sit there like an overly ripe plum. Assist me!'

Ramses helped his ostensible employer stand up and gave Gunter a quizzical look. Gunter led them to a lavatory and murmured solicitously as Sethos went into the small room. Ramses noted the presence of an armed guard leaning against the penultimate door. It was not one of the doors that he and David had investigated the previous day. It seemed logical that it opened on steps leading down to the cellar – or *keller*, if one preferred. The presence of the guard indicated there was something worth guarding, most likely a prisoner. Unless Gunter had a very bad habit of kidnapping people off the streets of Cairo, the obvious victim was David.

'I believe I should send for the physician,' Gunter said as he and Ramses returned to the dining room. 'Professor Doyle is not well. What sort of pills is he taking?'

'Nitroglycerine, for his heart. I am reluctant to tell him that the bottle is empty. If he is not more robust when he returns, I agree that you should send someone to collect the physician. The professor will be furious.'

'Did he tell you any more of the rumours from Giza?'

Ramses shook his head. 'I asked him for particulars, but he refused to elaborate and pointed out that I am here solely to assist him in the writing of his memoirs. We are in Egypt because he desired to refresh his memories of his postgraduate years, when he was present at various excavations and tomb openings. He usually dictates to me immediately after breakfast until tea time. I spend evenings at my typewriter. While he was at Giza, I made use of the opportunity to catch up and review the last few chapters. Professor Doyle has a sharp recollection of minutiae. We are nearly finished with Egypt and the Sudan. We are preparing to begin on chapter fifty-three, when he opted to spend a year in Siberia investigating the Middle Holocene hunter-gatherers of the Lake Baikal region.'

'Oh,' Gunter said. He did not sound intrigued.

'We are leaving tomorrow on a ship to Istanbul. Once we have traversed the Black Sea, we will travel by train. The Trans-Siberian will be most tiresome, I fear, and without the highly acclaimed luxuries of the Orient Express.' Ramses paused to listen for any sounds emanating from the lavatory. The time for improvisation was rapidly nearing. He and Sethos had anticipated a variety of scenarios based on Gunter's reaction, but Ramses knew quite well that human nature was unpredictable – and potentially volatile. 'Have you been to Siberia, Herr Gunter? I've been told that it is frigid and hostile, populated by peasants. Oddly, it is snowless, but temperatures may go below sixty degrees centigrade. It will be challenging to type with frozen fingers.'

Gunter did not pretend to listen as Ramses prattled on about Siberia. The latter was rapidly running out of Siberian facts when Gunter interrupted him. 'I must ask you to check on Professor Doyle. It has been five minutes since he went to the lavatory.'

'An excellent idea. If you will excuse me, I shall do so immediately.'

Ramses went down the hallway and tapped on the door. 'Professor Doyle, is there anything I can do for you?'

The door banged open. 'Get out of my way, Higginsnort! I am capable of walking without your inadequate attempts to steer me.' Sethos's steps resounded as he moved slowly to the doorway of the dining room. 'Gunter, be a good man and find me a glass of brandy.'

'Sir,' Gunter said, alarmed, 'your face is flushed and your breathing is laboured. I insist on sending for a physician!'

Sethos put his hand on his chest. 'Poppycock! I will not have some unknown man poking at me. Higginsnort, bring me—' He crumpled to the floor like a deflated balloon. As his eyes closed, he let out a piteous moan.

'Oh my God!' Ramses exclaimed as he kneeled next to Sethos. 'Professor Doyle, can you hear me? What should I do?' He glanced up. 'Herr Gunter, you must send for an ambulance! I fear this is a heart attack. He had one in the spring and it nearly killed him. I warned him that travelling was stressful, but he refused to listen to me. How far is the nearest hospital?'

Gunter went to the front door and barked an order at an unseen person. Ramses was relieved to hear the words 'Rettungswagen' and 'Krankenhaus', which strongly suggested that Gunter had fallen for the melodramatic enactment (and failed to see the smudges of red makeup on Sethos's collar). 'The hospital is only blocks away, so the ambulance and its attendants should be here in a matter of minutes. Is there anything we can do in the meanwhile? You said the pill bottle is empty. Could some of the pills have spilled in the bottom of his briefcase?'

'I will search it, but I sorted through it only this morning, looking for some of his notes about an oasis in the Western Desert.' Ramses rose and went across the hall to the parlour, pausing to glance at the guard. He picked up the briefcase, left the room and waited in the hallway until he heard voices from the porch. The butler opened the front door and stepped back as four burly men in hospital garb nearly ran him down with a gurney. They shouted in Arabic, demanding to know the whereabouts of the patient and his condition. The butler cringed as the gurney ran over his foot. Gunter came out of the dining room and attempted to seize control, adding to the vocal frenzy.

It was going quite well, Ramses thought gleefully. Sethos had coached (and paid) his players well to provide an adequate diversion, and they were as committed as the cast of a Shakespearean play. The butler, now furious, screeched when he was shoved into the wall. Gunter raised his voice as he continued to issue orders that were ignored. The ambulance crew raised their voices, too.

Ramses took a deep breath and grabbed the gurney. 'Get this out of the way! Your patient is in that room. You need to examine him before you transport him to the hospital, and this contraption is blocking the doorway.' Grimacing at Gunter, he wheeled the gurney down the hallway and stopped when the guard stepped forward. 'Do not just stand there and watch as if a cricket game is in progress. I fear for Herr Gunter's safety.'

'I must to stay here. I have my orders.'

'But you will not have an employer to pay you if Herr Gunter ends up in the hospital – or worse! I have no idea why you state that you must stay here, but I will do so while you subdue those hospital attendants.'

As soon as the guard headed for the dining room, from which shouts and profanities emanated, Ramses opened the door and went down a short flight of stairs. Despite the limited light, he had no difficulty spotting David bound securely to a chair.

'About time,' David said. 'I've run out of poetry to quote and have been reduced to counting beetles and cockroaches. The beetles outnumber—'

Ramses untied David and yanked him up. 'Are you still under the influence of drugs? If I must, I will drag you up the stairs but it may be quite uncomfortable.'

David took a cautious step. 'I seem to be able to walk under my own power. How are we going to get past Gunter's guards? From what

I heard when they thought I was unconscious, I received the distinct impression that they were in the house and yard waiting for you.'

'I will enlighten you later,' Ramses said as he propelled David up the stairs to the door. He looked at the hallway, which was now vacant, the attendants, the guard and Gunter having taken the fracas into the dining room. 'There is a hammock of sorts just below the flat surface of the gurney. Squirm your way into it and try not to wiggle.'

'Are you insane?'

'Would you prefer to remain in the basement and conduct cockroach races?'

Cursing under his breath, David eventually managed to position himself in the hammock. Ramses took the sheet at the end of the gurney and draped it so that David was not visible, and then wheeled it to the doorway of the dining room. Sethos remained on the floor, his eyes closed. Two of the attendants were berating Gunter, whose face was as red as that of Sethos, while the other two fussed over Sethos and made lewd accusations about each other's parentage. The guard hovered, unsure how to intervene.

'Put the patient on the gurney!' yelled Ramses, struggling to maintain his purported Welsh accent. 'You must get him to the hospital immediately!'

'Yes, you idiots!' added Gunter. 'I will ride with you to make sure that he is given the best medical care available. Pick him up gently.'

Sethos had coached his amateur actors, who began to shout that such things were not allowed and were illegal and medically perilous and contrary to their procedure. They picked up their patient, not as gently as they might have, and carried him to the gurney. 'We go now!' one of them pronounced with a growl.

The four attendants carried the gurney down the porch steps and wheeled it to the open doors of an ambulance. Ramses held his breath as they lifted it, apprehensive that Gunter might catch a glimpse of David. Luckily, the light was inadequate for anyone to see more than a bulky contour. As two of the attendants began to clamber into the back with their patient, a barrage of shots resonated from behind the embassy.

'*Verdamnis!*' shrieked Gunter. 'Go find out what's happening!'

The guards in the shrubbery emerged and raced towards the back-yard, firing randomly and more likely to harm one another than an intruder. Ramses leapt into the back of the ambulance and slammed the doors closed. 'Drive!' he yelled. He clung to the gurney as the ambulance spun in the gravel and then sped through the gates to the street.

Sethos, who had been flung off the gurney, began to laugh loudly. 'Well done, my Welsh lad.'

'Is it possible,' David's voice said, 'to explain what is happening? I must admit I am a trifle curious. I was assaulted outside the hotel and regained consciousness only an hour ago. Had I not heard a German utterance from one of the assailants, I would have no idea where I was or why.'

'You will have to wait,' said Ramses. 'We have arrived at the entrance to the hospital, where a carriage is awaiting us. Get yourself out of that contraption before we are noticed. I will pay our participants for their hearty enthusiasm and willingness to steal an ambulance.'

David grunted as he struggled out of the hammock and fell on top of Sethos. 'I recognise your voice, but who the hell is this?'

Ramses left them to extricate themselves from the tangle of arms, legs and medical devices. After he had paid the men, who were still clad in hospital garb as they dissolved into the darkness, he gestured for the carriage to approach. David was glaring at both of his companions as they climbed inside and sank back against the peeling leather upholstery. Sethos sat with the serenity of a statue of Buddha in front of a temple.

David gasped as he realised the identity of the Master Criminal. 'Ramses, why the devil is he here?'

'The same reason that I am here, which was to rescue you before Gunter decided you were of no further value.' He ran his finger across his throat. 'They would have left your corpse in the desert for scavengers.'

Sethos's moustache twitched. 'I acted purely out of altruism, although if our scheme was exposed, I was not inclined to play the martyr. That's why I permitted Higginsnort here to take a predominant role. He has fancied himself to be a martyr in many other dire situations.'

'Higginsnort?' David said, amused.

'Tidy yourself!' Ramses snapped. 'You are covered in dust and cobwebs, and your hair is poking up. Our family has a reputation to maintain at Shepheard's, you know.'

'Your mother would be so proud of you, Higginsnort.' Sethos laughed so loudly that the carriage driver turned around to stare at him.

⸙

THROUGHOUT THE NIGHT, Nefret and I took turns looking in on Herr Morgenstern. His immersion in the cool water had a beneficial effect, lowering his body temperature and reducing the fierce ruddiness of his complexion. Dawn was approaching when I went into the cabin and found him astir.

'You are improving steadily, Herr Morgenstern,' I said as I handed him a towel. 'Would you prefer to lie on the bed?'

His eyes squinted as he attempted to identify me in the residue of fading moonlight. 'Ach, Frau Emerson, I have once again made a fool of myself, although I do not seem to recollect specific details. I rode on a camel, a most dreadful creature, out into the desert, but I do not know what happened after that.' He sighed plaintively. 'I wish I could explain my behaviour. I am not the sort to abandon my work for a frivolous jaunt.'

Nefret must have heard our conversation. She came into the room, displaying minimal enthusiasm, and said, 'I am glad to see you are recuperating, Herr Morgenstern. Based on your earlier condition, I had only a small flicker of hope that you might survive the night. Let us help you into dry clothes so that you can get proper bed rest. Aunt Amelia, do we need to call the Professor?'

'I do not think it wise to interrupt his sleep.' I said this mildly, but I was imagining Emerson's belligerent reaction. He was not, as my Readers know, amiable when roused, especially when a nemesis was the cause of the disruption. 'Herr Morgenstern, do your best to stand up. Nefret and I will hold your arms while you climb out of the bathtub and make your way to the bed. Ramses's nightshirt will suffice; I will fetch it. I think you are strong enough to change your garments if Nefret and I help you stand up.'

He put his hands on the rim and struggled to rise to his feet. Both Nefret and I grasped his arms, and with much grunting from all of us, we navigated him the few steps to the bed, where I had placed the nightshirt. Nefret and I turned our heads while he peeled off his wet thobe, which clung to his body in a diaphanous skin. 'Please put on the clean nightshirt, Herr Morgenstern, it might be a bit short, but should do.'

'You are so kind, Frau Emerson and Fraulein Forth, and I am so humiliated. I have behaved abominably and should be dispossessed of the firman. As soon as there is adequate daylight, I will cross the river and go to Minya to send a telegram to the Service des Antiquités informing them of my imminent departure.'

Which meant, I realised, the excavation would be halted until M. Maspero found a candidate to assume charge. From what he had said in his office in Cairo, Emerson was not at the top of the list. Every moment that the site was unguarded would be an opportunity for the thieves loitering at the perimeter. I had already recognised Farouk, Asmar, Agha and, of course, Sethos; I had no doubt many of their ruthless colleagues were arriving daily.

'We will discuss this after you have rested,' I said. I beckoned to Nefret and we went into the passageway. 'This is quite a dilemma. Who knows how long it may take for M. Maspero to come up with a suitable replacement? For reasons I do not understand, he has insinuated that he will not turn over the excavation to Emerson, who is by far most suitable for this and any other prestigious position in Egyptology.'

'Then we shall keep Herr Morgenstern here despite his tendency to depart,' she said sensibly. 'We must encourage him to feel as though he is now capable of supervising the site, while the Professor discreetly manages the workmen and protects the more valuable discoveries.'

'Emerson is not the epitome of discretion,' I pointed out.

'You must make him understand that if he loses his temper with Herr Morgenstern, he will find himself twiddling his thumbs until a replacement arrives. Next week, next month, or whenever. He is a reasonable man.'

'He is also an impatient man with no tolerance for incompetency and indolence. You and I need to stay close by him in case Herr Morgenstern pulls another stunt that results in disaster. I wish Ramses and David were here. They could assist in keeping the workmen in line and keeping the rascals away from the site. Whatever can be the cause of their delay in Cairo?'

'Please excuse me, Aunt Amelia. I am in need of a few more hours of sleep before I attempt to come up with an explanation for anything Ramses does.' She went into her cabin and closed the door.

After a moment of contemplation concerning her current attitude towards my son, I decided that I was too agitated for further sleep. I went to the upper deck and gazed at a sky streaked with feathery pink and orange clouds. The cliffs were tinged with a golden diadem. The silence was profound. I wished that Abdullah was beside me, offering comfort if not enlightenment, but he appeared only in my dreams. He came of his own accord; he could not be beckoned at my whim.

A hand touched my shoulder. I spun around, fists readied to defend myself. Emerson caught my hand before I could punch him on the nose. 'Peabody,' he said, 'why are you here by yourself at this unlikely hour?'

'When I went to look in on our patient, I found him much improved.

Nefret and I helped him to bed. She returned to her cabin, and I came up here to admire the sunrise. As you can see, Emerson, it is a spectacular display of God's palette.'

'Fatima will not be serving breakfast for at least another hour.'

'I am not in the mood to partake of sustenance, although a cup of tea might be nice.'

'Then you shall have one, even if I have to make it myself.'

'And risk Fatima's wrath? You are a brave man, my dear husband.'

'Perhaps not that brave,' he murmured as he took my hand.

I WAS ENJOYING a generous serving of fluffy scrambled eggs when Nefret joined us in the dining room. She glanced at Emerson, who was lost in his own thoughts, and said, 'Herr Morgenstern is sleeping soundly. I did not want to disturb him, but I could see from the doorway that his complexion is normal – or as normal as it can be considering the extent of his sunburn. Skin is already flaking on his nose. He is a lucky man to have survived the heatstroke.'

'Lucky that Peabody found him,' Emerson muttered.

'For the second time,' I said as I refilled his coffee cup. 'He simply cannot keep vanishing like this, first in Cairo and then in the Eastern Desert. Had he not serendipitously encountered the Bedouin tribe, he would have lasted no more than another hour. We need to craft a collar and put him on a leash, or tether him to a stake.'

Nefret frowned. 'I think it might be more practical to confine him to the boat until he regains better control of his behaviour. Daoud can guard the plank. He is capable of flicking Herr Morgenstern into the water with one finger, and undoubtedly will take pride in doing so.' She sat down and rubbed her face. 'I studied chemistry and pharmacology during my first term, and I have forgotten much of the material. To some extent, his symptoms could be those of a mental disease called "*la folie circulaire*", or circular insanity, consisting of alternating bouts of mania and melancholia. As I do not have easy access to the books here, I shall send a telegram to my professor in Paris for details.'

'Balderdash.' Emerson held out his cup for more coffee. He considers himself to be the epitome of even-temperedness. Those with the audacity to contradict him are more than aware of his temper, but they hardly consider it to be even. The word 'tempestuous' comes to mind.

'We have seen him in a manic mode,' I said, 'but not in the grasp of melancholia, unless his bleating for "his" Nefertiti qualifies. I do agree that we need to confine him, if only to prevent further troubles. You have had the opportunity to observe him. Is there any discernible method to his madness?'

Nefret paused as Fatima set down a plate of eggs, bread and fruit. 'I don't know, Aunt Amelia. We have no idea what might have taken place prior to his unscheduled trip to Cairo. We know why he went, but something must have taken place after he met with Harun and negotiated a price for one or more forgeries. He could have taken up temporary residence at the Deutsche Orient-Gesellschaft or even the German embassy. Instead, he was living on the streets and scavenging for food. Why would he do such a thing?'

'When he returned here, he seemed to be of sound mind. His memory was riddled with gaps, I admit, but he was able to function for a brief period. Then yesterday something snapped that sent him into an appalling display of brotherly love. Had Emerson not intervened, the workmen might have attacked him. Based on Mr Dullard's account, he had been inebriated the previous night. Could he have had an allergic reaction to the schnapps?'

'Ridiculous,' inserted Emerson. 'He probably learned to drink schnapps on his grandfather's knee.'

I could not repress a chuckle as I envisioned Herr Morgenstern, who weighed in the range of sixteen stone, seated on the lap of his frail, ninety-year-old grandfather. 'Merely a supposition,' I said. 'When I found him on the pavement across from the hotel, I did not smell alcohol on his breath – nor did I yesterday morning. In truth, he was entirely too exuberant for a man with a hangover.'

Nefret started to speak, but stopped when our cabin steward entered the dining room and handed a telegram to Emerson.

Emerson tore it open and scanned it. 'It is from Ramses. He and David are fine, and will return tomorrow.' His fist hit the table, rattling the china. 'It is about time! I need both of them here, not gadding about Cairo like harebrained schoolboys.'

'They were hardly gadding about,' I said resolutely. 'They have been attempting to locate Harun's new workshop, a Herculean labour in the maze of Cairo. Ramses is too cautious to admit success or defeat in a telegram.'

Nefret stood up, her breakfast barely touched. 'I assume we will be departing shortly for the site. I need to instruct Daoud to prevent Herr Morgenstern from leaving the boat. Fatima can look in on him occasionally, and prepare a tray for him when he regains his appetite.' She gave me a concerned look. 'Aunt Amelia, you look tired. You suffered from the heat as well as Herr Morgenstern. Perhaps you should rest and join us later.'

I looked helplessly at Emerson. His face was so tanned that it was difficult to distinguish the blush spreading across his cheeks. Neither of us was able to offer a glib explanation. I exhaled only after Nefret had left the room. 'She is not an innocent young girl,' I said. 'She has been married and experienced intimacy.'

Emerson gazed at me. 'As have we, Peabody. I can only hope she finds herself in a relationship such as ours.'

FOURTEEN

E MERSON AND I walked through the cultivation, hand in hand, cheerfully theorising about what we might unearth in Thutmose's studio. Before his departure for Cairo, Herr Morgenstern had uncovered partial plaster casts of faces and heads, the ivory horse blinkers and pieces of shattered vases. The most valuable item thus far, the bust of Nefertiti, was lost to us at the present time. We agreed that it was unproductive to speculate about what Ramses and David had accomplished in Cairo. The morning train was notoriously unreliable, stopping at every village (and camel crossing), but might appear late in the day. If not, the night train would arrive before dawn and they could enlighten us over breakfast.

At Emerson's request, Selim had taken charge of the excavation. He had assigned some of our crew to continue at the Workmen's Village, and brought others with him. Herr Morgenstern's *reis*, Abdul, pouted in the shade of a rock wall. The fellahin loitered nearby, as well as the usual suspects; if Sethos was among them, he was indistinguishable. It all seemed serenely quotidian. Emerson refrained from giving Selim a vigorous handshake, perhaps because of the previous day's offensive display of camaraderie. Nefret joined them, and the three were soon engrossed in a spirited quarrel concerning the optimal camera angles to delineate the interior of the studio.

Mr Buddle stood nearby, notebook in hand. As I approached him, he glanced up briefly and then resumed recording data, presumably for his patron. I opted to interpret his failure to exhibit overt hostility as an invitation to join him. He might not have seen it in that precise manner.

'Good morning, Mr Buddle,' I said with a smile. 'What do you find worthy of notation?'

'Everything that happens, even if it turns out to lack consequence. Mr Ridgemont requested meticulous documentation of the excavation.'

I allowed my smile to diminish. 'How difficult this has been for you, what with Herr von Raubritter's murder and Herr Morgenstern's inexplicable behaviour. Had you met either one of them prior to your arrival in Amarna?'

'Not that I recall, Mrs Emerson.' He closed the notebook and tucked it in a pocket of his white coat. 'If I may be so bold, I would like to know what you suspect is causing Herr Morgenstern to lose control of his sensibilities. I examined his credentials and found them impressive. His reputation is excellent – or it was until he fled to Cairo. There are rumours afoot that he took something of great value with him. I sent a telegram to Mr Ridgemont, but I do not know how he can advise me from his manor house in Kent. This should have been a simple task, even though there is a substantial amount of money invested in the endeavour. I have failed miserably.' He took out a handkerchief to blot his eyes, and then vigorously blew his nose. 'Please excuse me for this vulgar exhibition of emotional debility. I have been in Mr Ridgemont's employment for eleven years, but now I fear for my future. Who will hire me without a letter of recommendation from my previous employer?'

'I do sympathise, Mr Buddle.' Inwardly, I was delighted to exploit his weakness, which gave me an upper edge. 'Let us find a place in the shade to continue our discourse.' I took his arm and led him to the spotty protection of a palm tree, doing my best to ignore his snuffles. A true gentleman may shed a tear, but he does not snuffle. When we were seated, I offered him my flask. 'Do try a nip of whisky. It has a soothing effect at times like this.'

He peered over his shoulder as though he feared that Mr Ridgemont was lurking in the distant foliage. 'As a rule, I do not imbibe beverages of an alcoholic nature, with the exception of an occasional glass of wine at dinner. Thank you, Mrs Emerson.' He took a substantial swallow from the flask, and then leaned against the tree trunk with a sigh. 'When I was a lad, I dreamed of becoming a world-renowned cricket player. I was reared in Gloucestershire and idolised W. G. Grace, the greatest cricketer of the nineteenth century. Sadly, I lacked the requisite physique. Later I became interested in studying law, but I could not afford to attend university. I undertook an apprenticeship as a bookkeeper, and might have made a career of it had my mentor not absconded with the payroll of a manufacturing company. His reputation was destroyed, and mine was tarnished. Now I am nothing but an exalted errand boy who hovers in a corner awaiting instructions from Mr Ridgemont.' He once again utilised his handkerchief to wipe away his tears while he engaged in another drink of whisky.

I did feel a scintilla of sympathy for him, despite his rude demeanour (and my emptied flask). 'All is not lost, Mr Buddle. As you can see, Emerson has the site under control and will uncover more artifacts. Herr Morgenstern will remain on our dahabeeyah until we are confident that he is capable of resuming his position. When he does, Emerson will continue to supervise from a distance. It is unfortunate that Eric von Raubritter was murdered. What do you know about him?'

'Nothing, nothing at all. He arrived shortly after Herr Morgenstern left for Cairo, and announced that he was taking over temporarily. It seemed to me that he had no idea whatsoever how to instruct the workmen.'

'He did not reside in the dig house. Do you have any idea where he was staying?'

Mr Buddle shrugged. 'I barely spoke to the man. At the end of the day a small boat transports me across the Nile to a more civilised dwelling, although, as one would expect, it is well below my standards. Von Raubritter must have found a place somewhere around here.' His eyes turned on me with beady suspicion. 'What do you know about him?'

'Very little,' I admitted. 'He was a German citizen and in good standing with the police force in Darmstadt. I have no clue whether or not he was acquainted with Herr Morgenstern before his appearance on the scene. It is certainly peculiar that he claimed to have his authorisation.'

'I cannot see that it mattered, since he is dead.'

'I am certain that it mattered to him,' I said acerbically. 'His head was bashed in and his body buried in the sand. Had it not been for a fluke of rigor mortis, he might have lain there until the inevitable stench was detected by predatory animals. I have seen the remains after the jackals and vultures have had their way. It is quite gruesome.'

He flinched and said, 'Well, of course. I apologise if I seem to be blasé about his horrible death, and I wish I could give you more information about him. It seems likely that he was staying in the vicinity of the workmen's makeshift campsite downstream and became embroiled in some sort of conflict with them.'

'Anything is possible, I suppose. After all, we found your name written on a card in the pocket of an assassin who broke into my bath chamber. When I shared that information with you, you were indeed blasé. Have you any explanation?'

'How could I? I have no idea who this man was. Upon arrival in Alexandria, I took a train to Cairo and stayed for only two days in a decent hotel. I did a spot of sightseeing and subsequently joined Herr Morgenstern here at the site. I did not speak to anyone at the hotel, except for staff, and I had no encounters of significance with the locals.'

'Have you ever been to Cornwall?'

He blinked at me. 'Not that I recollect, and if I was taken there as a child, it was not memorable. What is the importance of Cornwall?'

'That is where we think this assassin resided, along with his four brothers and a step-brother,' I replied. I saw no reason to elaborate on their dwindling number. 'They have sworn vengeance on my son and me because of an ill-fated occurrence in the past. You must take precautions, Mr Buddle.'

'If you say so, Mrs Emerson, although my life has been so mundane that I cannot imagine why anyone would bother to assassinate me. I have neither friends nor enemies.'

I did not offer a contradiction. 'What can you tell me about Herr Morgenstern's abrupt departure to Cairo?'

'Almost nothing, regrettably. Had not one of the workmen encountered him by chance the next morning at the train station in Minya, purchasing a ticket to Cairo, we would have no idea where he had gone. During the previous day, work was proceeding steadily in Thutmose's studio.' He took out his notebook and flipped through the pages. 'Ah, here it is. One of the men uncovered a broken cast of a male head. There was conjecture that it might have been that of Akhenaton. Herr Morgenstern ordered the men to retreat while he knelt in the sand to examine it more closely, and a quarter of an hour later he told them to depart for the day. He removed the piece, set down a bucket to mark the location and took it with him to the dig house. That was the last time I saw him until his recent return.'

'Why did you not accompany him in order to get a better look at it?' I asked.

Mr Buddle took off his hat and ran his fingers through his bristly hair. It reminded me of closely cropped hay on a sunburned field. He noticed my gaze and replaced his hat before he responded. 'I requested as much, but he brushed me aside like a pesky mosquito. He was exhilarated, chortling to himself in German. I did hear him use the word "schnapps" as he strolled towards the dig house.'

'A partial cast of a man who may or may have not been Akhenaton is hardly worthy of celebration.'

'You might ask the missionary chap. I saw him heading that way as I walked to the river. A most unfortunate product of nature's perverse humour, I must say. When they first laid eyes on him, many of the workmen were convinced he was a fiend from the netherworld. I my-self envisioned him to be the offspring of a bear and a gorilla. When he spoke, it was all I could do to refrain from laughing.'

'We must not stoop to amuse ourselves at his expense,' I said distractedly, pondering the significance of Mr Dullard's presence that evening. It was hard to envision a warm friendship between the stuffy Teutonic Egyptologist and the hirsute missionary (and former vagabond wrestler). Herr Morgenstern must have been desperate for companionship.

'Bloody hell!' snarled Mr Buddle, then gave me a horrified look. 'I beg your pardon, Mrs Emerson. I dearly pray I did not offend you. It is that woman, that irritating, simpering woman with no more sense than a guinea hen!'

It did not require a quick wit to realise of whom he spoke. I gritted my teeth as Miss Smith approached, swathed in lilac silk and ruffles. She sported a matching parasol and dainty shoes.

'Good morning, Mrs Emerson and Mr Buddle,' she trilled, fluttering her eyelashes. 'Isn't this exciting?'

I forced myself to return her smile. 'What do you find exciting about this? Archaeology can be a very dull process, and most of what is found is composed of fragments and shards. Nonetheless, they must be mea-sured, photographed, recorded and stored for future analysis, should they be deemed of some consequence. The basement of the Egyptian Museum is filled with unlabelled boxes of fragments. Most tombs have been robbed several times in prior centuries and more recent times. It is rare to come upon a site that has not been looted.'

Miss Smith pursed her lips for a moment. 'I am sure that is true, Mrs Emerson, but I am a neophyte in the field. I am not yet ready to take a cynical view of what may prove to be a spine-tingling adventure. Do you find this boring, Mr Buddle?'

'I find your expectations unrealistic. I have been here every day since the excavation commenced, and I can assure you that no one has uncovered a golden sceptre or a necklace of precious jewels. That is, dear lady, the stuff of fiction. I suggest you return home to write your capricious little books.'

'Then you will be disappointed,' she said. 'I am basking in the opportunity to expose myself to the culture so that my books will better reflect the realities of life in the desert.'

I spoke before Mr Buddle seized the chance to lecture her about her foolhardy endeavour. 'If you will excuse me, I am going back to the site to assist my husband. Perhaps you will stop by this evening, Miss Smith? I look forward to seeing you then.' I did not add that *I* intended to lecture her about her foolhardy endeavour, even if it took all night. With Emerson and Nefret to support me, I might be able to persuade her of her folly – not that Emerson would be happy to see Miss Smith again.

Miss Smith deftly slipped her arm through mine. 'A splendid idea, dear Mrs Emerson. I do have something I would like to discuss with you in private.'

Resigned, I allowed her to accompany me. Reis Abdul was in a much better mood, having been invited to work alongside Selim. The workmen were carefully brushing sand into buckets and dumping them beyond the bounds of the sculptor's studio. The fellahin observed silently. And standing on a flat rock, his powerfully sculpted arms crossed and his feet planted squarely, his black hair glittering in the sunlight, his profile more regal than any pharaoh, stood my beloved Emerson. All he lacked was his pith helmet, which he had discarded. It was a habit I had yet to discourage, despite my efforts over the years. This is not to say I have yet to concede the point, of course.

'I was wondering,' Miss Smith said, 'if I dare impose upon your hospitality by inquiring if you might consider including Mr Dullard in your dinner party? Your opinion is of immense value to me. My affection for him is growing stronger, but I cannot trust my judgement in matters of the heart. This will give you an opportunity to assess his sincerity and worthiness. I would be ever so grateful, Mrs Emerson.'

I was stunned by her audacity, and was preparing to say as much when it occurred to me that I had questions for Mr Dullard. He must have been the last person to see Herr Morgenstern on the eve of the latter's departure to Cairo, according to Mr Buddle. Emerson would be incensed by the addition of Mr Dullard; he had already made known to me his distaste for Miss Smith. I could not fault him for that, since I found her to be exasperating.

'Yes, if I encounter him, I will proffer an invitation,' I said. 'He must have enthralling stories of his exploits as a missionary in an Arab country. He is fortunate to have found solace in the Coptic village.'

'How kind you are, Mrs Emerson! I trust you will take the opportunity to evaluate his character. It will mean the world to me to have your approval.'

I disengaged my arm. 'We shall see. At the moment, I need to join my husband to assist in the excavation. I anticipate spending the morning sifting through that mound of sand. As you can imagine, my many years of work such as this have given me keen insight into the potential archaeological value of whatever I come across.'

Miss Smith's eyes widened. 'I am in awe of your perspicacity.'

I resisted the urge to step on her lilac shoe.

AS I ANTICIPATED, Emerson was infuriated when I announced my intentions to expand the dinner party. 'This will not do, Peabody!' he roared with such vehemence that it echoed from the cliffs. 'I refuse to have that pious and pretentious ape at my dining table! I have resigned myself to putting up with that nauseatingly coy woman for two hours, but I cannot tolerate Dullard for two seconds. Under no circumstances are you to invite him!'

I explained why I intended to do so, tactfully omitting Miss Smith's involvement. 'It is vexing to imagine such a fraternal kinship between Herr Morgenstern and Mr Dullard, but it seems to have existed for some time. It is possible that our hairy missionary can elaborate on

Herr Morgenstern's peculiar behaviour. You have the fortitude of a conqueror, Emerson. Surely you will be able to temper your aversion to the two during a simple dinner party.' I gave him a mischievous smile. 'You have matured greatly since the evening you threw the contents of a glass of wine into the face of the Marquess of Salisbury, who was the former prime minister.'

'The man was an ass!' exclaimed Emerson, flushing with ire. 'He opposed home rule for Ireland and suffrage for working-class men. He instigated the war against the Boers, resulting in seventy-five thousand casualties – a third of them women and children. Did you think I intended to offer a toast to him?'

'I saw your jaw tighten and your eyebrows lower as he pontificated at length. I was grateful that I was not seated next to him. If you recall, and I'm sure you do, I was wearing a particularly fetching blue silk gown. Red wine splatters would have ruined it.'

'Er, yes,' he mumbled, despite his general obliviousness to my wardrobe. (He does notice when I am not wearing any of it.)

'Then it is settled,' I said firmly. 'There he is, coming from the river. I shall invite him to join us this evening. All you need be is polite. I will take it upon myself to question him artfully about his relationship with Herr Morgenstern, who is recovering under Nefret's diligent attention. I will have a dinner tray sent to him in hopes that Mr Dullard will speak more freely about him if he is not present at the table.'

'I cannot make any promises as to how I will react when he pipes up in that intolerable squeak.'

While Emerson huffed and rumbled ominously, I did my best not to predict what might occur at the dinner table. My premonitions are not always welcome, especially those concerning airborne fruit.

NEFRET HAD REMAINED on the boat to monitor Herr Morgenstern's condition. She joined us in the dining room for the midday meal.

'His body temperature is nearing normal,' she announced as we sat down.

Fatima brought in a tureen of chilled cucumber soup. 'Then he should leave – that man. He is in Ramses's room. This is bad, very bad. What if Ramses and David should appear? Where would they sleep?'

'They did not catch the night train, or they would be here,' Emerson said as he poked his finger in the soup and tasted it. 'This is delicious, Fatima, but I am in the mood for a substantial sandwich. Are there any leftovers from the roast?'

She eyed the soup, then Emerson. The door slammed as she returned to the kitchen, but her muttered invectives were audible. I ladled soup into two bowls and passed one to Nefret, who was struggling not to laugh at Emerson's transparent ruse.

'Soup is not meant to be cold,' he said in his defense.

'The great chefs of Paris would beg to differ.' I took a spoonful to my mouth. 'It truly is delicious, but not worthy of further debate.' I informed Nefret of the impending dinner guests and my decision to keep Herr Morgenstern stashed out of sight in the boys' quarters.

'He is coherent,' she replied, 'but sporadically. When I questioned him about Nefertiti, he drifted into a convoluted story about his experiences in Syria. I do not believe he was pretending to be confused.'

'Of course he was!' thundered Emerson. 'And where is that damnable woman with my sandwich? Am I obliged to barge into the kitchen and prepare it myself?'

'You are free to do as you wish, Emerson, but I recommend patience. If you insult Fatima, you are apt to be served cold eggs for a week. Nefret, have you heard from your professor in Paris?'

Ignoring the grumble from the end of the table, she said, 'Not yet. I shall go to Minya tomorrow as I had no time today and send a telegram to Dr Willoughby. I studied what material I have with me and at the clinic in Luxor, and ruled out opiate derivatives. They dull brain activity and cause dizziness and drowsiness. Amphetamines, in contrast, stimulate the central nervous system. They can cause confusion, anxiety and a false sense of well-being. The research is in its infancy and no one has found a medical application. You cannot buy a bottle of pills or a potion at a chemist's shop.'

'The symptoms reflect Herr Morgenstern's behaviour,' I said slowly. I paused as Fatima stomped into the dining room and slammed down a plate in front of Emerson. A lump of beef slathered in horseradish sauce had been squashed between two rounds of charred pita bread. It looked most unappetising.

'Hmph,' Emerson grunted.

I put down my spoon. 'I must let Fatima know that we have a second guest for dinner. It would be so comforting if David and Ramses were on the train at this moment. What can they be doing in Cairo, Emerson? Breaking into the German embassy? Kidnapping the ambassador? Surely if they had been arrested, Mr Russell would have sent a telegram.'

'Do not underestimate them,' he said before chomping down on the sandwich. Horseradish sauce dribbled down his shirt. Nefret and I managed to contain our laughter as he ineffectually wiped the mess with his napkin. 'Damnation! All I requested was a simple sandwich. How difficult can that be?'

I excused myself and hurried into the kitchen before I broke into a wide grin. Although Emerson is very fond of my even, white teeth, it did not seem prudent to allow him a glimpse of them at that moment. Fatima and I discussed the menu. I told her about the second guest and the faint possibility that Ramses and David might arrive in time for dinner. Once we were in accord, I returned to our cabin to refresh myself. Emerson had flung his soiled shirt on the floor and was putting on a clean one. I was not concerned about the stain, since I was more accustomed to dealing with bloody discolourations. 'I will need Daoud's company this afternoon,' I said.

Emerson stared at me. 'Are you intending to go galloping into the desert once again, Peabody?'

'I am going to the camp where the workmen live. Mr Buddle seems to think von Raubritter was staying there. We need to find out why he came to Amarna and took control of the excavation. If indeed he had a tent or rented a hut, he may have left personal letters or a journal that will further our knowledge. Daoud can take me there in the small boat and serve as my bodyguard.'

'I don't like it,' he said flatly. 'You are much safer with me.'

'Of course I am, dear, but it is vital that we determine von Raubritter's role. You cannot oversee the work in progress and accompany me at the same time. Daoud can protect me quite adequately, and translate should the need arise. We should be back in only a few hours.'

'In time to dress for dinner?' Emerson said with a grimace.

'Please remember to wear your pith helmet, dear.' I kissed him on the cheek and went to find my overly conscientious bodyguard, who was eating a civilised sandwich on the top deck. 'Do you know where Herr Morgenstern's workmen are staying?'

'Downstream, not too far. Sometimes at night I can hear them.' His jaw tightened. 'It is not a place for ladies, Sitt Hakkim.'

'We shall see.' I asked him to prepare our boat. It lacks the lithe elegance of a felucca with its voluminous sail that allows it to skim swiftly across the water. When I came aboard, Daoud raised the makeshift sail and managed to catch a faint breeze. We proceeded down the Nile in a slow fashion, as if in a royal regatta on the Thames. I was a bit sorry that I had chosen my pith helmet rather than a stylish hat.

Daoud navigated the boat to a sandbar. 'It is not far from here,' he said as he offered me his hand.

'Nicely done,' I said once I was ashore. 'Is this the path?'

He nodded reluctantly. 'I do not understand why we have come here, Sitt Hakim. The workmen are uneducated and smelly. Also, they are at the site. You will find nobody here.'

'Perhaps not, but it's possible that some of the men brought their wives. We need to determine if von Raubritter was staying among them. If so, I will search his dwelling for information.'

Daoud bowed, but not before I caught a glimpse of his scowl. He led the way between the palm trees and acacias to a collection of tents, crudely built mud huts, circles of stones filled with ashes and clothing drying on branches. It was uncannily silent.

'*As-salaam-alaykum*, I am searching for information. There is a reward for anyone who can help me,' I said loudly.

'There is no one here,' pronounced Daoud. 'Let us go back to the boat and return to the dahabeeyah.'

I shook my head. 'Not yet. I feel a tingle in my spine that tells me I am being watched by someone nearby. You need to step back and stop glowering.' I approached a hut that had been severely damaged by the recent rainstorm. The roof sagged precariously and the exterior walls were bowed. 'Hello!' I called in a friendly voice.

A stout young woman draped in a black robe came out of a neighbouring hut. Her eyes were ringed with kohl and her upper lip obscured by a faint moustache. '*Masa el-kheir*,' she whispered.

'And good afternoon to you, madam. I am Amelia Peabody Emerson. Daoud, ask her if a young German man was staying in this vicinity. His name was von Raubritter and he had a scar on his cheek.' With my finger, I drew a line from my cheekbone to the corner of my mouth. 'Like this.'

While they conversed, I scrutinised her for any hint of masculinity in her face or hands. My Readers know by now that I am keenly aware of Sethos's dexterity in matters of illusion and disguise. However, the woman was no taller than I. The suppleness of her skin was that of a girl scarcely past puberty.

'What did she say?' I asked Daoud.

'She says that the pale man with a scar was living in a very fine tent behind these huts. He paid her to cook for him. Her husband told her that the man was dead, which makes her sad.'

'Ask her to show us his tent,' I said as I took out several coins and offered them to her.

She beckoned us to follow her, and we did. The canvas tent was held upright at either end by two poles, the sides secured by ropes threaded through metal grommets and staked. I estimated the interior to be the size of my sewing room. Daoud untied the twine that held the front flaps together.

I stepped forward, but then halted. 'Does she know if the pale man had any visitors?'

Daoud repeated my question in Arabic. The woman's lips puckered as she looked down at her toes. Eventually, and with obvious reticence, she nodded.

'Can she describe the visitor?' I asked.

The woman shrugged, and then trotted away in the direction of what I presumed was the hut inhabited by her and her husband. 'Well, then,' I said as I bestirred my inimitable courage to enter the tent, 'shall we have a look inside?'

Daoud yanked back the tent flap and peered into the poorly lit space. 'Back away, Sitt Hakim. I will deal with this intruder.'

I was too familiar with his method of dealing with people whom he deemed to be suspect. 'No, I will handle this myself.' I stepped into the tent and found myself exchanging leery looks with an unfamiliar woman in her early thirties. She was sitting cross-legged on a cot, dressed in khaki trousers and a blouse stained with perspiration. Her dull blond hair was in need of shampoo. Her forehead, cheeks and chin were sunburned and already blistering. 'Who are you?' I said, astounded.

'Who are you?' she responded with a German accent. 'You are the *Schuldige* . . . the trespasser. This tent belongs to Eric von Raubritter.'

'He is not in a position to object to my presence. I am Amelia Emerson, currently involved in the excavation at Amarna.'

'Liezel Hasenkamp, a colleague. I came here to make certain that he was enjoying his holiday. Now I have learned of his death. Most tragic, *ja*? He was a good and kind man. I am so sorry.' Her face was puckered as she looked away. 'He and I were . . . very close.'

Her avowal of grief was convincing, I decided as I glanced around the relatively spacious interior of the tent. On one side was the cot with a pillow and a light cotton blanket. Clothes were folded neatly in an open suitcase. The contents of a second suitcase had been spilled on the floor, and appeared to be female apparel. A table had been constructed from planks of wood resting on mud bricks; a chair made with the same materials looked precarious at best. I held back a gasp as my eyes focused on a stack of notebooks on the table. 'Goodness gracious,' I said lightly, 'I do believe that's a chamber pot behind the suitcase. Surely he did not bring it with him from Germany. What do you think, Liezel?'

'How should I know? Why are you here, Frau Emerson? Were you planning to steal some of Eric's possessions?'

The growl from behind me implied that Daoud was not pleased with her impertinence and was likely to shake her until her teeth clattered. I gave him a stern glance. 'Don't be ridiculous,' I said coldly, my arms crossed. 'I am well known in the field of Egyptology and held in high esteem. I came to find an explanation for Herr von Raubritter's presence here. From what I have been told, he claimed that Herr Morgenstern, who had left for Cairo, instructed him to take charge of the excavation. That was a falsehood. Your so-called colleague knew nothing about archaeology. What was his profession?'

Liezel looked down at the sand-strewn canvas floor. 'He was a researcher, but he was interested in archaeology. He had several books with photographs of Egyptian temples, tombs and hieroglyphs. I know nothing about his relationship with Herr Morgenstern. Maybe they met at some time and Eric was invited to this hot, filthy, dreadful place to observe the operation.'

'A researcher? Please be more specific.'

'It's complicated – and boring. Eric admitted as much. He loved to travel around the world and was eager to come to Egypt – it was more exciting than his research.'

I gave her a piercing stare. 'Cairo is crowded with tourists, but very few of them set up tents in Amarna. Herr Morgenstern claimed not to recognise Herr von Raubritter's name or even a photograph of him. You have said that his work was too complicated to explain, but I am neither uneducated nor ignorant. What was the application of his research? I am quite sure it was not Akhenaton.'

She covered her face with her hands and began to sob. The gasps and ragged inhalations were disturbing, but I felt only a twinge of remorse for speaking to her as I had done. I refrained from tapping my foot as I waited for her outburst to subside. Daoud's eyebrows were lowered and his mouth curled downward in sympathy. It might have been amusing, I thought, if he smothered her in a hug of sympathy. There have been incidents when his intentions have been overly zealous.

I took a handkerchief from one of my pockets and dropped it in Liezel's lap. 'Wipe your eyes,' I said gently. 'I will ask the woman who lives nearby to bring you food and water. Tomorrow you need to accompany the workmen to the site so that I can enlighten you about Eric's demise and tell you how to deal with the police in Minya. You will have to contact the German embassy to arrange to have Herr von Raubritter's remains shipped back to Germany.'

The volume of her distress rose to an uncomfortable level of decibels. I hooked Daoud's arm and propelled him out of the tent. It was possible that I had underestimated a German's capability to express grief. I suppose I should have lingered to comfort her, but I needed to return to the *Amelia* in order to freshen up before the dinner guests arrived. I could almost hear Emerson snorting with derision.

FIFTEEN

HEN I ARRIVED at the dahabeeyah, I encountered Emerson in our quarters. He had washed away the day's accumulation of dust and perspiration, shaved and changed into clean trousers and a white shirt. He was enthusiastic about assisting me with a sponge bath, and I feared we would be late to receive our guests. Shortly thereafter, we reassembled ourselves and went up to the top deck. Emerson brought me a whisky and soda while I described my encounter with Liezel. 'Her story,' I continued, 'was flimsy and made very little sense. She claims that she came to Egypt to find out if von Raubritter was enjoying his holiday. Even if there is a glimmer of truth in that, how did she know that he was in Amarna?'

'It is possible that he wrote her a letter that included specific information about his location, but that does not explain why she would expend her time, energy and a not-insubstantial amount of money to find him. She said they were colleagues. It would be helpful to know the topic of their research.'

'She refused to elaborate, which was suspicious in itself.' I paused to think as I gazed at the exquisite hues of the sunset reflecting in the distance of the Western Desert. 'I told her to come to the site tomorrow morning so that I can advise her about retrieving von Raubritter's body in Minya and arranging for its return to Germany for a proper burial. I presume she will need to communicate with Mr Russell, the Deutsche Orient-Gesellschaft and the German embassy.'

Emerson grimaced. 'Paperwork and bureaucrats be damned! It may take weeks before his body can be transported. I hope you do not intend to accompany her on her thankless tasks, Peabody. I need you here to offer your expertise. Furthermore, two of the Godwin brothers may be skulking nearby, waiting for the opportunity to cause you grief. I cannot allow that to happen. I would be forever lost without you to scold me, laugh at me, argue with me and, and see to my shirts,' finished my spouse, who was not given to verbal displays of emotion.

I was inundated with warmth as we regarded each other. I had formulated a response when a voice from below interrupted us.

'Ahoy!' called Miss Smith. 'May we come aboard?'

Ignoring an exasperated grunt from Emerson, I stood up and peered over the railing. 'Please do,' I called in a falsely jolly fashion, 'and you, too, Mr Dullard. We shall come down at once and escort you to the salon for an aperitif.'

In spite of my assertion that we did not dress elaborately for dinner, Miss Smith wore a daring red silk gown and numerous strands of pearls. Her makeup had been applied with a heavier hand than usual; the pink circles on her cheeks clashed with her scarlet lips. Had I not known she was an author, I might have ascribed to her a less savoury profession. In contrast, Mr Dullard's brown suit and necktie were decidedly dull. He had trimmed his hair and beard, but the overall transformation was negligible. Not even Meryma'at, the eighteenth dynasty barber of the Temple of Amun, could have triumphed over such a copious quantity of hair. I caught myself speculating if Mr Dullard could hear it grow in the night. I could not repress a shudder of revulsion, but sternly reminded myself that he was the victim of a genetic malfunction.

'So kind of you to invite me,' he squeaked.

'I am pleased that you are joining us,' I said as I glanced back at Emerson. 'Is that not so, my dear? You are always in the mood for convivial conversation.' I was relieved that his reply was inaudible.

I beckoned our guests to follow me to the salon, where Fatima had placed decanters of sherry and whisky. Miss Smith promptly requested sherry. Mr Dullard tugged on his beard and finally acknowledged that he might enjoy a nip of the same. Once we were settled, I smiled at the missionary. 'Is everything well at Deir el-Mowass?'

'I believe so. Although there is great poverty among them, the Copts remain dedicated to their faith and charitable to their brethren.'

Emerson raised an eyebrow. 'So you are living off their benevolence? How fortunate for you that they provide you with food and lodging.'

'Indeed,' interjected Miss Smith. 'They have accepted Mr Dullard as their spiritual leader, their beacon of piety and submission to the Almighty Lord. If you met them, you would see their affection for him.'

'Yes,' I said firmly before Emerson had the opportunity to respond in what might have been a sardonic tone. 'Our few encounters with members of the Coptic faith have been amiable. They have shown great courage for a minority, surrounded by those who adhere to their Moslem beliefs.'

'Only because the Moslems do not bother with them and they are all used to living together,' Emerson said.

Mr Dullard's eyes narrowed. 'That may change, Professor. In the future, the Copts will become a factor as the probability of war looms.'

'They are not so numerous. Should they attempt to instigate a rebellion – and for what reason, one might ask – no one will notice.'

Mr Dullard gulped down the remainder of the sherry and refilled his glass. 'You are uninformed, I am sorry to say. There is unrest afoot.'

I stood up before the exchange escalated into fisticuffs. 'Shall we go in the dining room? Our cook can be very testy if she is kept waiting to serve dinner. Nefret will be joining us and is looking forward to being introduced.' This was not particularly true, but courtesy forbade me from repeating her scathing (and hilarious) remarks about each of them. I led the way to the table, which had been set with our third-best silver (our first- and second-best silver were safely stored in Kent), crystal wineglasses, linen napkins and fresh flowers. I put Emerson at the head of the table, where he always presides over meals, and indicated to our guests that they were to sit across from each other. When Nefret demurely entered, I directed her to the chair between Emerson and Mr Dullard. I had already decided to do so in order to create a distance between the two men. Should an argument arise, she had volunteered to douse both of them with wine.

'Miss Smith,' I murmured, 'this is our protégé, Dr Nefret Forth. I believe she has already met Mr Dullard.'

'Nefret, my dear,' simpered Miss Smith, 'how is your patient? I was told that you retrieved him from the brink of death. I am amazed that a pretty young girl like yourself can succeed in a male profession. I am too timorous. I fear I would faint were I to be confronted with a bloodied patient, be he wounded or deceased.'

Mr Dullard cleared his throat. 'I must disagree with you, Miss Smith. You displayed admirable courage when you left the security of the steamer to take up residence among the pagans.'

'Pagans?' I retorted. 'The men, women and children who live in Amarna are devout Moslems. They adhere to the teachings of the Koran and pray more often than Christians.'

'They pray to Allah, a false god.'

Despite my stern look, Emerson was unable to constrain himself. 'Children are indoctrinated to believe one thing or another, based on their culture. If you had been born in India, you would worship Brahma, Vishnu and Shiva.'

'Heresy!' retorted Mr Dullard.

'Nefret,' I said, noticing with a modicum of alarm that she had gripped the stem of her wineglass, 'you failed to answer Miss Smith's question. Perhaps you might relate what you told us earlier about his condition.'

She nodded. 'Yes, of course, Aunt Amelia. Herr Morgenstern, who preferred to dine in his cabin tonight, is recovering from the heatstroke that afflicted him in the desert. His body temperature is normal, but his mind is at times confused. He doesn't seem to remember why he went to Cairo or what happened to him while he was there.'

Mahmoud, our steward, came out of the kitchen with a platter of Nile perch in a lemon sauce. I waited impatiently until we had all been served and our wineglasses filled, and then said, 'Mr Dullard, you were at the dig house with Herr Morgenstern the night before he left on the train to Cairo. Did he show you the partial cast he removed from the site?'

'This fish is divine,' Miss Smith commented. 'So fresh and flaky. It brings back memories of Brighton, a lovely city, where I dined with a direct descendant of the Duke of Cumberland. She invited me because she is enamoured of my books.'

Mr Dullard beamed at her. 'How could she not be?'

Trying to keep the subject on track was as frustrating as swatting at flies on a honeypot. I could tell from Emerson's expression that he was eager to further the religious debate. Although it would be pointless, I was disposed to allow him to do so – after I had interrogated Mr Dullard. Once the fish plates were removed, I said, 'I am pleased that you found the fish to your liking, Miss Smith. We are still concerned about Herr Morgenstern. You did accompany him to the dig house, did you not, Mr Dullard? Did he speak of his plan to go to Cairo?'

Mr Dullard again tugged on his beard while he thought. 'No, he said nothing out of the ordinary. When I asked to see what he had uncovered at the site, I was told that it might be of significance if it proved to be Akhenaton. Since my opinion was of no value, he did not show it to me. We had a meal of tinned meat and stale biscuits.'

'And schnapps,' I said. 'Here is Mahmoud with what I hope will be a satisfactory main course. Fatima purchases chickens and vegetables from the village.'

Emerson smirked. 'Did she procure an extra chicken in order to perform a ritual when the moon is full? Pagans are known to drink fresh blood and—'

'Do try the baba ghanoush,' Nefret interrupted. 'It is made from aubergine and garlic. It does not look especially appetising, but it is very tasty. Fatima uses her *tata*'s recipe.'

Mr Dullard did not need encouragement to try it – or any of the other dishes. He filled his plate to a precipitous height and began to eat noisily. The wine decanter was within his reach, regrettably. Miss Smith turned to look at me, her lips pursed in disapproval. I declined to respond. Conversation dwindled to a discussion of the weather, occasionally very hot but usually tolerable. Mahmoud removed our plates and poured coffee while we passed around a platter of fruit, cheeses and biscuits. I prefer simple menus on a daily basis, although our meals are most elaborate on holidays.

At my request, Emerson offered brandy. I waited until Mr Dullard drained his glass before saying, 'Do you recall Herr Morgenstern's mood that evening?'

'He was cheerful,' Mr Dullard said as he sadly regarded his empty snifter. 'Might I have another trickle of brandy?'

Emerson obliged, albeit with a martyred sigh. Nefret, Miss Smith and I politely declined. I accepted that I had learned nothing from Mr Dullard, nor was I likely to despite his obvious intoxication. It was time to put my beloved husband out of his misery. 'This has been delightful, but we awake before sunrise in order to take advantage of the cooler temperature. Thank you so much for your company.'

'We must thank you for your kind invitation,' twittered Miss Smith. 'I never dreamed I would dine with such illustrious persons. I shall write a letter to my editor, relating all the details. He will be most impressed.' She put her hand on Mr Dullard's shoulder. 'Come along, it is getting late.'

Mr Dullard wobbled to his feet and thanked us profusely for our hospitality. He then thanked Nefret for saving Herr Morgenstern's life, and might have gone into the kitchen to thank Fatima for her baba ghanoush had not Miss Smith taken his arm and steered him towards the door. I followed them to the deck and discreetly tried to help Mr Dullard down our narrow pier. He shook off my hand and staggered towards the shore, zigzagging precariously. I hurried after him to prevent him from toppling into the water. I was not overly concerned that he would be attacked by crocodiles, but I had no idea if he could swim.

Miss Smith joined us on solid ground. 'I am worried that he will not be able to row his boat across the Nile. What shall we do with him, Mrs Emerson?'

'I have no idea.'

'Oh dear,' she began, then gasped. 'What is that noise?'

I looked in the direction of the cultivation. The thickness of the trees and bushes allowed very little moonlight to penetrate. 'A horse's hooves in the distance, but coming closer. I think it wise to return to the dahabeeyah immediately.'

'I shall protect you!' proclaimed Mr Dullard in his high-pitched voice. It was not reassuring, to be candid. He was large, but he was unlikely to be able to subdue a galloping horse.

I stared intently into the shadows. 'There is a rider, but I cannot make out his features. He seems to be wearing a blue or black thobe and a turban, and he has some type of sword in his hand.' I yanked Miss Smith's arm. 'We must retreat now!'

'Who could it be?' she asked me in a tremulous voice.

I tightened my grasp. 'Let us discuss that from the safety of the da-habeeyah. We must retreat! Mr Dullard, listen to me!'

Only a few trees were separating us from the rider and his horse when Mr Dullard snatched up a rock and hurled it with the velocity of a celebrated bowler. 'Stop, you villain!' he shrieked.

I do not know if the missile or the shriek caused the horse to rear up in alarm. It came down hard and veered into the trees. The rider had risen on the saddle to keep his balance, and failed to duck when the horse almost collided with an acacia tree. Unfortunately, a V-shaped branch caught the man by his neck; as the horse disappeared, the rid-er's feet swung like a pendulum below him.

'Holy mother of Jesus,' said Mr Dullard in a more subdued voice.

Miss Smith fell to her knees. 'What have you done? This is – this is unspeakable!' She covered her face with her hands and began to sway.

'How could you? How could you do such a terrible thing?'

'We must ascertain if he is alive,' I said unsteadily.

Emerson appeared at my side. 'Stay here,' he ordered us. 'I do not think he could have survived, but I will find out in a moment.'

Mr Dullard was motionless, his mouth agape. Miss Smith was moaning as she continued to sway. I waited until Emerson was half-way to the tree before I caught up with him. 'What a bizarre scene,' I commented when he glowered at me. 'I was surprised by Mr Dullard's quick response, for which I am grateful.'

'Feeling in need of fresh air, I was on the top deck and saw every-thing. David slew Goliath with a stone from a sling. Mr Dullard's ac-tions were less poetic, but effective.' He stopped and looked up at the rider's face. "The bugger appears to have died from a broken neck. His eyes are rounded with terror. As much as I would prefer to leave him here, I suppose I should haul him down so that he might rest in peace if the nocturnal predators keep their distance. One of our men can stand guard until the police come in the morning.'

As I stepped forward for a closer look, I heard a crunch under my shoe. I did not require a premonition to identify the source of the sound. 'Here is his monocle, Emerson. It is too late to introduce you properly to Absalom. I suspect you will find his calling card in his pocket.'

Emerson clasped the man's legs and lifted him until the limp body was freed from the branch then unceremoniously dropped him, flipped him onto his back, and pulled up the thobe, which covered a pair of Western trousers. After a quick search of the man's pock-ets, Emerson removed a small rectangle of cardboard and said, 'He is Absalom. We shall not mourn his death, Peabody. His scimitar flew under that palm tree on the other side of the path. Dash it, I am obli-gated to thank that damned missionary for saving your life! I wish I had been beside you.'

'You must acknowledge Mr Dullard's bravery. Please try to do so without snorting under your breath or scowling.' I could not prevent myself from trembling as the scene replayed itself in my mind. Emerson caught me around my waist as my knees buckled. My face against his manly chest, I allowed a few tears to dampen his shirt. 'There remains another one of these beastly brothers. This is intolerable, Emerson. We can only wait for the next assassination attempt.'

'That is true, my darling Peabody.' His voice deepened. 'I would like nothing better than to track down that bl— blasted scoundrel, thrash him until he cries piteously and let him rot in a cell. The accommodations at the Tura prison are said to be unspeakably filthy and overrun with vermin. If you are feeling stronger, we must return to the boat to deal with this. Should the jackals arrive before the guard, I shall not be overwhelmed with remorse.'

I slipped out of Emerson's embrace and bent down to examine Absalom's features. I noted a resemblance to Judas. Both had broad foreheads and prominent eyebrows, flabby lips and a plethora of pockmarks. I had only a glimpse of Guy's face before he hurled the stick of dynamite in our direction, but recalled his concave cheeks and thin nose. I never saw Cromwell, who had been concealed by the crowd at the train station. Geoffery had been a handsome fellow, popular with the young ladies and their chaperones. Even Nefret had fallen for his charming demeanour.

'These Godwin brothers seem to come in all sizes, how curious,' I said as I patted at a slight protruberance under his thobe. Moving aside the opening at the throat I found that he wore a tailored waistcoat beneath, and I slipped my hand into its pocket. I was rewarded with a small card. 'This has something written upon it but it is too dark to read.'

Emerson has the eyesight of a nocturnal predator. He took the card and examined it. 'It is a name. Would you care to guess, Peabody?'

'Octavius Buddle,' I said wearily. 'I questioned him earlier today. He was adamant that he knew of no one who might desire to assassinate him, yet his name appears again and again.'

'He must lead a very boring life. At one point, you and our son had five would-be assassins plotting to murder you – and they were not the first ones. Ramses seems to wind up in danger every season. You have made many enemies, too.'

'And you have not, Father of Curses?'

'Egyptology can be a perilous occupation. We must go back now so that I can inform the authorities of what has happened.' He kept his arm around my waist as we walked towards the pier. 'Why is that woman ululating like a bereaved widow? She will alarm everyone in the village, and possibly Luxor.'

'She writes about violence in a pedestrian manner. Her sheikh may slice off the head of a marauding Turk, but he is never splattered with blood. I doubt she has ever encountered brutality or carnage.' My mind flashed back to the conversation she and I had over tea at Shepheard's, when she blithely described how her heroine had strangled a man with her scarf. 'In real life, that is.'

Miss Smith rose to her feet as we neared. 'He is dead, isn't he?'

'From a broken neck,' I said. 'Would you care to go aboard and have a brandy to calm your nerves? We are all very upset by what took place.'

'I prefer to go to my hut,' she replied, 'but I am afraid.'

Mr Dullard clumsily took a step in her direction, but froze when she glowered at him. 'I will protect you,' he declared.

'Not in your condition,' she said sharply.

Emerson patted her shoulder. 'Daoud will escort you and remain outside your dwelling for the remainder of the night. Our maid will come in the morning to help you pack. It is too late for you to rejoin the passengers on the steamer, so you must take the train back to Cairo.'

'You are so kind, Professor Emerson. I will feel much safer with a man to protect me. However, I have no use for a maid tomorrow because I am not ready to leave Amarna. I came here for adventure – and have experienced it beyond my wildest expectations.'

Mr Dullard tried again. 'I will protect you, Miss Smith.'

'I think not!' she snapped. 'You have dishonoured your vow of temperance. You will be fortunate if your Copts take you back into their fold.'

'Temperance? I vowed to serve my God, whose son turned water into wine at the marriage in Cana. We cannot know if he continued to perform such miracles elsewhere.'

'Like turning the Sea of Galilee into beer?' Emerson suggested.

I was too drained to listen to another verbal altercation. I gestured to Daoud to approach us, and instructed him to look after Miss Smith. After Emerson assured him that I would be well protected, Daoud scooped up Miss Smith as if she were a large bag of potatoes and began to walk down the path, despite her shrill objections. Mr Dullard trotted after them. After we reboarded the dahabeeyah, Emerson sent a cabin steward to stand guard over Absalom's body.

Nefret embraced me. 'Aunt Amelia! What happened?'

I related the events, including the identity of the attacker. 'The Godwin brothers are indefatigable, I must say. I cannot think why Mr Buddle might be among their targets. He is such an innocuous fellow. What could he have done to merit such enmity? Perhaps Mr Ridgemont did something vile to the Godwin family, and Mr Buddle is considered to be his representative. Ramses and I are at the pinnacle of their list, their first priorities. Mr Buddle's time would come once they have eliminated us. In the morning, I will take him aside and reiterate my warning.'

Emerson handed me a snifter of brandy. 'You will stay on board until the last Godwin has been exposed and defeated, Peabody.'

'What if this Flitworthy character is a pirate? I will be much safer at your side, Emerson, and I must have the opportunity to speak to Liezel and Mr Buddle.'

'I will speak to them.'

'But will they listen to you? I shall stay within an arm's length of you until Daoud recovers from his night outside Miss Smith's hut. He will accompany me the rest of the day. He must be aggravated that he was on the deck when Absalom charged, and eager to have a chance to pummel the remaining Godwin.'

Nefret sighed. 'I agree with my dear Professor, but I know you cannot be easily dissuaded. I need to look in on Herr Morgenstern before I retire.' She kissed each of us on the cheek and left the salon, muttering to herself.

From Manuscript H

RAMSES, STILL IN the personage of Higginsnort, nodded at Baehler as he crossed the hotel lobby and went upstairs to the diminutive room. David had opted to use the basement entry, and was washing his upper body. He conceded the washbowl with a chuckle.

'Bear in mind this disguise was necessary,' Ramses said sourly as he tugged at the plastic pouches glued onto his cheeks with gum arabic. 'Unless, of course, you would have preferred to remain in the basement of the German embassy until Herr Gunter arranged to have you tortured. Because of you, I am in debt to Sethos. It pains me to admit that the plan and its implementation were his doing.'

'What do you intend to tell your father?'

'As little as possible.' Ramses grimaced as he ripped off the last pouch. 'Obviously, we cannot remain here. I will retrieve the two copies from Baehler's supply closet and meet you in the basement. Damn that scoundrel Harun! Who knows how many more copies are in antiquities shops? Ten? Twenty? We must assume that the original bust of Nefertiti is in his new workshop wherever the hell that may be!'

David finished buttoning his shirt. 'I agree that we should move to another location, but I doubt we will be safer in any of the hotels, shabby or grandiose. Gunter will anticipate that and have his spies on the alert. When was the last time a desk clerk refused to accept a bribe? Not in this century or the one before it. My cousin Tahir has an apartment in the vicinity of the train station. We can stay there until it is time to catch the night train.'

'We can stay there until we locate Harun and throttle him,' Ramses retorted as he scrubbed his face. 'It behooves me to send a telegram to my parents, saying that we are well and will be staying a few more days.' He dropped the Higginsnort apparel on the floor and dressed in his own clothes. 'Do not panic if it takes me a while to meet you in the basement. Baehler will have to fetch a hammer, and perhaps a crowbar. He will not be pleased.'

David gave him a mock salute. Ramses departed the room and headed for the stairs, considering how best to transport the Nefertiti forgeries as he approached the front desk. One of them was in a bag, the other wrapped in thin paper.

'You have received a telegram, Mr Emerson,' Baehler said with an obsequious smile. 'Had I known you were in your room, I would have had it delivered to you.'

Ramses put the envelope in his coat pocket. 'I need my parcels. Do you still have the hammer, or do you need to send for it? I am in a bit of a hurry.'

'Anything to please your exalted mother.' Baehler reached into a drawer and produced a hammer. Ramses attacked the nails he had pounded into the door earlier, ignoring groans from behind him as the hammerhead scarred the wood. He gathered up the two hefty parcels, announced that he would be checking out within the hour, and started back in the direction of the stairs. Once he could no longer be seen from the desk, he went down to the basement.

David was waiting for him. 'Do you recall the comment that we might need a steamer trunk to carry our collection of copies of Nefertiti? Well, I have found one. According to the tag, it belongs to a Miss Annabelle Hadley of Somerset. It is empty. We can borrow it temporarily and send it back to the hotel before she becomes aware of its absence.'

Ramses was relieved to place the copies in the steamer trunk. 'I wish Thutmose had chosen a smaller size to honour Queen Nefertiti, something in the range of twenty pounds instead of forty-odd pounds. If we chance upon another ten of them, we will require help to load the trunk onto the train.'

'Baksheesh can work wonders,' David said as he closed the lid and gestured at Ramses to help him carry the trunk out to the alley. 'Based on recent history, it is not prudent for me to be seen on the corner by Shepheard's. You need to flag down a taxi or carriage and direct it here.'

'So that I might be set upon by Gunter's thugs, armed with hypodermic needles?'

'At least you are forewarned.'

'I am touched by your concern.' Ramses went down the alley and turned the corner. When he reached the busy street in front of the hotel, he shouted at a carriage driver to pull to the kerb, and instructed the man to turn down the side street and into the alley. David was waiting next to the trunk. With the driver's assistance, the trunk was secured behind the passenger seat. The driver took them to Tahir's address, and after an offer of baksheesh, helped them unload the trunk.

Ramses and David carried it to the second floor of the building. David knocked persistently until the door was opened and Tahir greeted them in Arabic. After he and David embraced, he insisted on helping them move the trunk into his apartment.

'This,' David said, also speaking Arabic, 'is a friend of mine. It is better if you do not know his name.'

Tahir sucked in a breath. In stilted English, he said, 'But I recognise him. He is the Brother of Demons.'

'You are not to mention my presence here,' Ramses said sternly. 'Or David's, for that matter. There are unpleasant people who would like to hurt us. You will be safer if no one knows we are here.' He smiled and held out his hand. 'You may call me Ramses, my friend.'

'Thank you, Brother of' – Tahir caught himself – 'Ramses. Please accept my little hospitality and please ignore the state of our home – it is not always thus. My wife has gone visiting to her parents.'

Ramses took the telegram out of his pocket and read it. 'Father demands that we return immediately to Amarna. No extraneous details, as usual. It is amazing how thunderous a piece of paper can be.' He wadded up the paper and tossed it at an overflowing wastebasket. 'David, you stay here, where you are safe from Gunter's henchmen. I shall go to the telegraph office to send a reply. After that, I will go to a café and hope that I encounter Latif along the way. He has an uncanny ability to sense my whereabouts when I am in Cairo. He may have learned something about the location of Harun's hideout.'

'I will be one step behind you,' David stated, his arms crossed. 'Aunt Amelia would expect no less of me. Besides that, I should hate to miss the fun if one of the Godwin brothers leaps out of the alley, brandishing a knife. I calculate that two of them remain.'

Tahir's eyes were round as he bade them a safe outing. Ramses and David went down to the street and walked briskly to the telegraph of-fice. After dictating a message that they intended to remain in Cairo for at least another day, they strolled to the café where they had pre-viously encountered Latif. They selected a street table, ordered coffee and chattered about nothing of significance as they idly watched the pedestrians in the growing darkness.

'Would you like to make another wager?' said Ramses.

'I underestimated your magnetism last time,' David replied, laugh-ing. 'You are as adept as the Pied Piper, who lured away the rats of Hamelin.'

'Folklore, along with ogres and fairies. Patience may be a virtue, but it can be vexing. Where in damnation can Latif be? Bah, this coffee is vile!'

'He is across the street, unsuccessfully attempting to conceal him-self in a doorway. Your scowl must frighten him, Brother of Demons. You look as though you might rip off the head of anyone who comes within range.' David waved at the small figure crouched in the shad-ows.

Latif scampered between the cabs and carriages, and approached with a wary look. '*Masa el-kheir*,' he whispered, his eyes lowered re-spectfully.

'Good evening to you,' said Ramses. 'Have you seen or heard of anything that might be of interest to me?'

Latif nodded. 'I have been watching the shop around the corner from the museum. A young man, very nervous, with only a few whiskers on his chin, went inside with something wrapped in a kaf-fiyeh. It was this big.' He held his hands at shoulder width. 'When he came outside without it, I followed him. He bought fruit from a vendor, stopped at a corner to gossip with his friends and finally made his way to a building on the edge of the river. A big building, not so big as the Citadel of Saladin or Ismailia Square, but big. Shall I take you there?'

'You are a clever boy,' said Ramses. 'Please tell us more about the location of the building and what surrounds it.'

David beckoned a waiter. 'Bring this boy a glass of tea and a large slice of basbousa.'

'*Shukran*,' Latif said as he sat down. 'The building is near where the ships dock to unload crates. There are many warehouses, some of them vacant, some not. I saw the man go into one, but I dared not go near it. It is built of brick and the windows are covered with pieces of wood.' He licked his lips as the waiter put down the tea and pastry. 'I will be happy to take you there in only one minute.'

'Take your time,' Ramses said, amused by the crumbs already accumulating on the boy's ragged shirt. 'David, do you think we should retrieve this latest bust of Nefertiti before we visit Harun?'

'It could be the original, stolen by an apprentice,' David said with a shrug.

'I was merely wondering if we should add it to our collection. This apprentice would not have dared return to the workshop if he had taken it. On the other hand, he cannot be of exemplary intelligence. One would think Harun should have realised the steady depletion of the copies by now.'

'Unless Harun is responsible for sending the apprentices to sell the copies before we locate him. He was threatened by the Father of Curses, and surely is aware that the Brother of Demons is searching for him all over Cairo.'

'Along with the Master Criminal,' Ramses said glumly. 'Latif, has anyone else been inquiring about the location of Harun's workshop?'

'My friend Saleem told me that he was stopped by a tall man with a great, bushy beard who was looking for Harun. Saleem was frightened and ran away. He is a coward. I would have kicked the man before I ran away.'

Ramses gazed at David. 'I'm not surprised that Sethos is as eager as we to find this workshop and lay his hands on the original bust. He was in the alley behind the German embassy when we exited with all due haste. He must have believed that Gunter possessed it, and was plotting to steal it when we upstaged him.'

'He did not attempt to take it from us,' David commented as he lit his pipe. 'He had a gun, after all. He could have forced us to stop and . . . well . . .'

'Were it not for his inexplicable adulation of my mother, he probably would have done so. Now we are one step ahead of him. It is not too far to the Egyptian Museum. I suggest we go to the tourist shop and purchase the bust. If it is the original, then we may be able to catch the night train. If not, then we proceed to the warehouse to deal with Harun. Latif, we will require your services for the next few hours. You will be rewarded generously for your ingenuity.'

'*Shukran*,' Latif said cheerfully as tea dribbled down his chin. 'I am ready.'

Ramses paid the bill. To the lad's delight, they took a carriage to the shop, and then went inside. The proprietor cringed when Ramses nudged aside the tourists and approached.

'*Masa el-kheir*, Brother of Demons,' he whimpered. 'I am most grateful for your presence in my unworthy shop. Please tell me how I can accommodate you.'

'Produce the bust of Nefertiti that you purchased earlier.'

'I do not know of what you speak. I have a very fine shabti from the tomb of Taharqa. May I show it to you?'

Ramses spread his hands on the counter and leaned forward. 'I am not in the mood to listen to your evasions. Bring me the bust or face my fury!' Once the bust was placed on the counter, he growled in frustration. 'Now we possess three copies, damn it! You can see where the apprentice nicked her throat. He attempted to patch it with plaster and repaint it, but it is flawed.'

'Take it,' begged the proprietor. 'It is rubbish, and I must protect my reputation. Please let me wrap it for you, Brother of Demons.'

David had bent down to examine the nick. 'Only you would notice it,' he said as he straightened up. 'If we are to take this damn thing, we need a bag. Surely one can be found in the back room.'

'That's right,' Latif said, his thin arms crossed. 'Bring us a bag or the Brother of Demons destroys you! I promise there will be blood!'

Ramses and David exchanged grins as the few tourists idling in the shop stampeded for the door. The proprietor mumbled under his breath as he searched behind the counter for a bag and reluctantly produced one. Ramses demanded to know how much he had paid for the forgery.

'It is yours. I want nothing to do with it – what I paid does not matter. Just take it, Brother of Demons.'

'Then I will pay for the scruffy bag,' Ramses said, dropping a few coins on the counter. 'Had this been the original, I would have had you arrested for dealing in stolen antiquities. That is, as you must know, illegal.'

Latif insisted on carrying the bag as they left the shop. 'Now we go to the warehouse, yes? If someone attempts to attack us, I will kick him so hard that he will howl from pain.'

David flagged down another carriage. 'You will have to give the driver directions, Latif. Once we have identified the warehouse, you must remain in the carriage and take this bag to my cousin's apartment. I will write down the address for you.'

The carriage wound through increasingly bleak and narrow streets as Latif gleefully shouted instructions. After a quarter of an hour, he told the driver to halt. 'This is where I stopped. The building is just around the corner. I want to come with you, Brother of Demons! I am small, but I am strong and quick.'

'Yes, you are,' Ramses said gravely, 'but you have an important assignment, which is to take this bag to a place where it will be secure. Here is some money if you have to pay anyone to store it, and the rest is for you.' He handed a handful of coins to the boy. 'I am sure we shall meet again, Latif. Show the address to the driver and keep your head down.' To the carriage driver, he said, 'I will pay you now, but if you fail to take my prodigy to his destination, I will find you sooner or later to discuss the matter.'

'*Aywa*,' the driver said nervously. 'I will do as the Brother of Demons requests.'

Latif sighed as he sank back against the cushion. Ramses and David exited the carriage, waited until it drove away and went around the corner. The warehouse loomed in the darkness, but glimmers of light escaped through the boarded windows. As they approached, they could hear steady clinks, indicative of chisels on limestone. They moved stealthily to the nearest window to peer into the interior. The only furnishings in the vast room were a long table and half a dozen stools.

'I see Harun, that bloody bastard,' said Ramses, 'and three apprentices. What I do not see is the bust of Nefertiti.'

'Nor do I, but it has to be there. Otherwise, we have wasted a great deal of time collecting forgeries – and being targets of gunfire and upsetting Mr Baehler. I have an unsightly bruise on my arm from the hypodermic needle. We are in debt to Sethos, which makes my stomach churn. Look! Harun has stepped aside. On the table there are two busts, distressingly similar. Shall we retrieve them?'

'With caution.' Ramses continued to a door and tested the knob. 'It is locked, and the door is sturdy. If we break through it, Harun may have time to snatch up the original Nefertiti and disappear through a back door. I am not inclined to waste more time searching for his next workshop. Let us circle the building.'

David had already reached the far end of the brick facade. 'I see no windows or doors on the side,' he said as he returned. 'If this was used for storage, there must be a large entrance where the crates were unloaded.'

They went to the backside of the building and located a set of double doors facing an alley. A rancid odour came from discarded food and rotting fish. The doors were flimsy and yielded when Ramses pushed them open a few feet. They slipped inside and crept into a dark corner.

'Do you see anyone other than Harun and his apprentices?' Ramses asked softly.

'I do not see an armed guard, if that is what you're asking. It does not preclude the possibility that one is sitting in the shadows.'

'True,' Ramses acknowledged grimly, 'but there is only one way to find out. Harun is fluttering around what must be the original Nefertiti. His apprentices are working on rough blocks of limestone. He has completed a skilful copy, worthy of his reputation as a master forger. I will circle around this way, and you go the other way. If neither of us encounters a guard, we can rush the table and grab the two busts. We can determine which one came from Thutmose's studio when we are in a more affable circumstance.'

David's teeth glinted in the darkness. 'And as for Harun? He has defied the Father of Curses and inconvenienced us. Is he to be punished?'

'He is an old man. I cannot cause him physical pain, but I will do whatever it takes to achieve our goal. Should he attempt to thwart us, he will do so at his own peril. You go left and I will go right. When I signal you, both of us will storm the middle of the room, bellowing like savages.'

David nodded and silently disappeared into the darkness. Ramses went in the opposite direction, his ears attuned for any sound other than the apprentices' murmurs and the incessant clinks of their chisels. Harun was offering harsh criticisms of their work, berating them for their slowness and lack of attention to detail. His reedy voice echoed in the vastness of the interior, as if it were a cavern.

Ramses stopped at what he felt was the optimum vantage point. He could see David across the room from him, crouched next to a broken crate. He took several deep breaths as adrenaline surged into his veins.

Harun would not be able to offer significant resistance. The three apprentices were no older than twenty, and had no motivation to risk physical violence in order to protect Nefertiti and her twin sister.

His hands clenched, Ramses let out a bloodcurdling cry as he ran towards Harun. 'You have insulted the Father of Curses, you wretched, snivelling dog! I, Brother of Demons, have come to seek vengeance in his name!'

'The Brother of Demons cannot be denied!' shouted David as he emerged, his face contorted into a grimace of ferocity.

Harun's jaw dropped. After a second of hesitation, he scuttled under the table. 'I meant no insult, no insult to anyone,' he screeched. 'Take her!'

The apprentices darted for the front door, babbling shrilly as they pushed one another aside. The bar on the door was thrown to the floor. They continued to scuffle as they opened the door and ran for the street.

'This is too easy,' Ramses said as he picked up one of the busts.

'I concur.' David grabbed the second one. 'Shall we be on our way?'

⚜

I WAS EXHAUSTED the next morning, my sleep continually interrupted by nightmares that featured an anonymous rider who bore down on me with the fury of a Valkyrie. Emerson, who had been repeatedly awakened by my outbursts, drained three cups of coffee without speaking. Fatima tiptoed out of the kitchen with our breakfast plates and mutely set them in front of us.

Nefret came into the dining room, gave me a hug and took her place at the table. 'What a horrid night,' she said. 'I can think of nothing pleasant to say about Miss Smith and Mr Dullard, both of whom are obnoxious. The episode with Absalom must have been terrifying.' She smiled wanly. 'And then, Aunt Amelia, you were haunted by bad dreams all night. I could hear your utterances through the wall, and the Professor's efforts to comfort you. I am so sorry I brought the Godwins into our milieu. Had I not been so angry at Ramses – if I had demanded an explanation from him – if I had not behaved so impulsively . . .' She wiped her eyes with a napkin. 'I hope Geoffrey is suffering in the underworld, rejected by Osiris and compelled to wander among the grotesque monsters and supernatural beasts!'

'With four of his brothers,' muttered Emerson. He looked at his plate with a puzzled expression. 'How did this appear?'

'Eat while it is warm,' I said. 'Nefret, my dear girl, you must stop blaming yourself. No one could have anticipated Geoffrey's dark side. Have you spoken to Herr Morgenstern this morning?'

'He continues to recuperate. I asked if he would like to have breakfast with us, but he declined and went back to sleep.' She spread butter and marmalade on a pita and began to nibble. 'I will encourage him to join us for tea.'

'An excellent idea,' I murmured as I sipped coffee and considered my next plan. 'Nefret, I will need you this morning at the excavation. I told the German girl, Liezel, that I would help her make arrangements to have von Raubritter's body returned to his hometown. Once I have interrogated her, it might be best for you to accompany her to Minya to deal with the authorities.'

Emerson banged down his coffee cup. 'I need Nefret at the site to assist with the photography. I cannot have her running little errands that very well might take up the rest of the day.'

'Shall I go?' I ask sweetly. 'Does that mean that you will accompany us, too?'

'Don't be ridiculous!' he sputtered. 'Morgenstern remains incapacitated. Until he regains his senses, which might take weeks or months, I am in charge. You have promised to remain at my side until the fifth – and I hope last – assassin has been rendered harmless.'

'I will instruct one of the cabin stewards to restrain Herr Morgenstern,' Nefret said without enthusiasm, 'and go with Liezel to deal with the preliminary paperwork. Selim and I can discuss the best placement of the cameras and reflective screens when we first arrive at the site.'

Emerson's brow was furrowed, but he merely rumbled under his breath. I retreated to our cabin, changed into my practical clothing and went to the kitchen to have a word with Fatima about nourishment for our unwanted houseguest. Emerson and Nefret had already disembarked and were waiting for me at the end of the pier. Daoud followed me closely as I joined them. I suspected, given the opportunity, he would be breathing down my neck the rest of the day. He would not.

Selim was supervising the workmen when we arrived at the site of Thutmose's studio. Mr Buddle had found a sheltered spot in which to observe and take notes. I was eager to speak to him about the grisly events of the previous evening (and about the card we had found in Absalom's pocket), but I concluded it could wait. I turned around abruptly, nearly stepping on Daoud's toes. 'I need you to go to the workmen's camp and bring back the German girl, her luggage and all the possessions of von Raubritter. Leave the tent and camping equipment for the workmen. Do be polite, please, but if she resists, be gentle. Emerson is nearby, so you need not be concerned about my safety.'

I could see the displeasure in his expression as he stalked towards the path that led to the collection of tents and temporary huts. Nefret and Selim were engaged in a spirited disagreement about the reflective screens. Emerson squatted in the sand, examining a shard of pottery, while Abdul flittered nearby. Had Ramses and David been present, I would have deemed this to be the paragon of archaeological harmony.

SIXTEEN

From Manuscript H

'AREN'T WE CLEVER?' said David as he, Ramses and Tahir drank tea in Tahir's sitting room. 'We now have five busts of that blasted queen, comprising four forgeries and the original – unless it is a perfect forgery.'

'It is the original. The other one is an exemplary forgery with only two nearly indistinguishable flaws. Harun's work merits his reputation.' Ramses winced. 'I estimate their collective weight to be more than two hundred pounds. Miss Annabelle Hadley's steamer trunk may prove inadequate for such an onerous load.'

'Do you speak of Queen Nefertiti?' Tahir gasped. 'I have heard rumours . . .'

'Everybody has heard rumours,' Ramses retorted coolly. 'I heard a rumor that Howard Carter has sworn to find Tutankhamen's tomb within the decade. He is more likely to find mummified cats.' He turned to David. 'I have wrapped each bust with towels, newspapers, and our clothing. It may take us hours to transport the trunk from here to the train station.'

'Which gives that bastard Helmut Gunter all day to find us. He will have his thugs at the train station, as well. It will be a bit of a challenge to fend them off while struggling with the trunk. Latif will not be an adequate bodyguard.'

'I will come with you!' Tahir leapt to his feet.

'Thank you.' Ramses tugged on his chin as he contemplated the dilemma. His foes would be armed with hypodermic needles as well as brawn. Based on David's recollection of his attack in front of Shepheard's Hotel and the number of armed guards surrounding the embassy when he had been rescued, there could be as many as a dozen of them. 'I am going to recruit a large number of men to accompany us. David, you must stay here on the off chance that Gunter has discovered where we are. Defend the door with a footstool. I shall be back in time for us to take the night train.'

'How do you intend to find these recruits?' asked David, eyeing the footstool with doubt.

'I shall think of something,' Ramses replied loftily as he left the apartment and walked down the sunlit pavement to a café frequented by locals. He selected an outdoor table, ordered coffee and pensively watched the pedestrians. When Latif appeared, not unexpectedly, Ramses gestured for him to sit down. 'You did an excellent job of delivering the parcels as instructed,' he said with a smile. 'Order whatever you would like.'

'Thank you, Brother of Demons. What else can I do for you? Are there more parcels to be found in Cairo? I can go to every shop that sells fake statues to tourists. There are so many shops that it may take me all day, but I will gladly do it for you.' He stopped and looked at the menu written on a chalkboard. 'As soon as I finish eating, anyway.'

'I do have another mission for you, but only after you have enjoyed your meal. I want you to spread the word among the able-bodied men in the area that I, Brother of Demons, will pay five pounds English to the man who best assists me to transport a trunk to the train station this evening. Everyone else who protects us will receive handsome baksheesh.'

'Five pounds! That is a fortune. I will do it for one.'

Ramses maintained a sombre expression. 'That is kind of you, but I still require at least a dozen . . . recruits. Tell them that I will remain here for an hour or more to enlighten them with the details. Now decide what you would like to eat and I will order it for you.'

LIEZEL HASENKAMP LOOKED exhausted as she emerged from the path that led to the workmen's makeshift campsite. She carried a worn suitcase. Daoud followed her, laden with von Raubritter's luggage and paraphernalia. I beckoned to her, and when she joined me, said, 'I hope Daoud did not disturb your rest, but it is imperative that you begin the ordeal of paperwork at the police station in Minya this morning.' It did not seem prudent to add that decomposition was a major factor. 'The authorities here are unlike their German counterpoints; they move ponderously and require everything to be done in triplicate. I have asked my daughter Nefret to accompany you.'

'*Danke*,' she said dispiritedly. 'I was unable to sleep last night. What happened to my dear Eric was so vile, so pointless. He would never have done anything to harm another person. Why would someone do such a thing to him?'

'We are doing our utmost to bring the villain to justice,' I said. 'Why don't we sit down in the shade so that we can talk about it?'

Liezel blotted her eyes with a sodden handkerchief. 'I fear I can be of little enlightenment. Eric asked me to come here, so I did as soon as I could. I envisioned romance under the starry sky.' Tears inundated her eyes. 'I did not envision this tragedy, Mrs Emerson.'

I took her arm and steered her towards an oblong of shade from the wall of a semicollapsed building. 'Would you like a drink of water?' I asked as I offered her my canteen. After she had done as I suggested, I replaced the cap. 'Dehydration is dangerous, even when the temperature is moderate. I am sure that you are aware of this, since you are a scientist. Precisely what field are you in? Scientific specialities range from agronomy to zoology.'

'I am a research chemist, as was Eric. We met at a laboratory in Darmstadt and became friends. Very close friends. We discussed marriage, but my parents were concerned because of my age – twenty at the time. I came here to this desolate place to tell Eric that I was ready to accept his proposal.' She bowed her head and began to sob.

She was highly emotional, I thought irritably. I would have preferred at least an element of Germanic stoicism rather than this propensity for weeping. I waited until she had calmed herself and proffered my little flask. 'Would you like a small sip of whisky, Liezel? It might help you retain your composure.'

'*Nein danke.* I must maintain a clear head at the police station. Since Eric and I were not married, I do not know if I have the legal right to have his body transported to Cairo and then Germany.'

'Surely the German embassy will be of help.'

'That is true. I have met the ambassador, who seems to be an affable man. I shall telegraph him if I cannot persuade the local police to cooperate. He will have contacts with the Egyptian authorities.'

I was relieved that her innate self-control had asserted itself, at least temporarily. She sounded as though she could go into battle with the ambassador and the government bureaucrats. 'When did you meet the ambassador?'

Liezel pursed her lips as she thought. 'Several months ago. He and an entourage of German officials that included ambassadors, high-ranking military officers, aides and attachés toured the laboratory and made inquiries about the research projects in various departments. Ours was of nominal interest, since it is in a very preliminary stage. They were more enamoured of those with potential military applications. I am worried that some of it will be used in the near future. There is great unrest in Germany and other European countries.'

'Yes,' I said with a grimace. 'It is unfortunate that countries are ruled by men, who are contentious by nature. From birth they take great pride in stroking their egos by evincing superiority in all matters, including the most trivial ones. If women were in charge, they would sit down and negotiate rather than declare senseless wars that result in mutilation and death. They would do so over tea and scones.'

'But they are not in charge and most likely never will be.' She stood up and brushed the sand off her skirt. 'I have enjoyed our conversation, Mrs Emerson, but now I must square my shoulders and face the arduous ordeal awaiting me.'

'Come along and I will introduce you to Nefret. Despite her delicate countenance, she is not only fluent in Arabic, but also formidable when dealing with the bureaucracy. I don't recall that you told me your specific area of research, Liezel.'

'Eric and I were experimenting with methylenedioxy-based compounds to ascertain if they might be of use in the control of abnormal bleeding. The lab rats' behaviour has been erratic and unpredictable, so we have been unable to test it on human beings. Thus far we have failed to find a safe, functional application.'

I was unable to comment, since I had no idea what she was talking about. Such occurrences rarely happen, but my command of convoluted chemicals was negligible. 'Here is Nefret. I have told her of your situation and she will gladly help you. She is a medical doctor. Perhaps you and she can discuss your research at some time during the day.'

I introduced them, and then said, 'Nefret, please take Liezel to the dahabeeyah so that Fatima can prepare her a proper breakfast. Afterwards, the cabin steward will take you across the Nile to Minya. Daoud will follow shortly with von Raubritter's luggage.' Once the girls were out of earshot, I joined Daoud. 'Are these all of his possessions?' I felt as if I were a salivating crow that had landed on a succulent carcass. I struggled to restrain myself from flinging open the suitcase.

'I left the tent and camp equipment for the workmen's wives,' he said stiffly. 'I could hear them squabbling as we left. Everything else I have brought to you, Sitt Hakim.'

Items of clothing had been stuffed in the suitcase without regard for organisation. The notebooks I had seen in the tent were at the bottom of the mess. I made a mental note never to allow Daoud to pack for me in the future, should a hasty exodus be necessitated. I took out the notebooks and sat down on a stone to peruse their contents. Some of them were filled with scribbled chemical formulas that were incomprehensible. Others had amateurish sketches and diagrams of the dig site and its surrounding structures, with notations about discoveries of insignificant shards of pottery. Von Raubritter had been diligent, if ineffective. The last notebook comprised a journal. I retreated to the shade to study it.

It was written in German. My fundamental aptitude in foreign languages includes French, Spanish, Italian, Greek, Arabic, Hebrew, Aramaic and of course Egyptian hieroglyphs. Although I am able to (haltingly) read Egyptological works in German, I have never taken to German with keenness because I find it to be unpleasantly guttural. If I were to devote hours to translating the journal, I could make limited headway with it. However, my brilliant husband was semifluent in all languages imaginable. I closed the journal and ascertained his location in the middle of Thutmose's studio. Without turning, he sensed my advance.

'Peabody,' he boomed with enthusiasm, 'we have come across the most remarkable discovery – a sealed chamber beneath the floor! It may contain sculptures like statues of Akhenaton and his six acknowledged daughters, or a portrayal of Kiya, mother of Tutankhamen.'

'Why would Thutmose not have placed the bust of Nefertiti in this serdab?'

Emerson shrugged. 'It is challenging to understand the motives of an eighteenth-dynasty artist. Perhaps he felt an imminent threat and did not have time to store the bust in the serdab, or intended to take it with him when he fled.'

'Reasonable explanations,' I said, nodding, 'worthy of the greatest Egyptologist of the century.' I realised that he was ecstatic about the prospect of opening the serdab; his sapphirine eyes shone with the intensity of lighthouse beacons. Translating von Raubritter's journal would be noticeably less intriguing than a potential trove of flawless sculptures. 'How soon can you open it?'

'Tomorrow morning, if all goes well. The workmen are removing the sand on and around the lid, which is composed of a very heavy slab of stone. It must be relocated with precision so that the contents are not imperilled. Let me show it to you, Peabody.'

'I am eager to see it, but I require a bit of assistance first.' I handed him the journal and explained my inability to comprehend all but the basic vocabulary and structure. 'This may help us determine why von Raubritter came here – and why he was murdered.'

His indecision was painful to observe. The prospect of uncovering a stash of masterpieces by a renowned sculptor was aphrodisiacal. Translating a journal to search for clues to the identity of a murderer fell in the realm of a pesky moral imperative. I could almost see a dark cloud forming above his curly black hair. (He had, as always, lost or discarded his pith helmet.)

'It will only take a few minutes,' I said soothingly. 'Selim is quite capable of overseeing the excavation. We cannot allow von Raubritter's death to go unpunished. Let us find a place to sit nearby, Emerson. You are the only person present who is capable of translating what may turn out to be of grave consequence.'

He snorted, but took the notebook from me, and we retreated to a location at a sensible distance from Mr Buddle's perennial perch. He plunked down in the sand, opened the notebook and flipped through the pages. I forced myself to stay silent despite the urge to demand that he commence to read.

'Tedious and boring,' Emerson muttered, 'but I will read it to you in its entirety. Try to stay awake, Peabody. The young man's prose, to be delicate, is constipated.' He began on the first page, and with only a few expletives when he stumbled across unfamiliar words, read the contents of the journal in a monotone.

To my dismay, there was no reference to past interactions with Morgenstern. Once in Cairo, von Raubritter had gone to the Department of Antiquities and presented himself as an amateur archaeologist. Maspero had suggested Amarna and made a furtive reference to Morgenstern's eccentric behaviour. Von Raubritter was excited (although he failed to elaborate why). After he arrived at Amarna, he learned of Morgenstern's absence. The workmen were in a foul mood because they feared they would not be paid in a timely manner. Abdul, the *reis*, was equally surly, as he had received limited instruction as how to pro-

ceed with the excavations. Von Raubritter had taken it upon himself to
coerce them to return to their jobs (despite his lack of education and
expertise in the field, upon which he elaborated at tiresome length),
until Morgenstern returned to resume his position. Von Raubritter had
written a letter to Liezel, begging her to come and help him confirm
his qualms that their joint research had been used for nefarious pur-
poses. He did not mention how or why the drug had been utilised, nor
did he imply intimacy beneath the starry sky.

The remainder of the journal dealt with grievances about the food,
the insects, the hostile workmen, the impossibility of a decent bath and
the dearth of civilised companionship. When Dullard appeared after a
week, von Raubritter had attempted to question him about his relationship with Morgenstern, but had received nothing beyond an avowal of
camaraderie based on lingual compatibility and the missionary's interest in archaeology. Von Raubritter intended to question him again.

I do not take defeat with grace. 'So there are no comments about
Mr Buddle?' I asked Emerson, my fingers crossed that he had skimmed
over paragraphs that he deemed irrelevant.

'Nothing,' he said, gazing at the site as if it were a reincarnation of
Nefertiti seated on a throne. 'My dear Peabody, I must return to Thutmose's studio before some idiotic workman dislodges a corner of the
stone atop the serdab. You do understand how significant this may be,
do you not? I am distressed that Morgenstern will not be present at the
opening.'

I knew that he was not at all distressed, and in reality was frantic
to see whatever was to be found in the serdab, having excavated it to
his exacting standards. And he was not averse to claiming some of the
glory of discovering it. Although Emerson professes to abhor publicity,
he is aware that notoriety (of the virtuous sort) leads to prestige and
therefore more desirable firmans. I must admit I relished the praise and
accolades awarded to him. 'You must take charge of the excavation. I
shall sit and ponder what was revealed or pointedly excluded from von
Raubritter's journal.'

'You have a suspect?' His question was sincere, but he was already on his feet and staring beyond me.

'I must make a list of everyone's appearances and disappearances. We will discuss it when we stop to have luncheon on the dahabeeyah.' I looked up at his scowling face. 'Or tea,' I amended quickly. 'Nefret has taken von Raubritter's fiancée to Minya to deal with the bureaucracy. Once the arrangements have been finalised, Liezel will take the train to Cairo. She claims to have met the ambassador, so I presume that he will offer her a guest room in the embassy. Nefret should be back in time for tea.'

Emerson's brow furrowed. 'Then there will be three of us for tea. If you inadvertently or otherwise invite anyone else, Peabody, I shall remain at this site until dawn to protect its integrity.'

'You are referring to Miss Smith and Mr Dullard. I acknowledge they were not the most endearing of dinner guests. Miss Smith is annoying, but I see no indication that she is involved with this mayhem. I feel quite differently about Mr Dullard. I cannot explain why.'

'A premonition?'

'Do not mock me, Emerson. My premonitions are usually well founded and accurate. Well, accurate to a degree. Human behaviour is serendipitous, not easily foreseeable. I need to interrogate him without raising his suspicions.'

'By all means, Peabody,' Emerson said with a smirk. 'He is emerging from the cultivation. Tackle him, tie him to a tree, have a donkey sit on him until he squeals. In any case, do not invite him for tea!' On that emphatic note, he strode away briskly to resume supervision of the excavation of the underground chamber. I could only pray that he would not be devastated after the lid was removed.

'Mrs Emerson,' Mr Dullard began in his grating, high-pitched voice, 'I must have a word with you. I fear I became somewhat inebriated last night and behaved in an uncouth manner. I beg your forgiveness, yours and Professor Emerson's.'

'You saved us from what might have been a fatal encounter with the horseman. For that, I must offer my gratitude. Have you had the opportunity to speak with Miss Smith? She was, shall we say, agitated by the event.'

Mr Dullard shuffled his feet. 'I have not approached her dwelling. Although I was impaired by the excess of alcohol, I recall harsh words from her. Have I sabotaged our budding relationship, Mrs Emerson? Should I crawl to her on my knees and plead my case? Would such a gesture be futile?'

I shook my head. 'I have no idea if she will forgive you or not. She and I are not close confidantes, and we have not spoken this morning. You must make your own decisions, Mr Dullard – just like when you decided to follow Morgenstern to Cairo. Do you have any idea where he was going?'

'Why would you think I followed him to Cairo?'

'Linear ratiocination. When you went to the dig house with him, you saw the bust of Nefertiti. Perhaps he told you his plan to have a forgery made so that he could keep the original for himself. He was besotted with it, was he not? After he found transport across the Nile and went to the train station, you followed him.'

Mr Dullard's eyes narrowed. 'He needed protection from thieves. When we arrived at the station in Cairo, he ordered a cab to take him to the Deutsche Orient-Gesellschaft. I found an inexpensive hotel for the night, and the next morning spent a few hours purchasing small gifts for my Coptic friends before I departed that afternoon. As for the bust of Nefertiti, he did show it to me before he placed it in a carpet bag. I assumed he was delivering it to the German embassy.'

'He never went to the D.O.G.,' I said flatly, 'or the embassy.'

'Then I have no idea where he did go. I am only repeating what I heard him say to the driver.'

'You did not appear at this site for a week. Where were you, Mr Dullard? Are you certain you did not remain in Cairo to keep an eye on Morgenstern?'

'No, I did not.' Droplets of perspiration appeared above his thick black eyebrows. 'I went to Deir el-Mowass to deliver my gifts. The Copts were grateful and thanked me for my generosity. You are very inquisitive, Mrs Emerson.'

I smiled sweetly. 'My husband would be the first to agree with you. His workmen have come across a serdab in Thutmose's studio, and they are preparing to open it soon. You will find it most intriguing.'

His smile was sour, but he said, 'I am certain that I will. Good day, Mrs Emerson.' His copious beard was bristling as he walked into the glare of the sunlight.

I began to make a list of people's whereabouts, sprinkling it with question marks and exclamation points. Mr Buddle had been here in Amarna at the time of von Raubritter's brutal murder, as had Mr Dullard. Morgenstern had relocated himself to the dig house. Abdul was staying at the campsite, and had voiced unhappiness at von Raubritter's presumptive conduct. I could not overlook my trio of ne'er-do-wells: Mahmud, Asmar and Mustafa. Miss Smith was twittering in her mud hovel. I hesitantly wrote down Sethos's name. I had no idea if he was still in Cairo, methodically tracking down the location of Harun's current workshop, or had returned to Amarna in pursuit of Morgenstern.

Alas, not one of them appeared to have an ascertainable motive to murder the young German chemist. In retrospect, when he told Emerson and me that he desired to talk to us, I should have insisted that he accompany us immediately to the dahabeeyah. In his journal, he referred to the letter he had written to Liezel in which he suspected that their experimental drug had been abused. He had not hinted how it had come to Amarna. I drew a tidy row of question marks while I thought. Morgenstern's purloin of the bust of Nefertiti had taken place before von Raubritter's arrival, and I doubted that anyone had bothered to enlighten him. My head was beginning to throb. The throbbing intensified as Mr Buddle drew near me.

'Mrs Emerson,' he said, tipping his hat, 'I have heard what happened last night. In fact, I have heard several versions, but I found all of them appalling. Why would this rider attempt to cause you harm in such a brutish attack?'

'He was one of the assassins who have besieged us since our arrival in Cairo. We have been most fortunate to dissuade them thus far.' I took a deep breath, determined not to allow him to see my shivers as sickening images invaded my mind. 'What is most curious, Mr Buddle, is that the horseman had a card in his pocket – with your name printed on it. When I informed you earlier that another assassin had a similar card, you failed to react. I am amazed that you are still alive, since you are an easy target.'

He took out a handkerchief and blotted his face. 'I have told you of my dreary life. My parents ignored me, my siblings never included me in their outings and my teachers could not remember my name. There is no possibility that I might have offended anyone, not even inadvertently. I am much too boring to garner the attention of an assassin – and as you have opined, I am as vulnerable as a pigeon in the park. The only rational explanation for my name on the cards is that these scoundrels believe I might lead them to an invaluable artifact. Of course, they are deeply misguided.'

'How could they know your name? Even if they learned that you were here as an agent of Ridgemont, why would they believe that you were handling such artifacts? I find it curious that they have doggedly attempted to assassinate my son and me, while ignoring you.'

'I can offer no hypotheses,' Mr Buddle said apologetically. 'You seem to know much more than I about these murderous men. If you will excuse me, Mrs Emerson, I must find out what is intriguing your husband. At the moment, he is on his knees with a brush.'

'Before you go, please allow me to ask you about von Raubritter. You must have been perturbed that an amateur had seized oversight of the firman. That could not be in the best interest of your patron.'

'What was I to do? The workmen required supervision, and I certainly could not provide even meek commentary. Yes, I became aware immediately that the German lad was incompetent, but he did compel the excavation to continue. I anticipated the return of Morgenstern at any time.'

I frowned at him. 'You have no idea why Morgenstern departed in the middle of the night?'

'That missionary chap claimed that Morgenstern had left at the behest of a woman in Cairo. I did not believe this fiddle-faddle, but I was unable to refute it. When he returned, I noted his . . . strange behaviour. However, I am here as a discreet and unobtrusive observer. Mr Ridgemont will be delighted to learn that Professor Emerson is in control of the site. I really must position myself to see this new discovery.'

The only way I could restrain him from walking away would be to leap on his back, which was unthinkable. I may be forthright in speech, but I am the epitome of courtesy. On occasion Emerson has claimed that I am blunt and reckless; he has never suggested that I am oblivious to refined interactions with others. It is one of his more endearing traits (despite his strident and prolonged lectures in the aftermath of certain minor events).

I was eager to examine the serdab. Mr Buddle and Mr Dullard stood as closely as they dared, leery of intruding into Emerson's domain. The habitual suspects and fellahin hovered behind them. How the word had spread so quickly was an enigma, yet typical of the lower echelon of Egyptian workers and idlers. My shoe size was undoubtedly well known, as was Emerson's addiction to his morning coffee. Gossiping was integral to their society. That is not to imply that the residents of Shepheard's Hotel allow a minuscule faux pas to take place without long-winded, acerbic commentary and condemnation.

I nudged my way through the crowd. Emerson's hands were on his hips and he was gloating as he looked down at the partially exposed lid. Some of the workmen had been assigned to other areas of the studio, but they were glancing back surreptitiously to assess the progress. I squeezed Emerson's shoulder. 'How very exciting this is,' I murmured as I considered what might be exposed to daylight after more than three centuries interred beneath the sand.

'We may find nothing but rubble,' he replied stoutly. 'Thutmose could have used it as a garbage pit, but more probably, it has already been looted. However, thieves would hardly have replaced the lid with precision. Morgenstern was not the first Egyptologist to examine this site, and no one found it.' His eyes regained their sparkle. 'Sand has been accumulating for three thousand years. I envisioned the studio as it was then, and instructed the workmen to dig deeply. The clank of a shovel confirmed my expectation.'

'I share your anticipation, Emerson. If you do not object, I would like to return to the dahabeeyah to analyse my notes. Nefret and I look forward to hearing more about this when we have tea this afternoon.' I stood on my toes to kiss his cheek, and then made my way back through the crowd. As I walked towards the cultivation, I was not taken aback when I noted one of our loyal workmen trailing after me. Until the fifth assassin was exposed and disarmed, I knew Emerson would arrange for me to be escorted. I insisted that the man join me, and inquired, in Arabic, after his family, who resided in a tiny village north of Luxor. His litany of births, marriages and deaths kept us occupied until we reached the gangplank. I thanked him and sent him back to the site.

Fatima came out of the kitchen as I entered the drawing room. 'Please do not be angry with me, Mrs Emerson! I did not know what to do! Mahmoud had taken Nefret and the young lady to Minya and was not here to assist me. I am so sorry if I have done something wrong.'

I caught her trembling hand. 'To begin, I do not know what you have done. Let us sit down and discuss it over glasses of tea. I need a few minutes to freshen up, and then I will join you at the dining table.'

Fatima scurried into the kitchen. I retreated to the marital chamber to tidy my hair and wipe my face with a damp washcloth. The latter was not easy, in that the wash basin was cluttered with so many flower petals that I could barely penetrate them to achieve access to the water. When Fatima is peeved with me, she leaves no more than two or three petals on the surface of the water. I was curious to hear what she had done to evoke a bouquet.

I went to the dining room and sat down. Seconds later she came out of the kitchen with tea and a plate of biscuits. I smiled and said, 'Sit down, Fatima, and please tell me what is troubling you.'

'That man – that German man! I did not know what to do,' she said, her face sagging despondently. 'If only you had been here, Mrs Emerson.'

My jaw dropped in what must have been an unattractive visage. I took a deep breath, exhaled, and said, 'Did he . . . er . . . make crude advances of an amorous intent? Oh, my poor Fatima, how dreadful! I will speak to Morgenstern most harshly and forbid him to leave his cabin. Professor Emerson will be livid when he learns of this. I cannot foretell how forcefully he will admonish the cad.'

'No,' Fatima said, 'I have spoken badly. Soon after the girls left, he came into the kitchen and applauded my cooking. He was dressed in Ramses's clothing. I almost laughed because they were ill fitting and he looked comical. He informed me that he was departing but looked forward to dining here again.' She took a drink of tea. 'I could not stop him. He is big and loud. I dared not speak.'

One of Emerson's more colourful expletives slipped out of my mouth. My Readers must rely on their imagination, since decorum prevents me from recording it. Morgenstern, a stout German with hearty features, had become as ephemeral as a spectre at the top of a staircase in a derelict manor house. His frequent disappearances were exasperating, to say the least, and I briefly indulged myself in an image of him chained to a bed frame.

'Did he say where he was going?' I asked Fatima.

'To his house. I offered to make him a meal so he would not leave, but he claimed that he was eager to resume his excavation as soon as he changed into his own clothes.'

I patted Fatima's hand. 'You did everything that you could to delay him. At least he did not ramble on about stealing a camel and adventuring into the Eastern Desert for whatever motivated him previously.'

More expletives came to mind as I trudged through the cultivation and the expanse of sand towards the dig house. It appeared that Morgenstern had regained his sensibility, in the same way he had after we restrained him in the hotel room in Cairo. He was quite reasonable after he returned to Amarna, yet within hours had lost his sanity once again. I increased my pace, ignoring the dampness under my blouse. His erratic behaviour was linked to the dig house in an obscure affiliation. I knew that mouldy bread and spoiled meat led to indelicate bodily ailments (mostly because of Ramses's experiments in his youth; his conclusions do not require elucidation). Yet Morgenstern had not been plagued with such ailments; with the exceptions of his malnourishment in Cairo and the heatstroke brought on by his inexplicable jaunt into the desert, he had appeared to be robust. As a hostess, I should have visited him in the boys' cabin, but I had been much too angry to inquire into his recovery.

The door to the dig house was ajar. I knocked perfunctorily and entered the main room. 'Herr Morgenstern,' I called, 'I have come to assure myself that you are well.'

Thankfully, he was dressed in suitable attire. His beard and hair were neatly groomed, and his girth regained (from Fatima's delectable food). 'Mrs Emerson! I am delighted to see you. How are you this morning? Is it not a *schöner Tag*, a beautiful day?'

'Yes, it is. It is heartening to find that you have recovered from the heatstroke. Your temperature was perilously high when I found you at the Bedouin camp. Why on earth did you decide to go there?' I could not bring myself to mention his bout of nudity.

He scratched his head. 'I cannot recall any of that, I regret to say. It was imperative at the time, and I succumbed to the impulse. From what I have been told, you saved me from expiring in a tent in the desert. I shall forever be in your service. May I offer you a cup of tea?'

'Very kind of you.' I sat down and beamed at him. I had no intention of eating or drinking anything from his kitchen, but I did want to linger in order to ask more questions.

'Ach, there are only ashes in the fireplace and I have no means to boil water. Would you care for a cup of schnapps?' He picked up a bottle and took a gulp. 'I am very fond of schnapps. It warms the soul and stimulates the mind.'

'Does it?' I inquired gently. 'It has been suggested that it muddles the mind.'

'The English have their tea; the Germans have their beer and schnapps. I have happy memories of attending Oktoberfests in Munchen with my compatriots. We would drink litres of beer and sing of our beloved fatherland. We feasted on pretzels, bratwursts, bierocks and strudel.' He took another gulp of schnapps as his eyes watered. He thumped his chest and began to warble what I surmised was the German national anthem, interspersed with belches.

I managed to retain an expression of admiration until he finally stopped. 'How stirring, Herr Morgenstern. You are very loyal to the land of your birth. This makes me wonder why you did not deliver the bust of Nefertiti to the Department des Antiquités, but instead took it to a well-known forger in order to have a passable replica made. Which one did you intend to keep?'

His eyes began to flicker. 'I was concerned that the Egyptian authorities would take possession of it and then store it in the basement of the Egyptian Museum. The beautiful queen deserves a place of honour in a German museum, where she can be cherished. My name would be on a brass plaque.'

'So you planned to offer the copy to the Department des Antiquités and smuggle the real one to Germany?' I was hard pressed to believe a word of it.

'Ja, that was my plan. Somehow I became confused and futilely searched the Khan el-Khalili for the forger's shop. I was unable to eat or sleep. I was outside Shepheard's Hotel because my mind associated it with comfort in the past. I do not know what would have become of me if you had not taken me inside.'

'Why did you not go to the German embassy?'

Morgenstern rubbed his temple with one hand while he utilised the other to take yet another drink of schnapps. 'I tried, Mrs Emerson, but I was dishevelled and my clothes were covered with filth. The guard at the entrance refused to allow me to pass. I have enjoyed our conversation, but it is now time for me to return to the excavation. I do not want Mr Ridgemont to conclude that I have been wasting his funds.' His voice dropped to a whisper. 'As you know, Mr Buddle claims he is here to protect his patron's investment, but in reality he is a spy for the Austro-Hungarian alliance. He has been sent by Franz Ferdinand himself in order to thwart further archaeological exploration until his empire seizes control of Egypt and all of North Africa.'

I blocked the front door. 'Herr Morgenstern, where did you learn of Mr Buddle's secret identity? I have seen no indication that he is any more than what he claims to be.'

He frowned. 'The scoundrel also works for the Ottomans. He is a nefarious double agent and a threat to your husband, as well as to me. When I find him, I shall beat him until blood gushes out of his mouth.'

He was in the grasp of paranoia, I realised with alarm. I gripped his shoulders and shoved him back into the room, uncertain that I could overpower him indefinitely. 'Herr Morgenstern, you must control these illogical feelings. Please sit down and allow me to rekindle the fire in order to make tea. Do you have a tin of biscuits?'

'Fatima made me a plentiful breakfast, so I have no desire for biscuits. We must hurry to the site before Buddle escapes with more precious artifacts. He is armed with a pistol. We must protect your husband, Mrs Emerson.'

'Well, yes, we must do something before there is more bloodshed,' I murmured, overwhelmed with a sense of helplessness. I felt a stab of sympathy for Fatima, who had found herself in this same situation. Morgenstern was bigger and stronger than I. He was delusional and paranoiac, a combination that might lead to a disastrous confrontation. The only element I found of some comfort was that he was not undressing while he blustered. 'Listen to me, Herr Morgenstern. You know that Emerson and I are your friends, and we will act in your best interests.'

He staggered forward, put his hands on my shoulders, and gave me a prolonged kiss on my lips. Ignoring my huff of outrage, he went out the door and began to run in the direction of Thutmose's studio. I could hear him chortling as I fought to regain my composure. There would be a scene of some sort, I thought with a sigh, although Buddle was in more danger than Emerson. I had no theory why Morgenstern had arrived at his wild accusations. I asked myself if I could have misjudged Buddle and failed to discern that he was a fanatical spy employed by the Austro-Hungarian and Ottoman empires. It did not seem probable. My next question was what to do. By now, Morgenstern was approaching the site and was focusing on Buddle, whom I hoped was positioned near Emerson. A melee might ensue, but my beloved husband would restrain Morgenstern before he carried out his intention of thrashing his illusionary opponent.

Pleased with my scenario, I turned my attention to the dig house. There were dusty tins of biscuits and potted meat in a corner of the counter. I did not find mouldy bread or spoiled meat and vegetables, thus negating my conjecture that Morgenstern had eaten something that affected his mind. My eyes narrowed as I looked at the bottle of schnapps. I took a sniff and did not perceive a peculiar redolence unless one considers peppermint flavouring to be abnormal. Prudence and a slight twinge of nausea dictated that I not taste it. I went into the bedrooms and the room he utilised as an office. The decor consisted of clutter everywhere; books, notebooks, stray papers and discarded clothing covered the floors. The ultimate room, reputedly for storage of artifacts, was secured with a padlock. Prudence departed. I stepped back and kicked the door with all the force I could muster. To my surprise, the bolt buckled and the door loosened from its hinges. A second kick freed it completely. My only regret was that I had no audience – even my son would have been impressed.

Crude shelves dominated the small space. On them were shards, pots, fragmented sculptures and the artifacts that von Raubritter had told us about during our first encounter. Everything was neatly labelled with a date and a location. Borchardt and Morgenstern had followed the canons of archaeological dictates. However, I doubted that Borchardt, before his departure due to a family crisis, had stockpiled a case of schnapps. Morgenstern was well prepared for the entire season. I could not recall any rumours that in the past he was unable to function in a professional manner because of his fondness for alcohol. (Egyptologists have been known to gossip, too.)

I decided not to attempt to reposition the door to the depository. There were no artifacts of great value. Arabs abstain from alcohol, so none of the workmen or idlers would be tempted to steal the case of schnapps. I fastidiously closed the front door, gazed in the direction of the site and then walked back to the dahabeeyah. Emerson could compel the retreat of a horde of barbarians merely by raising his voice, often described as thunder in the sky. It has been said that he could part the Red Sea if motivated. When I suggested as much, I was treated with a lengthy tirade about the historical inaccuracies and skewed mythology in the Bible.

Fatima was standing by the gangplank. 'Is all well, Mrs Emerson? Have you reasoned with that German man? I do not think the Professor will welcome him back to the site.'

'I did the best I could,' I replied. 'I was unable to thwart him, but I am confident that Professor Emerson will do so handily.' I continued into the salon, feeling inadequate. 'I would like a light meal, whatever is easy. I am going to the top deck to study my notes.' Although it was not yet midday, I detoured to our cabin and changed into a loose robe and slippers to relax in the breeze. I would, of course, put on a fetching tea gown before Nefret and Emerson appeared, but my sharpest cognitive acuity arose when I had no restraints from my usual (and often necessary) work attire.

When Fatima came up the steps with a tray, I thanked her and said, 'Did anyone pay a visit to Herr Morgenstern while he was recovering here?'

'Nefret made it clear that no one was to enter the cabin except Mahmoud, who brought trays of food and retrieved them later, and one of the girls to change the linen. That Englishwoman with the makeup of a . . . woman of ill-repute came by this morning after you, Nefret and Professor Emerson had finished breakfast and left. I told her that she could not visit that man. She cried, but I was stern.'

Miss Ermintrude de Vere Smith (a rather silly name, in my opinion) was no match for Fatima, who could stare down a charging bull. Emerson has been known to blink during confrontations with her. I have told him numerous times that tact was more effective, but to no avail. 'Did Miss Smith tell you why she wanted to see Herr Morgenstern?' I inquired.

'Only that she was concerned about his health. I told her that he was recovering and that she could not come further onto the deck.'

After Fatima left, I picked up a cucumber sandwich and nibbled pensively. I could think of no reason why Miss Smith would evince concern for the patient. To the best of my memory, they had exchanged few words. Had she concluded that Mr Dullard was no longer a viable suitor and had turned to Herr Morgenstern to replace him? The idea was so befuddling that I opened my notebook and drew an arrow with a question mark. Emerson, who abhorred romantic trivia, would not deign to debate the possibility. Nefret had met all three players in the love triangle, and might relish the opportunity to speculate with me.

I finished eating the sandwich, took a sip of tea, sank back into the pillows of the divan and succumbed to a nap.

SEVENTEEN

From Manuscript H

TAHIR PEERED OUT the window that fronted the street. 'There are dozens of men on the pavement, muttering to one another and frightening women who are burdened with bags and children. Are these the recruits you spoke of, Brother of Demons?'

Ramses nodded, having conceded that Tahir could never bring himself to use a more familiar form of address. 'Yes, but they are early. We do not want to arrive at the train station two hours before our departure. That will be our most vulnerable time, and we cannot rely on Gunter's rogues to duplicate Cromwell's fatal attempt to avoid being apprehended. Tahir, please go downstairs and remind my so-called recruits that I specified five o'clock.'

David waited until Tahir hurried out the door. 'I commend your success in the art of inspiring otherwise useless layabouts to protect us. They will outnumber those sent by Gunter to repossess his bust of Nefertiti, which I assume he believes is the original. Should we give him one of the forgeries as a gesture of repentance?'

'He fired a gun at us,' Ramses reminded him, 'and kidnapped you. The only thing I would give him is a bag of camel dung. Forty pounds of it, well ripened.' He went to the window and looked down. 'Tahir has had no impact on the increasing number of our bodyguards, now up to about forty. There will be little space on the platform at the train station for innocent travellers. I wonder if Sethos will be among them.'

'You wonder?' David said sardonically. 'Of course he will, although one cannot predict how he will be disguised. By now he must know that we possess the original sculpture. He will be on the same train, dressed as a rabbi, a wild-eyed dervish, a stout matriarch or a Slavic musician with a violin case. In case you have forgotten, Aunt Amelia refers to him as the Master of Disguise, among other things.'

Ramses snorted. 'I will recognise Sethos despite his best efforts. We will be in the last carriage before the freight car. He will not be able to get past us to pilfer the trunk, and he will be conspicuous if he departs the train at our customary unscheduled stop before Minya. Once we have deposited the trunk on the dahabeeyah, we will alert our staff to be on the lookout for him. Should Sethos attempt to sneak on board, my father will welcome the opportunity to express his animosity.'

'That he will. I look forward to observing from a safe distance. You may be obliged to restrain Aunt Amelia, who has an inexplicable tenderness for Sethos. Shall we have a final look at the contents of the trunk to make sure all the busts are well wrapped? They may be subjected to jostling.'

'That is a mild description of what may happen,' Ramses replied as he opened the trunk and viewed the contents. 'Tahir's wife will be distraught if we appropriate her draperies, so this will have to do. Let us have a final glass of tea before we enter the fray.'

'I would prefer something stronger, but I have already checked the cabinets without luck. Tahir is clearly an observant Moslem, worse luck. All we can do is fortify the tea with sugar.'

They drank the tea in silence, made sure that all their personal belongings were in the trunk and each took a side handle. 'Two hundred pounds?' David groaned. 'It feels as though there is a pygmy hippo hidden under the wadded newspapers.'

'Once we get it down to the street, we can delegate it to the most muscular recruits. That will give us a better opportunity to watch for Gunter's thugs. Now stop whining and try not to drop your end.'

With frequent stops to put down the trunk in order to catch their breath, they made it to the pavement. The men swarmed them, shouting for the attention of the Brother of Demons. Many offered to carry the trunk alone in order to receive the five pounds Ramses had promised. Others displayed knives and lengths of chain as weapons of protection. Latif wiggled his way through them to stand beside the trunk, his arms crossed as if he were a stone guardian of the Temple of Karnak.

'Quiet!' Ramses shouted, standing on the trunk. He pointed at two of the largest men. 'You will carry the trunk. The rest of you will sur-round them on all sides and watch for anyone who appears suspicious. I do not wish for blood to be shed unless it is necessary. Once we are at the train station and the trunk is loaded into the cargo car, I will distribute baksheesh to all and the reward to the man I deem most helpful.'

Screeches erupted as everyone reiterated his desire to carry the trunk. Pushing and shoving evolved into fistfights, and a goodly num-ber of the men were splayed on the pavement, cursing their supposed comrades. Pedestrians retreated hastily, and nearby shop owners be-gan to move their wares inside.

'Is this the militia you desired?' David asked with feigned ingenu-ousness.

'Hmph!' Ramses stood on the trunk and bellowed, 'Listen to me, you sorry excuses for rabid hyenas! Only those of you who pay at-tention to my directives will receive money. You are here to provide protection while we transport the trunk to the train station, not to pummel one another. Do you understand me? Remember that I am the Brother of Demons!'

The men lowered their fists and closed their mouths, although their expressions were resentful. Ramses stepped off the trunk and instructed the designated carriers to assume their places. He, David and Latif led the unruly assemblage through grimy backstreets to the train station. The platform was crowded, but not unusually so. Ramses selected a far corner for his temporary stronghold and motioned to his followers. Along the way, some of the fellahin had faded away, but the majority, motivated by avarice (and perhaps by their fear of the Brother of Demons) formed a barrier surrounding the trunk.

Ramses scrutinized his fellow travellers, who were staring at him. No one appeared to be plotting an assault. He admitted to himself that he had spoken impetuously when he claimed he could recognise Sethos in even the most devious disguise. The majority of the men, clad in thobes and kaffiyehs, had moustaches and beards that concealed their lower faces; the women were dressed in modest abayas, their hair invisible under hijabs. The foreign tourists were easily identified by their ordinary clothing and sunburned faces. Professor Ambrose Doyle, one of Sethos's most recent personae, was not present.

David had taken two bodyguards with him when he went to purchase tickets. He handed one to Ramses and said, 'If Gunter is nearby, he has concealed himself well. I had a brief glimpse of one of the thugs who accosted me outside the hotel, and I have not seen anyone else who is vaguely familiar. Do you think we will board the train and be on our way without incident?'

'*Inshallah*,' Ramses answered distractedly, still scanning the faces of those on the platform. 'I am sorry we did not have an opportunity to send a telegram informing my parents of our arrival.'

'Well, I did while you went on your recruitment excursion. Tahir promised to barricade the door and arm himself with the footstool. Nobody attempted to break inside the apartment.'

'While you exposed yourself to Gunter's thugs! Damnation, David, they would have tortured you until you told them where to find the bust of Nefertiti. Rescuing you the first time was exhilarating, but I doubt I will continue to feel that way if it becomes habitual. I am embarrassed that Sethos concocted the scheme and delegated me to be his underling.'

'You could have been kidnapped as easily,' David retorted with a scowl. 'Unless you believe yourself to be invincible, of course. You have been captured on occasion, if I recall.'

'Minor mishaps,' Ramses said. 'Keep watching for the German minions, and do not forget that there remain two Godwin assassins. We seem to have acquired a remarkable number of evil-minded enemies. Any or all of them could be nearby.'

'A comforting thought. I will feel much more relaxed when we are on the dahabeeyah, drinking whisky and soda on the top deck while Daoud bashes intruders.' He turned his head. 'I hear the train, although it is some distance away. Have you figured out how you intend to distribute the baksheesh and the grand prize?'

'I am hesitant to pay the recruits until the trunk is in the freight car and we are prepared to board the train. My father is so intimidating that none of them would defy his orders and depart without completing the mission. I can barely prevent them from brawling with one another.' He paused. 'The train should be here within a minute. It is best that we move quickly to lessen the possibility of an attempted attack. Tell the men who carried the trunk to position it at the far end of the platform. Everyone else needs to continue surrounding them.'

The train pulled into the station, the brakes squealing, the carriages rattling. A cacophony of blather broke out as those on the platform jostled for position by the train doors. The conductors opened the doors and shouted for the crowd to back away in order for the arriving passengers to exit. No one listened.

Ramses took in a deep breath as the stationmaster slid open the door of the final car. He and the others were forced to wait as crates, bundles of planks, luggage and bulky boxes were removed and stacked on the platform. Once the job was completed, he instructed the men holding the trunk to put it in the car. They were struggling to hoist it when a dozen men, light-skinned and fair-haired, loomed in the doorway, armed with iron bars and knives.

'Gunter's bastards!' David shouted. 'They must have gotten into the freight car at the previous station. Defend yourselves, but do not allow them to seize the trunk!'

Ramses grabbed the leg of one of the thugs and yanked him out of the car. The resounding thump as the man hit the platform was most satisfactory. Ramses's bodyguards rushed forward to disable the others in a similar fashion. Fists, iron bars and knives were wielded randomly as arms and legs flailed. Expletives in German and Arabic reverberated across the platform, sending the would-be passengers into the sanctuary of the station house. Policemen rushed forward and began to separate combatants.

'Get the trunk in the freight car!' Ramses roared as he punched an assailant on the nose. Blood splattered on both of them. The man howled as he escaped into the crowd. Ramses jumped onto the ledge of the car and helped lift the trunk to safety. Gunter's men were scrambling to flee while the police ineffectually yelled that everyone was under arrest.

Latif joined Ramses. 'We have beaten them, Brother of Demons! Your trunk is safe.'

'Only when David and I are seated in a compartment and the train has left the station,' replied Ramses with a confidence he did not feel. He had not spotted anyone who might be Sethos incognito, but it was implausible that the Master Criminal had conceded defeat. The bust of Nefertiti would be of tremendous value on the black market. Private collectors were rich, greedy and bereft of scruples.

David was arguing with the police officers when he glanced up at Ramses. 'Watch out!' he yelled. 'Behind you!'

Startled, Ramses turned as Latif leapt onto the back of a man holding up a dagger. The man froze, giving Ramses the opportunity to kick him in a most vulnerable location. Latif screamed as he clawed the man's face with the fury of a cornered wildcat. The assailant staggered forward and began to fall towards the platform.

Ramses grabbed Latif at the last second and stepped away from the ledge. 'Your hand is bleeding,' he said as he examined the boy. He took a handkerchief from his pocket and wrapped it around the wound.

'It is nothing. That man was going to stab you. I could not let that happen after all that you done for me, Brother of Demons. I only wish that I had found a weapon to knock him in the head.'

'You are a loyal and true friend, and you have earned the five pounds English. I am worried that if the others learn this, you will be robbed before the train departs, and also, the Germans and their thugs will be looking out for you. Therefore you must come with us and enjoy our hospitality until I determine what is best for you. Do you agree?'

'I have never been on a train, but I will try to be brave. What will happen to me if I come with you?'

Ramses smiled at him. 'In this case, plentiful food and a safe place to sleep. Jump down and join David, who will purchase a ticket for you. Once the two of you are on the train, I will pay my recruits.' He dragged the trunk into a corner, climbed down to the platform, secured the freight car door and began paying the men. He ignored demands to acknowledge the recipient of the reward, stating only that he kept his promise. Some of the men were glowering as he hurried up the steps to the carriage.

Ramses joined David and Latif in the ultimate compartment. Two students were playing backgammon on a game board balanced on their knees. An elderly woman stared straight ahead, her arms wrapped around a basket on her lap. Ramses scrutinised them. The boys had flawless skin and brown eyes, and the woman was so diminutive that her shoes dangled above the floor. He sat down across from David, who had a grip on Latif's wrist.

'He wants to wave goodbye and tell them of his triumph,' David explained with a grin. 'We don't want any of the men to jump aboard at the last moment and come looking for him, or seek revenge for incapacitating their colleague. You must be alert at all times, my boy. "Uneasy lies the head that wears a crown." In your case, the crown is worth a small fortune.' He saw that the three passengers were gaping at him. 'Contrary to what you may think, the lad is not a direct descendant of King Henry IV of England. His fortune awaits the demise of his pudgy and unsightly patron, Lord Higginsnort, who made millions of pounds importing kumquats from India.'

Ramses rolled his eyes but remained silent as the train began to pull away from the station.

∾⋎∾

NEFRET AWAKENED ME with a kiss on my forehead. 'It is time for tea, dear. The Professor is stomping around the salon, frantic to return to the site and the serdab. What an exhilarating discovery! How could all of the previous Egyptologists have failed to discover it?'

I sat up and rubbed my eyes. 'Emerson has no peers in the field. He availed himself of his perspicacity, as always. We should go downstairs before he takes out his frustration on the furniture. He has a very bad habit of plopping down on innocent chairs, and then berating me for their frailty.' Eschewing a change of clothes in light of my spouse's state of mind, I hastily tidied my hair and washed my face before joining him.

Emerson made no effort to temper his frustration. 'I am in no mood to twiddle my thumbs while you nap on the top deck, Peabody. Nefret, did you rid us of the fraulein? There are too many stray people as it is.' He raised his voice. 'Fatima, we are ready for tea!'

Fatima was holding a tray as she stopped in the doorway. 'There is no need to shout at me. I know that it is time for tea. I have always known when it is time for tea. If you believe that I am unreliable, you are free to prepare it yourself.'

I refrained from returning to the top deck to bask in solitude. 'This looks delicious, Fatima. Please put the tray within reach of the Professor so that he can gobble down the cakes and sandwiches and return to the site.' After I had poured tea for Nefret and Emerson, I served myself and sat down.

'So what did I miss?' Nefret said as she took a sandwich from the platter. 'Did you make any progress with the serdab, Professor?'

'Not as much as I would have if that blasted Morgenstern had not appeared,' growled Emerson. 'The workmen are still angry with him, and they would have caused an uproar had the missionary fellow not dragged him away from the site. None of us could understand his gibberish. How did he escape from the dahabeeyah?'

I studied a sliced egg sandwich while I considered how best to explain without further upsetting him. 'He told Fatima that he was leaving and went to the dig house. I found him there. He was lucid when I arrived, but began to deteriorate rapidly. I was unable to detain him. I assumed that you could do whatever was necessary, Emerson, so I searched the dig house and returned to the dahabeeyah to think.'

'I may be able to help explain his behaviour,' Nefret volunteered. 'While Liezel and I sat on a bench at the police station, waiting interminably for someone from the German embassy to send a telegram authorising her to have the body transported to Cairo, I asked about her research. She and von Raubritter were experimenting with a drug that has a complicated formula but is commonly known as MDMA. Merck, a pharmaceutical company located in Darmstadt, has applied for a patent, despite the fact that the drug has no acceptable medical or therapeutic applications. It can, however, produce grave side effects. Many of the lab animals displayed confusion, memory loss and psychosis.'

Emerson laughed. 'Did these lab animals submit to psychoanalysis? Did they forget their names and addresses?'

'They dashed themselves against the bars of their cages,' Nefret replied stiffly, 'and were unable to navigate a familiar maze that led to food. Morgenstern has exhibited many of the symptoms. Liezel could not explain how he might have received doses of MDMA. Surely he would not have taken it voluntarily.'

I put down my teacup. 'Liezel told me earlier that the laboratory was visited by German military officers, ambassadors and assorted aides. One of them might have stolen some vials of it.'

'You suspect the German ambassador to Egypt?' Emerson scoffed. He can be quite sarcastic when he is in the grips of impatience. It is a reaction that I have almost given up attempting to mellow over the years.

'Well, no,' I was obliged to respond, 'and even if he were the culprit, how could he have dosed Morgenstern on so many occasions? The only constant in Morgenstern's life is peppermint schnapps. When I first encountered him this morning, he was rational but kept gulping from a bottle on the counter. He has a case of the vile stuff in the storeroom.'

'Someone might have tampered with the bottles,' said Nefret, abruptly putting her teacup aside.

Emerson swallowed a sandwich. 'You have rescued him too many times, Peabody. Should he decide to wander off into the desert again, or climb the bluff to frolic in the tombs, let him do so. The important thing is that he stays away from the site until the serdab is opened and the contents removed and catalogued. I do not trust him to behave in a professional manner.'

'We could bring him back to the dahabeeyah until he is no longer under the influence of that drug,' I proposed.

Nefret gave us a dimpled grin. 'That will make things crowded, since Ramses and David are taking the night train. David sent a telegram to the office in Minya requesting that the boat and Daoud meet them.'

Emerson's eyes brightened, but he hid his emotional response with a harrumph. 'Do they have the bust of Nefertiti?'

I felt a powerful outpouring of relief. I knew they had been in danger in Cairo, and in the past they had not proven themselves to take sensible precautions – if any at all. 'What matters is that they are safe and on their way here.'

'David's telegram was terse,' Nefret said. 'I have not laid eyes on this bust, and I don't give a whit about it.'

'If you had seen it, you might feel differently,' I said softly.

Emerson picked up the last of the sandwiches and announced that he was returning to the site. He was mumbling threats about thrashing Morgenstern as he left the room.

'Is there any way to test the schnapps?' I asked Nefret.

She shook her head. 'My clinic in Luxor does not have the equipment to do that, and it would take weeks, or even months, to mail a sample to the hospital in Paris and receive a response. I could drink a small quantity of the schnapps to see what effect it might have on me.'

'Absolutely not! I forbid you from considering it. I have observed the deleterious effect it has had on Morganstern, and I will not allow you to put yourself at risk. You are very dear to us, Nefret.'

'It was just a thought,' she said, giggling at the fierceness of my expression. 'Shall we go to the top deck and partake of something other than tea? I have had a wearisome day. Liezel burst into tears frequently, to the alarm of the police officers. She demanded to see von Raubritter's corpse. I tried to deter her, but she insisted, then fainted into my arms and had to be carried out of the makeshift morgue – which is cooled only by a fan and a very few blocks of ice. I was exhausted by the time she climbed on the train, with the luggage and coffin stored in the cargo car. The German embassy promised that someone would meet her at the Cairo station.'

'Eric was a nice chap,' I commented as we went up the steps. I told her about his journal and its reference to the drug. 'He did not clarify why he came to Egypt instead of . . . some other country whose ambassadors had been in the laboratory. He ended up in Amarna because M. Maspero repeated rumours that Morgenstern had been behaving strangely.'

Nefret made drinks and handed one to me. 'Liezel told me that he chose this country because he suspected the ambassador to Egypt or one of his attachés had stolen a quantity of MDMA. You told us that Ramses and David had an encounter with an attaché at the embassy. If he is the guilty party, how could he have put the drug in the bottles of schnapps?'

I gazed at the placid water of the Nile, awaiting inspiration. It eluded me. 'Mr Buddle has been monitoring the excavation since its inception. I shall ask him if anyone from the embassy visited the site and found reason to go to the dig house, but it does not seem probable. That leaves Buddle himself and Dullard, the hirsute missionary.'

'I cannot imagine Mr Buddle as a cheerful drinking companion,' Nefret said wryly. 'He is as rigid as a stela, and he may write his notes in hieroglyphs.'

'He could have gone to the dig house to ascertain that all the artifacts were properly listed, but that does not explain how he could have put this MDMA in the bottles of peppermint schnapps. Nor does it explain how he came to possess it. I suppose the attaché might have bribed him – or claimed that it was a vitamin supplement to keep Morgenstern healthy.' I recalled previous conversations. 'Buddle does not strike me as gullible or unintelligent. He is dedicated to defending his patron's financial investment.'

'That leaves Mr Dullard, who certainly can be congenial with adequate alcohol consumption. He and Morgenstern are friendly.'

'He admitted that he accompanied Morgenstern to the dig house after the bust of Nefertiti was uncovered. They surely celebrated. When Morgenstern came up with the idea of going to Cairo so that Harun could make a copy, Dullard followed him. He claimed that he did so in order to protect Morgenstern from thieves. After he heard his so-called friend order a cab to the Deutsche Orient-Gesellschaft, he said that he checked into a cheap hotel and departed the following day for Deir el-Mowass to present gifts to the Copts. We could attempt to verify that, but I am sceptical that we will hear the truth.'

'How did Morgenstern know about Harun?' asked Nefret.

I was reluctant to disenchant her, but I could think of no way to ignore her question. 'Many Egyptologists are aware of his skills. I cannot say whether or not any of them have used his services, but it is likely that a few museum pieces are forgeries. Emerson and I have heard rumours since we first came to Egypt. I would never malign our fellow Egyptologists by mentioning their names.'

'Morgenstern must have heard the rumours, too. Did he intend to keep the original?'

I shrugged. 'This morning I asked him, and it seemed as if he illegally wanted to keep the original and leave a copy in its place here in Egypt.

According to others, including Harun, he was more than passionate about the bust. He was obsessed with it.'

'So,' Nefret said pensively, 'Mr Dullard could have induced Morgenstern to drink schnapps and suggested the possibility of a duplicate. Dullard followed him to Cairo and then kept supplying him with laced schnapps. When you spotted Morgenstern across from the hotel, he was dazed and in horrific physical shape from wandering around the city without food or shelter. After he spent some time without access to the drug, he became rational, if confused about what had happened. Memory loss is one of the symptoms.'

'Yes, and when he returned to Amarna and surprised us at breakfast, he was fine. Then he took up residence at the dig house, and soon after that began to display bizarre symptoms again. That blasted schnapps!' I forced myself not to dwell on the unwise camel ride into the Eastern Desert. 'I am beginning to feel confident that Dullard is the culprit, but I cannot think why or how he got his hands on the stolen MDMA. What could be his motive for such sabotage?'

'To acquire the bust of Nefertiti, but he claimed to be an amateur enthusiast. On the other hand, Morgenstern might have chortled about its value on the black market. Dullard took a vow of piety. He may not have taken one of poverty, and he clearly did not take one of abstinence.'

'Or celibacy,' I added tartly.

Nefret's cheeks reddened. 'You don't believe that he and Miss Smith . . . ? I shudder to imagine it.'

'No, I do not, but their relationship was deepening, and might have led to an engagement. I cannot predict what might have occurred had that disastrous scene not taken place last night. This morning Dullard pleaded for my forgiveness for his inebriation. Miss Smith attempted to visit Morgenstern, but was thwarted and has remained in her mud hovel. I dearly hope she has been packing her belongings in order to depart to Minya and await the next steamer – or take the earliest train to Cairo. I have no problem with either of those options. She has been a source of headaches from the moment of her arrival.'

'Perhaps I should offer to help her pack,' Nefret murmured.

'In the morning, while I coordinate transportation across the Nile. She need not depart on a camel. Mahmoud and Abdul can carry her trunks to the pier, cross the river with her and settle her into a hotel. It has been a while since she has had the opportunity to bathe in hot water and sleep on a mattress, even if it might be riddled with bedbugs. When she is back in her cosy cottage, her cat settled in her lap, she can write of her thrilling adventures in the desert, living among the wild and exotic Arabs and Bedouins.'

'If you will excuse me, I would like to see the serdab. I will drag the Professor back here when it is too dark to continue work. Selim can post guards at the site overnight.'

I embraced her and sent her away. Despite the archaeological fever that Emerson's new find had sparked, I felt duty bound to find out who was behind the problems at Amarna and the source of Herr Morgenstern's erratic behaviour, and resumed perusing my notes. Dullard, I concluded, was the most likely candidate to have spiked the bottles of peppermint schnapps. Subsequently, he had followed Morgenstern to Cairo and continued to supply him with the wicked drug until his victim had slipped away into gloomy and dangerous alleys. What I could not explain was why Dullard had been provided with the drug in the first place. Morgenstern had shown no peculiarities until he had taken the bust of Nefertiti to the dig house to gloat over her serene beauty. Dullard had encouraged him to partake of the schnapps; therefore Dullard already had the drug with him. No one could have anticipated the remarkable discovery. The most perplexing question was why the attaché had given him the drug and for what purpose. I realised that I needed to visit the Coptic village, but I would have to wait until the morning.

I had a more compelling mission for now, which was to alert Fatima of the predawn arrival of Ramses and David. Our breakfast would be lavish, as well as lunch, tea and dinner in the foreseeable future.

EIGHTEEN

From Manuscript H

RAMSES WAS UNABLE to sleep despite the soothing rhythm of the train as it rattled through the darkness. The students were slumped in their seats, and although the elderly woman remained erect, she was snoring loudly. Latif was sprawled across David's lap; both were lost in their dreams.

Bored and a bit hungry, Ramses left the carriage and walked through several more to the service bar. It was closed. He remembered that David had put chocolate bars in a paper bag that was now in the trunk with their clothes and the five Nefertiti busts. As he walked back towards their carriage, he spotted a conductor dozing on a stool. He gently shook the man's arm and in Arabic said, 'Excuse me, but can you tell me how much longer it will be before we get to Minya?'

After a jerk, the man opened his eyes and took out a pocket watch. He squinted at it, and then said, 'Less than an hour, Brother of Demons, unless a herd of camels wanders onto the tracks. That will cause a delay. The engineer has been told of your presence and will stop at your usual place after Minya. Is there anything I can do for you?'

There were times when Ramses would have preferred anonymity, but in this case he was pleased that he would not be obliged to go to the front of the train to have a word with the engineer. He thanked the conductor. It would be more than an hour and a half before they departed the train. Loading the trunk and crossing the Nile to the dahabeeyah would require another hour. After the train had left the Cairo station, David had gone to the service bar to purchase wara ainab and shawarmas for dinner. Latif's appetite for the stuffed grape leaves and sandwiches had left his spectators in awe. There was not so much as a crumb on the floor of the compartment.

When Ramses reached the final carriage, he hesitated in front of the door that opened into the freight car. On dire occasions that had lasted for days, he had gone without sustenance, and his body had not suffered. He reminded himself of this as the notion of chocolate gave rise to salivation. The aroma might awaken Latif, but they could share the booty.

'What the hell,' he said as he entered into the total darkness of the freight car. He had a mental map of the car and went directly to Miss Annabelle Hadley's purloined trunk. Reminding himself to make sure it was returned to her in a timely fashion, he knelt and opened it. He felt around until he brushed the paper sack of chocolate bars. He congratulated himself as he placed it in his pocket, but then sat back on his heels. The contents of the trunk were not arranged as he remembered – and his memory was reliably sharp. The trunk had been carried on the eroded streets of Cairo, and then lifted onto the freight car. Its contents would have shifted, but not relocated. He removed the wadded newspapers and oddments of clothing. The five busts were aligned at the bottom. The wrapping paper had been loosened, and the canvas bag was agape.

No one could have tampered with the contents of the trunk while it was being transported, he thought with a scowl. It was obvious that someone had disturbed its contents since then, and that could only mean that the culprit had hidden himself somewhere nearby. Ramses had been too distracted by the assailants from the German embassy to search behind the cargo for a lurker. The identity of the lurker was obvious. Sethos had entered the freight car at a previous station, perhaps alongside Gunter's henchmen.

Which meant that Sethos was present.

Ramses returned to the corridor and entered his compartment. He stepped over the students' legs to reach his seat and then leaned forward to tweak David's nose.

Startled, David awoke and stared at him. 'What is wrong with you?' David whispered angrily.

Ramses was reluctant to disturb the other passengers, especially Latif. He motioned for David to join him in the corridor. When David vehemently shook his head, Ramses repeated the gesture and hissed, 'Sethos!'

It took David a few minutes to extricate himself from Latif's arm and shoulder without awakening him. As Ramses had done, David stepped gingerly over the students' extended legs as he made his way out of the compartment. 'What about Sethos?' he demanded. 'Did you go for a stroll and spot him in another compartment? Did he join you for coffee at the service bar? What the hell is going on?'

'There is no need to be grumpy because I roused you from a dream about Lia,' Ramses replied. He related what he had discovered when he opened the trunk. 'I have concluded that Sethos is hiding in there. That is intolerable, even if he has been unable to identify the original bust of Nefertiti because of the darkness. We must take action.'

'I agree with you. Do you have any ideas how to proceed? As you said, it is very dark in there. We will not be able to see him – and he is likely to be armed with a pistol.'

'I do not care if he has a rifle with a bayonet!' Ramses declared as he opened the door to the freight car. As soon as he and David had stepped inside, Ramses closed the door and listened for a faint intake of breath. He had not expected the Master Criminal to expose his location so easily. The blackness was absolute. Reluctant to grapple with the oversized crates and luggage, since Sethos could track his and David's movements as they prowled, Ramses opted for a straightforward approach. 'Sethos, we know you are here! Eventually we will find you, and if necessary, drag you by your heels out of your hiding place. There is no need for any of us to crawl through spiderwebs or encounter scorpions. Well?'

'I care for neither spiderwebs nor scorpions,' said a voice from a back corner. 'I shall join you at the trunk. Your mother will be annoyed when she finds out that you stole it from the storeroom at Shepheard's Hotel.'

'We borrowed it,' David retorted loudly, 'and we will send it back as soon as it has been unloaded. Its owner will not have missed it.'

Ramses took David's arm and guided him to the trunk. He heard Sethos's padding footsteps approaching. 'There are still five busts at the bottom of the trunk, which implies that you were unable to identify the original.'

'Alas, that is true. The German hooligans allowed me to climb into the freight car with them when I gave them a generous bribe. After a cordial chat about the weather and such, they robbed me of my shoes, the remainder of my money, an electric torch and an exceedingly fine silk handkerchief from China. I retreated to a corner and they ignored me. Had they not taken my electric torch, I would have detected the original bust without hesitation. However, I did rule out three of the forgeries, and I knew you would notice the weight difference if I absconded with the other two.'

'I would have noticed the weight difference if you absconded with a pair of socks,' said Ramses scornfully.

Sethos chuckled. 'You think very highly of yourself, do you not, Higginsnort? If you could see me, you would realise that I am waggling my finger at you. Tut, tut, my boy! And this is a chance for you to see me as I really am. I did not feel it necessary to disguise myself, since I did not anticipate an encounter with you and David. So what do you intend to do with me?'

Ramses bit his lower lip to refrain from blurting out one of his father's more outrageous expletives. 'We could force you out to the corridor, where there is a dim light. Once we have studied your countenance, we will turn you over to a conductor who will demand to see your ticket. You will be detained until the train reaches the station at Minya.'

'A worthy proposal,' David said. 'Aunt Amelia and the Professor will be most interested in hearing a detailed description of you.'

'But not likely,' replied Sethos from the opposite side of the freight car. 'Give them my best wishes for a fruitful season.'

The sliding door opened, but there was insufficient light to see more than a silhouetted figure against the starlit sky. The figure paused, straightened his back and then vanished.

'Do you think he survived?' David said as he went to the door and looked down. 'I do not wish to feel guilty that we coerced him into a fatal plunge.'

Ramses slid the door closed. 'The train has been slowing down because of a curvature in the tracks. Sethos must have sensed it as well and chosen the moment. He has solved one problem, but if he was telling the truth, he has no shoes or money. It will be a long walk to Minya.'

⚘

OVER DINNER, EMERSON, Nefret and I had a lengthy conversation about Morgenstern and Dullard. The conversation did not begin until the dessert course was served, since Emerson could not contain his excitement about the serdab and carried on nonstop throughout the aperitifs and the entrée. It had been some time since he had been so endowed with enthusiasm, and I enjoyed watching his eyes glitter and his hands slice the air as he speculated about what might be revealed. I did not make an effort to divert him until he subsided and allowed me to offer my theory and expound upon it. Although I acknowledge the concept of coincidences, I emphasised Dullard's timely opportunities.

'Then you agree that he is responsible for sneaking the drug into the bottles of schnapps?' I asked Emerson.

He stroked his chin while he considered the question. 'Yes, Peabody, you must be right about this. What's more, that bl— blasted missionary was forced to murder von Raubritter to prevent him from confiding in us.'

'But we have no proof,' Nefret pointed out. 'No matter how hard you try to persuade the police of the logical explanation of Dullard's culpability, they will not act on it. They are dim-witted and lazy. Having spent the day with them, I can assure you that my assessment is accurate.'

I sighed. 'It is true that we have no proof. Our best chance is to go to the Coptic village to question its inhabitants, but they may be reluctant to speak freely about him. To them, he is a godly man filled with evangelical spirit.'

Emerson banged down his brandy snifter. 'Do not even think about going to the village, Peabody! I have asked you innumerable times not to wander off on your own. Has it slipped your mind that one assassin remains? Absalom followed us here, and there is no credible reason why the fifth brother would not have accompanied him. You are in danger whenever you are not within my sight.' He retrieved the snifter and took a gulp. 'Besides, I need you and Nefret to be present when we uncover the serdab and remove its contents. This will take us days.'

'But we must find proof of Dullard's guilt,' I protested. 'I will awaken early and be back here in time for breakfast.' He crossed his arms and gave me a steely look. 'The Copts might not confide in an unknown person, especially an official, and they will be more comfortable with a fellow Christian who is known to them, at least by reputation.' I returned the steely look. 'I will take Daoud with me on the off chance we might stumble upon the pesky assassin. His name is Flitworthy, if I recall correctly. Such a ridiculous name. He doesn't sound at all menacing.'

Emerson's eyes slitted like those of a viper. 'His name is of no importance if and when he attacks you, Peabody.'

Nefret fluttered her fingers. 'I would like to come, too. Daoud will have to remain at a distance, and two females will not seem intimidating to them, Aunt Amelia.'

'You will miss the arrival of Ramses and David,' Emerson said reproachfully. 'They will be deeply disappointed if you are not waving at them from the deck.'

I was amused by his final desperate attempt to dissuade me. 'They will be here long before dawn, and they will not be able to see me waving or dancing a jig. When they are on board, I will embrace them and send them to bed. That means I will be able to take Daoud with us. We will comprise a landing party as formidable as Trojan warriors.'

'I prefer to think of us as ferocious Amazon warriors,' Nefret corrected me.

Emerson was not amused. 'Then I shall be the one leading this party to Deir el-Mowass, even though it will delay work on the serdab.'

'No, my beloved husband,' I replied, trying not to make a horrified face, 'the Copts will not even come out of their houses if they see the Father of Curses. They most certainly will refuse to talk to us. I will win their trust with an avowal of religious fellowship.'

I WAS TOO excited to sleep. Emerson had escaped into slumber, intermittently uttering nonsensical phrases that I construed to be references to the serdab. I ardently hoped that Nefret and I would complete our mission and return to the dahabeeyah in time to join him, Ramses and David as they departed for the site. Emerson required caffeine in order to function, so although he might gulp down breakfast (to Fatima's dismay), he would have to drink several cups of coffee.

I sat up as I heard heavy footsteps on the deck, along with thumps and whispered exclamations. I put on my dressing gown and hurried out to the sitting room to greet Ramses and David. Once I had conveyed my extreme happiness with hugs and kisses, I noticed a young boy in the doorway. 'Who is this?' I inquired.

Ramses urged the boy to step forward. 'This is Latif, who saved me from an assault at the Cairo train station. He is going to stay with us until we decide what is best to do with him. Latif, this is my mother. You may call her Sitt Hakim. As for my father, call him "sir".'

'You are most welcome to stay here,' I said warmly. 'We will put a bed for you in the cabin that Ramses and David occupy when they are not gallivanting around the world. Danger does not follow them. They devote themselves to uncovering it.'

I would have continued had not Fatima rushed into the room with shrieks of joy and an effusive display of affection. Nefret followed at a more sedate pace and greeted them cheerfully. I introduced Latif, who was overwhelmed with shyness. I could not blame him. Fatima announced that she was headed for the kitchen to prepare a breakfast feast because, as everyone knew, the food in Cairo was not safe. David declined and said he needed to sleep. Ramses echoed him and took Latif by the hand to lead him to their cabin. Fatima scowled. In a firm yet kindly voice, I ordered her to return to her own bed until it was time to begin the meal preparations. As she left, I could almost hear her planning her schedule so that the dining table would be nearly invisible beneath all the platters of food. I gazed at the trunk that occupied a significant space in the room, then suggested to Nefret that we attempt to steal a few hours of sleep.

Emerson had managed to remain in his dream. I cuddled next to him, comforted by his warmth and the knowledge that Ramses and David were safe. I thought myself unable to sleep, but I must admit that I was wrong. Please note, my loyal Readers, that such admissions seldom happen.

I awakened when a hand flopped onto my bosom. I gently removed it and returned it to its owner, then climbed out of bed and put on an unpretentious frock. I would have preferred my sturdy khaki outfit, replete with my useful belt and boots, but I wanted the Copts to regard me as a simple, pious woman, who was visiting them as a fellow Christian. I tiptoed to Nefret's cabin and noted that her bed was unoccupied. I found her in the sitting room, groomed and dressed as I was.

'Daoud is waiting for us on the pier,' she said softly. 'It is not yet dawn, but there is enough light for him to navigate to whatever dock the Copts and Mr Dullard utilise. By the time we arrive, everybody should be up and about. I would like to be back here before the Professor has finished his third cup of coffee. The boys' presence will help keep him occupied.'

'I am as eager as you are. Fatima is already rattling around in the kitchen. She will insist that Emerson, Ramses, David and the lad do justice to her breakfast. Emerson will be forced to remain until she is satisfied, and that will take some time, no matter how much he protests. Shall we join Daoud?'

There was no breeze, which required Daoud to row downstream to a dilapidated pier that looked as though it might topple into the water of the Nile at any moment. Nefret and I climbed out of the boat and trod charily on the splintery, weathered planks until we were safely on terra firma. Daoud jumped into the shallow water and dragged the boat until it scraped on the rocky sandbar.

While we were traversing the river, I had contemplated how best to achieve rapport with the Copts. They claim their religious conversion to St Mark, who went to Alexandria early in the first century to spread Christianity. They were persecuted under the rule of the Roman Empire, and intermittently after the Arab conquests. Their history of survival was as precipitous as the undulating dunes of the Western Desert. At the present time, they lived peacefully in their Christian conclaves. I had explained my proposal to my companions, emphasising to Daoud that he needed to remain at the edge of the cultivation.

As we neared the village, I viewed the houses and estimated the population to be approximately five hundred. One of the larger houses displayed a cross above the door, indicating it was the place of worship. A dozen women were gathered around the community well delineated by a waist-high wall of mud bricks; they watched us with puckered brows of distrust. Most of them had never seen fair-skinned strangers. Nefret's blond hair, glimmering in the early rays of sunlight, resembled a halo, and her face was angelic.

'*Sabah el-kheir*,' she greeted them. '*Ana esmi Nefret.*'

'*Sabah el-kheir*,' I said with a cordial smile. '*Ana esmi Amelia.*'

As I mentioned earlier, my Arabic is functional but not fluently elegant, and not always attuned to the different dialects found in small villages. My pronunciation can be laughable, which is to say it often elicits laughter. I had primed Nefret to ask particular questions when the opportunity presented itself. I did my best to follow the ensuing rapid conversation in a very local dialect between Nefret and the group of women dressed in long robes and head scarves. I understood that we were invited to partake of tea in one of their houses, and nodded graciously. As I followed the women, I looked back at Daoud and shook my head. He scowled, but abided by my instruction that he not interfere unless I called for him.

The house was more spacious than the mud huts in Amarna. I was ushered to the seat of honour on a frayed hassock. Word had spread to neighbouring women, who crowded into the room. Nefret and I were presented with glasses of tea and a plate of sweet, buttery ghorayebahs, my favourite Egyptian biscuits. Nefret and the women chattered amiably while I tried not to make a glutton of myself.

The timbre of the conversation gradually changed. I had missed what Nefret had asked them, but I could tell that the women were disturbed. I recognised the words for 'Germans', 'Englishmen' and 'Egyptians'. Many of the women became so distraught that they raised their voices to drown out one another. Dullard's name began to be included in their tirades. I was flabbergasted; I had presumed his name would be said with reverence, not contempt. I caught the Arabic words for 'weapon' (*khaw*) and 'war' (*jihad*), a frightening combination that gave me a chill.

Nefret stood next to me and patted my shoulder. 'I think it best that we leave, Aunt Amelia. I will tell them you are feeling unwell due to your abundant consumption of ghorayebahs. The hostess will be flattered.' She resumed speaking in Arabic as we headed for the door.

'*Shukran*,' I called with a frail wave. The frailty was by no means the result of too many biscuits (after all, I had not eaten any breakfast); the references to war had unnerved me. Once we were away from the houses, I stopped. 'I could not follow the exchange with any exactitude. War? Are these few hundred Coptic Christians plotting to overthrow the government, or are they going to invade the Vatican?'

'Mr Dullard is trotting this way,' she replied urgently. 'Let us attempt to get to the pier before he catches up with us. I cannot respond to him with civility, and I think it is a sin to kick a missionary.'

I glanced up as Dullard increased his pace. 'I have read the Bible in its entirety, and kicking missionaries is not among the seven deadly sins. Please note that Daoud has assessed the situation and will be at our side long before Dullard – who has begun to retreat.' I linked my arm through hers. 'Now I desire to know what you learned.'

Her terse recitation stunned me. She caught me as I stumbled and obliged me to sit down until my mind stopped whirling. Daoud offered to carry me to our boat, but I waved him off.

'I need to hear this again,' I said to Nefret, 'but please go into greater detail. Dullard came to Deir el-Mowass about three months ago, correct?'

'Yes, in the guise of an evangelical missionary. Initially, his hirsute appearance and size frightened them, but they eventually accepted him into their community. He was given a small house and was provided with food, and participated in their religious services and holidays. All was well, according to the wives, until he began to have closed meetings with the husbands and young men in the evenings, serving them beer. He provided weapons and trained them how to use them. Often they would return home in abnormally high spirits, energised but unfocused. They spoke derisively of the British interests and control in Egypt.'

'Dullard is creating a militia,' I said, almost choking on the word. 'The Copts have always been gentle people who believe salvation lies in charity and the teachings of Jesus. He has converted them into insurgents by slipping that dreadful drug into whatever he served them. Unlike Moslems, their religion does not forbid alcoholic beverages. He is despicable!'

Nefret steadied me as we resumed our walk towards the pier. 'I would like nothing more than to send Daoud back to the village to put a stop to Dullard's vile scheme.'

'The only way Dullard could have come into possession of MDMA is to have been supplied with it by someone at the German embassy. His assignment must have been to motivate the Copts to be ready to rebel against the British authority in Egypt.' I paused to rub my temples. 'War is looming across Europe. If the Germans receive support from the Copts and other insurgents, they will be better able to seize Egypt and other North African countries. Dullard's loyalty lies with the Germans, if for no other reason than promises that he will be rewarded financially.'

'And we must stop him,' Nefret said in an ominous voice unlike herself.

I glanced at her in surprise. Nefret was the protectress of butterflies and wildflowers. At home in England, I had watched her return spiders to their webs and fledglings to their nests. She scooped up insects inside the house to release them in the garden. She had used her financial resources not only to build the clinic in Luxor, but also to support the local orphanage.

I was too taken aback to reply as Daoud helped us into the boat and we began the journey back to the dahabeeyah.

OUR ROUND-TRIP MISSION to Deir el-Mowass had taken most of two hours, but we were optimistic that Emerson and the boys had not found the courage to defy Fatima's demand that they partake of a hearty breakfast. As soon as Daoud guided the boat to our pier, we hurried into the dining room. Some of the platters had been removed to the sideboard, making space for five busts of Nefertiti in a tidy row.

'Good heavens!' I said, dazzled by the display. 'Is it conceivable that one of them is the original taken from Thutmose's studio?'

Ramses escorted me to a chair and fetched me a cup of coffee. Nefret was too confounded to move. David pulled out another chair and suggested that she sit down before she toppled over. She allowed herself to be seated, still staring at the busts. 'They are remarkably similar,' she said.

'Not to the trained eye,' said Ramses with what I considered to be insufferable condescension. 'Three of them have obvious flaws, and were produced by inept apprentices. One of the final two is the work of Harun, who is worthy of his reputation as the Master Forger.'

'He did a damned good job,' Emerson commented. 'I have not had the opportunity to scrutinise them at length, although I shall do so later.'

'How did you manage to acquire them?' I demanded.

David laughed. 'I can assure you, Aunt Amelia, that it was not a simple task. Thanks to Latif, we were able to find Harun's latest workshop.' He went on to describe their deafening screeches as they burst out of the shadows to grab the two busts. 'Ramses oversaw the transportation of the trunk to the train station, where we encountered scoundrels under orders from the German embassy. Latif diverted the last one, so we brought him with us. I will allow Ramses to elaborate about the train trip.'

Ramses did so with his typical impassivity.

'Sethos!' I gasped.

Emerson growled deep in his throat. 'Did you think he might concede, Peabody? Ramses should have deduced that the villain was on their trail. Very careless of you, son.'

'I am obliged to agree with you, sir,' Ramses replied.

'It is time to depart for the site.' Emerson looked at Nefret and me. 'I presuppose that you intend to change into more suitable attire. I anticipate a long, arduous day.' He smiled at Latif, who was oblivious to the exchange and was wolfing down lavish helpings of eggs, toast, hummus and pitta bread. 'We will cut trousers and find a shirt for you, and you will look like a professional archaeologist in my pith helmet.'

'There are extra ones in the back of our wardrobe,' I said coolly. 'Come along, Nefret. We will not be able to work if we are dressed like shop clerks or vicars' spinster daughters.'

'Or missionaries' wives,' Nefret added, dimpling.

Emerson harrumphed. 'While we walk to the site, you can tell us what you learned about that villainous missionary and his little flock of Coptic canaries – if they sang.'

'They may not have sung,' I said as I stood up, 'but they twittered. Nefret and I will freshen up and put on our garb. We will be ready to leave shortly. Please do not ruin any of your trousers, Emerson. I can only repair them with needle and thread so many times before they are reduced to tatters. The Vandergelts are coming for Christmas. I expect all of us to look respectable.'

'What is Christmas?' asked Latif between bites.

Ramses gestured at the boy to rise. 'I will explain while we help you change clothes.'

Emerson was drinking coffee when I returned to the dining room. My belt of useful items clinked like wind chimes as I poured myself a cup of coffee and prepared a plate of tepid eggs. I ate with ravenous disregard for proper etiquette. He politely kept his gaze fixated on the five busts that comprised our current centrepiece. Neither of us looked up as Nefret scooped up the last of the eggs.

As soon as Ramses, David and Latif appeared, Emerson announced that we were leaving. I slipped a pita sandwich wrapped in a napkin into my pocket as I rose. We walked down the pier and took the path through the cultivation. Nefret repeated what she had told me about Dullard's ploy to convince the Copts of Deir el-Mowass to arise against the British when German soldiers swept into Egypt to take control of the government.

David stiffened with anger. 'The Copts are delusional if they believe this will lead to Egyptian autonomy. King Abbas II is already under threat of being ousted by Lord Kitchener. The Ottomans refuse to acknowledge that Egypt is a British protectorate. Well-armed troops from various factions will collide in Alexandria, Cairo and destinations to the south.'

'It will be a bloody mess – bloody in that military and civilian lives will be lost,' Emerson said grimly. 'It is beyond our control.'

'The only thing we can do is stop Dullard,' I replied. 'Furthermore, he must be brought to justice for the murder of Eric von Raubritter.'

Nefret's shoulders slumped. 'We have no proof.'

'To hell with that!' Emerson exclaimed. I anticipated a further outburst of profanities and condemnations concerning the necessity of proof, so I was taken by surprise when he fell silent. A glance over my shoulder confirmed that our entourage was being followed by a number of the Arab men and women who resided in huts along the path.

Nefret put her hand on my arm, and in a low voice said, 'Miss Smith did not emerge when our boisterous parade passed by her sad little hut. Is it possible that she has packed her belongings and fled to Minya?'

My current upheaval of emotions depleted into cold reality. 'I would engage in a rambunctious celebration if that were true. Emerson would don his tuxedo and waltz with me on the top deck as we drank champagne. Mr Buddle might produce a smile. Dullard would be heartbroken, but that is of no concern to us – especially if he is incarcerated in a prison in Cairo.'

She gave me a puckish grin. 'Would you like me to go back to her hut and find out whether she has vacated it?'

'No,' I said, 'I cannot bear the thought that you will find her applying makeup in preparation to join us. This will be my beloved Emerson's moment of ecstasy when he directs the workmen to remove the slab and expose the contents of the serdab. Although I do not believe in telepathy, I will send a strong message to Miss Smith to stay away from the site.'

'Let us hope the message is received.'

'*Inshallah*,' I murmured as we resumed walking.

When we arrived at Thutmose's studio, I saw that Selim had organised the workmen. Emerson gave him a hearty handshake, and went to stand next to the serdab. He selected the most muscular workmen and positioned them around the stone slab.

'Make sure you can grip beneath the lid,' he said. His voice was steady, but I could hear an undertone of anxiety. He squatted at the head of the stone and put his hands under it. 'On my command, we will lift it and slide it to that side. Are you ready? Now!'

The workmen, as well as my husband, grunted and cursed as the slab was raised far enough to move it off the stone edges of the serdab. 'Serdab' is the Arabic word for 'cellar'; in tombs it denotes burial chambers for statues, replete with slits so that the statues could keep an eye on things. This was a more traditional cellar.

Emerson took out his electric torch to illuminate the contents. The rest of us crowded around him as best we could.

'Bloody hell!' he barked.

NINETEEN

I PEERED INTO THE serdab. 'I see only two of them, Emerson. The dining room table may not be able hold the additional weight.'

'Which would be a total of approximately three hundred pounds,' Ramses remarked. 'We could leave them here for future Egyptologists to discover.'

Emerson flung his pith helmet against a crumbling wall. 'I have a reputation to uphold, and I will not allow it to be tainted by rumours that I failed to excavate with professional precision! Selim, bring me the ladder. You and Nefret must take photographs before we disturb the contents. Were Thutmose to appear, I would throttle him.' He stomped away, cursing under his breath (although his profanities were audible to all of us, including the fellahin, Mr Buddle and the omnipresent thieves).

Nefret and Selim descended and began to discuss how best to position the reflecting screens to capture the light. David retreated to smoke his pipe. Ramses and I shrugged at each other. I knew from experience that it was wise to maintain a distance until Emerson's diatribe ran its course. Since he was capable of carrying on for hours, I could only pray that his innate inquisitiveness would lure him back to the serdab.

Nefret emerged and looked warily at Emerson's backside. 'There are many items that may be of great consequence, and the workmanship is extraordinary,' she said loudly to me. 'We dared not touch them, but we saw many sculptures. One appears to be of Nefertiti with an infant boy in her arms.'

'Could it be Tutankhamen?' I asked.

'Ridiculous!' Emerson barked over my shoulder. 'Nefertiti had six daughters. Tutankhamen's father was presumably Akhenaton, but the mother was either a sister or cousin of his. Quite possibly Tutankhamen married one of his half-sisters, making the situation more incestuous.'

I was quite aware that incest was commonplace among the pharaohs, having been engaged in exhaustive discussions about this with my husband, son and brother-in-law. Nonetheless, Nefret and I listened meekly as he expounded on the topic and its political implications. I noticed that the redness of his face was lessening and his voice had resumed its normal decibel level (high but tolerable). When he paused to take a breath, I took advantage of it and said, 'Selim is looking about for you, Emerson. He most likely needs your approval before he and Nefret begin to set up their equipment. You must go to him.' I saw no reason to add that I was yearning to eat the pita sandwich I had stashed in my pocket.

I did not have the opportunity to do so. Herr Morgenstern, now as welcome as an infestation of lice, came bounding through the spectators, his round cheeks flushed and his eyes bulging. 'Hallo, hallo!' he shouted. 'I have astonishing news to share with you. I received a telegram from Herr Maspero informing me that Herr Borchardt will be here within days to resume supervision of the firman. I knew that my position was temporary, but I did not anticipate that it would be so stressful. I am eager to return to Cairo to deal with an incompleted . . . task.'

'Searching for Harun's studio?' I suggested nicely.

A trickle of saliva escaped his mouth. 'I know nothing of this person, Mrs Emerson. It is a personal matter. I have packed my belongings and arranged to be taken to the train station in Minya. It has been an honour to work alongside you and your esteemed husband. *Auf Wiedersehen!'*

He winked at me, startled Nefret with a sloppy kiss and then disappeared through the crowd of spectators.

'I smelled peppermint on his breath,' Nefret said to me, shaking her head. 'Let us hope he is able to make his way to the safety of the Deutsche Orient-Gesellschaft house before he becomes disorientated.'

'He is no longer our responsibility. I must inform Emerson of Borchardt's imminent arrival. It will have a major impact on how we proceed today.' I found Emerson in a dialogue with Selim and related the news.

His reaction was not discreet. 'Damnation! Selim, have the workmen disperse the gawkers with whatever force is required. After that, inform them that they are to take a rest in the shade until their presence is required. Peabody, ask this God of yours why he is intent on complicating my life. He must have a streak of sadism.'

'He has better things to do than beleaguer you,' I replied acerbically. 'I suggest we have a conference at the dahabeeyah.'

Apparently Emerson was not enamoured with my proposal. His manly voice echoed against the cliffs as he ordered the crowd to leave. I noticed that Mr Buddle complied immediately, his notebook clutched to his chest. Selim and the workmen reinforced the message with physical encouragement. Once we were free of eavesdroppers and spies, we sat down in a shaded spot. Contrary to his usual dictatorial stance, Emerson explained the situation and asked for our thoughts.

'Morgenstern cannot claim credit for discovering the bust of Nefertiti,' I asserted. 'If he ever remembers that he uncovered it, he would be obliged to admit that he stole it in order to have a forged copy to present to the Department des Antiquités.'

'And I cannot claim that I discovered it,' Emerson said. 'That would be morally reprehensible.'

Ramses cleared his throat. 'Borchardt should have that honour. You could tell him about the serdab that you found. No one will believe that you did not remove the lid—'

'There were at least fifty witnesses,' David inserted.

'You did so merely out of curiosity,' Ramses continued smoothly, 'but acknowledged that it was Borchardt's prerogative to continue the work.'

'What's more, he will find the bust of Nefertiti,' I said.

Nefret wrinkled her nose. 'On the dining room table, in a row with the four forgeries?'

Emerson harrumphed. 'In the serdab, with Thutmose's earlier efforts.' He propped his head on his fist as he thought. 'Ramses, go to the dahabeeyah and bring back the bust of Nefertiti in a bag. I will conceal it in the serdab so that it is not visible at first glance. Borchardt has a reputation for meticulous diligence. He will deduce that the other two busts were made by Thutmose as well.'

'As you wish, Father.' He and Emerson exchanged a guarded look that I was unable to interpret. Or did not wish to interpret, I will admit to my Readers.

'Now,' Emerson announced, 'we shall resume excavating in other areas of the studio. Thutmose buried objects that may be worthy of our attention. Latif, this is your opportunity to be an archaeologist. Selim will provide you with a trowel and teach you as you go along, so that you can dig scientifically and not just for ancient treasures in the sand. David, keep a close watch on him. I will tell our workmen to return.'

I told Emerson that I desired to climb down the ladder to the bottom of the serdab to have a look before the lid was replaced. He opened his mouth to protest, but closed it and strode towards the huddled workmen. Nefret gave me the electric torch and cautioned me about the ladder that consisted of dubious lengths of wood and somewhat rotted rungs. Having descended into deep tombs by less sturdy ladders, I proceeded with confidence.

I knelt to examine the two busts of Nefertiti. Neither captured the incomparable allure of the masterpiece that Morgenstern had taken to Cairo. One had a large nose. The second had a small headpiece and lacked perfect symmetry. Thutmose must have been scolded by Queen Nefertiti when he presented each one, and thus relegated them to the serdab. The statue of Nefertiti and a male newborn reflected an intimacy between them. I wondered if Borchardt might consider my hypothesis that the baby could be Tutankhamen. I utilised the beam of light to admire colourfully painted pottery jars, a box inlaid with gold and ivory and a shining broad collar of semiprecious stones that had once adorned one of the busts. I emerged from the serdab, my mind swirling with glittering images, and noted that the workmen had resumed their assigned duties. Emerson's arms were crossed and his expression was unusually dour. He pretended not to notice me.

Shortly thereafter, Ramses returned with a misshapen canvas bag and disappeared down the ladder. The bag was flat when he reappeared. Emerson instructed some of the men to lift the stone slab back onto the serdab.

The workmen chanced upon various artifacts and put them in their allotted baskets. Latif was determined to prove his worthiness; he squealed in delight when his trowel encountered an object. He and David scooped away sand until they exposed a shard of blue-painted pottery, typical of the Amarna period. We toiled well past our customary luncheon respite, and I began to worry that Emerson would not allow us to stop for tea on the dahabeeyah. I had shared my pita with Nefret, but neither of us had eaten an ample breakfast.

I was working the sieve and gathering together the smaller objects when I glanced up and saw Dullard coming towards us. Luckily for him, Emerson and Ramses were occupied at the back of the studio. Nefret positioned herself behind me.

'My dear Mrs Emerson,' Dullard began in his grating voice, 'I am so sorry that I did not have the opportunity to speak to you when you visited the Coptic village. I was told that you and Dr Forth partook of tea and biscuits in one of the homes.'

Nefret stared at him. 'Yes, and we were made aware of your wicked scheme. We shall notify the proper authorities in Cairo so that you will be arrested for fomenting a rebellion.'

'I have no idea of what you speak. I am a man of God, not a rabble-rouser. I meet with my fellow Christians to teach them how to lead virtuous lives. I encourage the men to respect their wives and treat them with deference.'

'You supplied them with weapons,' I corrected him coldly, 'and trained them while they were unable to think clearly. What puzzles me is how you gained access to that drug from the Merck laboratory in Darmstadt. Surely you were not included in the German ambassador's entourage. Eric von Raubritter would have described you in his journal, and Liezel Hasenkamp would have told us of your – er – remarkable physical appearance.'

'I fear you have been in the sun too long,' he responded. 'Both of you should sit in the shade until you regain your common sense.'

Nefret clenched her fists. 'We know that you murdered von Raubritter before he could confide in us about the drug.'

'I adhere to the Ten Commandments, one of which forbids taking the life of another person. "Thou shalt not kill", to be precise. You have no evidence that I harmed that young man.'

I was unwilling to admit that we lacked any evidence whatsoever. I looked away as I searched my wits for a response. 'Oh, but we do,' I said, resorting to mendacity. 'Dr Forth examined his body when it was in the morgue in Minya. She immediately noticed black hairs embedded in the wounds. Von Raubritter had blond hair.' I leaned forward and tugged on his beard until I retrieved a sample. 'Black hair like this, Mr Dullard.'

Nefret, no amateur in the art of fabrication, nodded vigorously. 'I took samples of the hair and will send his and yours to the authorities in Cairo. They will compare them under a microscope.'

He began to back away. 'I had no choice. Von Raubritter attacked me as I was going to the dig house to make sure that it had not been vandalised during Herr Morgenstern's absence. I am certain that he intended to steal whatever he could find and sell it on the black market. I had no choice but to defend myself, despite the fact he was much younger.'

'You were twice his size,' I said. 'Had your story been true – which it is not – you could have restrained him easily. No, Mr Dullard, you murdered him to protect yourself from the exposure of your despicable scheme.'

'You may revel in your ludicrous theory if it amuses you,' he retorted shrilly, 'but I will not stand here and listen to it! I shall return to Deir el-Mowass to pack my meagre belongings and find another Coptic village where I will be regarded as a righteous spokesman for God's glory. Good day to you, Mrs Emerson and Dr Forth.' He turned around and began to trot in the direction of the river.

'Is there anything in the Bible about lying to missionaries?' Nefret asked me with feigned trepidation.

'Not that I recall.' I beckoned Daoud and said to him, 'Dullard admitted that he murdered the young German. We must delay him until he has been arrested and taken into custody at the police station. They can decide what to do with him until I send and receive telegrams from Mr Russell.'

Daoud, who had participated in our conversation as he rowed us back to the dahabeeyah, beamed at me. 'As you wish, Sitt Hakim. I shall retrieve our boat at once and pursue him.' He hurried away, chirping like a bushy-tailed jird. Daoud is happiest when he has been given an assignment that does not preclude carnage.

'Well?' Emerson demanded as he came towards us. His hearing is remarkably acute, and I knew that he had overheard most of the conversation. 'He confessed to the murder of von Raubritter. Nefret, I am impressed that you had the wherewithal to pluck black hairs from the corpse to provide proof of his guilt.'

'Thank you, Professor.' She looked at me for help.

'You have taught her well,' I said smoothly. 'Let us return to the dahabeeyah for tea, Emerson. I am beginning to feel a bit faint. Allow me to mention that Nefret and I have had little to eat today.'

Ramses, who shared many genetic traits with his father, including the ability to eavesdrop, advanced. 'Shall I escort you and Nefret, Mother?'

I would have readily agreed, but Emerson said, 'I need you here, Ramses. We must ensure that the site is not disturbed in our absence, however brief it may be. Peabody, you and Nefret will be accompanied by Ilyas. He has been warned about the possibility of attack by the ultimate assassin and will be alert.'

'Have you forgotten the little pistol on my belt?' I said coolly.

Emerson snorted. 'For many years I have heard it clang every time you took a step. Consider the likelihood that you will be fumbling to disengage it when a blade plunges into your back.' He paused and looked away, his eyes blinking rapidly. After a moment, he turned to me. 'You must be protected, Peabody. I cannot conceive of life without you.'

I found myself blinking, too. 'Very well, Emerson, Nefret and I will welcome the presence of Ilyas as we walk to the dahabeeyah, and invite him to join us for tea. Latif is unaccustomed to the harshness of the sun. We will take him with us as well.'

Latif slipped his hand into mine. 'I will protect you, *ya* Sitt Hakim. If a bad man springs out from behind a tree, I will jump on his back and scratch his face until he begs for mercy. Then I will knock him to the ground and stomp on him.'

'Thank you,' I said solemnly.

As soon as we were on board the dahabeeyah, I alerted Fatima that there would be four for tea. Ilyas was painfully uncomfortable now that his duty was done and took refuge in a corner. Latif, who now considered himself a bona fide member of our party, went to console his newfound friend. Nefret and I went to our respective cabins to freshen ourselves. I changed into more comfortable attire and splashed water on my face. Nefret had done the same, and we were in the sitting room when Fatima arrived with a laden platter of cakes and delicate sandwiches. Mahmoud followed with a tray for the teapot, cups and saucers.

My stomach fluttered with anticipation as I served the tea. Ilyas sat on the edge of a chair and held the porcelain cup as if it were a precious antiquity. Nefret gently admonished Latif to exhibit courtesy and self-control. She did not look at me as I stuffed a sandwich in my mouth, took a gulp of tea and reached for a cream cake. She did, however, load her plate with sandwiches before she sat down next to me on the settee.

'I have been dreaming of this moment all day,' she admitted happily. 'If we had not learned of Borchardt's advent, the Professor would have commenced the removal of the contents of the serdab. He would have kept us busy until it was so dark that we were colliding into one another.'

'We have worked in moonlight,' I said. 'When Emerson's enthusiasm is at its peak, he allows nothing to interfere. We have slept in tombs infested with bats and in tents that provided no protection from mosquitoes, rain, snakes or scorpions. This is why everyone recognises that he is the greatest Egyptologist of the century.'

'I am in need of a nap,' Nefret said. 'If you share my fatigue, I will send Ilyas back to the site.'

I put my hand to my lips to cover a yawn. 'An excellent idea, my dear. I shall go to the upper deck and recline on a chaise while I ponder recent events. Latif, would you prefer to remain here and have a cooking class with Fatima?'

He swallowed the cake he had jammed into his mouth. 'No, *ya* Sitt,' he sputtered, crumbs arcing across the room. 'I would rather learn to be archaeologist so that someday I will be famous like Mr Professor Emerson. Get up, Ilyas, and let us be on our way.' Had he not been pre-pubescent, he would have sounded like Emerson.

I stifled my laughter until they had gone down the plank. 'I am relieved that Emerson is his idol, as opposed to someone like Sethos, who would train the boy to be a pickpocket and a thief.'

'Do you believe we are rid of the Master Criminal?' asked Nefret.

'In the same way that I believe in fairies and ambulatory mummies. Ramses and David are convinced that he leapt out of the freight car, but keep in mind that it was very dark. Sethos stood in the doorway and then vanished. They may have fallen for the most rational explanation of his action. Sethos has a remarkable history of creating illusions to satisfy his audience.'

'I prefer to believe that he is limping towards Minya,' she replied with a toss of her chin. She went into her cabin and closed the door.

I sadly noted that the cakes and sandwiches had vanished. Fatima and I had already discussed the menu for dinner, so I went up the steps to the top deck and collapsed gracefully on a chaise. When I closed my eyes, I could not banish an image of Queen Nefertiti regarding me with reproof. Her unspoken accusation had validity, in that the inferior forgeries of her bust had been scattered across Cairo like cheap tourist trinkets. 'But you will have a place of honour in the Egyptian Museum,' I told her.

'Or in a German museum,' she retorted bitterly. 'Are you confident that Borchardt will not smuggle Thutmose's masterpiece out of Egypt? Surely you have not forgotten that the Rosetta Stone is in the British Museum, along with the Elgin Marbles.'

'I will grant that,' I said, unable to refute her assertion – and yes, Readers, I was aware that I was carrying on a conversation with an illusion. I have found it helpful to express my thoughts aloud. Doing so encourages me to analyse and amend my conjectures. Emerson has perfected the knack of pretending to listen to me while he considers the next day's activity at an excavation. He is often taken by surprise when I politely request that he put on his evening clothes for a social event that evening.

I could see by Nefertiti's glare that she was displeased by my re-sponse. 'We have no reason to distrust Borchardt,' I continued in an at-tempt to placate her. She had been, after all, the co-regent with Akhen-aton and possibly a pharaoh in her own right. One should not argue with long-deceased pharaohs.

Her lips tightened. 'You may trust Borchardt, but I do not. Have you examined all of the busts on the table in your dining room? Careful study may lead to enlightenment.'

'We know that they were made by Harun and his apprentices. Only one of the forgeries is nearly perfect.' I stood and poured myself a glass of water while I contemplated her intimation that we had overlooked something.

I was so engrossed that I nearly tripped when a voice called, 'Mrs Emerson, are you here? I have taken it upon myself to come without an invitation. Please forgive me if I have interrupted your conversation.'

I regained my balance and looked at the top of the stairs. 'No, Miss Smith, I was simply musing aloud. Is there something I can do for you?' I didn't add that the only thing I wanted to do for her was wave as she left for Minya.

She was wearing a lime green gown, a gaudy scarf and an emerald tiara. Her lipstick had been applied by an unsteady hand and the red circles on her cheeks were asymmetrical. She realised that I was staring at her. 'I apologise for my appearance, Mrs Emerson. I have not been myself since the horrific experience two nights ago. I have been unable to sleep or eat. I have come to beg for your advice about Mr Dullard.' I gestured for her to sit down and joined her. She sat down with a thud and began to wring her hands. 'He may have saved our lives, but at the expense of another's. Shall I forgive him?'

'Allow me to offer you a glass of water,' I said to stall before enlightening her with the sordid story of Dullard's treachery.

'Very kind of you, Mrs Emerson. I would prefer a wee drop of sherry to calm my nerves. I am not unfamiliar with violence. Do you recall my book in which Lady Whitbread was attacked in her tent and forced to decapitate the Sheikh's evil twin brother to protect her virtue?'

'I may have missed that one,' I murmured, beginning to feel uneasy.

'When I return home to England, I shall send you a copy. In another book, the heroine suspects that the sheikh murdered her brother, and is determined to seek revenge. She creeps up behind him, wraps her scarf around his neck, and would have succeeded in strangling him had he not in his last gasp persuaded her of his innocence.' She took a gulp of the sherry that I had handed her. 'Family loyalty is the basis of civilisation. I understand that you have a son named Ramses.'

My uneasiness escalated. 'Yes, and I am very proud of him.'

'Despite the fact that he has engaged in murder?'

'Ramses has a kind heart and does everything possible to avoid causing physical pain to his enemies.'

'Although I write under the pen name Miss Ermintrude de Vere Smith, I have been married twice and have had sons of my own. I understand your need to defend Ramses, but he is not a chivalrous knight.' She went to the cart and replenished her drink. 'You have had many encounters of a murderous nature, have you not? You may dismiss them by claiming self-defence, but I know better.'

Panic overrode uneasiness. 'Shall we return to a discussion of Mr Dullard? I regret to say that I have learned some disturbing information about him. He is an agent of someone at the German embassy—'

'Do you honestly believe that I have affection for him?' Her laugh was bitter. 'He is nothing but a pawn, providing me with an excuse to remain in Amarna. Poor, naive Miss Smith, hopelessly besotted with a disgustingly hairy missionary with the voice of a petulant toddler.'

I needed Queen Nefertiti to come to my rescue, but the odds were poor. 'I did not know that you write under a pen name, but I understand that is a common practice among authors. Ermintrude de Vere Smith is a peculiar choice.'

She bristled. 'My given name is Ermintrude. It is a combination of Hermione and Gertrude, my great-grandmothers.'

Enlightenment took its own sweet time but finally settled in my brain. I had already seen the steely side of her nature, as well as her melodramatic display when Absalom succumbed to the tree branch. Only a mother could feel such agony. 'Did you name your sons after relatives?'

'Hardly!' she retorted with a sniff.

'Nor did I name my son after a pharaoh. He himself chose his nickname. How many sons did you have, Mrs Godwin?' The question, offered with a friendly smile, was rhetorical.

She remained by the cart. 'Six, but five of them died at the hands of you and your son.'

'Five of them died because of their zealousness and incompetency. Vendettas are not without inherent danger.' I stood up and moved to the far side of the deck. 'This conversation is finished. Return to your hut, pack your trunks and hire some men to convey you and your belongings to Minya. Once you are there, take the train to Cairo and on to Alexandria. Book the next available passage to England and go back to your cottage in the Cotswolds or Cornwall or wherever it is.'

'That is what I intend to do after I have disposed of you, Mrs Emerson. I shall eagerly wait to read your obituary in *The Times*. Ramses's will follow soon thereafter.' She narrowed the gap between us (the upper deck was rather small), her hands curled.

'I am not afraid of you, Miss Smith or whatever name you prefer. Your mind is distorted with fury.' I reminded myself that maniacs can evince incredible strength.

'Murderer!' she screamed as she lunged at me.

I stepped aside and permitted her momentum to propel her over the railing. No more than a second passed before there was loud splash. I hurried downstairs and went to the deck. Nefret, Fatima and Mahmoud were already there, jostling for position. I scanned the water for any sign of her, but the surface was unruffled.

'Who – what?' Fatima gasped.

I waited until my heart stopped hammering. 'Miss Smith came by unexpectedly. What has happened to her? Why can we not see her? I did not have the opportunity to ask her if she could swim.'

'Before you pushed her?' Nefret asked in a tremulous voice.

'Don't be absurd! Why has she not struggled to the surface?'

Mahmoud touched my arm. 'Earlier in the day I saw several crocodiles sunning themselves on the sandbank. They are no longer there.'

I gazed at the unoccupied sandbank. 'I believe that I would like to sit down now and will appreciate assistance.' Fatima and Mahmoud held my arms as I staggered into the sitting room. Nefret brought me a snifter of brandy, sat next to me and said, 'Would you be so kind as to begin at the beginning?'

I wondered how my small audience might react if I said, 'If you must know, I was arguing with Queen Nefertiti when Miss Smith interrupted us.'

TWENTY

EFRET MUST HAVE sent a message to the site, because Emerson, David, Ramses and Latif arrived within a quarter of an hour. Emerson helped me to my feet and led me into our cabin.

His embrace was fierce. 'My dearest Peabody, you could have been killed by that nasty woman. I am so sorry that you were forced to be there, but I cannot say that I shall mourn her demise. Sobek, the deity reputedly associated with crocodiles, chose not to save her. There was nothing you could do.'

I was too comforted by his closeness to admit that I should have attempted to find a way to rescue Miss Smith, also known as Mrs Godwin – mother of the five assassins bent on deadly revenge. 'I regret that it happened.'

'There was nothing you could do,' he repeated. 'If you had dived into the water to pull her up, you would have been the crocodiles' dessert.'

After further interactions of a comforting nature, Emerson and I went to the top deck to join the others. Latif was sulking because his drink consisted solely of soda water. David showed us his copy of a relief found in the studio. Ramses scowled as he studied the hieroglyphs. Emerson sat and regarded me with his sapphirine eyes, his lips upcurled in a gentle smile. I found it difficult to follow the general conversation. I caught Nefret staring at Ramses, her expression indecipherable.

Daoud came up the stairs and stopped. He would have remained there had I not said, 'Please tell us about Mr Dullard. Were you successful in following him after he fled towards the Nile?'

'Yes, Sitt Hakim,' he said, visibly offended. He does not like his abilities to be doubted. 'I took the boat from our pier and rowed downstream with all my strength. I soon caught sight of him and shouted at him to beach his boat. Instead, he foolishly attempted to escape me by rowing towards a swamp. This behaviour made no sense. I followed and saw that he was obscured by tall reeds. Again, I shouted at him. He stood up and aimed a gun at me, but his boat capsized and he fell into the water.'

'So you hauled him out,' Emerson said, 'and delivered him to the police station in Minya. Well done, Daoud. We can always rely on you.'

Daoud lowered his head. 'The reeds are beset with huge ra'ad fish, the electric catfish, as well as crocodiles. Once he fell in and was shocked by the fish that are more than two and a half feet long he was done for. What the fish did not destroy, the crocodiles surely would. It would have been futile to attempt to retrieve any of his body parts. Aware that the heaving mass of fish and crocodiles could flip over my boat, I retreated with haste.'

I bit my lip. The Nile had claimed two victims, neither of whom could be deemed saintly. I was appalled by the violent nature of their deaths. Emerson put his arm around my shoulder.

Nefret had gone to the railing to stare at the rippling brown water. Ramses stood up as if to join her, but sat down again and downed the contents of his glass. David glanced at him, and then went to her side.

'Remember that Miss Smith had come here to kill me,' I said, breaking the silence. 'Dullard's scheme would have resulted in bloodshed and the loss of lives. We cannot blame ourselves because their wickedness resulted in their deaths. In a day or two, I will go to Cairo and meet with Mr Russell.'

Emerson bounded to his feet. 'Once again, Peabody, you have forgotten the existence of the fifth assassin. You will go nowhere without me.'

'And me,' Daoud asserted firmly.

'I do believe it is time for dinner. Fatima has toiled all day in the kitchen. We owe her the respect of dining at a fashionable hour.'

No one protested. We went to the dining room and took our seats at the table. I winced as I regarded the forgeries of the Nefertiti bust, currently down to four. I observed that all of us, with the exception of Latif, kept glancing at them as we ate.

'What are we going to do with the damned things?' Emerson said as he served brandy.

Ramses scratched his chin. 'We can't allow them to go back into circulation. Supposedly, Borchardt has not yet discovered the original.'

'It would be difficult to explain the existence of the forgeries,' David said, 'although we deserve a souvenir after all that we have been through to retrieve the copies from Harun's slimy hands.'

'We could keep one,' I suggested. 'Not here, of course, but in our house in England. The Department des Antiquités has permitted us to retain a few pieces from our excavations over the years.'

Emerson arched his eyebrows. 'It will be less complicated if it travels in one of our trunks. I do not intend to spend hours in Maspero's office, trying to explain its origin.'

'Will I fit in one of your trunks, Mr Professor Emerson?' asked Latif. He turned his large brown eyes on me. 'I do not know where this England place is, but I am sure that I will like it. I will be a servant and sleep on the floor of your cellar. I will be very good at scrubbing floors after you teach me, ya Sitt.'

'Come stand beside me,' Ramses said. 'Selim and I had a long talk about your future. He has become very fond of you, and believes that his sister and her husband will welcome you into their family. You will go to school to learn how to read and write. You will study geography, history and science. It is vital that a great archaeologist is educated about the world.'

'I will run away,' Latif vowed with a dark look.

'If you do, you will risk the displeasure of the Father of Curses. You will also disappoint me.'

I smiled at him. 'You will remain here for Christmas and the rest of the season.'

David held up his glass. 'Let us offer a toast to Latif's future. He will have an opportunity to become the greatest Egyptologist of the latter part of the twentieth century.'

Nefret raised her glass. 'We should commemorate this moment with a solemn ceremony on the deck.'

'An excellent idea,' Ramses said. 'I can carry two of the busts, and David will bring the other. They were created by Egyptian ingenuity. It is only fitting that they will always reside within its boundaries.'

'Wait just a moment,' I said as they all stood up. 'From what you told us earlier, you and David found one of these in a locked cabinet in the office of the German ambassador's attaché. Morgenstern was too addled to have told him anything. The only other person who knew of its existence was Dullard. There is the link.'

Emerson stroked his chin. 'This attaché stole the drug when he was included in the tour of the Merck laboratory. He wanted Dullard to experiment on the Coptic community to find out if they could be useful in a war. Dullard must have had a vial of it when he saw what Morgenstern had discovered. I am beginning to think kindly of the denizens in the swamp.'

I was prepared to admonish him for his lack of charity, but chose to stand up and follow the rest of our group out to the deck. David and Ramses threw two of the blatant forgeries into the water and offered the third to me. When I declined, Latif mentioned that he had spent hours searching for shops all over Cairo that specialised in antiquities. He crowed at the sound of the splash.

THE FOLLOWING MORNING we were able to enjoy a plentiful break-fast while Emerson concentrated on coffee. I would have preferred to spend the morning alone, trying to assimilate the events of the previous day, but Emerson insisted that I accompany him to the site. Selim conferred with him, and ordered our men to go back to the original site to continue excavating there. The remaining workmen were visibly pleased when they were told that Borchardt would take charge soon. Morgenstern had infuriated them. It is true that my beloved husband has been known to express his temper when he is not pleased, and this excavation had been a series of frustrations. Ramses, David and Nefret meekly accepted their assigned duties. Latif scampered about, leaping on and off rocks and offering everyone his assistance. He, like Emerson, had discarded his pith helmet.

'I must have a word with Mr Buddle,' I told Emerson. 'He deserves to be informed so that he can send a telegram to his patron.'

'I do not trust that man. Based on what you have told me about him, he is so arrogant that he fancies himself above danger. I am going to interrogate each workman to assure myself that he is not that bl—blasted assassin. Stay within my sight, Peabody.'

'Of couse, my dear.'

Mr Buddle put down his notebook as I approached him. 'Once again, I have heard disturbing rumours. Can you tell me if any of them are true?'

I sat down on a convenient rock. 'Regrettably, most of what you have heard is true.' I elaborated at length, but glossed over the more gruesome details. 'I feel remorse that I did not recognise Dullard's involvement earlier. I could have saved Morgenstern from his ludicrous adventures. He is gone now, and I shall pray that he does not imperil himself before he runs out of peppermint schnapps.'

'I feel similar remorse that I was unable to persuade Miss Smith to depart Amarna. I am aghast that she attempted to hurt you, Mrs Emerson.'

'She did admit that she had borne six sons. One of them, Geoffrey, was married briefly to my goddaughter. Nefret was in a disturbed state of mind at the time, and allowed herself to be blinded by his charming demeanour and handsome features. We failed to see the evil in his heart.'

'That is often the case, is it not? We prefer to think the best of people. Sometimes we are wrong.'

'I am seldom wrong,' I said. 'Emerson thinks you are a fool, but I believe otherwise. You are sly, and you revel in misleading people. You found out that a man named Ridgemont was funding the excavation. You presented yourself as his agent, and no one was in a position to question this. You chose to call yourself Octavius Buddle. Your real name is Flitworthy. Why did your mother opt to burden you with such a preposterous name? This is not to say that I would have chosen to call my offspring Judas, Guy, Cromwell and Absalom.'

'I was christened Rasputin. I cannot remember why I chose to call myself Octavius. I have always thought it has a melodic cadence.' He stood up, gripped my arm and propelled me to my feet. 'Your husband and the other members of your family seem to be distracted. None of them is looking this way. They cannot see the pistol that I am pressing against your ribcage.'

'You are the sorriest excuse for an assassin that I have ever met,' I said as we went behind a formation of boulders. 'Your brothers were failures, but they did display a certain amount of panache.'

Buddle gave me a wry look. 'Assassination is not as easy as one would think. My brothers were reckless, too fanatical to consider the consequences of their attempts.'

I had a minor epiphany. 'When you dressed in a black robe and tried to lure me into the wadi, you should have been more aware of the impending flash flood. I took refuge on a ledge on the cliff. What did you do?'

'I was fortunate to scramble out of the wadi before I was swept away.'

'Would you have killed me?' I asked bluntly.

He lowered the gun. 'I do not know what I might have done that day, Mrs Emerson. You have displayed empathy and kindheartedness. On the other hand, my foremost duty is to uphold the honour of the Godwin family.'

'The Godwin family is sorely lacking in honour.'

'And sadly lacking in numbers.' Buddle stared into the distance, his brow furrowed. 'I am the only one left.'

I unhooked the tin cup that forms part of my belt of tools, having been obliged to replace it after my meeting with the Bedouin sheikh. I had done so promptly, since I have always considered it unladylike to swig liquid from a bottle or canteen. I poured whisky into the cup and pretended to drink.

Buddle watched me with a sardonic smile. 'Are you sufficiently fortified, Mrs Emerson? Then . . .' A gloat spread across his face as he raised the pistol.

I dashed the liquid directly into his eyes. I have been informed that the sensation is not at all agreeable. His behaviour bore this out. He staggered back, pressing his hands to his face and crying loudly. I picked up my parasol and brought it down on his head with as much force as I could muster.

After this it was simply a matter of tying his hands and feet with the cords from my belt of tools. I then seated myself on a rock and awaited the advent of my rescuers.

There was a teaspoon or two of whisky left in the flask . . .

Crocodile on the Sandbank

Elizabeth Peters

In this first adventure, our headstrong heroine decides to use her substantial inheritance to see the world. On her travels, she rescues a gentlewoman in distress – Evelyn Barton-Forbes – and the two become friends. The two companions continue to Egypt where they face mysteries, mummies and the redoubtable Radcliffe Emerson, an outspoken archaeologist, who doesn't need women to help him solve mysteries – or at least that's what he thinks!

Curse of the Pharaohs

Elizabeth Peters

When a cry of help goes out from a colleague in distress, Amelia Peabody is only too happy to drop everything in England and travel out to Egypt to help.

The colleague in question is Lady Baskerville, whose husband Sir Henry has died suddenly, under bizarre circumstances, at the site of a tomb in Luxor. Little wonder, then, that the newspapers are proclaiming: 'The Curse of the Pharaohs has struck!'

On arrival in Luxor, Amelia and her husband Emerson find the camp in disarray and the workers terrified by the appearance of an apparition that Amelia promptly christens 'The Lady in White'. Yet this does not deter her from seeking the truth behind Sir Henry's death. Armed with nothing more than her trusty parasol, Amelia sets about bringing order from chaos . . . and herself much closer to danger.

The Mummy Case

Elizabeth Peters

The irascible husband of Victorian Egyptologist Amelia Peabody is living up to his reputation as 'The Father of Curses'. Denied permission to dig at the pyramids of Dahshoor, Emerson is awarded instead the 'pyramids' of Mazghunah – countless mounds of rubble in the middle of nowhere. Nothing in this barren spot seems of any interest – that is, until a murder takes place in Cairo, and a sinister-looking Egyptian spotted at the crime scene turns up in Mazghunah. After his appearance, Amelia can't resist following his trail. But at the same time she has to keep an eagle eye on her wayward son Rameses and his elegant and calculating cat, and also look into the mysterious disappearance of a mummy case . . .